A
Harlequin
Romance

WELCOME
TO THE WONDERFUL WORLD
of Harlequin Romances!

Interesting, informative and entertaining,
each Harlequin Romance portrays an appealing
love story. Harlequin Romances take you
to faraway places — places with real people
facing real love situations — and
you become part of their story.

As publishers of Harlequin Romances, we're extremely
proud of our books (we've been publishing
them since 1954). We're proud also that Harlequin
Romances are North America's most-read
paperback romances.

Eight new titles are released every month and are
sold at nearly all book-selling stores across
Canada and the United States.

A free catalogue listing all available Harlequin Romances
can be yours by writing to the

HARLEQUIN READER SERVICE,
M.P.O. Box 707, Niagara Falls, N.Y. 14302.
Canadian address: Stratford, Ontario, Canada.

or use order coupon at back of book.

We sincerely hope you enjoy reading
this Harlequin Romance.

Yours truly,

THE PUBLISHERS
    Harlequin Romances

BRIDE OF THE RIF

by

MARGARET ROME

HARLEQUIN BOOKS

TORONTO
WINNIPEG

Original hard cover edition published in 1972
by Mills & Boon Limited, 17-19 Foley Street,
London W1A 1DR, England

© Margaret Rome 1972

Harlequin edition published December 1972

SBN 373-01645-X

Printed in Canada

CHAPTER I

THE bows of the luxury cruise ship *African Queen* were cleaving the waters of the warm Mediterranean en route for Tangier. Her upper decks were ablaze with lights, laughter, music and happy voices spiralled noisily aloft, then were hushed – swallowed into the surrounding darkness of the tropical night. It was playtime for the passengers aboard, the time of day when children slept and relieved parents were allowed to snatch a few hours of pleasure not attuned to the demands of their offspring; time for the middle-aged to sink gratefully in the depths of the nearest comfortable chairs and to relive in retrospect the wonders revealed on earlier sightseeing excursions; and for teenagers, the much looked-forward-to hour when the day's exploratory skirmishes with the opposite sex, the tentative smiles and interested glances, reached fruition in the seclusion of the upper boat deck.

By comparison, the atmosphere inside an upper deck lounge contrasted sharply. There, the only sound that impinged upon the concentrated hush enveloping the room was the thrumming of the air-conditioning and now then a smothered cough – quickly suppressed when the culprit was made aware of accusing eyes swivelling momentarily towards him, then back again to the card game taking place inside a circle made up of eager, enthralled spectators. Sara Battle did not so much as blink when her companion called his opponent's bluff.

"I'll see you," he challenged casually in the vernacular familiar to card-playing addicts. No evidence of prize money was apparent, no chips littered the table nor was there any currency in sight, but the watchers gasped as they acknowledged the cool professionalism, the casual indifference to the winning or losing of an invisible stake which they were aware amounted to a small fortune, displayed by the handsome, elderly gentleman and his aloofly beautiful young companion.

The young Spaniard who had been challenged bit his lip and hesitated momentarily, then, with a defiant flourish, he spread his cards face uppermost on the table. "Three aces and two queens!" he offered a trifle wildly. "You've beaten me every night this week, Colonel, but this time I think it is my turn to scoop the pool!"

Dismayed shock caused Sara's wrist to jerk and connect with the stem of a wine glass set near to hand. Luckily, she managed to grab it in time to prevent its contents from spilling over the table, and the sigh of relief that rippled over the waiting crowd owed its origin more to a release from tension than to any dismay felt at the thought of damage caused by spilt wine. But almost immediately attention was again riveted upon the two players. Sara made a valiant effort for control and her features resumed their usual mask of composure, but she could not suppress the quiver of relief that relaxed her mouth when the Colonel, with his customary aplomb, spread out a Royal Flush and countered mildly, "I think not, Don Alvaro, tomorrow night, perhaps...?"

Colonel Battle took the following storm of congratulations in his stride, but even within the circle of admiring well-wishers Sara was conscious of a wave of disapproval emanating from a man standing aloofly apart who made no attempt to add his congratulations to those of the excited throng. As she glanced up their eyes collided, and his look of frowning distaste sent a shiver through her tense body. Each night for the better part of a week he had appeared in the lounge just as the games were about to start, and his forbidding presence had acted as a spur on her already tender conscience so that her usually nimble fingers had become numb as she shuffled and dealt the cards and her quick wits had become so dulled the Colonel had twice sharply reprimanded her for making some stupid move. Only that evening, before they left the dining-room to start playing, he had reproved her,

"I hope I can rely upon you to pay attention tonight, Sara, because if I can't I would prefer that you drop out of the game altogether rather than saddle me with a partner whose moves would shame a beginner at a village whist drive. What ails you, girl, are you sicken-

7

ing for something?" She had known she could not
hope to fight his deliberate obtuseness. Many times she
had tried, and failed, to get him to see her point of
view, but there was no way of penetrating his stubborn
refusal to see reason. Perhaps that was why her argument had lacked spirit when she had replied.

"Yes, I am sick! Sick of travelling around the world,
sick of having no permanent home – no chance to put
down roots – and most of all I'm sick of playing cards,
especially when I know it's our only means of existence
and that we have to *win to live!*" The Colonel's mous-
tache had bristled and for a moment Sara had shared
the same feeling of trepidation that had been felt by
many young subalterns unfortunate enough to have in-
curred the Colonel's wrath while under his command.
He had then drawn himself stiffly erect and, in a manner reminiscent of the way in which he had enforced
discipline during his many years' service in India, had
snapped,

"You're being impertinent, dammit, and I will not
tolerate impertinence!" He had glared at her across the
table, making no attempt to hide his fury so quickly,
and before his peppery temper could escalate into a
second eruption, she had risen to her feet and with as
much dignity as she could muster had begun walking
towards the exit. Luckily, very few passengers had
opted for the second sitting for dinner and the dining-
room was fairly empty, but even so a rush of shamed
colour had stained her cheeks as she had weaved her

way between the tables, pretending to ignore the many curious glances.

Once inside her cabin she had paced the floor, furiously angry, wondering, not for the first time, why she tolerated such an alien existence. For five years, since the age of fifteen, she had accompanied her grandfather on his everlasting cruises. At first it had felt as if a dream had come true. For as long as she could remember an orphanage had been her home. When she was a mere infant her father and mother, both only children, had been killed together in a car crash. The authorities had tried without success to find some relative who might claim the child who had been thrown, still in her carrycot, unharmed out of the crushed car. But when no one had come forward she had been taken to the local orphanage where for fifteen years she had grown up thinking herself completely alone in the world. Then had come the wonderful day when she had been summoned to the matron's office where a visitor had been waiting to meet her. She had felt instinctively drawn towards the elderly gentleman who was introduced as her grandfather because even though at first sight he had looked stern – even forbidding – his hands when he had taken hold of hers had been shaking with suppressed feeling and as he had bent down to kiss her proffered cheek his eyes had filled with unashamed tears of emotion.

Explanations had followed much later, after the dust of the orphanage had dropped for the last time from her feet and she had been escorted by her grandfather into the cabin she was to occupy for the duration of her very first cruise. She had been too excited to take in his words, too grateful to him for transporting her into a Cinderella world to wonder at his earlier lack of concern for his family, and so she had accepted without question the circumstances she had outlined as an excuse for his neglect. To her, it sounded quite feasible that on being discharged from the Army he should have chosen to remain in India to try to find some occupation which would enable him to stay in the country he had come to love. But India had had nothing to offer the man who had spent the better part of his life in her service, and then had begun his years of drifting. The fact that he had ceased to receive letters from his only son had caused him some misgivings, he had told her, but being a poor correspondent himself, he had shrugged off niggling doubts and nursed an inward conviction that his son was probably too busy with his own affairs to bother about a father he had not seen for years. It had been mere chance, when the ship on which he had been travelling had made an unscheduled stop at a London port, that caused him to come ashore on a lightning visit only to discover that Sara, the last of the Battles, had for years been languishing in the care of kind, but unavoidably austere, officialdom. . . .

She had been inside the cabin only a few minutes when a tap on the door had heralded the crisp command: "Sara, open up, I wish to speak to you!" With a shrug, her temper no longer at flash point, she had moved obediently towards the door.

"Come in, Gramps," purposely she had used the affectionate term that never failed to please him, then found herself having to suppress a smile when his scowling countenance had softened into a sheepish smile. With a lightning change of mood so characteristic of the Battles he had reached out to hug her before ruefully apologizing. "I'm sorry about that disgusting display of temper, child, forgive me. . . .?"

She had answered his request with a smiling nod, but even so his brow had creased into worry furrows and his arms had dropped from her shoulders. Testily, he had begun to grope in his pocket for the case that held his cheroots and without his customary request for permission he had lighted one, then blown a savage stream of smoke from pursed lips before making the surprising admission,

"You're perfectly right, you know, Sara, I should be horsewhipped for introducing you into the sort of life we've led all these years." She had tried to contradict, but he had silenced her with a gesture. "No, somehow, without realizing myself quite how it happened, I slipped into the routine of a professional gambler. It was the only thing I was good at, you see." After a dejected shrug he had qualified hastily, "Other than military practices, that is. I pride myself I did my job well in the Army, but," the glowing tip of his cheroot had been examined minutely while he sought for words to

11

justify his weakness, "the Army doesn't equip one for the ardours of civilian life. Unknowingly, soldiers become cosseted from such things as money worries, where to live, where to work ... To a regular soldier the Army is a home, family, employer, and when you are cast out – no longer needed," he grimaced bitterly, "it's similar to a non-swimmer being thrown in at the deep end. One clutches at any straw for survival."

Quickly, Sara had moved to his side, her face contrite. "Stop it, Gramps, do you hear? I won't have you blaming yourself. You've been wonderful to me and I'll always love you for it, always!" Her last words had ended in a choked sob and she had leant her head upon his chest to hide from him the tears she was fiercely ashamed of.

"Don't try to whitewash my actions!" he had clamped, determined, once having admitted his guilt, to purge his soul completely. "I've used you abominably and you know it! From the age of sixteen the only art you've been taught is that of playing cards. I've passed on to you every bit of skill I possess and you've learnt your lessons well – I'd defy any man in the world to better you when you are playing on form. But you're right to feel ashamed, because it's not exactly the sort of skill one looks for in a young and beautiful girl. You have a right to expect better things and in future, dammit, I'll see to it that changes are made. You've partnered me for the last time, Sara. From now on I play alone!"

12

Her head had jerked up at these words. His face had looked flushed, too highly flushed, and she had felt a twinge of fear. He was so upright and so handsome still, with brilliant, far-seeing eyes and thick iron-grey hair, that she was apt to forget he was far from young. If anything should happen to him she would be once more on her own. The thought was unbearable. Anxiety had made her voice sharp as she had demanded,

"Sit down and stop talking foolishly, Gramps. You know you couldn't bear to live anywhere else but afloat, and card-playing is the only way we have of stretching your pension far enough to pay my fare. I've a right to earn my keep, so of course I must help out! Besides that," she had faltered ... "I like to play."

His blue eyes had looked straight through her, deep into her innermost soul. "Little liar," he had grunted. "You're a disgrace to your namesake and you know it!" She had smiled wanly at this reference to an oft-repeated private joke. Many times he had quoted to her a passage from one of Lamb's "Essays of Elia" in which a character named Sarah Battle considered that "Whist was her life's business; her duty; the thing she came into the world to do, and she did it. She unbent her mind afterwards over a book". But while Sara often took refuge in a book she did so in an effort to rid herself of the guilty remorse she felt each time she relieved some amateurish card-player of his money.

When a vagrant sigh had escaped her the Colonel's

frown had deepened and a determined line had appeared between his bushy eyebrows. "I meant what I said, Sara," he had growled roughly, "in future I play alone. And I promise you," his direct look had been as binding as a pledge, "that as soon as we have sufficient funds we'll leave this life behind us and settle down somewhere ashore. Will that please you, d'you think, my love?"

Half laughing, half crying, she had run to hug him.

"Oh, Gramps!" For a moment she was quite incapable of forcing the words of delighted agreement passed the lump in her throat, but when she did finally manage to speak he was left in no doubt of her joy and heartfelt relief. "You'll never regret your decision, Gramps, I promise you," she had babbled happily. "We'll find a house somewhere — near the sea, or perhaps in the country where you can go for long walks and fish or shoot game — and I'll cook and clean and look after you so well you'll wonder why we wasted all these years! Oh!" a visible shudder had run through her tense young body, "just think how wonderful it will be when there's no more need to pretend we're rich, bored tourists who advocate playing for stake money merely to add more spice to the game! If you only knew how much I've hated the subterfuge we've had to practise in order to avoid being exposed as gamblers . . . the deceit, the lies, the occasions when we've even had to sink so low as to *bribe* members of the crew not to give us away to the captain . . ."

She had faltered to a stop when she had felt him go rigid. Her outburst had shaken him to the very depths, her vehement words had stripped bare his way of life and for the first time he was forced into facing reality – to see himself portrayed not as the cultured sophisticate he imagined himself but as a petty adventurer, a cheap gamester who, if his intentions were known, would never again be allowed aboard any ship belonging to a reputable shipping line. Appalled by her own insensitivity, she had tried to stutter an apology. "Gramps, I've hurt you! ... I didn't mean ..." But her words had not seemed to penetrate; with granite-hard features, his lips compressed into lines of shock, he had turned from her and marched, with his back ramrod straight, out of the cabin ...

The clamour of excited voices escalated into a discordant babble and Sara suddenly felt that if she did not get away she would scream. Her grandfather was still enclosed within a circle of congratulatory onlookers, and her silent antagonist had disappeared, so she slipped out of the lounge and sped towards the bow of the ship, searching the deeply-shadowed deck as she ran for a corner that might offer the solitude she craved. When at last she found a deserted spot she leant against the rail and waited until her thumping heartbeats had subsided and her riotous thoughts could be marshalled into some semblance of order.

She was worried, dreadfully worried. The Colonel had stuck to his resolution not to allow her to play that evening, so she had had no other option but to sit, rebelliously, watching the game. Gradually, a sense of foreboding had begun to plague her. No reason, other than some sixth sense, was responsible for the depression that descended like a dark cloud, causing her to cast many worried glances in her grandfather's direction. But he seemed to have recovered his former spirits – indeed, he radiated such an aura of well-being her fears were calmed – until she noticed his feverish flush and the light of reckless abandon that had replaced the grave intentness he usually displayed when a game was in progress. A faint suspicion that he might have been drinking was dismissed instantly; he never drank before a game. Not even the relief she had felt when the young Spaniard, Don Alvaro de Leon, a reckless young man who always insisted upon playing for enormous stakes – had been beaten was enough to dispel the sense of impending doom that gripped her so mercilessly she found herself trembling as she stood gripping the ship's rail with hands grown suddenly cold.

When an icy voice snaked out of the darkness she spun on her heel with a frightened gasp.

"You look like a sea wraith standing there, *señorita*. I was almost afraid to speak in case you should vanish over the side at the sound of my voice. Why are you so edgy, I wonder? Could it be that you are plagued with remorse?"

Her startled eyes fastened upon the shadow that was moving towards her out of the darkness and when it was near enough to take substance she backed away and choked out a confused: "*You!*"

"Yes, it is I, *señorita,*" he bowed distantly. "Don Felipe de Panza, cousin of the young fool Don Alvaro de Leon whom you helped to rob this evening!" As she stared mesmerized at the tall, haughty Spaniard whose silent disapproval had plagued her for a week Sara wondered wildly if she was experiencing a nightmare from which she would shortly waken. But there was nothing ethereal about the man who now stood mere inches away, searching her face with anger-dark eyes that contained in their depths a smouldering flicker of danger.

"Well, do you deny my accusation?" the hateful voice continued, "or are you searching for excuses — an exercise at which I am sure you are adept."

"Please," her constricted throat refused to allow more than a whisper, "I don't understand. Are you accusing me of cheating?"

"As an accomplice you are every bit as guilty as your," he paused, then drawled with distaste, "companion. It was he who did the actual switching of cards, but please do not ask me to believe that your unfortunate accident with the wine glass was not intended as a deliberate diversion created solely to enable him to change his hand during the few seconds that all eyes were upon you!"

When his outrageous meaning finally penetrated she erupted into a flare of white-hot anger. Her bronze cap

of hair seemed fairly to bristle and her eyes, twin orbs
of sparkling emerald, lighted furiously upon his darkly-
etched features in the manner of trained artillery with
sights set to blast him from the face of the earth.

"How dare you!" Even as she spoke her hand connected with his lean cheek in a slap hard enough to rock
him on his heels. Surprise was the element responsible
for the success of her attack, and for the amazement
that held him silent while a dull red mark spread across
his cheek.

"You she-devil!" He reached out and caught her
shoulders in a bruising grip. Tight-lipped with fury, he
bit out: "If you were a man I would kill you for that!"

"And if I were a man," she twisted abortively in his
grasp, "I'd never rest until I'd made you eat the disgusting lies you've just spoken!"

"Lies, are they?" Her heart almost stopped beating
when he jerked her head erect and forced her to face
the full battery of his rage. "Then if they are lies, why
is your accomplice being escorted at this very minute
to the captain's cabin to answer the charge of cheating
which I personally have laid against him?"

"No!" Her eyes distended with horror as his words
reverberated like a crash of doom in her ears. Through
narrowed eyes he watched the signs of shocked incredulity and unbelieving dismay that drained every drop
of colour from her face. When his grasp slackened she
twisted from his hands and retreated to stand pressed,
like an animal at bay, against the ship's rail. For a

18

second she fought gallantly to suppress tears, then, after a shuddering sigh, she flung at him accusingly, "If what you say is true, if you really have done such a despicable thing – *I shall hate you for the rest of my life!*"

CHAPTER II

Sara ran all the way to the captain's quarters, hoping dementedly that what Felipe de Panza had said would prove to be a lie, that the threat he had uttered in his anger had been born of a vicious desire to frighten her. But when she reached the captain's cabin and flung open the door, forgetting in her anxiety to knock, the words she heard confirmed what she had inwardly suspected – not even in anger would the arrogant Spaniard be prepared to lie.

The captain's stern voice was directing her grandfather: "Not only did you blatantly disregard company rules by inveigling fellow passengers into playing for stake money, but worse, much worse, you set out deliberately to cheat and rob those who were unfortunate enough to be conned into playing your game!" His eyes flickered momentarily across to Sara, acknowledging her presence without giving her a chance to intervene. "If it were not for your granddaughter here," he nodded in her direction, "I would be tempted to put you ashore at the next port of call and leave you to your own devices, but because of her – and *only* because of her – I'll be lenient. You can both remain aboard until the cruise is ended, but you will not at any time be allowed to mix with the rest of the passengers. The crew will be instructed to see that my orders are carried out, so I would advise you not to disobey my command, because if you do I shall have no alternative but to carry out my original intention which was to order you off this ship!"

At these words, Sara's temper boiled over. Taking a hurried step forward, she blazed up at him, "How dare you accuse my grandfather of cheating! He may have broken your rules, but cheat? Never!"

The captain returned her furious look with unrelenting firmness. "I'm sorry, Miss Battle, but your grandfather was seen by the passenger who reported him to switch cards. It seems this same gentleman has been keeping a very close watch on Colonel Battle because he was somewhat sceptical of his unusually long run of luck. He suspected him of being a cardsharper, and tonight his suspicions were confirmed. Naturally, he reported what he had seen to me, and when your grandfather submitted to a search by one of my officers a playing card was found lodged in the lining of his coat sleeve."

Sara fought waves of shock to protest. "But finding a solitary card upon his person doesn't prove anything. It's only Señor Panza's word against my grandfather's . . ."

The captain was not used to having his decisions questioned. Frostily, he replied, "Don Felipe is a well-known and greatly respected member of a very old Spanish-Moroccan family. I have the honour of having been personally acquainted with him for many years and can vouch that he is a just, honest man of great integrity; not a man who would bring serious charges against another without being very sure of his facts, but one I would trust without doubt or question. So, Miss Battle, as I have no intention of discussing the matter further, I will be obliged if you and your grandfather will go to your cabins so that I can continue with my work."

It was a peremptory dismissal; the captain was not the most tolerant of men and the contempt that showed in the manner in which he turned his back and began rifling through the papers on his desk would have been found galling by all but the most insensitive. To the Colonel, who up until then had seemed rendered speechless, the captain's attitude was intolerable and he gave vent to his resentment in a burst of blustering defiance. With a roar reminiscent of the barrack square, he attacked the startled captain.

"You, sir, can keep your favours for those spineless enough to accept them! You have the audacity to set yourself up as judge and jury – I've been tried, found guilty, and sentenced – all upon the word of one Felipe de Panza who you yourself admit is a personal friend of yours! Well, I don't intend that the matter shall end here. Tomorrow, I shall write to the chairman of the Line and complain forcibly about the treatment I've received on this ship! And as for your ridiculous decree that we must spend the rest of this cruise segregated from the rest of the passengers – I refuse absolutely to accept it! What have you to say to that, sir! "

Sara closed her eyes and prayed the captain would be lenient. Although she agreed with every word her grandfather had said, she could not help but wish he had chosen a more diplomatic way in which to put his objections before a man who, if anything, seemed even more arbitrary than he was himself. She felt a sick feeling in the pit of her stomach when the captain's haughty face flushed a dull red, and was hardly surprised at his icy reply.

"I say this, Colonel! Tomorrow we dock at Tangier. Please see to it that all your belongings are packed ready to be transported ashore first thing tomorrow morning. You've worn out your welcome aboard this ship! "

The next morning she felt a fierce gladness when she realized they were to be spared the humiliation of being banished in the sight of curious eyes. The ship was anchored off Tangier when an early breakfast was served to her in her cabin by a blank-faced steward who informed her that a tender would be waiting to take herself and the Colonel ashore in an hour. Between them, they had quite a lot of baggage. The life they led necessitated smart, up-to-date clothes to help perpetuate a wealthy image, but as she had packed everything possible the previous night, when the time

came for them to disembark they were able to board the
tender without fuss and without any but a handful of
passengers taking a pre-breakfast stroll around deck
being any the wiser.

She sat stiff-backed, fighting a wave of humiliated
tears, as the tender sped away from the ship and the
coastline of rocky cliffs and sandy beaches grew gradually nearer. But by the time she was being helped on to
the quayside at Tangier she was sufficiently composed
to pretend an interest when the Colonel pointed out to
her an old Arab town perched on top of the hill sweeping down towards the harbour. When he hailed a taxi
and began directing the driver to one of Tangier's most
expensive hotels, she began an involuntary protest, but
then she bit her lip and managed to remain silent while
she inwardly resolved that before the day was over she
would confront him not only with a demand for an
explanation of the catastrophic events leading up to
their banishment from the ship, but also for a detailed
and truthful account of the state of their finances.

The room she was given was quietly luxurious. Cool
white walls, white lace bedspread, and a white lattice-
work canopied bed were saved from monastic severity
by a vividly patterned tiled floor. Tall windows with
protective white shutters opened on to a view of bright
blue sea, bobbing yachts, and a sweep of green hillside
crammed with white-painted villas each surounded by
an expanse of garden profuse with blossoms of riotous
colour. As she stood absorbing the view a vagrant

breeze whisked bronze tendrils of hair across her furrowed brow, then advanced to tease with a dry-sounding rustle the leaves of a large potted palm stood effectively against the stark walls. The rustling sound interrupted her train of thought, and with a decisive gesture she turned on her heel and made towards the door. Unpacking would have to wait. Too many questions were seething around in her mind – questions which, for the sake of sanity, her grandfather must be made to answer immediately!

His room was just along the corridor from her own and in a matter of seconds she was outside his door demanding to be let in. When, after a few hesitant seconds, he appeared, she saw by his expression he was braced for argument, so without preliminary she began her attack.

"I have some questions that must be answered, Grandfather," she told him firmly as she settled down in a chair and showed every indication of refusing to budge until she received satisfaction. He looked affronted, he was usually the one who gave the orders and she the one who obeyed them, but the sparkle in her green eyes warned him to be cautious, and suddenly, after a moment of rebellious silence, his stern mouth relaxed into a smile and he sat down facing her. His manner, when he began searching his pockets for his cheroot case, appeared nonchalant, but to her dismay she saw that his hands were trembling.

"You're right, my dear, the hour of evil is upon me,

explanations can be put off no longer. But I warn you – you will not like that you're about to hear."

A chill sidled down Sara's spine even as she confidently assured him, "You have no need to deny the accusations made against you, Grandfather – you're quite incapable of cheating, I know that. What I want you to tell me is how the misunderstanding occurred in the first place, and what steps you intend taking to clear your name. Señor Panza must not be allowed to get away with his despicable actions, he must be made to publicly apologize for daring to sully your good name with such a foul fabrication of lies!" She stopped, her breast heaving, her face flushed with angry indignation, and glared across at him as if he were the instigator of her fury rather than the insolent Spaniard whose name she had spat out as if the mere mention of it burnt her tongue.

Under her furious gaze he seemed visibly to wilt. Stilts could have been kicked out from under him as he sagged against the back of his chair. Misty film clouded his eyes and lines appeared around his mouth which she had never suspected were there. His usually stabbing look was a mere flickering of his eyelids as he glanced up and then quickly away before nerving himself to take some tremendous strain.

"Señor Panza didn't lie, Sara," he told her heavily. "I did wrong, God help me, but I did it with the best of motives. Unfortunately, I was found out."

Incredulously, she stammered, "Grandfather! This

is no time for jokes, please don't tease . . ." Her words ended in a choked gasp when she saw his face whiten and his knuckles stand out as he gripped the arm of his chair.

Compulsion to justify his actions, to banish the shocked horror from her eyes, brought words tumbling from his lips. "I did it for us, Sara, so that we might realize a dream. Alvaro de Leon is a compulsive gambler – a wealthy playboy with money to burn. The amount staked on the game we played was a trivial amount to him, but to us it represented a cottage in the country, a chance to settle down and live a normal life with normal people! " When her fixed gaze did not alter he sighed and began to plead. "Try not to blame me too much, Sara. Despicable though my action might seem, it was not premeditated, I swear it! Alvaro had a good hand – I sensed that – but I was only an ace away from having an unbeatable one, a royal flush, and your accident with the wine glass seemed a God-sent opportunity which I seized upon almost without thinking. In the space of a split second, the thought became deed and for the first time in my life I cheated an opponent. Do you believe that, Sara?" he urged with a momentary return of his customary dignity. "Do you believe me when I say it was the one and only time in my life I've ever cheated?"

His bowed head and agonized eyes were too much for her. With a passionate cry she dropped to her knees beside him and cradled his drooping body in her strong young arms. "Of course I believe you, Gramps!" she rasped through a throat tight with compassion. "It was all my fault for trying to change your way of life simply to satisfy my own selfish whims! You took me from the orphanage and introduced me to a life of luxury such as I'd never dared dream about. Travel, good food, beautiful clothes, you gave me all of these as well as an abundance of love, and I repaid you with dissatisfaction and continuous nagging to change your ways. Don't dare to reproach yourself ever again, Gramps. The blame is mine – all mine!"

He murmured soft denials while he stroked her bent head and waited until her storm of remorseful tears was spent, then when she was calm enough to think clearly he supplied the answers to the other question she had intended to ask.

"About money, Sara . . ."

"Yes, Gramps?" She went very still.

He cleared his throat and began, "We have very little capital left – enough to pay our hotel bill for little more than a week, in fact." When she drew in a gulping breath to speak, he hurried on, "I know what you're going to say, and I don't agree. You would have us move into some cheap sleazy hotel without decent food and no air-conditioning, but to my mind that would merely be prolonging the agony. I much prefer to live in a decent hotel for a week rather than exist in an inferior one for a month."

"But what will happen when the money is finished?"

she asked in a voice registering panic at the hint of returning obstinacy she saw in his outthrust chin.

"I have a plan," he returned confidently. "It's a huge gamble, I admit, but desperate situations call for desperate measures. The Club Aziz in Tangiers has always been an exceptionally lucky place for me. I intend going there tonight, taking what cash we can spare, and I guarantee, my love, I'll bring back enough money to get us back to England and, if my luck runs true to form, some to spare!"

She stared at him with wide, frightened eyes, wondering if she had heard aright. To be stranded in a place like Tangier with hardly any money was bad enough, but to deliberately contemplate risking what little they had on a card game was criminally foolish! Only then did she realize how deep the gambling bug had bitten into her grandfather's soul. In a voice she found difficult to control, she charged him,

"You'll do no such thing, do you hear me?" When his chin lifted a degree higher, she stood up and held out a trembling hand. "I want every penny we possess in my keeping and I want it now, Grandfather. For both our sakes, I must insist that you hand it over immediately!"

For an agonizing moment she thought he was going to refuse, but then, with an offended shrug, he pulled his wallet from his pocket and threw it down in disgust upon the table. "Take it!" he flung across his shoulder as he strode furiously from the room. "I never thought

I'd see the day when a Battle would succumb to cowardice! I hate to quote clichés, but as you well know 'Live for today' is a motto I've always found pleasing. Think on it, Sara. You have plenty of time before the club opens in which to change your mind!' "

For the rest of the day his parting words reverberated in her mind, but her resolution never faltered. If she had been under his influence during her most formative years perhaps his devil-may-care attitude, his reckless disregard of the need for caution, would have rubbed off on her, but orphanages rarely breed frivolity, nor even over-confidence, and Sara's unherently cautious nature revolted against encouraging him in his rash venture. To occupy her mind – and to avoid running the risk of being subjected once more to the influence of his persuasive tongue – she decided to explore Tangier. Shore excursions had not been included in the itinerary of their life aboard the luxury cruise ships because they were expensive extras and, in any case, as the Colonel had stated bluntly: "Pickings are better aboard."

She thrilled to many new sights and sounds as she wandered unaccompanied through the steep, narrow streets of the old town. Everywhere she looked, old contrasted with new, women in European clothes mingled with veiled Arab women; pale-skinned merchants in expensive suits rubbed shoulders with dark, fierce-eyed men in *djellabahs* who wore their robes with aristocratic arrogance; donkeys with full panniers sauntered along in the path of monster cars whose abundant chromework drew the sun like a magnet so that eyes had to be averted from stabbing rays reflected from gleaming coachwork. She was enthralled by her first sight of a water-carrier in his elaborate, crazy gear. On his head he wore a wide brown and red straw hat hung all around with charms and baubles. As he walked, small bells and glass ornaments jingled at every step, and added to that was the clashing of brass cups which he wore on a long string around his neck. When he swung towards her she took his piercing cry as an effort to attract her custom, but although she was thirsty she dared not chance drinking the water he carried in a goatskin slung over his shoulder. Firmly, she shook her head and was relieved to see him turn without demur and stroll away looking like a cross between a clown and a walking fountain, ringing his handbell vigorously as he went.

After wandering for hours, oblivious to time, it was a relief to find a garden with seats placed at strategic spots for the benefit of the public. A burning feeling at the back of her heel had begun throbbing in earnest, so she tottered over to the nearest vacant seat and eased her sandal strap away from what she imagined must be the beginnings of a blister. The garden was high on a hill overlooking a wonderful view of shipping far below in the Straits. In the distance she could make out the outline of the Rock of Gibraltar, and opposite, a mere ten minutes away by plane, was the brown, parched coast of Spain. She frowned, her pleasure spoilt by a transient reminder of something unpleasant. Reluctantly, she began recalling to mind the lean facial contours, the firm mouth and despising eyes of Felipe de Panza. A lump lodged in her throat as she remembered the utter contempt in his voice when he had accused her. Ignorant of the truth, she had stood up well to his searing indictment, had retaliated nobly in defence of her own and her grandfather's honour, but she flinched when she remembered the pistol-sharp sound of her open palm connecting with his lean cheek. The proud señor would never forgive that humiliating slap . . .

Shivering, even under the caress of the hot African sun, she began limping out of the gardens to make her way back to the hotel. The scarlet of hibiscus, the purple and crimson of bougainvillea, the silvery eucalyptus trees and the green leaves and golden fruit of the orange trees all merged into a kaleidoscope of colour when a sudden rush of tears blurred her vision. In the midst of her dejection a thought brought a measure of relief: for one thing, at least, she could thank the captain – his edict that they should leave the ship had spared her the ordeal of a second meeting with Señor Panza – the idea of having to endure his scathing condemnation while knowing it to be *deserved* would have been more than her proud spirit could have borne.

The Colonel was very morose that evening at dinner; he evinced no interest whatsoever in the account Sara gave him of her afternoon's activities, but answered merely in monosyllables without bothering to look up from the food he was moodily pushing around his plate, Finally she lost patience with him.

"Are you going to sulk all evening, Grandfather? Because if you are I might as well go straight up to my room."

He shrugged, unrepentant. "And I might as well do the same. I wouldn't care to sit in the bar knowing I dared not allow myself to become involved with people. I've been hard up many times in my life, but never so much that I couldn't afford to buy an acquaintance a drink!"

Sara felt remorse. By depriving him of his money she had hurt his pride as well as his pocket and his aggrieved attitude was his way of showing it. "Very well, Gramps," she sighed, "you shall have your money back if you'll give me your solemn promise not to be extravagant. You do realize," she leant forward to give emphasis to her plea, "that this money is all that stands between us and starvation?"

His eyes lit up as she handed over the wallet she was carrying in her handbag for safe keeping. "Of course, I realize that fact only too well, child! You've no need to worry, I intend to make this money stretch as far as possible."

She left him contentedly sipping an after-dinner brandy and went upstairs, meaning to spend the evening with a book. But the written words danced meaninglessly before her eyes, refusing to make sense while chaotic thoughts chased through her mind. Finally, after deciding that physical effort was needed to counteract the tension building up inside her, she tossed it aside and went into the bathroom to wash her hair. Shampooing, setting and drying out helped to dispose of the better part of the evening and by the time her glossy bronze hair was combed to perfection footsteps outside the hotel, together with jovial goodnights exchanged between friends, denoted the return of fellow guests from their evening activities.

She sighed, conscious of her own loneliness. She had made very few friends aboard ship and certainly no lasting friendships. Not from any lack of opportunity, because the atmosphere aboard ship is the friendliest in the world; nowhere does one mix more freely or advance more quickly into deep relationships. It was for that very reason she had had to don a mask of reserve, to gain an undeserved reputation for aloofness; it was the only way to save herself the embarrassment of having to evade confidences, or even telling lies, in order to avoid making public the fact that she and her grandfather had no permanent home, no solid, respectable background. Impatiently, she threw down the comb and swung sharply away from the sight of her mournful eyes and drooping mouth reflected in the mirror; she needed company to help restore her spirits and in that respect, at least, her grandfather never failed her.

There was no sound coming from inside his room

when she knocked tentatively upon his door. She knocked again, sharply this time, and when still she received no answer her heart began to pound with heavy, frightened thuds. For no particular reason her grandfather's last words popped into her mind. *I intend to make this money stretch as far as possible*, and only at that moment did she recognize a possible *double entendre*, to begin to suspect that they might have been chosen deliberately to hide his true intention which, by his own admission, was to risk every penny they owned on a game of chance!

With frantic haste she picked up the telephone, but when the desk clerk asked politely if he could be of assistance she found it impossible to keep her voice steady when she asked him to page Colonel Battle.

"Colonel Battle? He left the hotel about two hours ago. I telephoned myself for a taxi to take him to the Club Aziz."

The blood slowly drained from her face as she digested his words. The shock was so great that for a second she could not move or speak, and it was only when the desk clerk's anxious voice had asked for the third time whether she was all right that she found the courage to whisper, "Please will you get me a taxi? I must go after him."

"But, Miss Battle," he sounded perturbed, "the Club Aziz is not one I would recommend that you visit without an escort. What if your grandfather should have left . . . ?"

Her brittle laugh startled him as much as the hardness of her answer. "He'll be there – get me that taxi immediately!"

Even the taxi driver seemed reluctant to leave her when he finally drew up in front of a badly illuminated house surrounded by depths of shadow in which a dozen different dangers might have lurked. The street was narrow, dark and crooked, the roofs of the houses just saved from touching by a narrow slit of sky only one shade lighter than the inky depths of the old town beneath. But she refused to be dissuaded from entering the club, nor, as she had just enough money to pay his fare, would she allow him to wait, so when she ran up the steps and disappeared through the entrance he shrugged his shoulders at the folly of the English and drove away.

She hardly noticed the extreme garishness of her surroundings as she moved quickly towards a flight of stairs leading upwards. From sounds she could hear as she ascended, she judged it was not the sort of place her grandfather would visit from choice: his taste leant towards quieter, more dignified surroundings, and the high-pitched female voices that were rising above tortured strains of music coming from an inferior band somewhere above were ample indication that whatever luck he had been favoured with on previous visits to the Club must have been great enough to overcome his distaste for the prevailing unsavoury background. She had reached the top of the stairs and was about to enter the main room of the club when a black-sleeved arm was thrust in front of her.

"I'm sorry, *mademoiselle*," a pleasantly accented voice informed her, "but you cannot be permitted entry without showing proof of membership." The young Frenchman who barred her way looked as if he would be more at home in wide open spaces, his vibrant eyes echoed the blue of summer seas and his tanned, handsome features evidenced that he was no stranger to sun and spray.

"Please," she stammered, appealing to the hint of sympathy she saw in his eyes, "I must find my grandfather. I was told he came here."

The young man's smile faded when he heard the tremble in her voice and his expression became grave. "Then we must do what we can to assist you, *mademoiselle*. But first, let me introduce myself. I am Marc Rochefort, temporary assistant manager of this club. I will be happy to enquire around the premises for your grandfather if you will tell me his name?"

"Oh, thank you so much, *monsieur*, if only you would! My grandfather's name is Colonel Benjamin Battle."

"Then our search is ended before it is begun." Sara saw relief in his smile. "There is a card game taking place in one of our private rooms and only minutes ago I heard one of the gentlemen inside being addressed by that very name. Come –" He held out a guiding hand. "Let me show you the way."

She followed him along a corridor and when he stopped outside a door and indicated that they had arrived her body stiffened with apprehension. She was shaking when she stepped inside the room, hardly daring to search for her grandfather amongst the men who sat around a circular table, totally engrossed, for fear of what she should see written on his face. When she eventually did nerve herself to single him out her heart plummeted. There was no need to count the pitiful stack of chips that lay in front of him; his expression was enough to warn her that the thing she had tried to prevent had already happened. Even as her eyes swept over him, noting his grey pallor, the nervous twitching of his lips, he looked up and saw her.

"Sara!" He half rose from his seat as he croaked out her name then, for long, terrible moments his mouth worked as he fought for speech. Before her horrified eyes he seemed to crumple, then, with one last penitent look, he toppled forward to lie spreadeagled across the table. The next moment the room was in an uproar. Sara knew she screamed, because the sound of it echoed in her ears for hours afterwards, but her limbs refused to obey the instinct to move and she could do nothing but stand with shock-widened eyes watching her grandfather being lifted from the table and lowered gently on to a settee. As Marc Rochefort swiftly loosened the constricting tie from about the Colonel's neck, he rapped out an order to one of the men to fetch a doctor, then almost in the same breath commanded another to fetch brandy. When this was brought, he put an arm behind the Colonel's shoulders to lever him forward and manage to force a few drops of the spirit through his blue lips.

When Sara saw his eyes flicker, the blood began to flow once more through her veins and with a sob of relief she ran forward and dropped to her knees beside him.

"Gramps," she quavered. "Oh, Gramps darling, are you all right? How do you feel?"

He responded to her frightened appeal by moving his hand a fraction towards her so that she could clasp it in her own. His lips moved, but his breath was coming in laboured gasps and the effort to speak seemed quite beyond him. Marc pressed her shoulder, warning her not to encourage him to talk, so for ten long minutes until the doctor arrived she sat quietly, his hand in hers, devouring his pain-whitened face with eyes full of dawning fear.

Marc took her to an adjoining room when the doctor arrived and insisted that she should sip a glassful of brandy while she waited for the results of his examination. She was hardly conscious of her surroundings, much less of the man who had taken her so competently into his charge, but she obediently swallowed a minute quantity of the spirit although without once moving her eyes from the door behind which her grandfather was lying.

As soon as the doctor reappeared, she jumped up and

ran towards him. "How is he? Please, tell me quickly.
. . ."

Again, Marc Rochefort's steadying hand was there
to support her when the doctor answered gravely, "He
has suffered a severe heart attack. I have given him an
injection which will help alleviate the pain, but he is
very weak. However, he insists upon seeing you; Miss
Battle, and to avoid over-exciting him I had to agree.
An ambulance should arrive within the next few minutes, so until then you may sit with him."

With a quickly gasped: "Thank you, doctor," she
ran past him into the room. Blinds had been drawn across the windows and one small lamp cast a dim pool
of light on to the colonel's drawn, but now peaceful
face. He opened his eyes when she tip-toed across to
the bed and for a fractional second his glance went
beyond her to where Marc Rochefort stood. His puzzled
eyes assessed him, then slowly lightened with relief,
but his attention was all for Sara when he enunciated
slowly, "I'm sorry for the mess I've made of things,
child. Please forgive me?" She shook her head in violent repudiation of his need to apologize and buried
her tear-stained face against his arm. But he persisted,
and she was forced to listen. "You are so like your
mother, Sara, so lovely . . . But she never approved of
me, you know. She would have much preferred, if she
had known, that you should spend the rest of your life
in that orphanage rather than come under my influence,
and who could blame her? I've been selfish," he laboured

on even when she gestured him to be quiet, "so selfish and so criminally stupid I don't deserve to be forgiven ..." When his voice petered out she lifted her head with a startled jerk, but he made a tremendous effort and continued, "We've always had to fight for survival, you and I," a faint mockery of his usual grin lifted the corners of his mouth. "Battle by name and battle by nature, eh?" he quipped with a pitiful attempt at humour. "But at least you have an indomitable spirit and the fiery nature you inherited from me will help you combat the hostilities of life; I comfort myself with the thought that whatever rigours lay ahead you will meet them with unbowed head and an unbroken spirit." She shivered at the finality of his words. Her lips parted to assure him of her love and complete dependence upon him, but before she could speak the doctor strode into the room followed by two attendants who transferred the Colonel to a stretcher, then took him downstairs to a waiting ambulance.

She was allowed to go with him in the ambulance, and Marc insisted upon accompanying her. All during the long night while she sat tense and silent in the hospital waiting room, jumping at every footstep and flinching at every unexpected sound, he talked continuously as though in an effort to release her from her nightmare thoughts.

She was grateful for his understanding, for his lack of curiosity towards herself and her grandfather, and most of all for his company during her long vigil, and she turned instinctively to Marc to hold her hand while she nerved herself to meet the approaching doctor.

The doctor looked haggard when he entered the room, his white coat creased and his hair flopping untidily across his furrowed brow. His eyes were so full of pity that she knew he was searching for words to soften a blow, so she put him out of his misery. White to the lips, and feeling unbearably cold, she whispered, "He's dead, isn't he . . .?"

"Yes," he sighed. "We did everything we could; he lost consciousness almost as soon as we arrived here and although we fought all night to preserve a last flicker of life, it was no use . . ."

She mustered all her courage and choked, "He believed in living one day at a time. I'm glad he managed to live this one to the full." Then she turned towards Marc and was enfolded into his waiting arms.

CHAPTER III

OF necessity, interment is swift in the tropics and twenty-four hours later Sara was trying to cope with the bewildering knowledge that she was now totally alone in the world. The situation would have been daunting enough in her own country where at least she would have known where to begin to pick up the threads of her shattered life, but here in Tangier – a cosmopolitan city teeming with foreigners, birds of passage too engrossed in their own affairs to give a second thought to a stranded, bereft girl whose only assets were a trunkful of expensive clothes and an aptitude for playing cards – it was frightening in the extreme. If it had not been for Marc Rochefort she might have floundered in a welter of despair; even when he suggested a possible solution she was too numbed with shock to properly appreciate his plan.

They were lunching together at her hotel when he broached the subject of her future. Watching as she prodded a fork through untouched food on her plate, he frowned and chided gently, "Please try to eat something, Sara, you've had nothing for two whole days. Won't you make an effort – to please me?"

Her eyes were vague when they lifted to his face.

"What . . . what did you say?" She shook her head and made an effort to concentrate. "I'm sorry, Marc, I wasn't listening, I'm afraid. I wonder you bother to seek me out when I'm such depressing company."

"I am worried about you, Sara," he said. "Forgive me if I intrude, but I must ask. Have you sufficient money for your needs?"

She swallowed hard. "I have the money from the chips you cashed belonging to Gramps." She faltered at the memory of that fateful last game, then hurried on, "There's enough to pay my hotel bill, but there are funeral expenses to be met and my fare home . . . perhaps if I sell some of my clothes . . . I shall have to find a job, but first of all I must move from this hotel and try to find somewhere less expensive. Perhaps you know of a cheap *pension* in the French quarter, Marc? All I shall need is one room."

He frowned. "I could ask the *propriétaire* of my *pension*, but you would find it a great change from what you have been used to." He glanced quickly around their luxurious surroundings, comparing them with the clean but strictly functional amenities of his own lodgings, and wondered how the contrast would strike her.

She read his mind. "I am sure your *pension* will be no more spartan than the orphanage where I spent the first fifteen years of my life. I haven't always been used to luxury such as this."

His eyebrows rose in surprise. She fitted so perfectly

the part of an indulged child of fortune that it was hard to imagine her in any other setting but one of wealth. Her clothes were expertly styled and obviously expensive, her shoes and handbags looked as if they had cost as much as he earned in a month, and it was hardly possible to believe that her skilfully manicured hands with their perfectly shaped nails could ever have carried out menial tasks. Her disclosure helped to stifle the doubts he felt about the suggestion he intended to put to her. So he cleared his throat and offered: "There is a vacancy at the club for a croupier, if you are interested?"

Her first instinctive reaction was one of dismay. The club's brash atmosphere and coarse clientele had repelled her at first sight and the thought of becoming part of it was abhorrent. When he saw her hesitation, he pressed on, "I know the Club Aziz isn't your scene, Sara, but I would be constantly at your side to protect you from any unpleasantness, although, to be fair, I doubt if there would be any. Our patrons are not out of the top drawer, I admit, and some of them do tend to over-indulge themselves with liquor, but on the whole they are well behaved and I'm certain that when you get to know them you'll find them as likeable as I do myself. Certainly, I would not like the idea of your working there alone, but you'll be quite safe under my eye and the money offered is too good to be overlooked – far more than you'll get anywhere else in Tangier."

A refusal stopped on her lips at this reminder. She

had no skill to offer any employer; gambling was all she knew, and much as she longed to cut free from the association she was sickeningly aware that she had no choice but to carry on, for a while at least, if she were to survive. Silently, he watched signs of inward conflict chase across her expressive face. "Very well, Marc, I'll do it."

"Good!" He reached across the table to give her hand a reassuring squeeze. "I'm selfishly glad to hear you say so because it means I shall see more of you than I would have done if you had decided to opt for a job during the day. I'll hire a boat, we'll swim together, and sunbathe, and I'll show you parts of Morocco the ordinary tourist doesn't know exists. You won't regret your decision, Sara, I promise you. We are going to have a marvellous time!"

He proved to be a man of his word. During the weeks that followed he gave all his spare time to banishing painful memories from her mind. He introduced her to his many friends amongst the predominantly French-speaking hoteliers of the town. She moved from her hotel into the house of Madame Blais, Marc's landlady, a small, amply-proportioned Frenchwoman whose heart was bigger than her frame, and when sun-filled days were followed by nights of feverish activity as she threw herself into learning the intricacies of her new job, her agony gradually faded and she began once more to be able to face the world with a modicum of self-confidence.

Her extensive wardrobe was a decided asset to her job. Each night she dressed carefully before going to the club, taking as much care with her hair and her make-up as she would have done if she were about to attend some important function. Her perfectionism paid off in a surprising way. The management noted that die-hard drinkers whose behaviour had given them much trouble in the past seemed very anxious to gain favour with the new croupier and rather than risk seeing her delightful nose turned upwards at the sight of them, they were curtailing their intake of alcohol to within reasonable limits. This change caused no loss of revenue, because the table Sara managed was crowded with eager gamblers almost from the first night she took over and in no time at all word of her charm and skill circulated and became a magnet that drew clients from all over Tangier into the Club Aziz.

Marc was delighted with her success and told her so one night as they drove to the club. He took his eyes off the road long enough to admire the rich emerald sheen of her dress as it contrasted eye-catchingly against burnished hair piled high over her forehead and swept into a sophisticated pleat at the back of her head.

"I'm not surprised the club is being inundated with requests for membership," he teased. "Your appearance has not only bemused the clients, it has brought out in them a latent desire to appear as gentlemen – in your eyes at least." He chuckled and drew deeply on his cigarette. "There has even been a suggestion from one

47

of our directors that we rename the club – he thought
The Lorelei might be apt. Are you flattered?"

The grin was wiped from his face when she replied
in a tight voice, "No, I'm not flattered to be linked to
a siren who lures men to their doom! No one knows
better than I how near to disaster is a man with gambling in his blood. Isn't it bad enough that I'm forced to
earn my living encouraging men to gamble without having to endure jokes about a situation which is already
tormenting my conscience?"

He muttered a soft imprecation and drew the car
into the side of the road. Catching hold of her shoulders,
he forced her round to face him, his usually merry eyes
dark with dismay. "You sound as if you hate your job,
Sara? I had no idea . . . I thought you had enjoyed these
past few weeks . . ."

She drew in a deep breath and admitted shakily, "I
do hate it, Marc, not the club, nor the people I meet
there, but having to encourage men to become victims
of the gambling syndrome. It's a disease, Marc, a horrible, gripping disease that grabs a man's soul and takes
him over completely! You may find it hard to understand because you've never been bitten by the bug, but
for the past few years I've lived in the centre of an
international brotherhood that ordinary card-players
know nothing about. It's not just money that entices
hardened gamblers to the tables – the excitement of
bluffing an opponent gets into a man's blood! Many
times I've watched my grandfather going through the

ritual of looking into a man's face and smiling even though the cards in his hand amounted to practically nothing – and smiling the same way when he was certain he was going to win. It's a cat and mouse situation where the biggest bluffer takes all. The trouble is, once a man becomes hooked he's hooked for life and then, as my grandfather used to say, is when Old Nick takes over." With bitterness, she jerked out, "And I'm the go-between – the one who makes it all possible! "

"No, Sara! " He shook her. "You have magnified the situation out of all proportion. The club is not the den of iniquity you imply, it is merely a place of relaxation, somewhere to while away a few pleasant hours! " But when she shook her head, unconvinced, he had to recognize the guilt and remorse that plagued her. "Very well," he conceded, "if you feel so strongly that what you are doing is wrong, and I cannot convince you otherwise, you must stop working at the club." She began a protest, but he held up his hand for silence. "You need not worry about finding another job. I have friends who will help you if," he became thoughtful, "it should become necessary."

"You know I can't leave," she appealed despairingly. "I still need the money for my fare to England and I wouldn't earn half as much doing any other job."

"Must you return to England? Couldn't you, instead, come with me to France as my wife?"

"Marc! I never once thought . . . I like you tremendously, but . . ."

He pulled her forward into a quick comforting embrace. "I understand, please don't distress yourself, Sara. I've loved you since the first night we met and I've hoped ever since that you might come to love me, but I see now I was foolishly optimistic. I hesitated to tell you earlier," he confessed, "because I think I knew inwardly what your answer would be. However, my father has sent word that he wishes me to return home to take over the running of the business. It seems he has not been well lately, and his doctors have advised him to rest. Naturally, I shall have to go, but I put off making a final decision so that I might have more time with you." He flicked away a tear that clung to the edge of her gold-tipped lashes and forced himself to look away from her infinitely kissable mouth that was trembling with the hurt she was feeling for his sake. "Although I must accept that you cannot return my love, Sara, I have one favour to ask of you which, for the sake of my peace of mind, I hope you will not refuse. Will you allow me to pay your fare back to England? If you cannot bring yourself to accept, then I must cable my father not to expect my return just yet because I refuse absolutely to leave you alone in Tangier."

She met his intent look and realized he was deadly serious. For one wild moment she was tempted to accept his unexpected offer of marriage. He was everything a girl could wish for, handsome, attentive, kind, and so thoughtful of her feelings that she despised herself for not being able to spare his. She could not return his love because her own feelings were dead, she told herself fretfully; she was nothing but a shell, a vacuum, empty of all emotion.

Marc deserved only the best, and the little she had to offer was an insult to his generous nature. But it was inconceivable that he should ignore the wishes of his father simply because her pride baulked at the idea of taking his money. For his sake, she had to overcome her scruples.

"Thank you, Marc," she replied with dignity. "I can accept your offer of money because, contrary to what you believe, I do love you. There's no one in the world closer to my heart. You're a wonderful, very dear friend and I should hate to have to stay here in Tangier without you."

"Sara." Gently he lifted up her chin and touched her lips with his own. It was a sweet kiss, haunting as a goodbye, and it brought a rush of tears to her eyes. But he would not allow them to fall. Deliberately, he dispersed the atmosphere of almost unbearable emotion by ordering firmly, "No tears, *ma petite*, we have customers to think about, remember? They come to see you looking radiant, so for the short time you will be remaining at the club we must try not to disappoint them, eh?" His tanned, handsome face was blurred by tears, but she managed to satisfy his demands by nodding agreement before he started up the car and drove off in the direction of the club.

It was even more hectic than usual that night, and

Sara was kept so busy she had no time to dwell upon the unhappy fact that she was shortly to be deprived of Marc's bolstering presence. She had quickly learned the routine of the club, and had progressed from presiding over chemin de fer, baccarat, and roulette until, by popular demand, she now worked almost exclusively at the table set aside for the confirmed addicts – the poker-players. It was midnight when the game that was in progress broke up and she was able to slip away to take a half hour's break before play re-commenced, to continue until the early hours of the morning. She was making her way to Marc's office where she knew a tray of coffee and sandwiches would be waiting, when a familiar voice called her name. Blood pounded in her ears as she slowly turned to face the man who had hailed her.

"Sara! Sara Battle! What a pleasant surprise, I had no idea you were in Tangier!"

"Señor de Leon! I, too, am surprised. I thought you were still aboard the *African Queen*. What brings you here?"

The young Spaniard dismissed the question she so badly wanted answered and flashed her a wide smile.

"Alvaro, please. We were not so formal aboard ship and Señor de Leon sounds as if you no longer consider me a friend! I had nothing to do with the unfortunate misunderstanding that was the cause of yourself and the Colonel having to leave the ship, I hope you believe that? Where is the Colonel, by the way? I would very much like to match skills with him again." They were surrounded by noise, hemmed in with people, and being jostled on all sides so that coherent conversation was impossible, so after a slight hesitation she suggested:

"Would you care to join me for coffee? We can go into the office and talk without interruption."

A few minutes later, settled in a comfortable chair and supplied with coffee, he repeated his former question. "Is the Colonel here? I would very much like to meet him again."

"No, he isn't," she answered abruptly, knowing herself incapable of discussing her grandfather's death without showing distress. The pain of it was still too new, the wound too tender to stand even slight probing, so she deliberately allowed him to misunderstand.

"Oh, I'm sorry to hear that," Alvaro frowned his disappointment. "I have never played against a cleverer opponent and I was so looking forward to a return bout. I shall never forget our last game," he missed her sudden flinch. "It was, without a doubt, the most exciting I have ever played and, although I lost, I feel I excelled myself that evening simply because the Colonel's skill brought out the best in me."

"You didn't lose," she whispered. "My grandfather cheated, you know that."

He shrugged. "What of it? I might have done the same in the circumstances. I've no doubt he needed the money desperately or it would never have happened. Certainly, I would never accept my cousin's ridiculous assertion that the Colonel was a professional cheat – he was too much of a gentleman. No, he was tempted and he fell, but I have too many weaknesses of my own ever to judge him. Only a person such as my cousin Felipe, who has never been known to digress from his rigid standards, has a right to condemn us lesser mortals," he bit out savagely.

She strove to sound casual, but her hands were tightly clasped when she asked, "And where's your cousin now? Is he with you in Tangier or did he continue the cruise alone?"

"Felipe on a cruise?" he laughed without humour. "I assure you, *señorita*, my cousin would not waste his precious hours on such a frivolous project. His presence aboard ship was deliberate. He was following his usual practice of tracking me down simply to exert his authority as head of the family and order me to return home where, as he so grimly put it, he intends to see that I shoulder my share of responsibilities. Our family is one of the richest in Morocco, yet he thinks he can compel me to work in the vineyards like a common labourer. I must learn the business from the bottom up, he says, otherwise my allowance will be cut to nothing!" He glowered into his empty coffee cup, but after a few moments' silence his frown vanished and he chuckled. "But I have fooled him. He thinks I am asleep, worn out with honest toil, and look at me," he waved his hand to encompass his surroundings. "How his temper would erupt if he could see me now!"

Sara heard him out, feeling growing dismay. It took great effort of will to question him further. "Where is your home, Alvaro? Is it near Tangier?"

He nodded. "Actually, we have several. My mother and Felipe's, who are both widowed, live together at our family estate just across the Straits in Spain itself. We also have extensive vineyards to the east of Tangier, on the slopes of the Rif mountains – a benighted spot where nothing ever happens – and that is where my dear cousin thinks I am at this very moment incarcerated while he himself is preparing to entertain at his villa on the outskirts of Tangier a young woman whom he has decided I will marry. What a hope! " he exclaimed furiously. "Do you wonder I am tempted to choose the most unsuitable bride I can find as a lesson to him that we are now living in the twentieth century? I must find some way to impress upon him that I refuse to recognize his right to decide when, where, and even whom I am to marry! "

Sara was appalled. She had been left in no doubt that his cousin Felipe was an arrogant, forceful man, but that he should think himself qualified to choose the woman his cousin should marry was too imperious even for him. Alvaro's resentment found an echo in her own heart. Reckless and ineffectual he might be, but he deserved better than to have to live his life under the thumb of a despot, a man whose tremendous conceit made him intolerant of the weaknesses of others.

Alvaro was gratified by the sudden warmth she generated as she offered him more coffee and hastened to light a cigarette he raised to his lips. He was used to such attentions from the opposite sex, but up until now Sara's manner had held a hint of aloofness, a cool contemplation that had at times left him feeling uncomfortable and slightly inadequate. He preened himself, certain her change of heart was a tribute to hidden qualities she had only just recognized, completely unaware that she saw him as a victim of oppression, a martyr who needed help to escape the clutches of the man she blamed for the untimely death of her grandfather.

CHAPTER IV

Two days later Marc left for Paris. He booked on the first available flight after receiving a telegram which told him his father's condition had deteriorated and that he was asking to see him. Sara accompanied him to the airport and waited with him in the lounge until his flight was announced.

"Are you sure you don't mind being left alone, Sara?" he asked for the umpteenth time, glancing again at the hands of his watch that were creeping inexorably towards the time of separation.

"Of course not," she said with a smile. "Madame Blais will look after me and I promise you I'll book a passage for home as soon as they find replacements for us at the club. You know we agreed we couldn't both leave at a moment's notice, it would put the management in too much of a spot, so I'll stay on for another few weeks, at least, to give them time to engage new staff. So please, Marc, do stop worrying. I'll be perfectly all right, I assure you."

He jumped to his feet when an announcer's voice boomed across the lounge informing him and his fellow passengers that it was time to assemble at the departure gate. Grasping her shoulders, he questioned with renewed urgency, "The cheque – your passage money – is it safe? Do you have it with you?"

"Oh, Marc!" Knowing he would not leave until he had assured himself that she still had the cheque he had given her the previous evening, she scrabbled in her bag and withdrew it with so much haste that it escaped her light-fingered touch and fluttered to the floor, coming to rest at the feet of one of the approaching crowd. Both she and Marc made a dart towards the precious piece of paper, but the man whose shoe it touched was quicker. Even before it had time to settle, he picked it up and began scanning its contents with eyes so intent Sara knew they were missing neither her name nor the amount payable to her from the account of one Marc Rochefort. She pulled up short, her heart somersaulting, then like the clashing of swords her eyes met those of the man who was holding the cheque between thumb and forefinger as if its proximity was offending.

"Yours, I think, Miss Battle," he offered icily, his patrician features mirroring distaste.

She wanted to scream a denial of the conclusion he had so obviously formed. Each time they met it seemed she was surrounded by incriminating circumstances and now, if looks could be taken as evidence, she was once more being judged a ruthless gold-digger out to prey upon the susceptibilities of men. She had never hated him more than when she had to swallow his unspoken insults and accept meekly the cheque he was holding out towards her.

"Thank you, Señor de Panza." She snatched the damning piece of paper from his hand and thrust it into her bag before slipping her hand through Marc's arm and edging him in the direction of the departure gate. "Please excuse us, we must go or my friend will miss his plane."

Felipe de Panza bowed, his quick glance taking in every detail of Marc's distrait appearance, then he turned to walk back to his waiting companion.

She missed Marc dreadfully, but never more so than the first evening when she worked alone in the club. Without her having realized it he had become a buffer; his protective manner had served to warn off anyone who would have attempted a more familiar approach towards the attractive new croupier, with the result that, once his absence was noted, she began to sense disturbing undercurrents in remarks addressed to her by some of the club's more unsavoury characters.

She was dealing cards, preparatory to beginning a round of poker with three of the club's most valued clients – Tangier businessmen who discarded respectability as quickly as unwanted cloaks once they crossed the threshold where their names were synonymous with reckless gambling. One of the men, hard-eyed, softly-spoken and of obvious mixed parentage, had tried often to ingratiate himself in the past, without success, but this evening his manner was so much more familiar, his lascivious eyes so revealing, that Sara knew he was aware of, and was rejoicing in, the absence of her protector. She suppressed a shudder when his hand reached out to enclose hers in a clasp that was moist and clammy.

"May I have the pleasure of your company at supper tonight, my dear?" he hissed through teeth so large and tobacco-stained she was reminded of weathered tombstones.

Her face felt stiff as she tried to smile. "You are very kind, but I already have a supper engagement."

"So?" The angry flicker in his eyes told her he knew she lied. "May I ask with whom?" His clasp tightened when she tried to withdraw her hand, and when her quick desperate glance of appeal towards his two companions was met with broad grins her heart sank. She had no wish to make a scene; instinct told her that in a showdown with the management her own value would balance lightly against the weight of currency poured into the club by her three tormentors, and although Marc's generosity had helped enormously, she was still in need of money to pay one or two outstanding debts, so she dared not risk being dismissed.

"A . . . friend," she faltered, attempting once more to tug her hand free of its trap.

"But your friend Marc Rochefort left today," he persisted with enjoyment, "and everyone knows you have no other close friend in Tangier."

"Then everyone is wrong, *amigo!*" The voice came from behind her, and she spun round quickly to meet the laughing eyes of Alvaro de Leon. Then, as his glance slewed round to her companion, his smile faded and in a voice incredibly like his cousin's he observed, "The *señorita* does not seem to find your company amusing, gentlemen, so perhaps it would be as well if you were to seek your pleasures elsewhere." The following undignified scramble to vacate seats underlined forcibly the power wielded in Tangier by Alvaro's family; a family of money and position, the possession of which seemed to give even to its weakest member the strength of Atlas, in the sight of these men, at least.

She was shaking so much she was barely coherent when she thanked him. "I'm so grateful for your help, Alvaro. That man – he was so horrible, I couldn't cope..."

"Then why do you try?" A frown sat uneasily upon his usually cheerful face. "I simply do not understand, *señorita,* what you are doing in this place. It is not for you, ladies do not frequent such places as the Club Aziz! Why, in my country, if a girl were to be seen even entering such an establishment she would be forever damned in the eyes of the family of any prospective suitor. Never would she be allowed to live down the disgrace!"

Her sense of humour revived at the sight of his shocked face; for all his earlier bravado, his tirade against the resistance of his cousin to modern trends, Alvaro himself was still a century behind in his attitude towards women.

"Then perhaps it's just as well I have no suitor at

my heels," she teased. "Just imagine how it would shock your cousin, for instance, if you were to tell him you were paying court to a girl who earns her living as a croupier in the most notorious club in Tangier! The mind boggles at picturing his reaction."

To her surprise he did not join in her laughter, but sat staring at her across the table, his eyes fastened upon her face with startled intensity.

"Is something wrong, Alvaro? Why are you staring at me like that?"

He jerked back to reality, but his eyes were still feverishly bright when he leant across to urge. "Sara, let's get out of here, we must go where we can talk!"

"But that's not possible. I have work to do, I can't just walk out on my job, surely you realize that?"

He snapped his fingers to show his contempt of her work, then jumped to his feet and ordered, "Please go and get your wrap. If you insist, I will arrange that you are given permission to have the rest of the evening off, but it is not really necessary as you will realize when I have talked to you. Hurry now, I expect to see you in the foyer in five minutes."

Without resenting his arbitrary manner, she found herself hurrying to do his bidding. Centuries of aristocratic lineage lay behind the arrogance which in his cousin Felipe was ever-present and therefore insupportable, but which in Alvaro was rather endearing and not in the least offensive. She was not really surprised when she reached the foyer to find he had with him an affable director who was waiting to assure her that she had his permission to absent herself for the rest of the evening. With a speed that left her breathless, she was then ushered into Alvaro's car and driven at breakneck haste towards some unspecified destination.

He did not speak until the town was far beneath them, hundreds of feet below where he brought the car to rest on a steep hill looking down and across the Straits to Spain. Below, dozens of different coloured lights twinkled from a miscellany of shipping crowding the harbour, while above, huge stars encircled a sickle of pale gold moon that rested against a backcloth of midnight blue sky. Silence surrounded them, a silence she made no effort to break when she sensed his careful searching for words with which to explain his extraordinary actions. She watched him nibble his thumb, seemingly engrossed in his thoughts to the exclusion of herself, until finally curiosity overwhelmed her and she gave him a verbal prod.

"I'm waiting for an explanation, Alvaro. Why have you brought me here, and what is it you have to discuss with me that is so important that I suspect I've almost jeopardized my job to hear it?"

"Job?" he questioned vaguely, then with a wave of his hand he dismissed the subject as being of no importance.

"Well, really!" she began indignantly, "you might not think it important, but I certainly do! Do you realize . . ."

"Would you consider working for me?" he interrupted.

"Doing what?" she asked, breathless with surprise.

His voice was full of suppressed excitement when he raced out the words. "Something far more congenial than the work you are doing now and much less strenuous. You suggested the idea to me yourself when we were talking in the club earlier, and the more I think of it the more convinced I am that it is the solution I have been searching for. I know my idea is unconventional, but I hope you will not think it insulting because it is certainly not intended to be. Look, Sara, we both know my cousin Felipe has formed a totally wrong impression of you and I've thought of a way of making him suffer for his damnable tendency to jump to conclusions. I want you to agree to pose as my fiancée for a short while — a few weeks should be long enough to convince him that I mean business and that I no longer intend to allow him to make all my decisions. I will *not* be told whom I shall marry," his fist thumped into the palm of his hand with a force that jarred, "and if I can introduce you to Felipe as my future bride he will have no option but to concede defeat and to send that infant he has brought here to either approve or disapprove of myself as a suitable husband back to where she came from!"

Sara, who was fighting a losing battle against surprise and astonishment, marshalled her senses into sufficient order to ask, "You mean you've never even met this girl he wants you to marry, she's so much a stranger you don't even know her name?"

He shrugged and answered sulkily, "Her name is Isabella Savedra. She is distinctly connected – a sixth or seventh cousin, I'm not sure, and I care even less. We played together as children," he frowned at the memory, "but as far as I am concerned she could not be more of a stranger. My mother and Felipe have arranged it all between them and even though I have stated firmly and irrevocably that I will have nothing whatsoever to do with her they refuse to listen. Felipe is determined, and my great fear is that his persistence will one day wear me down until I finally find myself bound in marriage to a total stranger." He whipped round, full of urgency. "Say you will help me to fight Felipe! Please, Sara, you are my only hope, don't let me down!"

For long seconds her horror-filled eyes were held by his fixed gaze as he silently pleaded with her not to reject his idea. Her mind seethed in an agony of indecision; she dared not allow her thoughts to dwell too long upon Felipe de Panza lest the surge of bitter feeling his memory engendered should overrule the Christian beliefs nurtured within her from childhood. It was wrong to hate, wrong to desire revenge, wrong to plan the downfall even of an enemy – but the appalling truth was that, wrong or not, she *did* hate, she *did* desire to see the pride of her grandfather's executioner ground into the dust! Beads of sweat formed on her brow as she struggled to reach a decision. Never before had the forces of evil beaten so strongly within her, it was as if the devil himself mocked her puny efforts to retain sanity and his downfall was brought about only because she envisaged his face as a replica of Felipe de Panza's. In her fevered imaginings she saw his dark, satanic face laughing his contempt of her scruples and the will to submit was overcome only by forcing herself to admit that hate is self-destructive and that to succumb to it would be to afford him yet another victory. It was a relief to gasp out,

"No, Alvaro, I'm sorry, I can't do it!"

The light died out of his eyes as he sank back against his seat, bitterly disappointed. "I don't see why not," he muttered, his bottom lip protruding in a childlike pout. "It can't be that you have any regard for Felipe – he treated you and your grandfather abominably. Not that he knew the Colonel was your grandfather," he admitted carelessly.

"What do you mean?" she questioned sharply.

He looked uncomfortable for a moment, then blurted out. "From a reference he once made to yourself and your *travelling companion* I assumed he knew nothing of your relationship with the Colonel and, that being so, he had as usual put the worst possible construction upon your close association."

Her heart was thumping so hard she felt a sickening pain, but no trace of it showed in her tone when she stated. "Your cousin's opinion of me is even worse than I had thought. He has accused me openly of being a thief and a cardsharper, he has silently condemned me as a mercenery adventuress and now," her voice cracked on a forced laugh, "now you tell me he even doubts my virtue! Oh, Alvaro," she began to laugh wildly, "how funny, how very, very funny!"

He was completely out of his depth, as much bewildered by her laughter as he was by the flood of tears that followed, and all he could think of doing was cradle her trembling body until her sobbing was spent and she lay silent and still in his arms. He was astonished that the information he had disclosed, primarily to make her angry, should have had such a devastating effect, and while the silence lengthened he was forming belated apologies for his clumsiness.

But the need to apologize was forgotten when she spoke against his shoulder. "I've changed my mind, Alvaro, I'd like to take up your offer." She felt his surprised jerk, but allowed him no more than a gasp before carrying on. "But there is a condition..."

"Yes? Anything..." he urged.

Her face was still pressed against his shoulder, muffling her voice, but he was conscious of great stress when she formed the words.

"Gramps is dead. Before I do as you ask, I must have your promise never to speak of him to your cousin, neither to mention his death nor to disclose his relationship to myself. Do you agree?"

He fought down shocked remorse to make the ragged reply. "I'm terribly sorry, Sara. Of course I will never speak of him, and especially not to Felipe, I give you my word."

The villa, with its white marble floors, terraces, and swimming pool shimmering in the sun, had the appearance and ambience of a Moorish pavilion. The focal point of the house was the terrace room where a large white leather and wood seat took up most of the space in the centre and stools and loungers with scatterings of gaily-coloured cushions beckoned relaxing guests to gather like butterflies to blossoms.

Sara had caught a quick glimpse of activity around the turquoise waters of the pool before Alvaro ushered her into the more formal room where she now waited to be presented, as his fiancée, to the head of his family. To ease her nervousness, she wandered around the room supposedly examining the many beautiful pictures that hung around its walls, but in reality seeing nothing at all. Blind panic grew with every second of Alvaro's absence as she began picturing in her mind the confrontation with Felipe which he had insisted had to take place that day.

She ran nervous fingers across the gold velvet covering of a settee that ran the full length of two walls, then hastily erased with the palm of her hand the trail of fingermarks she had left on the soft material. An enormous fringed carpet deadened her footsteps as she moved restlessly towards a marble table holding a Moorish lamp delicately traced in metal, squired by two gold candlesticks containing virgin white candles. The carpet came to an abrupt end just before she reached her objective, and the loud staccato beat of her heels against the marble-tiled floor was so unexpected the sound set her heart racing. Her knees were shaking so much she sank down on to a large soft pouffe, only to jump up again at the thought that it might not be such an advantageous position in which to begin a formal meeting.

She smoothed her dress, fretting at Alvaro's extended absence. The smell of orange blossom coming from a tree outside the open window was overpowering and for one dreadful moment she felt certain she was going to be sick. Her hands were pressed to her fluttering stomach when the door was suddenly thrown open, and when her green eyes, enormous in a pale face, met those of Felipe de Panza she felt immediately and paralysingly afraid. For a split second as they faced one another no holds were barred, his look, glowering dark with contempt, took in every detail of her appearance – the delicate green cloud of dress that caught a slight draught from the open door and clung to her slender curves as if deliberately flouting their perfection before eyes determined to find fault, the smooth tanned flesh of her arms, bare except for a gold slave bangle snapped around her wrist to emphasise fragile hands and slender gold-tipped fingernails, and her burnished coronet of hair that looked afire with trapped sunlight.

He had been swimming. His hair was tousled, rubbed through with a hasty towel, so that the dark glistening spirals falling across his brow afforded his usually suave features an aura of carefree vitality. But the contrasting fury in his eyes and in his tightly compressed mouth told her that he had already spoken to Alvaro and that the news he had been given had left him feeling anything but carefree. She braced herself against attack. Their confrontations had been few, but each had held an element of battle, a battle that now threatened to escalate into a full-scale war from which she sensed she would emerge with scars even greater than those she had suffered in earlier skirmishes.

Her grandfather had always maintained that attack was the finest form of defence, so with an aplomb that inwardly amazed her she directed him a cool smile and mocked sweetly, "I see Alvaro has acquainted you with our news. Have you come to offer your good wishes for our future happiness?"

His answering retort would have annihilated her completely if it had been allowed to be voiced, but even as a quickly indrawn breath hissed between his teeth preparatory, she had no doubt, to delivering a blistering tirade, a young breathless voice spoke from somewhere behind him.

"Oh, there you are, Felipe! We were wondering where you had disappeared to. Alvaro has arrived, did you know?" When the slim figure of a girl dressed in a towelled robe only partially covering a one-piece bathing suit stepped into view Sara knew instinctively that she was looking at Isabel Savedra. She was a ripe, lucious beauty with lovely flashing eyes and jet black hair and she projected the unconscious, almost puritanical sex appeal so often possessed by nubile Spanish girls. She was also shy, as was revealed when her footsteps faltered to a halt and her cheeks flooded a becoming shade of pink at the sight of Sara.

"Forgive me if I intrude, Felipe," she stumbled, her eyes downcast. "I did not know you were not alone."

Sara, however unwillingly, had to admire his superb self-control. With complete mastery, he banished the anger from his face and took hold of Isabel's hand to draw her forward into the room. "Isabel, let me introduce you to Miss Battle – Sara," he amended quickly, then, with a hard look towards her, he stressed, "A *family* friend." His look dared her to deny his assertion, dared her to disillusion the shy young girl whose voice had trilled with delight when voicing Alvaro's name, and so, although hating to allow him even one small victory, she found herself smiling agreement as she stepped forward to shake the hand Isabel immediately held out towards her.

"How do you do, Sara. Won't you come outside and join us around the pool?" she coaxed, with a quick glance at Felipe. He was forced to second the invitation or seem churlish, and Sara felt she had the advantage when, with stiff politeness, he bowed to the inevitable.

"Yes, certainly you must join us. You are no doubt anxious to meet Alvaro's mother and she, in turn, would never forgive me if I allowed you to go without an introduction."

The quick flickering of her eyelashes told him she was disconcerted, and the knowledge seemed to afford him much satisfaction. Alvaro had made no mention of his mother's presence at the villa, she was prepared to meet only one adversary, Felipe, whose forceful personality was ample strain without the added burden of a possessive mother. But her discomfiture was only momentary, she had pledged herself to help Alvaro extricate himself from his family's bondage and the sympathy and indignation she felt on his behalf gave her the courage she so badly needed to face further opposition. So she tipped up her chin and met his sardonic smile with outward nonchalance before stepping past him to follow Isabel, who was already leading the way.

"One moment, *señorita*," he checked her hurrying footsteps. "Before we proceed I must warn you, as I have already warned Alvaro, there must be no mention of your supposed engagement before I have had time to prepare my aunt for the announcement. Because of his usual lack of consideration, my cousin has had to be reminded that his mother's health has been causing us much worry. He knows, but has chosen to ignore, that her doctor has ordered complete rest and freedom from stress if her tired heart is to last out another year. At the moment she is happy, convinced her son is at last ready to settle down with the girl she expects him to marry – Isabel – and I intend to see to it that she stays happy, at least until her strength has been sufficiently built up to allow her to cope with the changed situation."

His words caught her heart with the sting of a lash, their underlying threat unmistakable. "And how do you propose to do that?" she tilted, defiantly determined to oppose what she was convinced was no more than emotional blackmail, a ploy he had thought up on the spur of the moment in an effort to baulk Alvaro's bid for freedom.

"There is no time to discuss ways and means," he rapped as Isabel's voice called out to them. "Just bear in mind that if you do not do as I direct both Alvaro and yourself will be very, very sorry!"

Her cheeks were still wildly flushed when they finally reached the small group that sat lazily around the cool blue-green waters of the pool. To her surprise Alvaro was one of them. When she appeared Isabel jumped to her feet and leant down to whisper in the ear of the white-haired old lady whose chair was next to hers. She looked up, removed her sunglasses, and extended her hand towards the somewhat timidly advancing Sara.

Ready as she was to meet unfriendliness, even cold hostility, Sara was completely taken aback when Alvaro's mother smiled a welcome which was undoubtedly genuine. "My dear," the eyes shaded by a mantilla of fine black lace were kind, "Isabel has just whispered to me that I am about to meet a very special friend of the family. As I know Alvaro has no time at the moment for anyone but Isabel, I have gladly guessed that the one it is who holds you so dear to his heart is my nephew Felipe." She cast a roguish glance around their astonished faces. "Why you all persist in treating me like a decrepit imbecile when you know how impossible I am to deceive I do not know! Sara, my dear – I may call you that, may I not? – will you please side with me against my incorrigible family and help me to convince them that far from inflicting harm upon my stupid old heart, the good news that my dear Felipe has at last been persuaded to part with his affection is a tonic I have long been waiting for.

"Come, kiss me, my dear," she proffered a smooth cheek, "then sit by me so that we may talk. I must have all the answers ready for Felipe's mother when I return to Spain or else be prepared to suffer her displeasure."

In various stages of shock, they all moved automatically into position. Sara threw one stunned glance towards Alvaro as he placed her chair next to his mother's, but his eyes slewed away with embarrassment and she had no choice but to accept the seat which, mercifully, was placed so that all she could see of Felipe was his rigid back and the shadow of his grimly etched profile.

Isabel moved a stool next to Alvaro's chair which was placed overlooking the glistening water, isolating them both on an island of solitude he was either too loath or too cowardly to abandon. Sara's fury at being placed in such an invidious position knew no bounds. Obviously, there had been a ring of truth in Felipe's assertion that his aunt was not in good health, but Doña Maria, as she had been introduced by Isabel, was a matriarch figure, a pampered old lady whose every whim had been allowed . . . up until now!

Felipe must have sensed her objective even as the thought was formed. As her lips opened to disabuse Alvaro's mother of her hastily formed conclusions he jumped to his feet to reach her side before the first defiant word could be spoken.

"Would you like to swim, *amiga*?" he asked, his hand digging so cruelly into the soft flesh of her shoulder she all but cried out with pain.

"Oh, but, Felipe . . . ! " Doña Maria moued.

"You will have plenty of time to get to know, Sara, Tia," he flashed her a white-toothed smile, "but later, when the sun is not so hot. Once you get into your stride your questions tend to develop on the lines of the Inquisition and I want Sara to try out the pool. So, to please me, will you try now to sleep, then this evening when you are more rested I promise I shall let you have her to yourself for as long as you wish." He bent over Sara with a tight set smile. "Are you agreeable, *chica*?"

She could not answer, her bottom lip was caught between her teeth biting back the pain his fingers were inflicting upon her tender flesh and so she nodded and gasped out: "Of course!" Feeling his merciless grip relax was a relief so great she could have fainted.

"Good, then that is settled," he straightened and re-returned his aunt's smile of agreement as he urged Sara to her feet. "Isabel has plenty of spare costumes, so if you'll follow me I'll show you where you can change."

The water felt blessedly cool against her fiery body when she slid into the pool dressed in a borrowed swimsuit which ought to have clashed with her hair but which instead created an unusual contrast of frosted pink against its rich rubiousness. She was so humiliated, so full of suppressed rage she would not have been surprised to feel the water sizzle around her suffused body. She cleaved the water with smooth, clean strokes, rejoicing at its satin caress against her flushed face, and surrendered for the moment to the sheer bliss of uncomplicated solitude. She had to think, to plan, and to reorganize her opinions about Alvaro whose spineless acceptance of his cousin's dictates had left her feeling terribly vulnerable. He would have to be discounted as an ally; though full of confidence the previous evening when outlining his ideas, once within his cousin's influence he became as wax in his hands. But she must carry out the plan he had originated. Alvaro needed to be protected from himself, even more so now that she knew the full extent of Felipe's dominance over his weak-willed young cousin.

She rolled over on her back. Closing her eyes against the sun's glare, she allowed herself to float along, paddling now and then with her hands to project her body languidly through the water. She was lost in the enjoyment of the moment, her troubles almost forgotten, when a turbulence around her set the water heaving and a second later Felipe's voice commanded,

"Swim with me to the far end of the pool where we will not be overheard. I want to talk to you!"

Reluctantly, she abandoned her state of happy euphoria and followed in his wake. She would have headed towards the steps rather than seek his assistance, but he reached the side long before she did and she could not evade the hand that reached out to pull her out of the water and on to a sunbathing raft placed at the pool's edge. He stretched out on the raft like a great cat, his muscles rippling with panther-like power as he adjusted his body to a comfortable position. She was very conscious of his bare brown limbs and of the breadth of his shoulders; their strength was indication that, if he wished, he might break her own slight body in two without exerting himself in the slightest.

To occupy her hands and to keep her eyes from straying towards his uncovered limbs, she flung off her pink cap and loosened her hair from its constricting pins so that it cascaded around her bent head, screening him from her sight but also hiding her own flushed cheeks from his keen eyes. She had no idea why she should feel so burnt up with shyness. On the sun deck aboard ship she had often been surrounded by men in various stages of undress and Marc, too, had many times swum with her wearing the same kind of black swimming briefs favoured by the *señor*, but somehow none of the others had projected the primitive aura she sensed around the dark Spaniard. In shedding his clothes he had also shed the veneer of culture that had made her feel able to oppose him. In his case, clothes had not merely made the man – they had helped to cloak the sheer animal virility beneath their surface. A quick breath caught in her throat: how had she even dared to contemplate contesting the will of this man whose victory was sure to be as swift and as merciless as his retribution? She swept the curtain of hair back from her face and forced herself to meet his cynical eyes. Cowardice had won; she intended to back out, to assure him she would leave his house immediately. But then fate decided otherwise.

"Well, Señorita Battle," he forestalled her, "how much is it going to cost me to be rid of you?"

"How . . . much . . . ?" she stumbled like a child grappling with new words.

"Come now," his jaw was granite hard, "spare me the preliminary games, I'm not in the mood for pretence. I wish to know what amount of money will be required to free my family from the embarrassment of your presence."

78

When his meaning became clear her previous decision sank without trace beneath a flood of furious anger.

"How dare you!" she whispered, her eyes mesmerized by a face as cold and unfeeling as a swaying cobra's. She felt battered by contempt when he returned with cold deliberation,

"I dare because I have previous knowledge of your methods. You do not seem to have much lasting success with the men you ensnare, *señorita*. What happened to your shipboard companion, for instance? Did he desert you, or had you no further use for him once your despicable tricks to extort money were uncovered? And the young man at the airport, what about him? You seem to have forgotten that I held in my hand evidence that he, too, had paid dearly for your favours!"

His words were missiles flung from his tongue without thought of mercy and his cold eyes did not soften when he saw how her slender body wilted beneath the weight of their bombardment. She had expected a fight, indeed she had come prepared for one, but only now did she fully realize how ill equipped she was to enter the arena with a man whose cutting tongue could reduce her spirit to ribbons with a single spate of words.

She lifted her shaking hands to her ashen face, only to have them jerked away in his hard grip.

"You haven't answered my question," he gritted. "Because of the urgency of the situation I am willing to let you name your own sum. If it were not for the fact that I am forced to consider the feelings of Alvaro's mother as well as those of his future wife I would leave him completely at your mercy. It would do the young fool good to learn his lesson the hard way, by personal experience, instead of always relying upon others to extricate him from the messes he gets himself into. You might well have been the making of Alvaro, *señorita*," he suddenly mocked. "He is still so naïve he thinks a pretty face indicates a pretty nature, but an entanglement with you would have soon disabused him of that idea! However," his mocking look disappeared with a return of grimness, "as speed is an essential essence of my plans, I must forgo that pleasure and insist that we come to an immediate agreement. How much? And do you prefer the money to be paid in cash or by cheque?"

She was quick to recognize the direction of his thoughts; if he could remove her from out of his family's orbit immediately her flying visit would soon be forgotten and her existence permanently erased from their memory. But if she stayed long enough to make friends with Doña Maria and Isabel he would run the risk of her disclosing everything to them, leaving him with some very awkward questions to answer.

She almost managed to smile when she straightened her drooping back and met his look with eyes that held newly aroused vengeance in their depths.

"I hadn't definitely decided to accept Alvaro's proposal," she told him hardly, "but you have helped me to reach a decision, *señor*. I'm not in love with your cousin, but my hatred for you goes so deep that I find myself willing to marry him simply to get even with you! So you can throw away your cheque book. As the future Señora de Leon I shall no doubt be furnished with ample money to supply my needs."

His expression evidenced the terrible passions she had aroused, and instinct forced her to her feet to flee from danger. His reaction was swift, but she managed to slip from the grip he only just managed to fasten upon her arm and dived into the water to swim faster than she had ever done in her life before towards the other end of the pool.

Half an hour later the group around the pool broke up, Doña Maria to escape the strengthening heat of the sun by seeking the coolness of her room and Isabel to go to the kitchen to inform the staff there would be two extra for dinner that evening. Of Felipe there was no sign, by the time Sara had reached the end of the pool and made haste to join the others he had disappeared from sight and had not been seen since.

Alvaro was just preparing to sidle out of view when Sara turned to speak sharply to him. "Alvaro, don't go, you must realize we have to talk!"

He shrugged. "Can't it wait until after dinner? I have some business in town that must be attended to today. I hadn't bargained on being delayed here so long. I must get back to Tangier immediately."

"Your business must wait!" she retorted, despising him for his attempt to avoid the awkward questions he knew she was about to ask. "But, in any case, there need be no delay in reaching Tangier, just give me a minute to change and I'll travel back with you. We can talk on the way."

He looked uncomfortable. "But we are both expected to dine here. You heard Felipe's promise to my mother, she will be most disappointed if you do not appear!"

"You needn't worry, Felipe has no intention of allowing me to stay," she broke in wryly. "No doubt he had already formed some excuse to offer your mother for my absence when he asked me how much it would cost to be rid of me immediately!"

"He asked you that?" Alvaro slowly enunciated, embarrassed colour seeping under his tan. She waited for a storm of protest on her behalf, confident that this disclosure was the prod he needed to bring out the spirit in his indolent nature, but she waited in vain. Instead of the indignant reaction she expected, all he did was drop down on to the nearest chair with a whistle of surprise and mutter helplessly: "Well, I'm damned! He said he intended being ruthless, but I'd no idea he would go that far!"

Sara's scalp prickled. "Would you mind telling me what else he had to say when you told him of our engagement?"

With a resigned shrug he settled back in his chair

and struggled to find less offensive words than those his cousin had used to convey his displeasure. "First, he threatened my complete destitution by saying he would throw me out of the family business, and after that he tried appealing to my sense of responsibility. It was my duty, he said, to marry Isabel as everyone expected it and both my mother's heart and hers would be broken if I refused to comply. When I remained adamantly opposed to the idea, he proceeded to outline in detail the many reasons why I should not become entangled – his words – with you. For a man who has met you only infrequently he has a surprising knowledge of your movements since you left the ship. Not only does he know about your job as a croupier at the Club Aziz, he knows also of your association with a man named Marc Rochefort who, according to him, has reason to regret ever having met you."

He slewed a quick glance over her set face and when she did not interrupt he carried on reluctantly, "Finally, when everything else had failed, he reminded me that my mother's health would be jeopardized by any sudden shock, such as she might receive if I acquainted her of my decision to marry you." With a shamefaced look, he leant forward to plead, "Sara, I swear that up until then I did not know the seriousness of her condition. When Felipe waved the doctor's report under my nose I realized it was out of the question to carry on with our plan. My mother can be stern at times, she often treats me like a child whose actions must always be vetted, but I love her dearly and could never do anything to harm her. That is why," he sighed, "I have decided to do as they ask – to marry Isabel. I could not live with myself if any action of mine were to bring about the death of my mother."

He was genuinely worried, and she could not find it in her heart to condemn him. But it hurt, the fact that her proud boast to Felipe had been so much hot air. How he would gloat when he found out . . .

"Alvaro!" She spoke so suddenly he jerked to attention. "Felipe can't be aware of your change of mind or he wouldn't have attempted to bribe me?" When he nodded affirmation she bounded on, "Then need he know just yet? If only to teach him a lesson, can't we keep him in the dark a little longer?"

He did not try to hide his dismay.

"But why, Sara? You've no idea what he is like when opposed, and already he's sworn to go to any lengths to break things up between us. He means every word, I assure you, so why tempt the devil?"

"You owe me this one favour, Alvaro! Felipe has humiliated and threatened me and in the cause of justice I mean to see that his actions do not go unpunished. Neither Isabel nor your mother need ever know," she coaxed. "It will be our secret, yours and mine."

His nervous fingers sought out his cigarette case, but when it was found he did not attempt to open it but merely drummed a nervous tattoo upon its surface as he tried not to become wooed over by her impassioned reasoning. Even as he hesitated, her sensitive mouth began to tremble and he knew then that he was beaten.

"Very well, you win," he sighed. "I'll say nothing to Felipe about my change of plan, but I warn you, Sara, you will be dicing with danger. My mother's hastily formed conclusion that you and he are more than friends puts you both in an untenable position – one Felipe will resent. If you insist upon driving him into a corner you will have no one but yourself to blame if you find the outcome unfavourable!"

They left the villa a short while later. Sara wanted to change for dinner, so Alvaro dropped her off at the *pension* with the promise that as soon as his business was concluded he would return to drive them both back to the villa in ample time for dinner.

Her hands trembled as she ransacked her wardrobe, seeking an extra special dress with appeal enough to help her get through the difficult evening ahead. But nothing inspiring came to light, so she unlocked the two large cabin trunks that were stacked, still unpacked, in a closet and continued searching. One dress after another was discarded as she burrowed through the collection of fabulous clothes that constituted the only profit accrued from her partnership with her grandfather. At last, she emerged satisfied, clutching one of her more recent purchases, a culotte fashioned out of finest nylon jersey, so insubstantial it rippled like a silken breeze through her fingers. Holding it against her body, she stepped eagerly towards the mirror and stared with satisfaction at the effect its multi-coloured greens, blues and golds had upon her copper hair and wide expectant eyes. "My choice of ammunition might not be as obvious as yours, *señor*," she murmured softly, "but let's hope it will prove to be just as deadly!"

She dared not dwell too long on her plan of revenge; the idea had been formulated not from conceit, but from the many advances she had received from men over the past few years. Men found her attractive, and Felipe de Panza was a man. It must therefore follow, she reasoned, that if she were in a position to bombard him with the wiles that came naturally to every woman, sooner or later a crack must show in his defences. She would work on him, subtly but intently, until he was completely disarmed, and then, when the moment was right, she would shatter his enormous self-esteem by laughing in his face! Just to think about it made her tremble with frightened anticipation, but she felt she was committed and there could be no turning back. As Alvaro's fiancée she was bound to see a lot of Felipe and so long as Alvaro kept his promise not to divulge his change of plan she could safely count on having ample time to ensure his cousin's downfall.

Alvaro picked her up as promised and they reached the villa with time to spare. He took her into a small salon and after supplying her with a drink and assuring her that she would soon be joined by the rest of the family, he excused himself and went up to his room to change. The windows of the salon opened out on to the garden, so she put down her glass and stepped outside to experience at close quarters the eternal marvel of the orange tree bearing ripe fruit and blossom at the same time. She sniffed deeply, revelling in the sweet, sharp tang, and leant forward to caress with an inquisitive finger the white, star-shaped blossoms that clung around the richly coloured globules of fruit.

"Good evening, *señorita!*" Even as the words shattered the evening calm a pair of hard hands clamped her waist and spun her round without thought of gentleness to face the *señor's* hard eyes.

"Let me go!" She fought him with instinctive resentment, his attack catching her completely off guard.

"Not until we finish the discussion you so abruptly terminated this afternoon," he suavely refused. "You were too quick for me then, but even if you should fight all night you will not be allowed to escape me this time." He pulled her forward and demanded with a steely glint, "Are you going to be sensible, or must I continue to employ brute force?"

"What other kind would you know of?" she spat furiously.

His amused laugh clashed with the thinly veiled dislike in his voice. "Am I to infer from that remark that you consider me a brute?" He lowered his head and sent a chill of fear through her by menacing softly, "You underestimate me, *señorita!*"

"No doubt!" She flung away from him and he allowed her to go, but his wary look was proof that he was ready to pounce if she should make the effort necessary. She heard the snap of his cigarette case and saw a flare of light in the dusk before he spoke again.

"Do you still insist upon carrying on with your mockery of an engagement to Alvaro, even though you know the pain it will cause his mother and Isabel?"

She swallowed hard. His presence was so dominating, the wide sweep of his shoulders under a white dinner jacket was intimidating and his pristine linen was a foil that threw into relief the granite hardness of his profile. "We . . . we have decided, Alvaro and I," she stammered, "to keep our engagement a secret for the time being as we are in no hurry to get married. In the meantime, I intend to become better acquainted with Doña Maria so that when we do actually decide upon a date she will perhaps have begun to like me enough to consider me acceptable as a daughter-in-law."

"*Madona mia!*" he hissed, his dark eyes flaming alive. "Have you no shame? I did not imagine that even you would contemplate carrying out such a deception against a frail old lady and an unsophisticated child! As for Alvaro, I must suppose the poor fool is so much in love he will agree to anything!" Further tumultuous words were crushed even as the cigarette he discarded was crushed beneath his foot. Exercising supreme control, his voice dangerously low, he asked, "Do you realize, I wonder, that I have it in my power to deprive Alvaro of the very substantial income he now enjoys? He holds a very junior position in our firm. One word from me and you could find yourself engaged to a pauper!"

"But wouldn't you then be defeating your own ends?" she enquired sweetly, experiencing for the first time a heady taste of power. "If you should be tempted to carry out such a threat would not the shock inflicted upon your aunt be greater than any she might be in danger of receiving from me?" She laughed up into his angry face and taunted, "You are out-manoeuvred, *señor*, so why don't you act as a gentleman should and admit to an honourable defeat?"

During dinner she made sure her eyes strayed as little as possible in his direction as he sat smouldering at the head of the table. She was not finished with him by any means, but she needed a breathing space in which to marshall her exultant thoughts and to muster her forces for the second attack that had to be timed to a nicety if the element of surprise that was its main ingredient was to inflict the maximum of damage. None of them guessed as they proceeded through each delicious course with relaxed enjoyment, that her mind was seething with activity, weighing up each remark that was addressed to her, just waiting the oportunity of an opening which would allow her to show her hand with maximum effect. Unwittingly, it was Doña Maria who paved the way when, with the persistence of the aged, she returned to the subject of Felipe and his supposed attachment. She spooned up the last of her *Zabaglione*, obviously relishing the delicate blending of chilled whipped cream and rich Marsala wine, then pushed away her glass with a satisfied sigh before questioning Sara,

"When did Felipe and yourself become acquainted, my dear? Was it recently, or has the rascal been keeping you to himself for some time?"

Sara knew without having to look in his direction that Felipe's head jerked suddenly erect and the conversation between himself and Isabel ceased abruptly while he waited to hear her reply. This was the chance she had been waiting for and she took it, though not without experiencing a thrill of exhilarating terror. Doña Maria was completely charmed by the rosy blush, downcast eyes and shy whisper that seemed to indicate to all those watching the confused happiness of a girl in love.

"I feel I have known Felipe all my life," she cooed with wicked enjoyment, "but in actual fact we met on the *African Queen* only a few short weeks ago."

"And it was love at first sight for both of you!" Doña Maria clapped with delight, completely carried away by the play upon her emotions. Sara chanced a swift glance towards Felipe and a surge of triumph drowned the inward fear she felt at the thought of his retaliation, but anything was worth enduring for the pleasure of seeing him so completely disconcerted. He had insisted upon her playing out the farce that afternoon, confident that by evening she would be gone, now he was hoist by his own petard and she was gaining great satisfaction from watching him writhe . . .

"Felipe, dare I ask, or am I being rather premature?" Doña Maria hesitated, flags of excited colour in her cheeks, then rushed on, "When is the wedding to be?"

Sara felt she had been struck in the solar plexus. Events were moving too rapidly, she had intended only to annoy Felipe not to trap him – that might turn out to be altogether too dangerous a manoeuvre!

Only Alvaro seemed to read correctly Felipe's set expression. Sending Sara a quick glance of warning, he attempted to smooth things over by reprimanding his mother. "Shame upon your curiosity, Mother! What Sara must be thinking of your prying I hardly dare to imagine."

His mother's face crumpled like a chastened child's at his uncustomary severity, leaving him feeling a complete moron. But even as his shoulders lifted in a masculine shrug of helplessness, Felipe's deliberately amused voice broke the strained silence.

"Why all the fuss?" he demanded, one dark eyebrow lifted quizzically. "You, Tia, shall have your answers as soon as I know them myself, whereas you, Alvaro," he turned on him with a meaning glint, "can safely leave Sara's feelings to me."

Sara gasped. The gauntlet was thrown down with a vengeance! Obviously Felipe was taking Alvaro's interference as a sign of jealousy and fear that he might betray the truth was forcing him to accept the need to act out the lie. She was left no time to wonder further. Felipe's hand burned through the flimsy material of her sleeve as he grasped her arm and began propelling her in the direction of the garden. Without giving her time to protest, he made their excuses.

"I am sure you will understand if Sara and I do not join you for coffee. I have much to say to her and the words will come much more easily in the garden. Don't you agree, *cara*?" he hissed in her ear.

Doña Maria's face brightened when a lovely rush of colour stained Sara's cheeks, and when she noted how incapable she seemed of tearing her eyes from the smile that twisted Felipe's mouth into lines of almost sardonic humour.

"Of course, of course!" she beamed.

Alvaro's reaction was to emit a harsh sound that died in his throat as soon as it was born and which to Sara sounded like a croak of commiseration.

She was marched without ceremony out of earshot. Prickles of sweat began to form on her brow, but she held her head erect as he piloted her in grim silence along the dark paths. It was only when he jerked to a halt and rasped out: "Now, tell me exactly what it is you are trying to achieve!" that her nerve went and she was left speechless looking up into his furious eyes.

He was so big, so dark, and so tight-lipped with anger that her mind refused to advance beyond those facts. Even when he shook her impatiently, as if he would rattle loose the words from her tongue, she continued to infuriate him by remaining mute. As the silence lengthened she tried desperately to release her paralysed vocal cords, but the words simply would not come. With an exasperated sigh he shook her again and as he did so his elbow caught the branches of an orange tree, dislodging blossoms that rained upon her bent head like a shower of tiny white stars.

He speared down at her and the sight of her mutely appealing face with its rich coronet of blossom spangled hair seemed to goad him further. With a sudden rough movement he tilted her chin. "Perhaps I've been a fool," he muttered through clenched teeth. "Is this what you are waiting for?" His hard mouth descended upon lips still partly open and for infinite hateful moments she was tortured by a kiss that spelled out far more effectively than words ever could the contempt she held in his eyes. He punished her thoroughly and cold-bloodedly until she was reduced to a helpless puppet in his arms. When finally he pushed her away, she staggered back until she felt the welcome solidarity of a tree trunk which offered her trembling body the support her limbs refused to supply. For long seconds she clung to it, even less capable of speech than she had been before his onslaught, and waited for the condemnation she was certain was to follow. But he, too, seemed to be labouring under some kind of strain; his compressed mouth, his outthrust jaw, and the fathomless darkness of his eyes all suggested furiously leashed anger, anger that was directed inwardly – *against himself*!

Relief surged through her veins like some instant

acting drug, relaxing her taut nerves and calming her mind's tumultuous clamouring so that she was again able to think. She had *not* imagined an infinitesimal hint of tenderness creeping in unawares at the end of that punishing kiss! His final rejection had been too swift, too hastily accomplished for a man who was supposed to be in complete control of his emotions! A shuddering sigh escaped her; right from the beginning she had suspected that her impulsive plan was doomed to failure, that its outcome would be ignominious defeat, but now...! Could it possibly be that the mighty Don's defences really *were* in danger of being breached?

CHAPTER V

FOR days afterwards a small enigmatic smile tugged at the corner of Sara's mouth, exciting the curiosity of all who saw it. She was certain that nothing could now go wrong, every move she made was destined to succeed. Doña Maria had again proved her worth as an ally, insisting she should move into the villa for the duration of her own stay, and Sara, though flying in the face of her host's unspoken disapproval, had quickly agreed.

But three days had gone by without her having had a chance to further her plans. She had spent her time chatting with Doña Maria and swimming with Isabel, trying to make up to them both for the absence of Alvaro, who had been ordered back to work at the plantation. Felipe, she had seen only at dinner each evening, when his cool calculating eyes and set features had given lie to the hopes she had nurtured since their last encounter. However, the fact that he was so obviously avoiding her gave some substance to her theory that he was not entirely immune to her presence, so she was content to bide her time, confident that within the relatively small confines of the villa he could not avoid her indefinitely.

A voice intruded upon her train of thought. They

were sitting on the terrace overlooking the pool, Doña Maria gently dozing in a chair placed between Sara's and Isabel's, when the younger girl stirred impatiently, then pouted, "I still do not understand why Felipe found it necessary to send Alvaro away. Surely the men employed in the vineyards are capable of carrying out their work without supervision? I think it mean of Felipe, I really do!"

"Someone has to give orders, child," Doña Maria opened sleepy eyes to reprove mildly. "Our estates are large and widely scattered, it is too much to expect Felipe to continue to carry the full burden alone. He was a mere boy when he took over the running of the business – much younger than Alvaro is now – but he did not hesitate to give up his pleasures when his father and my own dear husband died almost within a year of each other, and he has managed alone ever since. It is time he was allowed to relax and now that Alvaro has finally agreed to do his share I look forward to seeing Felipe recoup his lost years." She smiled across at Sara. "And with you to help him, my dear, I'm sure he will. Felipe as a young man was always so carefree and *vital*. I envy you the pleasure of his company when his youthful spirits are regained."

An image of Felipe's disapproving, aloof face flashed before Sara's eyes and it was with the utmost difficulty that she tried to imagine his grim features cast into a mould of gay abandon. Responsibilities had dampened any flair for enjoyment that might have existed in the younger Felipe; the fetters accepted willingly by the boy would be relinquished reluctantly by the man whose back had become accustomed to their weight.

Isabel's shrug conveyed all the selfishness of impatient youth. "But why so far away?" she wailed. "There are other vineyards nearer than those on the slopes of the Rif mountains. If Felipe had deliberately contrived to get rid of Alvaro could not have found a more desolate place of banishment. There are no towns near at hand, no means of communication other than by messenger, and absolutely no civilized people for miles around – just wild, barbaric Rifs and their families. Felipe is a heartless villain to expect Alvaro to exist in such desolation!"

She was obviously echoing Alvaro's own words, his dismay upon being told where he was to spend the next few weeks had been displayed for all to see and sharp words had been exchanged between himself and Felipe before he had reluctantly driven off with the threat that should he find it too unbearable he intended to return immediately. If Felipe were not so obsessed with the idea of removing Alvaro from her own vicinity, Sara chuckled with inward amusement, Alvaro's recent lack of resistance to the plan to marry him off to Isabel might have registered, but as it was his blind stubbornness was hindering his own plans.

Isabel sensed her amusement and was provoked by it. "I think it very unkind of you to regard my troubles

97

so lightly, Sara," she rebuked with offended dignity. "You who are lucky enough to have your fiancé near to hand ought to be able to spare a little sympathy for those less fortunate."

Sara reacted with an immediate apology. "I'm so sorry, Isabel. Please don't think me unsympathetic. I feel very deeply about your separation from Alvaro and would do anything in my power to help, surely you know that?"

Mollified, Isabel shrugged, then permitted herself a wan smile. "You have a right to feel happy. It is I who should feel ashamed of the jealousy that causes me to begrudge you the joy I cannot have myself. But I do miss Alvaro so!" She sighed, then seemed to drift away on a tide of memory with a dreamy soulful look. Doña Maria exchanged a conspiratorial grin with Sara. Isabel's nature was as volatile as any of her race, one minute soaring to the heights, the next scouring the depths, but she bore no malice and Sara found Doña Maria's fondness for Isabel echoed in her own heart at each stage of her progressing friendship with the younger girl.

"Is the heartless villain permitted to join you, or will my presence interrupt a further spate of confidences?" Felipe's dry question startled them, his fleeting look of contempt warning Sara that he had been there long enough to overhear her exchange with Isabel. Colour burned her cheeks. His appearance had again coincided with circumstances disadvantageous to herself and she

knew he was notching up yet another mark against her
– this time for treachery.

But her wild colour was viewed with delight by Doña
Maria, and even Isabel was generous enough to remark
without rancour, "It seems one of us, at least, welcomes
the sight of you, Felipe. I can only wish that I too had
cause to blush at the unexpected arrival of one who fills
my thoughts." She laughed, then relented. "But of
course you may join us, *amigo*! Heartless you may be,
but a villain you most certainly are not. Come, pull up
a chair and sit by me so that I can pester you for news
of Alvaro!"

He straightened from kissing the cheek his aunt had
proffered, but refused Isabel's offer. "Much as I
would like to I cannot spare more than a few minutes.
I have something of importance to discuss with
Sara, so if you will both excuse us while we go into the
library?"

Now that the opportunity to be alone with him had
arrived, Sara discovered a contrary streak that made
her feel extremely reluctant to comply. "Can't we
talk out here?" she offered desperately, hating the indomitable, cold look that was visible only to her.

"No, Sara," his tender smile deceived the others,
but underneath his velvet tone she recognized an iron
determination that would not be thwarted however
much evasion she might attempt.

"The child is shy, Felipe." Doña Maria's hand reached out to comfort Sara. "Do not allow this nephew

of mine to deceive you, my dear. When you have known him as long as I, you will realize that the flint-like exterior he shows to the world hides a heart as vulnerable as any child's."

Sara suffered his mocking laughter as he guided her through the house in the direction of the library. She could hardly blame his aunt for her totally inaccurate summing up of his character; his split personality was so cleverly concealed he appeared as two complete entities – one a saint, the other a reincarnation of the devil. His actions had been the cause of her grandfather's death, and yet she had to make herself appear attracted to him. She prayed for strength!

But such was the intentness of his thoughts he forgot even to offer her a chair. She stood watching while he paced the book-lined room with its aroma of leather and polished wood, his brow furrowed as if the opening he sought eluded him. Finally, his tone almost casual, he addressed her. "Your plans seem to be working well. I must congratulate you." A rabbit mesmerized by a snake could not have felt more stricken. How could he possibly have found out? She had mentioned her plan to no one, so how . . .? "Not only has my aunt taken a liking to you, she is continually singing your praises." With relief she heard him follow on. "No doubt she will still be shocked to learn that you and not Isabel are to be her son's bride, but the blow will not be so severe as it would have been had a total stranger been presented as her future daughter-in-law." He moved until his towering presence blocked everything from sight and she was forced to meet eyes that were appraising her with puzzling inscrutability. "Yes, your idea was very cleverly conceived. You have managed to make fools of us all."

She made an involuntary movement of dissent, for the picture of deception he painted was distasteful, but he surprised her into silence with the resigned admission, "I was wrong to oppose your engagement to Alvaro, I see that now. Obviously, it cannot be expected of him that he should give orders to others and yet be denied the right to make his own personal decisions. Both for his sake and for the sake of the business, I am forced to acknowledge the wrong I have done him – and you. I intend to make reparation as soon as possible. Can you be ready to accompany me on the journey to the plantation early tomorrow morning? Alvaro will need a lot of convincing that I mean what I say and your presence should act as an assurance that from now on his life is his to live as he wishes, without interference of any kind from me."

The uncharacteristic surrender was so staggering she could hardly take it in. At last Alvaro was to be free! The boy was to be allowed to become a man, to act, to decide, even to love as he fancied! It was great news. Her joy on his behalf knew no bounds, and that, together with the relief she felt at her own release from an unbearable situation, was responsible for her expression of supreme happiness. No need to tell Felipe of their bogus engagement; she would leave it to Alvaro to include that explanation amongst the many others which would have to be exchanged before the two cousins reached complete understanding.

"But that's wonderful news, *señor*!" His dark, quizzical look swept her rapturous face, but he forbore to comment. "I'll be very happy to accompany you tomorrow," she babbled on, her mind completely occupied with the thought of Alvaro's reaction to the news of his release from bondage. "Isabel can help me to pack..."

"Isabel must not be told!" he rapped with a return of his usual arrogance.

"No, of course not, I understand perfectly." Isabel would be bound to ask a lot of awkward questions if she knew of the journey that was about to be undertaken – questions Alvaro would be best left to answer.

"Wear something suitable for travelling in an open jeep," he ordered, "and pack a warm coat to wear at night when the wind blows cooler. Be ready to leave at sunrise – and remember, not a word to Isabel or to my aunt. When Alvaro returns he will tell them himself what he plans to do."

Dawn light was barely spearing the skyline when he drove the jeep to the front of the house where she was waiting. His cursory nod somehow conveyed an unspoken approval of the serviceable cream-coloured trouser suit she was wearing and the topcoat which was slung casually around her shoulders. She clambered up beside him and without exchanging a word of greeting they set off on the journey.

She knew there were two hundred miles of Rif Mountains stretching eastwards to the Algerian border and that the whole of the area they were to travel contained barely half a dozen towns of any importance, but she was not prepared for the beauty that was gradually unfolded as they travelled along the road towards Tetouan. She feasted her eyes upon sparkling blue sea that sometimes lapped its tideless caress against the golden sands of numerous deserted beaches and sometimes against cliffs splashed with gentle colour. Gradually, the mountain's far-off appeal grew nearer and soon they were traversing green rounded ranges, full of folds and curves smoothed down and eroded by heavy rains. The roads were bad, making the ride rather uncomfortable, but she had no intention of complaining. Every now and then she had sensed a quick, amused glance from her silent companion that told her he was anticipating hearing vocal evidence of her growing discomfiture, so she gritted her teeth and vowed never to allow him that particular satisfaction.

His attitude was puzzling. For the first hour he had remained morose, his mouth set in lines of uncompromising sternness, but as the miles between themselves and the villa lengthened his humour grew, melting the ice in his eyes and dispersing the granite hardness from his jaw. It was not until she heard him humming that her suspicions were really aroused, and by that time they were many miles from civilization, travelling a long, lonely road which for all she knew might stretch into infinity.

She did not attempt to disguise the sudden fear that clutched her heart when she charged him, "I don't believe you are taking me to Alvaro! You've tricked me – told me deliberate lies to get me away from the villa!"

Her fears were confirmed when he threw back his head and laughed. "How perceptive of you, *señorita*, and how perfectly correct is your assumption. I did manoeuvre you out of the villa because your tactics there were meeting with too much success. As for Alvaro, I expect that at this very moment he is being re-united with Isabel. I received word last night that he had left the plantation and was on his way home. We would no doubt have passed him if I had not calculated correctly and taken a different route from the one he has chosen. By this time he will have arrived at the villa and been told by either his mother or by Isabel that you are accompanying me on a long-awaited holiday. How will he react to that, do you think? However much he might wish it, he will be hard tried to believe that a girl who can disappear with another man as soon as his back is turned could be genuinely in love with himself!" He pulled up at the side of the road and gave her incredulous, angry face his full attention. Satisfaction sparkled in his eyes and as he watched her fight for control he showed every sign of savouring his victory to the full.

"You ... you fiend! You unspeakable barbarian! You're worse than the poor uncivilized wretches you employ – you at least have had the benefit of an education whereas they have the excuse of ignorance! Have you *no* scruples? Are you so self-obsessed, so much a victim of omnipotence that you think there are no rules you cannot break?" When she realized her tirade was having little effect, she lost control completely and raised her hand to strike. But with the speed of a whiplash her hand was captured and held forcefully away.

"Oh, no, *señorita*, not again!" he gritted. "Once before I suffered that indignity at your hands, but if you ever again attempt it I promise your punishment will be tailored to suit." With a swift change of mood he informed her carelessly, "Perhaps it will help to convince you that I mean what I say if I explain that I too have Rif blood in my veins. Many years ago, when Spaniards first invaded Morocco, one of my ancestors was captured and held prisoner by the Rif tribesmen. These people have always resented domination from any outside source. They fought many fierce campaigns against my own people and against the French, and even now it is not unknown for disturbances to occur in some parts of the mountains."

She blinked at the fantasy of it all, but she gave his words her complete attention. "Somehow," he went on, "this ancestor of mine infiltrated the hearts of these great, independent tribesmen and instead of being put to death he was accepted by them. In return, he showed

them how to cultivate their land so as to provide sufficient food to fill stomachs that up until then had always
felt hunger. He helped to nurse their sick and to edu-
cate their children, and as the years went by it was forgotten by all that he had ever been a prisoner. He married a beautiful Rif girl who gave him a son just before
she died. He then returned to Spain, for his child's sake,
but he made frequent journeys back to these mountains
to visit his friends. That is why my family have been
tolerated here all these years, *señorita*. Anyone who
bears the name Panza is regarded by them as a blood
brother. Have you now been sufficiently warned?"

Cold fear kept her silent as she withstood his probing stare. She believed his story implicitly. Now she
could understand his uncanny likeness to the tall,
haughty tribesmen who occasionally strode the streets
of Tangier, their cloaks flaring behind them with all the
arrogance expected of such a proud race. His face reflected the same cruelty, his eyes the same contempt,
his actions were carried out with the same callous disregard of inflicted pain . . . Her throat was tight when
she forced out the question,

"What do you intend doing with me?"

He recognized the echo of defeat in her question
and was pleased by it. For a long moment he remained
silent, seemingly savouring some devilish plan that afforded him endless pleasure, then his eyes swung towards her, bombarding her with reflected brilliance so
that her heart leapt with terrified anticipation.

"I'm going to marry you, *señorita*! Only according to the Rif custom, of course, but the ceremony will serve its purpose in that even Alvaro will hesitate to bring down the wrath of the Rifs upon his head by casting desirous eyes upon one of their brother's possessions!"

For the remainder of the journey Sara sat huddled in panic-stricken silence, convinced she was in the company of a madman. Too late now to wish she had heeded Alvaro's warning, too late to even attempt an explanation to the man whose Spanish reserve and fiery Arab blood mated in his veins so uneasily and with such devastating results. Doña Maria's assessment of his character could be excused. She had seen only the Spanish Don, considerate and courteous in the bosom of his family, whereas she seemed always fated to arouse the sleeping forces of wild recklessness that were a legacy from his beautiful pagan ancestress. In the midst of civilization this strain was subdued, subjugated by the demands of society, but how much effort would he make to contain it once he was back amongst his primitive brotherhood...?

When vine terraces appeared in view she knew their journey was almost over. Tall men clothed in ragged cotton shirts, their legs bound with rawhide strips of leather to protect them from briars and thistles, straightened from their labours to wave an enthusiastic greeting as they passed, but not even the menial tasks that occupied them, nor the poverty of their attire, could detract one whit from the untrammelled, almost swaggering image they projected.

The village was little more than a compound containing primitive huts, their walls made of mud or stone held together with mud mortar, and roughly roofed with reeds. A stockade made up of branches of thorn bushes woven among prickly pear surrounded the whole settlement and inside its perimeter sloe-eyed children tended the beasts that supplied milk, and chickens so scrawny they seemed barely capable of supplying eggs. With horn blaring, he drove into the centre of the compound and in a matter of seconds the jeep was engulfed by a crowd of squealing, happy children all anxious to greet him. Laughing with obvious enjoyment, he allowed them to crawl over him, suffering tugged hair, sharp elbows in his ribs, and sticky hands that reduced his immaculate bush shirt to a mass of crumpled linen.

Fighting off their attentions, he grabbed the bag he had stowed in the back of the jeep and when they saw it their mouths pursed into oohs and ahs of anticipation. They scrambled down, still screaming their excitement, and lined up in an orderly row as if taking part in a well-loved ritual.

He handed Sara the bag of sweets and instructed, "Give each of them an exact amount so there will be no squabbling, but be careful of that imp at the end of the row. He is crippled and his great soulful eyes underline his misfortune, but he is actually the soul of mischief and any favour he receives will be bragged about vociferously until the other children are riled into giving him a thrashing." She glanced along the line of children until she spotted at the end a small skeleton of a boy whose left leg was so deformed he could not have stood without the stick fashioned into a crutch that was tucked under his arm. Even as she watched, he sensed her interest and turned his liquid brown eyes in her direction. A lump lodged in her throat; he looked so solitary, so very much as she felt, she wanted to run and cuddle his racked little body in her arms.

"What is his name?" she asked, her voice betraying a suspicion of a quiver.

"Khairy," he answered, then with a quirk, "and it seems the cunning little devil has achieved yet another conquest. Weak, downtrodden males seem to hold a fascination for you, *señorita*. Perhaps it is hardly surprising I do not find favour in your eyes." He wheeled away, leaving her to distribute the sweets to the impatiently waiting children.

When they had been divided equally and to everyone's satisfaction, Khairy appointed himself her guide by attaching himself to her side and offering to show her around the village. She had the choice of either accepting or being left stranded – there was no sign of the *señor* – so she answered gratefully, "Thank you, Khairy, it will be nice to have a companion who can speak English. You are a very clever boy. Who taught you?"

He swelled with importance and his face showed boundless contempt of the rest of the children when he glanced in their direction. "My mother, and she in turn was taught by my father who was killed in a battle before I was born. He was the son of a Caid, a great and wise man, but after he was killed my mother returned here to her own people. I have been brought up with these ignorant Rifs, but one day when I am a man, I will take my mother back to my grandfather's kasbah at the oasis of El Safida." This was said with such conviction she had to believe him. His broken body caged a spirit as indomitable as her own and her optimism was revived by his remarkable courage.

"I'm sure you will, Khairy," she answered softly. "Your mother is a very lucky woman to have a son such as you."

His suspicious look told her he suspected her of laughing at him, but when she met his eyes with steady earnestness his face creased into a broad smile and his hand was pushed into hers with a heartwarming gesture of friendliness. "Come with me, *señorita*, I will take you to meet my mother. She, too, grows weary of gossiping peasants and her day will be brightened if she can speak with you." She followed him to one of the huts, but when he stepped inside to lead the way she hesitated, unsure whether or not she would be welcome. She was about to turn away when Khairy reappeared holding the hand of one of the most beautiful women Sara had ever seen. She was tall with a willowy, graceful carriage, and her head, braided with glossy black hair, was carried proudly erect, giving credence to the allusions of past grandeur made by her son. Her skin had the tint and the bloom of olives and her sad, lustrous eyes spoke of mystery and pain buried too deep ever to be forgotten.

"I am Zuela, mother of Khairy," she spoke with a charming lilt. "If you will honour us with a visit you are assured of a welcome." Sara stepped inside to be confronted with appalling poverty. There was just one large room divided by curtains of grass matting. The floor was of hard beaten earth and the solitary window was merely a frame with a wooden shutter. Round three sides of the room was a shelf of earth spread with mats and rugs which were evidently used as seats by day and as covers at night. Very little daylight penetrated, and as she groped her way forward Zuela moved to light an oil lamp which cast eerie shadows as it swung backwards and forwards at her touch. Sara wondered how dignity could possibly be maintained under such circumstances, and when Zuela politely asked if she would favour them by accepting some mint tea she was filled with admiration for the woman who moved inside her pitiful hut as if it had the ambience of the princely kasbah that once had been her home.

But the tea Sara gulped down was delicious, a much longed for refreshment made of green tea, mint and sugar that was nectar to her parched throat. She nodded grateful acceptance when offered a second cup.

"The *señorita* visits with the *señor*, Mother," Khairy offered. "His visit is to last perhaps as long as a week."

"That is good news." A hint of colour ran under Zuela's olive skin, but her voice was calm when she stated, "We are always pleased to receive a visit from Don Felipe. He has done much for our people." When Sara's eyebrows elevated, Zuela gently reproved, "Please do not blame the *señor* for the poverty that surrounds us. The Rif are an independent race who react unfavourably to change. They much prefer their own ways, even though they are primitive, and the *señor*'s greatest wisdom lies in his ability to accept our manners and customs. But even so, slowly, and by exercising extreme discretion, he has managed to improve our standard of hygiene and our knowledge of working the land. Doctors pay us regular visits to check upon our health and he has even managed to persuade some of the tribesmen to undergo dental treatment, something that could never have been achieved a few years ago."

"And I am to have an operation," put in Khairy. "When I am older and stronger the *señor* is taking me to a large hospital so that my leg may be straightened, is that not so, Mother?"

This time there was no mistaking the blush that set Zuela's cheeks afire. Sara's heart gave an inexplicable jolt as with sudden insight she became aware that the mere mention of Don Felipe's name was enough to arouse in Zuela an emotion so strong it was reflected in her eyes as an unmistakable glow.

A small commotion outside heralded the arrival of a young Arab boy whose frantic gesticulations made Sara sickeningly aware that her presence was required elsewhere. When Zuela confirmed this assumption it was as much as she could do to refrain from pleading for help to escape. But the instinct was crushed under a weight of fear that Zuela herself might be made to suffer for daring to interfere in the affairs of a man so highly regarded by these unpredictable Rifs. So, as casually as she was able, she thanked Zuela and her son for their hospitality before following her impatient guide outside into unexpected darkness. Night had fallen with its usual suddenness while she was being entertained inside the hut, and its denseness, coupled with the unfamiliarity of her surroundings, made her hesitate before groping her way forward in the direction taken by her swiftly retreating guide.

"Wait! Please wait . . ." she called after him, suffering a fear of the solitary gloom that was closing in on her with silent menace. But the boy either did not heed or was deaf to her cry, because the sound of his footsteps grew gradually fainter, then faded completely. She stood stock still, shivering, her heart pounding with dull, heavy thuds. She was ashamed of her fear, a long-forgotten relic of her childhood in the orphanage where pleas for a nightlight had been frowned upon as bids for extra attention. She had thought the fear long outgrown, but her leaden limbs and dry mouth were ample evidence that the deeply buried dread had

113

needed only favourable conditions to achieve its resurrection.

A sudden deepening of the gloom in front of her brought a scream of hysteria to her lips. The shadow moved forward with a muttered imprecation, then, to her indescribable relief, spoke soothingly.

"Do not be afraid, you are quite safe."

She almost collapsed into the arms of the Arab whose tall figure clad in a voluminous *djellaba* loomed like a monster out of the darkness. Half laughing, half crying, she clung to him while his strong arms cradled her shaking body and his hand, gentle as a woman's, stroked her hair with light, soothing strokes.

"I'm sorry," she gasped finally, experiencing a strong reluctance to leave the comfort of his arms but forcing herself nevertheless to step a pace away from him. She peered upwards, trying to pierce the darkness that veiled his features, but the moonless night defended its secret, leaving her with a sense of frustrated longing.

The shadow spoke again, his voice tender but with a hint of laughter. "The night has thrown many things in my path, but never before such an enjoyable experience. Things that come out of the darkness are often cruel, or predatory, and are almost always startling, but within the boundaries of our village you need not be afraid. Tell me, what dire misfortune did you imagine was about to befall you when I appeared? Did you suppose me a ghost, a wild animal, or perhaps a predatory male – sometimes the most dangerous of all the species?"

Strangely, his amusement did not anger her. His voice was too kind, his touch too compassionate, she knew she could trust him. Whether she had felt the lack of a sympathetic listener since the death of her grandfather, or whether it was the relief of his reassuring presence that loosened her tongue she was not sure, but she surprised herself by pouring out all the feelings of terror she had felt as a child when the dormitory lights had been switched off and enormous shadow giants had spread up and along the colour-washed walls, huge distorted shapes that watched unmovingly just waiting to pounce on the first unwary child who closed his eyes.

She expected some teasing remark when she faltered to a stop, but his shadow remained still and silent. "Have I been boring you?" she laughed lightly, even though grim memories had brought beads of sweat to her brow. He moved and she felt his hands upon her shoulders. She was drawn forward until her head rested against his chest, his hard, lithe body felt taut and somehow full of anger. Silently, he rocked her in his arms until peace flowed through her veins and her tense body was calm and relaxed. She felt his lips cool and firm upon her brow as he whispered, "Gallant child, brave little warrior!" She never again wanted to move. His arms were the haven she had sought, his strength the strength she had yearned to find in the men she had

known but which up until then she had never been even
remotely near to finding. She struggled to tell him so,
ached to find the words to describe her feelings of
wonder...

The sound of swiftly running footsteps encroached,
breaking the spell that bound her in spirit to the anony-
mous shadow who held her. She spun round as the boy
who had previously been sent to fetch her loomed into
sight and felt bereft as the arms that held her were
withdrawn, leaving a warm impression where they had
rested.

"All right, I'm coming," she assured the panting
boy, then turned to speak again to her unknown companion. But he had gone, melted into the night as silently as he had come, without waiting even to say good-
bye. A wave of desolation swept her and for seconds
she struggled with an onrush of tears. But he had not
completely gone, he had communicated to her a part of
himself, a courage, a sense of belonging, and the wonderful satisfaction of knowing that she had at last met
a man whose nature was as strong as it was gentle, a
man whose very tenderness was proof of masculine
assurance, the kind of man she had begun to doubt even
existed. With a springing step and shining eyes she followed the boy to where she was bidden.

As she suspected, it was Felipe who had summoned
her. She was led into a large, newly erected black tent
decorated internally with colourfully patterned carpets,
silken drapes and mounds of plump cushions – trea-

sures hoarded by the Rif families but surrendered willingly for the comfort of their guests. Ornate lamps cast a warm pool of light into the centre of the tent, but beyond its perimeter deep shadows stretched, giving an illusion of sinister depth to the surrounding darkness. She gave a startled gasp when Felipe's voice rasped out as he stepped from out of the shadows into the pool of light,

"I trust you have been sufficiently entertained during my absence?" Her wide eyes mirrored shock as they swung in his direction. The change in him was as incredible as it was startling. A striped *djellaba*, long, loose, with wide sleeves and a hood, adapted to his lean length as no other garment could. Wearing it, he assumed the very spirit of the desert and his stance – legs apart, arms akimbo – added strength to the illusion. But the turban skilfully twisted around his arrogantly held head seemed more than anything else to emphasise his return to the customs of the Arab people. Beneath it, his aquiline features had an added sombreness and his dark eyes glistened with primitive fire, newly released so doubly dangerous.

"Yes, thank you, I have had a most enjoyable visit." Her voice was not quite steady, but she discovered that actually she felt able to cope with his projected intimidation. Her earlier encounter had left her armoured, wrapped around in a cloak of security that not even harsh words could penetrate. She withstood his narrow-eyed glance, retreating behind an expression of dreamy unconcern that served to infuriate him.

"I would not have thought the villagers' pleasures sufficiently sophisticated for your taste," he accused her sarcastically.

"What do you know of my tastes?" she countered, incensed. "You do not know me half so well as you imagine, *señor,* nor are you ever likely to!"

He swallowed up the distance between them with one giant stride and smouldered down at her. "Did I imagine the incident aboard ship when you and your accomplice combined to cheat my cousin?" he challenged as if urging her to contradict. "Did my eyes deceive me when I picked up the incriminating cheque made out to yourself by a man you could only have known for mere weeks? And discounting all of that, did I not hear from your own lips the plan you conceived to fool not only my aunt and Isabel but also Alvaro himself! No, *señorita,* I would be a fool ever to allow myself to believe that one so practised in deceit could ever be deserving of mercy!" He swung on his heel, his cloak swirling around him like the wings of a swooping bat and bit out one final savage sentence.

"Sleep well, *señorita.* Tomorrow marks the beginning of a week of ceremonies which custom decrees must precede our much rejoiced-over wedding!"

CHAPTER VI

HAD it not been for Zuela, the activities of the following week would have driven Sara to distraction, wondering if each day's ceremony would be the last before the final act of marriage was performed. Zuela's explanations helped to keep her informed, but even so her nerves were frayed with anxiety and worry to such an extent that she was driven to pleading with Zuela for help to escape.

"Escape?" When Zuela's eyes betrayed a flash of quickly concealed hope Sara's heart leapt with optimism; she had not been wrong about the Arab girl's love for the *señor*; helping to remove a rival for his affections was an action she would hardly be foolish enough to reject. But she had underestimated the hold custom had upon the Arab people. Strongly held beliefs and superstitious fear handed down through generations could not be cast out lightly, not even in a moment of rebellion. Zuela's mouth trembled when she refused. "I'm sorry," she told Sara dully, "but I could not do such a thing to the *señor*."

"But I *hate* him!" Sara shouted in her aggravation. "I will not be forced into marrying a man I dislike, however obscure and meaningless the ceremony!"

119

"The wishes of the bride are never heeded," Zuela intoned without a flicker of emotion. "Indeed, the consent of the girl is neither required nor asked."

"*Oh!*" Sara's hands clasped and unclasped as she fought to contain the ravages of frustration. For days she had witnessed acts of tradition progressively carried out until now there was less than one day left before the marriage. *One day!* She flinched from reflecting upon the embarrassments she had already suffered and from imagining others that might be in store. How she had hated Felipe for not even attempting to conceal his amusement at the remarks passed by the chiefs of the village whose job it was to assess the value of his future bride. Their faces had registered dismay and not a little scorn as she had stood before them to be looked over by disparaging eyes. Grunting, and pulling mournfully at their beards, they had circled around her, ignoring her scarlet face, intent only upon their search for the signs of strength that were essentially desirable in a Rif bride. Finally, they had thrown up their arms, bewailing loudly some damning facet of her physical appearance. Felipe – and she still burned at the memory – had insisted upon translating their remarks even though he was convulsed with laughter.

"They look for two qualities, *señorita*. The first, youth, is an absolute essential and on that point they have no quarrel, but the second one is plumpness and on that point they say, and I quote: 'If an illness befalls a plump wife, at least something is left of her after-

120

wards; whereas in the case of the one who is already lean ...'" She had stomped away, furious, her ears beseiged by his unkind laughter.

Unconsciously, she made an impatient gesture and glared angrily around the inside of the tent where she and Zuela were relaxing against piles of silken cushions heaped about the floor. Her face softened when she saw Zuela's woebegone expression; she had no right to vent her spleen upon the girl who had been designated to serve her.

"Do cheer up, Zuela," she admonished. "You must learn not to take the things I say in temper so much to heart. I know you would help me if you could, and I understand that your loyalty to the *señor* must come before any duty to myself, so stop moping and smile, for heaven's sake!" Zuela's instant obedience to her command made her feel unbearably dictatorial, so in an effort to dispel some of her own ill humour she changed the subject. "Tell me again what must be endured before the *Dreaded Day*," she capitalized.

Zuela's hand, with fingers outspread, was brought into use as she began counting off previous days' happenings. "First, we had 'the cleaning of the wheat', you remember – four flags were hoisted on top of the *señor*'s house and the grain – barley, wheat and durra – that is to be used during the wedding was heaped up in the courtyard to be cleaned by all the unmarried girls of the village?" Sara nodded; she could hardly forget the village chief's barbaric machinations on that occasion. She had watched fascinated while he had sprinkled both the grain and the girls with water as a safeguard against evil spirits. He had then thrust a dagger into one of the heaps, and placed a bowl containing a mixture of raw egg and salt upon its summit; the dagger and salt, Zuela had explained, being directed against evil spirits and the eggs to ensure a happy wedded life. Eventually the bowl and its contents had been buried outside of the tent – which it was supposed would be shared by herself and the *señor* after the ceremony – so that it would be stepped upon by the bridal pair as they entered the tent together for the first time as man and wife.

"You don't need to remind me of number two," Sara interrupted shortly. "That was the night the *señor* and his companions engaged in a disgusting round of revelry that kept us all awake until the early hours."

"But every bridegroom must have a 'bridegroom's night'," Zuela protested. "He would not be considered manly if he did not!"

"Oh, don't bother to recap further," Sara interpolated when Zuela made to continue. "I want to know what happens next, not what has already gone before."

Looking a little unhappy, Zuela obeyed Sara's edict. "Well ..." she glanced apprehensively at her set face, "tomorrow, you will be thoroughly bathed by the women of the tribe before being painted with henna ..."

"*What!*" Sara jumped to her feet, bridling like an

122

aggravated terrier. "You don't seriously believe I would allow . . ."

"But it is necessary," Zuela showed obvious distress. "Such customs must be carefully observed, otherwise Yiblis, the devil, would make husband and wife fight, as he is never pleased about people getting married."

"Then for once I'm on his side," Sara spat. "I can understand why Yiblis, as you call him, should be angered at the thought of losing one of his own!"

"You can't mean the *señor*?" Zuela gasped a protest. "He is the kindest of men, one any woman would be honoured to have as a husband."

"Then I suggest you take my place!" Sara retorted with unthinking cruelty, too blinded by rage to choose her words. But when Zuela's face crumpled she felt ashamed and stricken with remorse. Quickly, she moved to put an arm around the Arab girl's shoulders and whispered an apology. "I'm sorry, Zuela, please try to forget I said that. I'm a stupid, unfeeling woman, and even if you do bring yourself to forgive me I'll never forgive myself."

Zuela's head lifted to show large tear-filled eyes. "You know," she whispered brokenly, "you know, and yet you ask for *my* forgiveness?"

"Yes, I've known for some time that you are in love with the *señor*," Sara smoothed the dark head that was bent with remorse, "but I feel sorrow for you, not anger. He is not worthy of being loved by someone as wonderful as you."

123

Zuela shook her head fiercely, but did not reply, and Sara's curiosity moved her to ask, "Why do you stay here when his nearness must be torture to you? Why don't you return to your husband's people where Khairy will be able to live the sort of life he is entitled to as the grandson of a Caid?"

Zuela drew a deep breath of pain. "I cannot," she choked. "They will kill him if he ever returns!"

"Kill Khairy?" Shock chilled Sara's blood.

Zuela nodded. "That is why I had to flee from my husband's people as soon as I was able after the birth. You see," she struggled for composure and prepared to explain, "my husband married out of his class, and that in itself is a crime punishable by death in the tribe to which he belongs. Only the intercession of his mother prevented the sentence from being carried out, and when, shortly afterwards, my husband was killed it was looked upon as Kismet – an act of fate. Then, when my child was born deformed, they claimed that he was invaded by *djinns* and that his misfortune was revenge by the gods for the wrong we had committed. Nothing but the execution of my child would appease the gods and exorcise the evil *djinns* contained within his body, they insisted, so I was left no choice but to flee with my child under cover of darkness to escape here to my own people."

Sara rocked back on her heels, wide-eyed with disbelief. "But that's incredible! An impossible situation!" she jerked.

"But not such a hopeless one as we once thought," Zuela smiled through her tears. "Señor Felipe has been in touch with my father-in-law, the Caid, who is old and very lonely, and he has promised that if Khairy can be restored to him in perfect physical health he will welcome him as his heir. A doctor friend of the *señor*'s has already examined Khairy and has held out hope that a series of operations will bring about a successful conclusion. So you need hardly wonder," she finished softly, her eyes tender with warmth of feeling, "why I love the *señor*. To me he is the most wonderful of men, the brightest star that shines in my heaven."

Sara flinched; the fervour and sentiment in Zuela's words found an echo in her own heart. For days she had searched the faces of the men of the village, hoping for a clue that might pinpoint the man whose memory had teased her thoughts every moment since their strange encounter. Many times her senses had leapt at the sound of a similar voice or at some vaguely familiar gesture, only to sink back under the blow of yet another disappointment. She could not explain even to herself the attraction he held for her, an attraction so vital that the memory of his touch made her quiver with inward longing and the echo of his words, played back again and again on the sound track of her mind, was a comfort to be hugged close, a treasured talisman that would guard her against Felipe de Panza and his barbaric intentions. She felt his presence so strongly that she was moved into action: today might be the day of their second meeting, but it would hardly be likely to occur within the confines of her tent.

"I'm going outside for some air, Zuela," she decided impetuously. "No, don't bother to come with me," she waved a protest when Zuela would have risen to accompany her. "I'd rather be alone. I need to think, so you might as well remain here as I'll be very morose company." With a smile and a wave, she slipped out of the tent before Zuela's protests could delay her.

Outside, the village had an air of festivity. Everywhere, women were preparing great mounds of food, stirring, dipping, tasting, all to the accompaniment of much chatter and excited laughter. Obviously, tomorrow was to be a great day for them, but Sara shuddered away from dwelling upon the significance it might hold for herself. Her progress through the village was slow as each group of women tried to persuade her to sample the delicacies they were preparing. The aroma of *tajin* – a stew of chicken, pigeon, mutton and beef left to simmer for hours upon a slow heat – was already wafting in the air, together with *harira*, a wonderful thick soup which she had already sampled. Kebabs of mutton, offal and small sausages were being expertly skewered ready to be roasted over glowing charcoal embers in company with whole sheep carcases that were lined up ready to be hoisted on to spits, then turned laboriously hour upon hour until succulently tender.

Her stomach began to knot with apprehension. So sure had she been that some last-minute intervention would baulk Felipe's plans, she had refused to allow herself to worry. But now, as she watched the final preparations going ahead, she had to face, with a sick feeling of dread, the possibility that by this same time tomorrow she could be the wife of the one man in the world she had come to detest.

She stumbled as she hurried away from the groups of laughing women, her mind too numb to register that her feet were leading her into danger. A line of horsemen, young Rif bloods resplendent in gay ceremonial colours, were lined up mounted on brightly caparisoned horses. A pistol shot rang into the air and sent them charging headlong in a frenzied gallop, with heads down and bodies bent low in the saddle to gain maximum speed, too intent upon the race to notice Sara's slight figure wandering blindly in the path of their horses' galloping hooves. A sound like the rumble of approaching thunder was the first indication she received of danger. Her head jerked up and with stricken eyes she saw the line of deadly hooves moving swiftly towards her. Too petrified to move, she stood waiting for death or, if fate were to be unkind, injuries too horrible to be borne. With a flash of almost Eastern fatalism she registered that this could be answer to her problems – Felipe de Panza was, after all, to be cheated of his prey!

The sound of hooves thundered in her ears, a cloud of dust enveloped her completely so that she never actually witnessed her own dramatic rescue when from out of nowhere and with the speed and determination of a man demented, a rider charged across the line of approaching horses to scoop her into his saddle before releasing a volley of rifle shots into the air. All she knew was that during the last terrifying seconds she closed her eyes, then felt herself lifted into the air and thrown across something hard and so unmercifully bumpy that every breath was knocked out of her body. Shots rang out, and she was jerked upright into steel-hard arms just in time to see a sea of horseflesh veer off course and go rushing past in a sweating, steaming wave. Sick and trembling with reaction, she clung to the rider who had snatched her into his arms and buried her face against his cloak while he galloped his horse away from what might have been her place of execution. She sobbed as she clung to the stiff, erect form that sat so tensely in the saddle, then gradually, fear was superseded by relief and by a contentment completely alien to the circumstances when she became aware that the arms holding her were communicating the same possessive, tender quality she had experienced only once before. She nestled against him, her head against his chest, happy to wait until she could savour to the full the wonderful moment when she would look for the first time upon the face of the man whose presence had haunted her dreams, the moment when shadow became substance and she would hear again the magic voice that had the power to disperse every nightmare that plagued her.

The conviction was so strong, she had to bite back

a cry of bitter disappointment when the rider drew in the reins and prepared to dismount. His harsh, clipped voice rasped her nerves when he commanded, "If you will loosen your grip on my shirt, *señorita*, I will help you down from the saddle!"

Her eyes were wide and deeply green with shock when they lifted to his face and it took tremendous effort to gather her wits and make the confused reply,

"I'm sorry, *señor*, I might have known it would be you."

"Of course," he answered lightly as he slid to the ground and opened his arms wide to receive her. "Who else has the same interest in keeping you alive? I always protect my property."

"I'm not your property," she clenched, hating the tears that clogged her throat and hating still more the need she felt to offer thanks to the hard-eyed man who had saved her from pain only so that he could inflict his own particular brand of torment at leisure. Without making any attempt to accept the assistance he offered, she remained looking down at him as she whispered: "I wish you had let me die . . .!"

His face darkened. The bright cloud of hair accentuating her pale cameo face, her vulnerable, drooping mouth and the veiled brilliance of her eyes all spoke of deep unhappiness. He could not doubt that her words were sincerely meant.

"Ah!" His smile held not a vestige of pleasure. "So my methods are achieving success? It is greatly satisfying to learn that you, who have not hesitated to use people to your own ends, are at last being made to suffer. I had wondered from your seeming insensibility if you were a fool, but fools do not suffer pangs of conscience, neither do they react satisfactorily to the more refined methods of punishment." He sounded driven. Although his words were hard, his eyes were tormented, as if some traumatic experience had stripped him for a moment of the hard core of dislike of herself that motivated all his actions.

She swayed in the saddle. Reaction, united with despair, had helped to crush every bit of fight from her aching body. He moved instinctively to catch her when she would have fallen and the small apology she murmured before she fainted into his arms was, ironically and quite unintentionally, the sharpest weapon she had ever used against him.

CHAPTER VII

Mutinous and tight-lipped, Sara sat within a circle of excited women all intent upon adorning her with every conceivable aid to beauty. She was far beyond the boundaries of fear; only mere hours ago she had been subjected to the humiliation of being rigorously scrubbed by the village washerwoman whose job it was to wash the bride clean of evil spirits, then half drowned as bucketful after bucketful of water was sluiced over her by the rest of her enthusiastic attendants. Rage was the primary emotion that held her as, like a trussed-up doll, she was dressed in her wedding finery and decorated with stars, crosses and other good luck emblems vital to the success of the ceremony.

Zuela was nowhere to be seen; she had faded out of sight at the arrival of the village women, leaving her to their untender mercies without a word of warning or even an explanation of what was to come. I'll have a few choice words to say to that young woman, Sara seethed inwardly. And to think I supposed her to be my friend! She eyed the giggling, pushing women coldly. She had quickly discovered the uselessness of trying to escape their ministrations. They had been given a job to do and no one was going to be allowed to say it had not

131

been done thoroughly even if, at times, its doing entailed the employment of brute force to subdue the temper of the bride the *señor* had so unwisely chosen. They were too simple to realize she was merely biding her time, Sara comforted herself as she prepared to seize the first opportunity of escaping that presented itself. It would be only too easy to evade them once they had been gulled into thinking her resistance had been subdued. She looked down with distaste upon the costume she had been forced to wear. Trousers made of light, filmy material gathered in at the ankles by jewelled bands, a scanty, bejewelled brassiere top that left little to the imagination, silken slippers and ornate strings of beads – all would better have graced the figure of a harem dancer.

The sound of men shouting sent the women scurrying to the door of the tent where they gathered with their backs towards Sara, forgetting in their curiosity the need for constant vigilance. Quick as a flash, she seized her chance and ran, uncaring of her insubstantial attire, not even stopping to plan her direction. She was through the gate of the stockade with many miles of empty road stretching in front of her before she heard a small commotion in the distance that told her she had been missed. Frantically, she searched the revealing landscape for cover. On the open road she would stand out distinctly and the sloping terraces of the vineyards to her left offered little or no shelter. Her only hope was to lose herself amongst the folds of hills, so she swung sharply right and raced as fast as her flimsy slippers would allow towards the nearest grass-covered shoulder. Her lungs felt ready for bursting when finally she flung herself down in the shade of a solitary tree and lay there panting for breath. She could hear nothing to indicate that she had been followed, so gradually her heartbeats subsided to a steadier pace and she relaxed and began to weigh up her position.

After sombre reflection she had to admit that her sense of victory was premature. She was stuck in the middle of the Rif mountains with neither food nor adequate clothing and without any means of contacting help. She clenched her teeth, determining never to go back to the camp; death from starvation or exposure was preferable to the fate that awaited her there. She stumbled to her feet, obeying an urge to put as many miles as possible between herself and Felipe de Panza and began trudging in the opposite direction. It was a terrible shock when she rounded the next hill to be confronted by an Arab stallion elegantly pawing the ground and tossing its mane while it waited the command of its master, who was sitting a few yards away, his white *djellaba* and turban contrasting starkly against inscrutable features.

"Well, are you ready to discuss terms of surrender?" he questioned dryly, one eyebrow quickening upwards as he studied her dishevelled, very revealing outfit.

She stared back at him. "How did you find me?" she

choked, her eyes swivelling to the silent hills as if accusing them of treachery.

"I've had you in sight from the minute you left camp," he stated with infuriating calmness, "but I decided to allow you time to realize how abortive is your attempt to escape. Are you convinced, or would you prefer to continue for a while? I'll be content to sit here until you are ready to beg for recapture."

"Beg? Never!" she trembled, catastrophically near to tears. "I'd rather wander till I drop than ask for mercy from you!" She took a grip upon her emotions and tilted, "But at least the whole camp now knows what I feel about you! Not even your barbaric brotherhood will be able to accept with an easy conscience a bride as unwilling as I have shown myself to be. You dare not force me to go through with the ceremony now!"

When he threw back his head and laughed she knew her reasoning was faulty. "On the contrary, *señorita*," he twinkled, "your actions have allayed the many misgivings my friends have felt about your suitability as a bride. Quite unknowingly, you conformed to Rif custom by fleeing from your bridegroom on the morning of the wedding – you have shown proof of a modest disposition, and that is a highly regarded trait." He stood up with one easy movement and strode across to look down upon her bent head. She was beaten and he knew it. Far above her, she heard him say almost kindly, "A good general knows when to surrender, *señorita.* Perhaps you are now ready to admit that you took on too practised an adversary?"

She was so dispirited that for one unguarded moment she was tempted to plead, but then, at the precise moment when her lips parted to speak, she remembered her grandfather's words: *Whatever adversities lie ahead, I know you will meet them with unbowed head and an unbroken spirit!* When her bright head suddenly tilted to show eyes defiant and sparkling green he betrayed a flash of unwilling admiration.

"I'm ready to go back, *señor*," she ejected through clenched teeth, "but I warn you not to become too complacent. I do not yet admit to being beaten!"

Back at the camp, everyone was gathered in the centre of the compound waiting for the final ceremony to begin. Felipe left her in the charge of the widely grinning attendants and after doing a quick tidying-up of her hair and costume they too disappeared, leaving her alone in the tent with a thumping heart and a mouth so dry she felt she would choke. She longed for Zuela to put in an appearance so that she might answer some of the questions throbbing through her mind, but it was Khairy who appeared at the door of the tent, dressed up to perform some function which, guessing from his puffed-up manner, held some vestige of importance.

"You are ready, *señorita*?" he quavered excitedly, obviously anxious for his part to begin.

"Yes, thank you, Khairy, but before we go won't

135

you tell me what your duties are to be?"

His chest swelled with pride. "I am to ride in front of your carriage, *señorita*. Always a boy is chosen to ride in front of the bride so that she may be helped to bring forth male offspring!"

Sara's cheeks were still burning when she was helped into the "bridal box" strapped on to a vicious-looking camel. It was a curious structure consisting of wooden framework draped in thick net to shield her from the evil eye. The camel was hung with embroidered rugs and tasselled trappings and musical bells tinkled as it was led slowly towards the crowd of waiting villagers. She did not remember much of the performing of the actual rites. There was a great deal of confusing ritual, a gold coin was pressed to her forehead to ensure prosperity and some brown-coloured paste was pressed first into Felipe's palm and then into her own, but she did not look, much less speak, to the man who was the instigator of the meaningless ceremony. It was only when two little girls came forward to present her with a basket containing henna, sugar plums and slippers that she remembered Zuela remarking that this gift symbolized her entry into the nuptial home and was the culminating act of the ceremony. Only then did she look up at Felipe. She was now his wife or, as more befitted the nature of the marriage, his chattel, his water-carrier, the provisional bearer of his sons . . .

She was not allowed time to analyse whether it was this thought that sent the blood racing madly through her veins or whether it was the lambent flame her quick glance surprised in the depths of his eyes. For long seconds their glances held and it seemed even in the midst of tumultuous rejoicing that they were quite alone while he stamped upon her his own private seal of ownership with a look so compelling and so full of possession that she shuddered from wondering just how much the strange ceremony had meant to the man whose Arab blood so influenced his actions – with such dire consequences to herself!

Feasting and humour were at their highest when a roll of drums was heard above the din being made by the villagers. It heralded the arrival of a small procession of boys who approached the gathering and took up their stand in the centre of the jostling merrymakers. The sound of the drums escalated into a mighty pounding, and a chant was taken up by the villagers when a veiled performer riding a camel was seen approaching. With slow and measured tread the camel, draped with heavy and expensive rugs, wended its way through the crowd. Sara's eyes widened as she recognized, even though veiled, that the rider was Zuela clothed in the dress of a bride.

The camel reached the centre of the space and the boys formed a ring around it; the music swelled to a very high note and every villager joined in, each throat working overtime as they were caught up in a spirit of emotional fervour. Sara watched intently as Zuela balanced herself upon her knees, then began to wave her arms and bend and sway her body in time to the music. Her movements became gradually more fluid, the chanting villagers egging her on to fantastic bodily expressions of emotion such as might be felt by a girl swept by the spirit of unwedded youth. Then presently the chanting became slower and the dance more dignified and more attuned to the symbolizing of married life with all its pain and joy. It was so beautifully and so sensitively portrayed that Sara felt an emotion so deep it was a lump in her throat. So much so that when finally a much slower note was introduced and the dance terminated in a portrayal of the oncoming of women's old age tears stung behind her eyelids and she had to swallow hard to overcome the effect the exquisitely performed dance had upon her senses.

Felipe's words were an intrusion when, after appraising her expressive face, he commented, "So, you are beginning to recognize that Rif customs do not benefit only the men of the tribe. Zuela has portrayed the ecstasy and the pain, the glory and the subjugation that are the inheritance of every bride whether cultivated or savage. The Rif are primitive in their passions, but every woman taken by them as a wife is counted fortunate in acquiring a faithful and devoted mate."

Sara looked up, full of sudden defiance. "In return for what?" she cocked. "Demonstrating a perfect obedience? Prostrating herself submissively before her husband in such a way as to have no will of her own? If that is Rif justice then you can keep it, *señor*. I prefer the more emancipated outlook of Western civilization!"

They were surrounded by feasting villagers, sitting next to the head men of the tribe, so it was impossible to argue without betraying animosity. He bent towards her, his teeth showing white as he flashed a smile, but his eyes so full of cold intent she shivered. "Rif justice, primitive though it might be, is more merciful than any you dispense. I have no doubt many of your past acquaintances would rejoice if they knew that at last you are on the receiving end of the same callous indifference you have meted out to them in the past!"

She glared back, feeling an urge to smack his despicably regal face, but a reminder of the reprisals he had threatened should that act ever be repeated stayed her hand. Instead, she had to be content with blasting scorn from her stormy eyes. Her belligerence was so marked that attention was riveted upon them both, so, blandly, and to her utter confusion, he lifted the most choice morsel from his plate and held it to her lips as an invitation to eat. There was complete silence from the assembled company as they waited for her reaction. "*Don't dare!*" he breathed, as her mouth pursed in a suggestion of refusal. His eyes never left her lips as they wavered, unsure of the threat behind his words, then finally parted to accept the proffered bite. Relief rippled through the watching men before they relaxed once more into enjoyment of their pleasures. The woman was untamed; they themselves would never countenance such a wife, but the *señor* seemed satisfied so all must be well. His needs were different from theirs, his standards strange, but in the words of one of their elders: "There must be much in the woman that only his eyes can see – after all, the hawk is not content to catch flies . . ."

It was both a relief and a strain when after darkness fell, she was escorted by women holding lighted torches to the doorway of the tent. She was left there alone and shivering while they circled the tent three times muttering incantations she was now able to recognize as efforts to ward off evil spirits. Her flimsy bridal apparel gave no protection against the wind that had sprung up with the sun's departure, and she gritted her teeth to stop them from chattering as cold, both physical and spiritual, chilled her body. She smothered a gasp when, encouraged by a mighty cheer, Felipe descended from out of the darkness to swoop her up in his arms and carry her into the tent. She clung to the folds of his cloak, forgetting in her distress to fear the body whose warmth she coveted. Even when he set her down she could not bear to withdraw from the comfort he emanated, and she signalled mute gratitude when he shrugged out of his cloak and slid it around her icy slimness.

"I'm sorry my forgetfulness has caused you physical distress," he clamped as his hands rubbed briskly over the heavy cloak to generate welcome heat. Her teeth chattered, so when she tried to reply he pulled her forward, cloak and all, into his arms, employing his vibrant body as a furnace to combat her frozen misery. For long minutes she basked in the comfort of his warmth, her head against the powerful heart that was radiating heat from his body to hers. She had become chilled to the bone during the short time she was exposed to the wind, and the sudden transition from cold to heat caused her to feel drowsy and to enter the same state of euphoria often experienced by a cosseted and terribly weary child.

"M . . . m . . . m," she sighed, and nestled closer, her heavy eyelids drooping over eyes bemused with the desire for sleep. He lifted her incredibly gently and strode across to the pile of cushions that made up her bed. Still wrapped around by his cloak, she was laid down, but when he straightened to leave her her fingers refused to be prised from the grip they had upon his shirt. Even in sleep, her hold was intense, so he had no choice but to sit cradling her like a slumbering child while he waited until she should awake.

The camp was still and silent when hours later her eyelids lifted over sleep-drugged eyes. She felt warm and cherished, cradled by reassuring arms. Still in the no-man's-land between sleep and full alertness, she sighed and snuggled closer, then smiled with complete contentment when the arms around her tightened protectively.

"Are you awake?" The whispered question set her quivering, but she remained silent, hardly daring to hope in case she might again repeat the mistake she had made once before. His sigh when she did not answer almost made her abandon pretence, but she was pleased she had not when his hand reached out to stroke her hair and she heard him whisper the words that convinced her she had at last found the shadowy presence who stalked her mind.

"*Brave little warrior!*" Only he had ever called her that! In a fever of impatience, hungry for the sight of the man whose memory tormented her, she turned to face him, only to fall back, incredulous, when she saw Felipe de Panza.

"Why did you use those words? How could you possibly know . . .?" The cry was wrung from her, disillusionment, pain, bitter disappointment, they were all contained in the agonized questions. The interior of the tent was dim, the lamps turned low so that the mellow pool of light surrounding them was hazed by confusing shadows cast by flickering wicks. But there was no doubting the identity of the man who stared back at her, betraying for one fleeting second a flash of acute desire. It was so quickly disguised she could almost have believed she had imagined it, were it not that his incriminating words still rang in her ears.

"It was you!" She sobbed out the accusation, her heart thudding hard against her ribs. "I suppose that, too, was part of my punishment. You were playing up to me and I thought . . ."

"You thought what?" His voice was barely recognizable when he breathed out the words. "When you

142

believed me to be a stranger you felt an attraction – perhaps even love?"

"Love *you*?" Her look radiated contempt. "You are a despot, a spoiler of people's lives, so how can you ever expect to know love?"

He jerked her forward to stare down at her with eyes mirroring cold passion. "If I know nothing of love then teach me!" he rasped, pulling her closer. Fear rose up inside her as she sensed danger. She was alone, completely unprotected from the desires of a man filled with dangerous madness!

Her puny defences were stormed with an ease that was frightening. Pinned against his hard strength, she was subjected to kisses of sweet steel that threatened to tear the heart from her body. Against her pulsating throat she heard his demented whisper, "You are a fever, a disease in my blood that's past cure or reason. I know you to be a cheat and a liar, Sara Battle, but at this moment in time I could not care less . . .!" And the numbing, terrifying truth was that as his lips clung to hers and his touch awakened within her a wild and joyous unrest she discovered that she did not care either.

The peak of emotion was almost reached when she was thrust suddenly at arm's length. He held her away, fighting visibly for control, then just as suddenly withdrew from her completely. Quivering uncontrollably, she watched through a mist of tears as he strode without a backward glance through the doorway of the tent, then with a moan of despair she sank down upon the cushions and began, even though convulsed with sobs, to search her mind for excuses that might allow her to forgive her own weakness in responding so fervently to the man she had pledged herself to hate.

CHAPTER VIII

THEY left the village early next morning to return to Tangier. Sara learned of Felipe's decision from Zuela who came to the tent to serve breakfast, a duty she performed in complete silence while managing, nevertheless, to project the sympathy she felt at the sight of Sara's wan face and tear-shadowed eyes. But she made no comment on the absence of the *señor*, whose breakfast she had also provided, but merely removed the superfluous dishes from the tray and deposited them outside before returning to sit quietly until Sara was ready to speak.

"I'm sorry, Zuela, I can't eat any more." She pushed away her plate with the food barely touched.

Zuela inclined her head, understanding perfectly, but anxiety moved her to protest, "You have far to go, *señora*, please try to eat just a little more."

With a dispirited hand Sara pushed back a heavy wave of hair that had fallen across her brow and struggled for a second to clarify Zuela's words. "Far to go?" she echoed stupidly.

"But yes," Zuela's dark eyes were sad. "Even now the *señor* is preparing to leave us, and he is hardly likely to leave behind his wife of so few hours. Tangier was mentioned, but his mood is such that no one dares to question him further. He seems very ... displeased, *señora*, but perhaps you could charm him into staying?" she appealed.

Sara's laugh held an element of hysteria and Zuela forbore to press the point. Something was very wrong, of that there was no doubt, and her heart ached for the girl whose expressive face reflected deep unhappiness.

"Is there anything I can do to help, *señora*?" she dared to ask, only to be disconcerted by the sharp reply.

"Yes, you can stop calling me *señora*. Also you can leave me alone, *for heaven's sake leave me alone!*"

Sara felt absolutely wretched as she watched Zuela's dignified departure, but she could not bear the company of anyone; even Zuela's gentle presence rasped like a file against her sensitive nerves. The news that they were leaving for Tangier should have brought her relief, but her mind was unable to grapple with any fact other than the one that had kept her awake, unbelieving and not a little distrait, all during the night. She was in love with Felipe! Not even by speaking the words aloud could she dispel the fantasy they contained. The hard conclusion had been reached during long hours of searching both her conscience and her heart until she had at last forced herself to face the truth she had been deliberately evading. It had not been mere coincidence that had ordained that her mysterious companion of the shadows should have the height and build of Felipe, nor that he should emanate the same sense of assurance. Deep down, without even admitting their existence, she had admired these qualities in the man who was her enemy, qualities personal to Felipe alone which she in her blind stubbornness had attempted to bestow upon a shadow rather than admit to them in the substance. For reasons of his own he had played up to her that night; he had listened, sympathized, even comforted, and on that solitary occasion, under the guise of strangers, their first meeting had been like a tryst made many years ago . . .

Khairy burst into the tent, scattering her thoughts and demanding her complete attention. "*Señora, señora*, my mother says you have to leave! I do not want you to leave, *señora*, I love you, my mother loves you. Please, please stay!" His black eyes were moist and his lip trembled as he searched her face for reassurance. His distress was echoed in her voice when she told him gently,

"I love you too, Khairy, and I count your mother one of my dearest friends, but I have no choice. If the *señor* has decided to leave then I must go with him."

"Spoken like a true Rif bride!" a hard voice mocked from the doorway. They both spun round to face Felipe, once more a son of Spain, his suit immaculately pressed and his dark head free of the Riffish turban that had more than any other thing emphasised his affinity to the Arab race.

Khairy ran towards him, ready to plead, but for once

147

the *señor* had no time to spare for him. His hard look was fastened upon Sara, taking in the bright mass of hair that tumbled around her peaked face, its colour contrasting sharply against skin that had the pallor of marble. Her mouth was unsteady with pain, and the green eyes from which all sparkle had fled seemed to aggravate him greatly, as was borne out by the curtness of the command that scythed across the width of the tent to deal her a pitiless blow.

"We are returning to Tangier immediately. I have no doubt the news will lend wings to your feet and that you will not keep me waiting longer than is absolutely necessary, but that will suit me admirably. My mission is accomplished and the sooner we leave the better!"

Mission accomplished! All during the return journey his words echoed in her mind. She was being taken back to Tangier to be held before Alvaro as a hostage to prevent him from ever again rebelling against marriage to Isabel. She was a marked woman; she could not have been more possessed if she had been branded, and Alvaro would never again dare to cast eyes in her direction. But the irony of it all! To think that if Felipe could have brought himself to believe her capable of telling the truth all this need never have happened . . .

He swung the jeep off the road and brought it to an abrupt halt. They had been travelling for some hours without once stopping and obviously he was feeling the need of refreshment. He unloaded fruit and a bottle

148

of wine from the back of the jeep and strode to the edge of a nearby stream where he spread out a blanket upon which he deposited the alfresco meal before returning to her. She was sitting still as a mouse, her hands folded in her lap, staring into the distance as if waiting for some symbol of hope to appear on the horizon.

"Come," he held out a hand to help her down, "there are things we must discuss before we reach the villa, and now is as good a time as any." Without argument, she climbed down from the jeep, so pointedly ignoring his proffered hand that a hint of angry colour ran under his skin. They ate in silence until the fruit was finished, then, when she refused wine, he poured out a measure for himself and studied her intently while he drank. When he did speak his words were so startling that she jumped.

"You are a very beautiful woman, Sara. It is not surprising you are likened to Lorelei who lured countless men to their doom."

Her face suffused by hot colour, she stammered, "Is . . . is there nothing you do not know about me, señor? Do you make it your business to collect every bit of gossip that comes your way?"

Lazily he rolled on his side and admitted, "From our first meeting I found you interesting. Women of your qualities are mercifully rare, especially within one's family circle. I cannot say I altogether blame you for wanting the respectability of Alvaro's name, and I hope that you, in turn, will understand my motives in preventing such an occurrence. However," he gave careful attention to the lighting of a cheroot, "now that the battle is won, I must confess I feel I owe you something. Why I should feel this way I cannot imagine, unless it is simply that the mock ceremony was not such a mockery after all and the rites, barbaric though they were, have impressed upon my conscience an obligation towards you that only a proper marriage will assuage." He swivelled towards her, cold mockery playing upon his lips at the sight of her obvious perplexity, and stressed, "I'm offering to marry you, *señorita*, legally and in the sight of my family and friends! Well, what have you to say? As Señora de Panza you will be even richer and more secure than you would be as Señora de Leon."

Her cheeks burned at the coolly offered insult. Her immediate impulse was to reject his proposal with words so searing that they would leave him in no doubt of the distaste she felt for his suggestion. But she pulled up sharply as she noticed the restless pulling on his cheroot that betrayed a tautness completely at odds with his relaxed body. Were his words perhaps not so illogical as they sounded? Her mind went back to the moment after the marriage ceremony when his look had burned possession upon her very soul. However lightly he had entered into the idea of a mock marriage, in that instant he had been profoundly moved. And later that evening when they were alone together, only tremendous will power had prevented him from taking what he so strongly desired – *what he felt was his by right to take*!

She felt no triumph at the discovery of his weakness. He wanted her so badly he was willing to hide his desire under a cloak of obligation, so deceiving himself that the outcome he sought had actually been thrust upon him. She had waited so long for the tide to turn in her favour, but now that the moment had arrived she hesitated to act upon it. When passion had been at its highest he had admitted she was a drug in his veins. Dared she take the chance of becoming his wife, allowing him to think her motives mercenary? Or had she the strength to refuse him, knowing that once back in Tangier she might never see him again?

"Well, what have you decided?" His tone was casual to the point of indifference.

She swallowed hard, then asked carefully, "Are you asking me to believe that you want to marry a person you despise – someone you believe to be a cheat, a gambler, a preyer upon men – simply to ease a fretful conscience?"

His dark eyes were slumbrous as they roved her fresh young beauty. As if compelled by an inner urge, he admitted, "Perhaps I am hoping that a marriage between us might produce some hidden compensations." Then his voice took on a quality of roughness as, impatient of prevarication, he demanded, "Are you or are you not to be Señora de Panza?"

For the life of her she could not hold back the breathless whisper: "To be!"

Her answer seemed to afford him little satisfaction. A blush spread all over her body as she was scrutinizing by eyes of pinpointed steel that roved her face seeking answers to unspoken questions. Her shame was such that she would have retracted, but then he sprang suddenly to his feet and stated so matter-of-factly: "Good, then we had better be on our way," that she was able to swallow her misgivings and follow him to the jeep to continue the journey.

Halfway to Tangier, he made a surprise detour, deserting the main road in favour of a secondary one that climbed upwards until they reached a pass affording a breathtaking panorama of softly rounded mountains, then shortly afterwards he took a left fork and as they continued along the steep road she saw in the distance tall minarets towering above the rooftops of a small town. He drove into the centre of a small circular "square" and pulled up outside a *parador* whose sign "Hotel de Chaouen" indicated the name of their stopping place.

"I thought you might welcome a chance to freshen up before arriving at the villa," he offered as explanation. "If you wait here I'll find out if they can oblige us with the use of a room and shower as well as providing us with lunch." He strode into the hotel, leaving her happily assessing what she could see of the delightful old town. It was magnificently positioned high on

152

the mountain tops, with innumerable streams running down to irrigate the flower-filled gardens so beloved by Moroccans. She sniffed deeply, inhaling perfume drifting from the flowering trees planted around the market place, and lifted her face to feel the caress of the breeze being breathed over the town from the surrounding mountains.

"We are in luck," he informed her as he returned to assist her from the jeep. "If you go inside someone will show you to your room while I make arrangements to have our luggage taken upstairs." With a spontaneous grin he added, "I am thankful that you are not like my aunt and Isabel in one respect at least. They have never been known to travel more than a few miles without a pile of luggage, whereas you seem to manage perfectly with one small suitcase." She flushed and shyly returned his smile before leaving him to enter the hotel where she was shown into a room, unobtrusively comfortable, its standards conforming to the Government-run *paradors* in Spain – reasonably priced halting places built in styles typical of their region. She flung off her jacket and stretched luxuriously; somehow her spirits had miraculously revived, and it had all to do with that unexpected grin of Felipe's. Strange how a smile can cure the wounding of a frown. How wonderful it would be to bask for ever in the warmth of his approval . . .

He knocked on her door just as she was giving a final brush to her hair. Her feet seemed hardly to touch the

153

ground as she sped to open it, eager to discover whether the upward quirk of his lips would tell her his humour was still mellow. He drew in a quick breath. She was aware that the pale yellow dress she had chosen to wear complemented her burnished hair to perfection, and that its simple lines drew tantalizing attention to the slenderness of her figure, but she did not know that happiness had lent to her movements the vibrant gracefulness of a young gazelle and had transformed the jewelled brilliance of her eyes to the softer, gentler glow reminiscent of an ocean's depths. For one startled moment his look betrayed flame, flame which was instantly suppressed but which lingered slumbrously as a lambent glow.

She felt a quiver of pleasure when his deeply timbred voice complimented: "You look enchanting. Nothing lunch has to offer will be half so delectable as the companion I am to share it with." He proffered an arm. "Are you quite ready?" Without daring to trust her voice, she took it in silence and allowed him to escort her downstairs.

They ate spicy soup served piping hot, followed by *pastilla* – pigeon and almond pie enclosed in flaky pastry made with butter – followed by various types of sweetmeats. It was only when they had been served with the mint tea that is the drink which inevitably accompanies every Moroccan meal that he leant back, well satisfied, to surprise her once again by offering casually, "As we are no longer in any hurry to reach Tangier, I

154

suggest we pay a visit to the *souks*. Chaouen is famous for its excellent local craftmanship, so I'm sure you will find it entertaining. Would you like that?"

The prospect of seeing at first hand one of the wonders of the East made her forget her nervousness and she reacted with a pleased anticipation that brought an indulgent smile to his lips. "Will there be snake-charmers, and jugglers and acrobats?" Her breathless question betrayed the hushed wonder of a child to whom such treats are rare. The once-a-year visits to the circus provided by the orphanage had been something of an aggravation, a whetting of the appetite for such novel entertainment that lingered still in the mind of the girl who should have long outgrown such childish pleasures. His smile betrayed his thoughts and embarrassed colour flared in her cheeks as she fought an onrush of foolishness. As expected, he laughed, but then he confused her by promising gravely,

"If there are no acrobats then I shall demand that they be sent for. You have been sufficiently deprived, and today we must try to make up for the magic stolen from your childhood." His lean fingers reached out to capture her hand that was plucking at a discarded napkin as he reminded her that it was he who had been the recipient of her frightened confidences on the night she had encountered him as a shadowy stranger. She looked away, confused by the complexity of the man whose charm was such he could quell the fury of a stallion as easily as he could charm a band of unruly

youngsters. She wanted to distrust him, to have time
to sort out in her mind the reasons behind his devastating change of attitude, but her worst enemy was her
own desire to be loved that was forcing from her mind
every niggling doubt about his motives. *Live for today*,
her grandfather had urged. Well, just this once, she
would take his advice!

To set foot in the labyrinth of alleyways comprising
the main *souk* was to step immediately into the Middle
Ages. From the very beginning of their tour Sara was
engrossed in the fascinating stalls and shops that held
for her a magic so intense she could not find adequate
words to express her pleasure. But her green eyes, wide
with wonder, reflected her feelings perfectly, so dispensing with any need for speech.

Felipe was an expert and considerate guide. He ela-
borated in depth as he explained the methods and materials used by the craftsmen who were manufacturing
and plying their wares in exactly the same way that their
ancestors had done hundreds of years before. He waited patiently while she hesitated before a potter at his
wheel, watching his nimble fingers shaping a mound of
wet clay into an elegant vase in a matter of seconds.
All around him were stacked finished products, glazed
and painted with colourful patterns of flowers or geo-
metrical designs – no two alike. They then wandered
passed spice perfumed grocers' shops; stalls piled high
with decorated leatherwork, and others offering beaten

156

metal trays, daggers with inlaid hilts and glittering, barbaric jewellery.

"You must have a memento of your first visit to the *souks*," Felipe's amused voice reached through her absorption as she rummaged through a pile of costume jewellery that had caught her attention. With an embarrassed flush, she hastily dropped the bracelet she was holding and replied,

"No, really, there's no need, just to look is enough." Narrowed eyes denoted his surprise at her reaction and she blushed deeper, hating the thought of being judged mercenary. Ignoring her protest, he sharply directed the grinning Arab to keep the rubbish he displayed for gullible tourists and to bring forward wares more worthy of the lady whose custom would make him the most honoured shopkeeper in the *souk*. Bowing, and with much gesticulation, he hastened to obey, and seconds later he reappeared carrying trays containing trinkets of such delicate beauty that Sara was enraptured.

"Do you have a preference?" he asked, his disparaging hand sorting through the glittering, gem-encrusted baubles.

"They're all so lovely," she breathed, then added a hasty protest, "and so expensive . . ."

"Nonsense!" he laughed. "Although this rogue would have us believe otherwise," he nodded towards the Arab who returned the nod vigorously, "these stones are far from perfect and so sell relatively cheaply." His dark glance disconcerted her as it swung to her face. "Did you really think I would consider such trinkets worthy of anything other than whimsical keepsakes? As my future wife," he watched with interest the slow tide of colour that rose under her clear skin, "you will wear only perfect stones brought to life by masterful cutting – a delicate science that uncovers hidden beauty." He flicked her wavering lashes with the tip of his finger as he continued. "Emeralds are a must, for eyes such as yours can only be matched by that costly and most coveted of stones – the fire emerald."

"You know a lot about precious stones?" she faltered, her taste in jewellery suddenly seeming terribly unsophisticated.

Smiling slightly, he admitted, "I have studied the subject, but only as a hobby. Colourful, sparkling stones have a strong appeal to the imagination, and I find it interesting that even in the days of Moses the Hebrews related the different coloured stones to various phases of life and nature ... What month were you born?" he disconcerted her by suddenly asking.

"April," she stammered. "April the seventh."

His lips quirked at some hidden joke. "Then your natal stone is the diamond, whose white colour symbolizes life, joy and innocence." She turned away to hide a glint of tears as the source of his amusement became clearly apparent. His words were sword-points of mockery, inflicted deliberately to cause pain. She must never again allow herself to be gulled into thinking his attitude towards her had softened; deep within him lurked an outraged conscience shrieking out against his acceptance of a girl whose character fell far short of the standard he himself had attained.

When he turned his attention once more to the choosing of a trinket she was composed enough to accept with a show of gratitude the slender pearl and diamond bracelet he finally selected. But when he clasped it around her wrist his fingers lingered, his caressing, easy strokes upon her smooth skin seeming to denote a pride in possession she found abhorrent. She did not want to be possessed for physical reasons; her heart cried out for understanding and for a love that would withstand the test of time and adversity. Instead of that, all she was offered was pride of ownership and a desire strong enough to overcome the better judgement of a man noted for his iron will.

It seemed no time at all before the sun began to set over the dusty, heat-scorched market place and the majority of stallholders began to pack up their wares. Sara swallowed her disappointment and resigned herself to returning to the hotel without having savoured the amusements she had so eagerly looked forward to – and which Felipe had all but promised. But he made no move to leave. He continued sauntering around, saying little, but with a humorous quirk to his lips that was annoying in its secrecy. Then suddenly, as if by magic, the whole square was filled with performers of every sort – musicians, jugglers, acrobats, swallowers of swords and boiling water, snake-charmers, dancers and, most remarkable of all, storytellers who gathered around them an audience of spellbound listeners who seemed impervious to the discordant noises assailing them from every side.

Felipe's smile widened into a broad grin as he enjoyed her dawning bewilderment. Speech was impossible, the racket being made by performers, collectors, audiences, water-sellers, cab-drivers and would-be guides was deafening. She watched with amazement as a young cyclist pedalled up to the crowd encircling a storyteller, dropped his bike and himself to the ground and became immediately absorbed in the storyteller who never for one moment allowed his grip upon his listeners to relax. "In a few minutes," Felipe spoke close in her ear, "he will reach a climax in his story and stop to pass around the hat." Sure enough he did, and the spell he had cast upon his audience was so great that they could not rid themselves quickly enough of the small coins needed to ensure that the tale would continue.

Felipe dispensed money liberally as they visited each performer; they joined hands and laughed together like children at the antics of the clowns and jugglers, watched spellbound the incredible feats performed by acrobats, and were impressed by the fluidity and grace of the dancers. Some enterprising businessman had built a rooftop café from which vantage point could be seen most of the spectator rings, and it was towards this that he was guiding her when she suddenly stopped, transfixed with horror, staring at a cardboard box lying directly in her path. She tried to scream a warning, but her throat was dry with fear as she watched a cobra's head lift fractionally above the box and begin swaying, its beady eyes fixed directly upon herself, its forked tongue darting horribly in and out as it waited for a victim. Just at that second Felipe saw it too, and with a speed that left her gasping he pushed her out of the way, seized a larger box from a pile of rubbish and thrust it over the writhing snake, effectively blocking its exit. The crowd around the nearby snake-charmer was scythed apart as Felipe strode his way through to grab the luckless man by the scruff of the neck. Biting anger was evident in his every word and gesture as he slated the man for his carelessness, shaking him every now and again to emphasise his displeasure. Finally he dropped the abject Arab in disgust and strode back to Sara, whose ashen face and uncontrollable trembling turned his anger to quick compassion. His arms were a haven, his voice caressingly tender as he rocked her in his arms and soothed gently,

"Forget it, *cara*, the danger is past, you no longer need to fear."

With deliberate effort she pulled herself together. "I'm sorry, but it was so horrible. I was terrified, I thought . . ."

"Hush," he erased the quiver from her mouth with a tender finger. They were quite alone, surrounded by noise but isolated in the depth of shadows between two

deserted stalls. The clamour of the market place faded
to a whisper as her eyes were drawn to linger, as if
hypnotized, by the flame in the depths of his eyes. With
a quick intake of breath he pulled her closer, and her
heart jerked alive when she felt his lips feathering
lightly across her brow. His voice was barely audible
when he murmured inconsequentially, "It would not
have struck, you know. Snakes like heat and the slightest drop in temperature makes them sluggish." Punctu-
ating his words with teasing kisses, he mused on, "The
disgruntled Arab probably threw the snake into its box
because it refused to perform and then forgot to put
on the lid. He deserved a verbal thrashing, don't you
think . . .?"

She nodded, too bemused even to think, then began
to tremble when his lips descended, firm and cool, to
begin the first exploratory kiss of tenderness they had
ever shared. Its sweetness made her senses soar, excitement raced through her veins so that she was able to
forget for a few short seconds that his kiss was a kiss
of ownership, his action a right to which any future
husband might think himself entitled.

"Lorelei," he sighed against her lips, "you are indeed
well named, *bella!*" She stiffened and pulled sharply
away, only to suffer being pulled back into steel-hard
arms that threatened to break her in two with force of
passion. Sharply, his eyes scoured her face, seeking a
reason for her withdrawal, but when she turned away
and refused to meet his challenge his arms dropped to

his sides and he accused bleakly, "So, though my wealth may be greater than Alvaro's my charm is not, eh?" When she did not reply, his voice grated out the instruction, "We must set off for Tangier immediately if we are to arrive before the household retires for the night. Tomorrow will be a big day for us. As soon as our betrothal is announced I shall move heaven and earth to expedite the date of our wedding." She flinched as if from a threat, but managed to hold back the scorching tears burning her throat. The day had been a delight, full of precious moments, but the sun had gone in and once more she felt the chill of his disapproval.

Just one room was illuminated when they pulled up outside the villa shortly before midnight. The night had turned cold and she was glad to obey when he curtly told her to go inside to see about food and hot drinks while he put away the jeep. She heard voices coming from the small salon and decided to announce their arrival first before proceeding to the kitchen in search of the servants. No flash of premonition prepared her for the surprise she received when with a smile of anticipation she flung open the door to confront Isabel and Alvaro who were talking to a stranger whose back was towards her. When Isabel cried out at the sight of her, the stranger turned swiftly and with a gasp of relief held out his arms.

"Sara! I've been worried sick, why on earth didn't you answer my letters?"

163

"Marc!" Half laughing, half crying, she ran into his arms to be hugged close with a fervour that communicated without words the anxiety and heartburning her silence had caused him. "I meant to write, Marc, honestly I did, but things happened so swiftly," she babbled happily between hugs that were forcing the breath from her body. "I'm sorry if you've been worried . . . How is your father? Are you back in Tangier for good . . .?" His kiss effectively silenced the many other questions she wanted to ask, and she surrendered to its warmth like a kitten to the fire, basking in the deep affection of the man whose regard she had missed more than she had realized.

"It is obvious, Sara, that you and this gentleman are old . . . *friends*." Felipe's clipped words and the emphasis he placed upon his last word robbed their greeting of its aura of friendship, leaving them feeling their relationship had been somehow tainted, smeared by a smutty finger. She knew Marc felt it too, when his arms dropped to his sides and he stepped in front of her to shield her from threatened unpleasantness.

"I don't believe I have had the pleasure?" She could hardly believe it was Marc who was speaking in a tone so frigid one could almost hear the ice splintering around his words. Felipe stood in the doorway, his eyes narrowed to slits, his manner arrogantly demanding an explanation. The antagonism between them both could be felt as they weighed each other up, their tempers so finely balanced the others were afraid to speak in case a careless word should detonate an explosion that might annihilate them all.

Felipe's set expression did not alter when he contradicted coldly, "Your lapse of memory is excusable, Monsieur Rochefort, our first meeting was brief and you had a plane to catch."

A flicker of puzzlement relaxed Marc's tense young face, then memory dawned. "But of course, you are the gentleman who rescued the cheque!"

"That is a matter I intend to discuss with you, *monsieur*," Felipe put in brusquely, leaving Sara frantically wondering what he intended saying to Marc. "At a time and place convenient to us both we must talk, but Sara and I have had a tiring journey, so if you will please excuse us . . .?"

The dismissal was so insultingly clear that Marc's colour rose, but to his credit he swallowed back an angry retort and began taking his leave with meticulous politeness, lingering only long enough to plead with Sara as he bent over her hand, "I must speak with you alone. May I see you tomorrow? Perhaps we could lunch together?"

Flags of colour were high in her cheeks when she defied the hard eyes that bored into her back and accepted gently, "Of course, Marc, I would enjoy lunching with you. Don't bother to call for me, I'll meet you outside the hotel at one o'clock, if that's all right with you?"

Marc shot a look of triumph at Felipe before bending his head to kiss the hand she held out to him.

"Perfect, *chérie*, I shall count the hours! I am staying at the *pension* if by chance you should want to get in touch with me. *Au revoir, ma petite,* until tomorrow!"

"I'm sorry to disappoint you, *monsieur*, but that will not be possible!" Marc's head jerked up when Felipe coldly addressed him. Blue eyes clashed with black across Sara's head, but Felipe forestalled Marc's angry protest by rebuking her with deceiving mildness, "Have you forgotten, *cara*, that tomorrow we will be kept busy with arrangements for our wedding? You must also have a ring," his laughter was dangerously light when he questioned an astonished Marc, "Would you believe any girl could forget such an important matter? I fear your surprise presence has driven all thought of our wedding from my fiancée's head!"

Isabel's squeal of delight drew attention away from Marc, who stood as if turned to stone, grey-faced with shocked disbelief. "You have fixed a date? Oh, what wonderful news!" As she ran to embrace Sara excited questions tumbled from her lips. "When is the wedding to be? Will it take place here, or in Spain? Can I be bridesmaid, Sara? I would so love to be a bridesmaid just once before I become a bride!"

Sara could not answer; she was staring mutely at Marc, willing him to understand that she would have given anything to have spared him the shock he had so obviously suffered. At that moment she hated Felipe for the deliberately callous way he had sent out to inflict the maximum of shock upon the man he obviously considered as a rival. His dog-in-the-manger attitude was unforgivable; the possession of herself had assumed paramount importance since his sensing of the interest of another man. Heaven help her, she thought bitterly, if she should ever digress when she was his wife. Already, in the light of a mere betrothal, she felt stamped with the hallmark of his domination.

Marc made a tremendous recovery. He still looked stunned, but he managed a smile as he took Sara's hand to ask, "Is this what you want, *petite*?" He jerked his head in Felipe's direction, not yet ready to meet his sardonic look. "Is he really the one who warms your heart?" The torment reflected in his eyes was almost her undoing. She was tempted to ease his hurt with a denial, but that would have meant raising his hopes yet again and she had suffered herself the agony and ecstasy of wishful thinking. So she spared him by being brutal. "Yes, Marc, Felipe is the one I am going to marry."

His head lifted, and with the expressionless face of a man who refuses to acknowledge pain, he addressed Felipe. "Congratulations, *señor*, you are in my opinion the luckiest man in the world. But be warned," his short laugh deceived no one, "if you should ever become careless of your good fortune there are those who will not hesitate to take it into their keeping."

Felipe's lips tightened, but he ignored the veiled threat and curtly repeated his earlier dismissal. "Thank

you, *monsieur*. But now, although I insist upon a future meeting, I must ask you again to excuse us as both Sara and I have had a long and tiresome journey ..."
Before he left Marc clicked his heels and bowed to each in turn, but as she watched his retreating figure Sara felt a sense of shame, a feeling that a cherished friendship had been somehow betrayed ...

Alvaro caught her by the arm when she would have rushed blindly past him to seek the solitude of her room. Isabel, after a perceptive look at her drawn face, had gone to order refreshments and Felipe was escorting Marc to the door to ensure, Sara had no doubt, that his unwelcome guest was speeded on his way. So they were quite alone when Alvaro voiced his incredulous question.

"Sara, what does all this mean? You're surely not seriously considering marriage to Felipe?" She flinched from his intense grip; carried away by amazement, he was completely unaware of the pain he was inflicting. Her green eyes took on a depth he could not fathom when she stumbled over words of explanation.

"Yes, Alvaro, I'm afraid I am. We ... I ... it's difficult to say exactly how it happened, I'm not quite sure myself, but ..."

"He's forcing you to marry him, isn't he?" Alvaro interrupted savagely. "He'd go even as far as that to get you away from me! But why are you allowing it, Sara, *why*? You hate him, you told me yourself you would never forgive the wrong he did your grandfather, and yet now you are asking me to believe you are willing to marry him. I utterly refuse to believe it! If you won't admit the real reason behind your decision then I shall go to Felipe and tell him everything. He has never attempted to hide his contempt of you and he must be made to drastically revise his opinion even if it means making him aware of the true facts!"

"No, Alvaro," an agitated quiver disturbed her mouth, "you promised me you would keep silent and you must keep your word."

He searched her pleading face with dismayed intensity. "But you *can't* marry him knowing he thinks ill of you, and knowing also that, being the man he is, he will never allow himself to love where he cannot respect. He must be told the truth, Sara, *he must!*"

"No! No!" She was trembling with reaction as she gasped out, "How can I tell him I set out deliberately to trick him? That I planned and schemed for his humiliation? He would never forgive me, you know that!"

"True," Alvaro nodded agreement, "but does it matter? Once you leave here you need never see him again."

She flinched, then swiftly lowered her lashes to hide the glint of tears. "Yes," she managed to whisper. "It matters, it matters terribly . . ."

Comprehension flashed across Alvaro's face as he expelled on a whispered breath, "*Madre de Dios!* You have not been foolish enough to fall in love with him?"

"It seems this is your night for bidding your ad-

169

mirers a last farewell!" Felipe's icy tone snaked out from the doorway. Sara's head jerked up, her tortured eyes flashing a mute yearning plea to be trusted, but when her look was met with glowering suspicion she turned and ran swiftly from the room, the sob catching in her throat sounding to Alvaro like the cry of a mortally wounded animal.

CHAPTER IX

ISABEL was chattering excitedly on and on, as she had done constantly since the announcement of the engagement and the swiftly advancing date of the wedding. They were in the small salon sorting through piles of patterns and batches of materials left there by the dressmaker who had been summoned to the villa by Doña Maria immediately she had been informed of their plans.

"Do you like this shade, Sara?" Isabel held a swathe of delicate pink organza against her sun-kissed complexion and waited for comment.

Sara tried to instil enthusiasm into her answer. "It is very becoming. Pink is a colour you should wear often."

Isabel gave a pleased nod and blushingly volunteered, "Alvaro said so, too, on the day he asked me to marry him. We were in the garden of my home in Catalonia," she confessed dreamily. "I had sensed weeks before that he intended to propose, so that day I purposely set out to make myself as attractive as possible in the hope that I might overcome his diffidence, and I succeeded beyond my wildest hopes."

"Shame on you for admitting to such guile!" Doña

171

Maria tried to look stern, but her lips twitched even as she reprimanded, "If I had known you were deliberately planning to ensnare my son I would never have agreed to Felipe sending him to work in your father's vineyards. Our intention was that he should go there to gain experience of the modern machinery recently installed there – not to be bombarded by wiles as old as Eve herself."

"Do you deny that you, too, were overjoyed when Alvaro told you of our betrothal?" Isabel met Doña Maria's twinkling eyes with serene complacency. "Indeed you cannot, because it was whispered to me by my mother that you had expressed just such a wish many years ago when Alvaro and I were mere babies."

Doña Maria was not in the least disconcerted. "Perhaps," she shrugged smilingly. "In the old days it was customary for families to choose their children's future partners when they were still mere infants. Nowadays, such action would not be tolerated by your modern generation, but it does not follow that we parents do not still hope and even, if the situation warrants, give a necessary push in the right direction."

All during the teasing interchange Sara listened with mounting dismay. Could it possibly be that Alvaro had lied when he accused Felipe and his mother of arranging a marriage for him behind his back? Isabel's words indicated that she had found no lack of ardour in a courtship Alvaro had denied ever existed! The thought of the wrong she might have done Felipe made her squirm inwardly; it was an effort to clear her throat and force out the question.

"I had no idea your courtship was of such long duration. How long have you been engaged, Isabel?"

"Simply *ages*!" she stressed, ignoring Doña Maria's tut-tut of denial. "You have no idea how fortunate you are to be marrying Felipe, who is a law unto himself, and who can make his own arrangements without fear of finding disfavour with his family. Alvaro and I were madly keen to be married six months ago, when he first proposed, but my family insisted upon us waiting so as to give them time to make arrangements for an elaborate affair which neither of us want. No wonder the poor dear took off in a temper and omitted even to write to me while he was away. Luckily," she smiled her relief, "Felipe was able to make him understand that the delay was a minor setback, a penance that had to be endured for the sake of keeping peace within the family, and so eventually he was persuaded to return." Suddenly she became pensive, the sparkle in her eyes dimmed by reflective memory. "I am grateful to Felipe," she stated soberly. "If it had not been for him I'm sure Alvaro would neither have forgiven nor understood."

When Doña Maria nodded agreement Sara realized with sudden insight the true extent of the debt they both owed to Felipe. Alvaro was their idol, in their eyes he could do no wrong, and because of that Felipe had never allowed them to discover the weaknesses that were only too apparent to those who knew his real character. She felt sickened by the lies that had tripped so lightly from his tongue, and by the way he had not hesitated to lay the blame for his own folly not only upon his cousin – whose back was broad – but also upon his mother. She wanted to berate them both for their stupidity, to tell them in no uncertain terms that the man they so readily excused had tried desperately to run away from his responsibilities towards the girl to whom he had proposed probably in a fit of pique or, what was even more likely, in an effort to relieve acute boredom. But of course she had to remain silent; the injustice she had so unknowingly done Felipe could not be rectified by destroying the peace of mind he had striven so hard to maintain. In a way, she could be grateful to Alvaro; if it were not for his lies she would not at this very moment be preparing for the wedding which was the outcome of Felipe's determination never to allow her to constitute a threat to the happiness of his family.

The following days passed in a nightmare rush of fittings with the dressmaker, whirlwind shopping bouts and the making of countless decisions ranging from the choosing of flowers for the bridal bouquet to the more mundane task of agreeing which sweet course should be served at the reception planned for the hundred or so guests who were to attend the wedding. Doña Maria had made herself responsible for drawing up the guest list which, at Sara's request, was cut to the very minimum. Even so, she was appalled by the number of people Doña Maria solemnly insisted were so closely related that their presence was essential if family honour were to be upheld.

"But no one could possibly have so many close relatives!" she protested to the adamant Doña Maria.

The old lady's lips pursed obstinately. "Nonsense, child! This list is a mere fifth of the size it would be were Felipe not in such a hurry to claim his bride." She raised distrait eyebrows and wailed, "Two more weeks would have given me sufficient time to arrange things to perfection, but no, seven days were all I was allowed and, knowing Felipe, if matters are not concluded in the time stated he will disconcert us all by dispensing with ceremony completely!" This possibility seemed to spur her on to greater effort; she held out her hand for the list Sara was scanning with unbelieving eyes and stood with pencil poised as she urged, "I must have the names of the people you wish to invite. The caterer insists that he must have the final number by this evening at the latest."

Not for the first time in her life Sara regretted her orphaned state. She longed to be able to match Felipe's list with a formidable one of her own full of names guaranteed to assure his relatives of the solidarity of her background – but the wish was pointless yearning. "Marc Rochefort and Madame Blais are the only two I shall be inviting," she answered firmly, steeling herself for the surprised outburst she knew she could expect. It was quite a few seconds before Doña Maria found her voice, only to be cheated out of expressing her dismay by a firm request projected from the direction of the doorway.

"Can you spare Sara for a few minutes, Tia? There is something I wish to discuss with her." Coolly, Felipe swept her from under his aunt's nose and guided her outside to the deserted patio. She went unwillingly. For the past few days she had been attempting a meeting with Marc, only to be baulked at every turn by urgent demands upon her time from one or other of the family. These requests had been so well timed, and so seemingly spontaneous; she had been forced to accede to them and it had taken her until yesterday to realize that she was the victim of a conspiracy aimed at keeping Marc and herself apart. She had no doubt that its instigator was Felipe, and consequently her tone was cool when she rejected his offer of a seat.

"No, thank you, I prefer to stand," she tossed over her shoulder as she walked towards the edge of the pool, hoping the contemplation of its cool blue waters might calm her throbbing nerves.

"Come here, Sara," he insisted gently, making no move to approach her physically. She obeyed reluctantly. "That's better!" He smiled slightly as he led her towards a dual swing seat with a gay protective canopy and waited until she was seated before taking his place beside her. She showed little interest when he reached into his pocket to withdraw a small suede-covered box. With one lean finger he snapped open the catch and in spite of herself her eyes were drawn to examine the ring displayed upon a cushion of bridal white satin. It had an Arabian Nights quality, a possession worthy of a sultan or a king, a liquid emerald orb from which a thousand scintillating sparks ricocheted from a centre of molten green fire. Not for the life of her could she imagine herself walking around with such a king's ransom anchored to one small finger!

Her mute response seemed to please him. As he lifted up her hand to slip the priceless gem upon her finger he laughed softly and murmured, "So you feel it too — an aura of mystery, a feeling that if this ring could speak it might tell many tales of intrigue, of battles for possession fought and won so that the victor might carry to his lady love a jewel fine enough to express his devotion. See," he tilted her hand so that the sun's rays were caught and devoured by green flame, "once more it lives! Such jewels are fashioned by man for woman and only a woman's touch can bring forth their true beauty."

Her hand lay within his, limp and icily cold. A thrill of superstitious fear chilled her as she fought a conviction that the ancient ring, though harmless to lovers, might bring down the wrath of the gods upon any misuser. Their engagement made a mockery of love, the ring was to be a symbol of that mockery — what dire curse might it evoke as a revenge against their hypocrisy?

He frowned when he felt the shudder that ran

through her body. "What is it? Don't you like the ring?" She nodded, too miserably afraid to lie, then forced through tight lips.

"You are quite determined to go through with the wedding, aren't you, Felipe? What pleasure do you expect to derive from a marriage to someone you can never love?" He brooded down at her, deliberating her question but seeming in no hurry to put her out of her misery. A sudden flare of anger gave courage to her tongue, and an accusation was voiced even before the impulse had properly registered. "I am your weakness, Felipe, the only weakness you have ever allowed, and how you despise yourself for it! You want me so much physically that you are willing to overlook my less satisfying qualities, but is that a good enough basis for marriage? I've changed my mind! For both our sakes, I am breaking off our engagement now, before it is too late!"

Her words were as match to tinder. Vibrant emotion leapt to life in eyes that seconds before had been pools of inscrutability. He hissed through a tightly compressed mouth: "It is already too late! You are mine, *you belong to me!*" She was pulled fiercely forward to meet lips that descended to plunder with kisses so harsh she tried to cry out. He punished her revolt unmercifully, extracting what satisfaction he could from lips that refused to respond and from a body fighting desperately not to succumb to a wave of passion so devastating that the sun whirled in the heavens and the ground heaved beneath her feet. The answer she had goaded from him was growled against her fiery cheek. "Every man is entitled to one reckless impulse in his lifetime, *chica*, and marriage to you will be mine!"

He released his hold and she backed away, too overwhelmed by her own feelings to protest and too afraid of his to ever again chance being on the receiving end of a passion so intense that it overcame every civilized impulse. However suspect his motives, he was determined to make her his wife – he believed he had some prior claim over her . . . and in a strange, fatalistic way she believed it too! Had there been some tangle of magic in the potions heaped upon them both during the pagan marriage ceremony? By the powers of the mystic East she had been ordained a Rif bride and it seemed that any attempt she made to deny her subjugation only served to set the gods laughing . . .

She jumped up and ran from him, too shaken to protest further, her thoughts chaotic beyond reason, and was relieved when, after an aeon of silence, she heard his retreating footsteps resound against the tiled floor. She sagged against a pillar, relieved beyond measure that hostilities had momentarily ceased, and allowed tears of weakness to trickle down her ashen cheeks.

She was still there an hour later when Alvaro sought her out. His glance quickened as he noted the signs of inward torment her hour of solitude had not been able to erase and his tone was rough with apology even as he accused, "I warned you, did I not, what dire consequences might result from any clash with Felipe? Why didn't you heed my warning, Sara?" he pleaded with concern. "No one has ever yet managed to best him, as I know to my cost, but you can't say you went into the fight ignorant of his ruthless methods."

She seemed to stare blankly through him, so that for a second he was unsure if his words had registered, but she forced a flush to his face when she rebuked quietly, "I recognized the strength of my enemy, but not the treachery of my friend. Alvaro, why did you lie to me? I opposed Felipe on your behalf as much as my own because I thought you were being tyrannized into marriage against your will. None of this need ever have happened if you had been honest with me."

Alvaro grumbled, "I never intended to propose to Isabel. For weeks I was stuck on her parents' farm, driven almost to distraction by lack of amusement. Naturally, we were thrown together a lot, but I never meant to propose, it just sort of happened. If Felipe had kept out of my affairs the engagement would by now have died a natural death, but it was *he* who insisted upon reviving it; he even went to the extent of chasing me halfway around the world to make sure I would be here when Isabel came to visit. The damned girl would have been fixed up with someone else long ago if he had not insisted upon interfering!"

Sara flinched for Isabel. Doubtless he would now marry her — the engagement had been made public and not even he would have the effrontery to back out now

— but Isabel deserved a better future than was augured with a man of such doubtful qualities. She found herself praying that the blinkers would stay on, that Isabel would never be deprived of the rose-coloured glasses that portrayed for her a giant where others saw a pygmy.

Her response disguised her distaste sufficiently well to bring relief flooding back to Alvaro's face. "I don't think you realize how fortunate you are in your choice of bride, Alvaro, but perhaps that is something time will remedy. It is too late now for recriminations. We are in the same boat, you and I, both betrothed to partners whom neither of us deserve."

He looked shocked, as if the idea of himself being in any way inferior was a notion too ridiculous to be entertained, then he shrugged lightly and admitted, "Of late, I have become very much attracted to Isabel, so much so that the idea of marriage is no longer repugnant."

"I'm glad." Sara's smile warmed his chastened spirit. "I hope you will both be very happy."

"But what of you, *amada*?" he questioned solemnly. "What wish shall I make for you?"

"Wish for an armistice, Alvaro," she sighed wearily. "All I can hope for now are reasonable terms of surrender . . ."

CHAPTER X

THE ancient, beautiful church seemed crowded to capacity as Sara was escorted down the aisle on the arm of Felipe's uncle. A thousand eyes were trained upon her pale, very lovely face framed by a veil of Spanish lace that had been worn throughout generations by every Panza bride. They assessed with approval her slight figure, looking in virginal white an insubstantial shadow as she glided past columns of black marble and oak-panelled walls towards the man who waited, gravely erect, until she reached his side. That her brilliant eyes were stunned passed without comment; it was fitting that she should be so aware of the extent of her good fortune. Felipe was, after all, the most eligible bachelor in the whole of Morocco.

She moved in a dream through the sea of faces that were turned so eagerly towards her, but clung to the sight of cherubic choirboys whose sweet voices soared high up to the domed ceiling in a hymn of praise that fitted her fantasy perfectly. The moment had actually arrived. For days now she had accepted that the inevitable must happen, she had ceased fighting against Felipe's domination and had allowed herself to float upon a tide of events which in the last days had developed into a flood. Now on the final wave, she was being cast up like a piece of flotsam at the feet of the man she was preparing, once more, to marry. An hysterical giggle rose in her throat as she wondered lightheadedly what effect the news that this was to be the second marriage ceremony they had participated in would have upon Felipe's starchy relatives. But the giggle died into a quiet gasp as, with a final reassuring squeeze, Felipe's uncle relinquished his hold upon her hand before passing it over into his nephew's firm keeping.

She dared a look at him, but immediately swept her lashes down over cheeks that were suddenly hot. She barely followed the ceremony; her confused mind was grappling with the magnitude of feeling she had glimpsed in that one quick look, and her senses whirled as she fearfully acknowledged that the odd flashes of feeling he occasionally allowed to escape him were the mere tip of an iceberg that, should it ever melt, would create devastation.

He put on a very convincing act for the benefit of his family. His responses were spoken firmly, but with an undertone of reverence that amazed her – in direct contrasted to her own which stumbled out in inaudible gasps – and his compelling eyes were upon her face during the whole of the service. During the reception he was understandably attentive. As they stood together to receive the congratulations and good wishes of their guests his arm encircled her waist and every now and then when a fit of trembling seized her his grasp tightened to communicate understanding and reassurance while at the same time his eyes forced her into sharing glances so intimate that she felt unbelievably cherished. His attitude was unbearably tantalizing. She yearned to be able to relax, to bask in his unaccustomed approval, but the certainty that once the guests had gone and they were again alone together he would revert to treating her as an expensive toy made her determined to remain aloof.

When he was called away to take a telephone message the relief from pressure was tremendous. So much so that when Marc seized the opportunity to speak to her he was dazzled by the welcome he received.

"Marc!" she almost stammered in her eagerness. "I'm so glad you managed to come."

"Did you ever doubt that I would?" he smiled, his eyebrows elevating with teasing enquiry. Then his smile was replaced by grave sincerity. "You look enchanting, Sara, ravishingly beautiful. I should hate Felipe for stealing you away from me, but I must admit in all honesty that you were never really mine." He sighed, then shook himself free of abortive regrets. "We had lunch together yesterday, Felipe and I, did you know?" Surprise robbed her of speech, so he nodded and continued, "Yes, we spent a most rewarding hour in each other's company. I no longer have any doubts about your choice of husband, *chérie*. If I cannot have you then there is no other I would rather see in my place. Be happy, Sara," he whispered quickly as he saw Felipe's advancing figure, "and think of me sometimes . . ."

He melted into the crowd before she could question his amazing change of opinion, and all during the ensuing rush to change into travelling clothes and even while she and Felipe ran the gauntlet of happy guests determined to give a hearty send-off to the honeymoon she was frantically wondering what confidences exchanged between the two men had resulted in dissolving their initial animosity to the extent of leaving them firm friends.

The villa where they were to begin their honeymoon was perched high upon a cliff overlooking a tiny bay. On either side of the bay promontories of rock ensured complete privacy; the beach being accessible only from steps cut out of the sheer cliff face. It belonged to a member of Felipe's family who had put it at their disposal for an indefinite period, insisting that they would be favouring him by making use of its amenities and by providing work for the two Arab boys he employed as servants. Darkness had fallen by the time they arrived, after a silent journey along a coast road which every now and then had offered glimpses of black velvet sea heaving under a scattering of glistening silver moonbeams. Her nervousness was very obvious, and Felipe's straight-cut mouth quirked upwards when, as he pulled up in front of the villa, her startled eyes leapt to his face, then hastily away again.

"Shall I carry you across the threshold, or would you prefer to walk?" he enquired dryly when she made no move to abandon the car. Hastily she scrambled from her seat, almost tripping in her eagerness to escape the underlying threat. Her face burned as his soft laughter reached her through the darkness and she bit her lip to prevent frightened tears from falling. She was too overwrought to admire the quiet opulence of the interior of the villa, and he frowned when she spun round in startled confusion when the Arab servant, whose approach had been silent, enquired whether they were ready to eat. In response to the questioning lift of Felipe's eyebrows she shook her head, then had grave misgivings when she heard him tell the boy that his services would not be required until morning.

She was standing by the window, tense as a bowstring, when he approached from behind to urge her kindly, "You are tired and not a little tense. Why don't you go to your room – a bath will relax you and later, when I've had my swim, I'll bring you up a drink that will help you to sleep."

Fear loosened her tongue. "Swim? In the dark . . .?"

Laughter was a low rumble in his throat. "But yes, do you find that so unusual? I often swim by moonlight."

Her wariness of water dated far back to the days in the orphanage when swimming had been allowed only under strict supervision and certainly in the broad light of day when any unforeseen danger could be spotted and swiftly averted.

"But there might be currents – and the cliff looks so terribly steep . . ." She faltered to a stop, her eyes

186

enormous. Suddenly he was very close, too close for peace of mind. Her body was suffused by fire when against her ear she felt the feathering of his lips as he breathed,

"And if I should break my neck tumbling down the cliff, or suffer any other of the unmentionable fears that are spinning through your mind, would you care, *cara* . . .?"

She spun away from him, too agitated to think clearly, and so humiliated by his amusement her only defence was to lash back with words. "Go for your swim!" she choked as she retreated in confusion. "I could not care less whatever the outcome may be!" But once in her room restless pacing gave lie to her hasty words. She was tormented by fears for his safety, but too proud and too sensitive of his laughter to do as her senses urged and fly out into the night in search of him. She forced herself to undress and take a shower, then with a negligée wrapped loosely around her, she sat staring into a mirror as she brushed her hair, seeing nothing of her fear-whitened face, but concentrating on every little sound coming from outside that might tell her he had returned safely. She heard the Arab boys talking quietly together as they set off towards the nearby village where their families lived, but for a long time afterwards no sound disturbed the still night and as the silence grew her fears were magnified out of all proportion. She glanced down at the great emerald she was agitatedly twisting around her finger and shivered; the green, cold stare could have come from the malevolent eye of Yiblis himself as he debated her punishment. She began to picture Felipe's lithe body lying crushed and broken at the foot of the hungry cliff, and a sob broke from her as she recalled hearing tales of strong swimmers being crippled by cramp, of others whose bodies had been tossed on distant shores after fighting a losing battle with vicious currents.

Rif superstition held her so fast in its grip that she failed to hear a light tap upon her door. When she did not reply Felipe entered quietly, carrying a tray holding a decanter and two glasses. He was wearing a silk dressing-gown, his hair roughly towelled but still glistening with sea-water. He glanced immediately over the curves of her body outlined by transparent white chiffon, but when his eyes lifted to her set features he frowned darkly. Quickly, he disposed of the tray and strode tight-lipped across the width of the room to take her by the shoulders. "*Madre de Dios!*" he hissed. "You have no need to look like that. I swear I have no intention of harming you!"

His demented words shocked her back to life and when she lifted tortured eyes to his face and whispered brokenly: "Oh, Felipe, thank God you are safe!" she betrayed a secret so momentous that a few taut, amazed seconds were necessary before complete understanding dawned. Then: "Sara . . . you really were afraid for me! Oh, my beloved, my own dearest love!" He moved with the speed of light, wasting no more

188

words, but gathering her up into an embrace that speared shivers of delight through her pliant body. Kisses of mingled longing and remorse were stormed upon her quivering mouth, her tear-wet cheeks, and tender, painfully aching throat. When she was allowed to, she whispered, "Felipe, I don't understand, you can't love me, it isn't possible ..." Protests that were silenced with typical Spanish arrogance without deigning even to afford them the importance of a denial. Then gradually, his kisses grew less wild and full of tender sweetness and she began to believe that the pinnacle of hope she had never dared aspire to was not merely a possibility but glorious reality. He caressed her with restrained ardour, whispering broken phrases of love that reached her through the growing heat of ecstasy, treating her with the gentle reverence of a passion deliberately leashed, by great power of will, so that fear should play no part in the final, glorious consummation both physical and spiritual. He understood completely her shy uncertainty; his demands were kind, his insistence tender, and he was rewarded by the breaking down of every last doubt as she surrendered entirely to the love he had demonstrated was as great and as unselfish as her own. The pounding of the sea became a roar that filled the room as she was lifted against his heart and carried towards fulfilment – the destiny ordained by the gods of the Rif who must at that very moment have been smiling ...

She was supremely happy, contentedly relaxed as she

toyed idly with the medallion nestling amongst the tangle of dark hairs that grew across his chest. "How long have you loved me, Felipe?" she questioned with pretended casualness. She heard him growl a laugh, then thrilled to his nearness as his bulk towered over her in the darkness.

"How like a woman!" he mocked. "Not satisfied with having ensnared me completely, you want the time, date and moment of my downfall. Does it matter, *cara*?" he nuzzled her throat. "Isn't the fact that our love exists sufficiently wonderful to fill your heart and mind for many years to come?"

She dimpled in the darkness. "Of course, but women like to be practical . . ."

"Curious, you mean," he contradicted with mock disgust.

But with all the rashness of Eve, she pressed him, confident he would deny her nothing. "Tell me . . ." she pleaded. He went very still. She immediately sensed his withdrawal and was appalled by her lack of sensitivity when she recognized the extent of the hurt she had so wilfully resurrected.

"I have always loved you," he told her with difficulty. "From the very first moment we met I was attracted, but I would not admit it even to myself." His arms reached out as if even now he was afraid she might try to escape, when he admitted, "You know how I misjudged you, my sweet Sara. I was a fool, a cretinous idiot, but even while I fought the emotion you aroused in me I was certain, deep down in my heart, that you were the only woman I could ever love." Her small surprised gasp caused him to tighten his hold, her closeness giving him comfort, as he relived a moment of agony. "It took a horde of galloping horses to drive home just how much you really meant to me," he murmured huskily. "If you had died beneath their hooves that day, my darling, my life would have ended in that same second. From that moment on I tried to heal the breach between us, but our every meeting was at sword's point and no matter how much I tried each attempted victory ended in defeat. I knew you hated me because of my treatment of your grandfather, and because of the drastic measures I had to employ to prevent you from slipping out of my grasp. Finally, I had to resort to intimidation in my bid to keep you near me." She smiled secretly at the hint of puzzlement in his voice when he pondered aloud, "My greatest surprise was when you agreed to my proposal. Overjoyed as I was, I could not understand why you did not immediately throw my offer of marriage back in my face! "

"But you are no longer puzzled, are you, my darling?" she teased, preparing herself for the retaliation she knew would follow. He did not disappoint her, and for a time conversation ceased while he chastised her with kisses. Wrapped in the warmth of his love, she could think of her grandfather without pain, and perhaps he sensed this when he chose that moment to speak of him again.

"I have Marc to thank for releasing me from my self-imposed purgatory. He explained many things that had puzzled me – he also told me about the circumstances surrounding your life with your grandfather." He paused, fighting a return of the hard anger he had felt when Marc had outlined the Colonel's shameless exploitation of his granddaughter's affection. She was not deceived by his silence; some day she might endeavour to make him understand, but at that moment all she could manage were the choked words: "He was a good man, Felipe, and I loved him dearly . . ." She waited, willing his anger to die, fearful that even now some spec re from the past might spoil the wonder of their love. Impulsively, she reached out to draw his head down against her breast and for long minutes he fought a silent battle she was not allowed to share. Finally, his mind at war, he startled her by grating out one last tormented question.

"Did you ever really want to marry Alvaro?"

"You need to ask me that . . . now?" she trembled, her obvious distress dissolving for ever the last shadow of misunderstanding that had plagued them. A great sigh rippled through his taut frame before he swept her close and muttered through mounting passion, "We have talked long enough, *cara!*" Eagerly, she opened her arms to receive him, and as she lifted her slender hand to caress his dark head with a possessiveness he adored the emerald upon her finger glittered, then flared suddenly into glorious, dazzling life.

THE FOLLOWING STATEMENT IS FROM
JOSEPH SCHULL, RCNVR OFFICER, 1941-
45, AND AUTHOR OF *THE FAR DISTANT
SHIPS*, THE OFFICIAL ACCOUNT OF CA-
NADIAN SECOND WORLD WAR NAVAL
OPERATIONS:

"I don't know Jim Lamb, but I wish I did. I think
his book is superb. For me, and I'm sure for anyone who had anything to do with the navy, the
whole thing comes alive again, just as it really
was. In its humor, its understanding, its vivid descriptions, its general warmth and realness, the
book encompasses the whole of those years—and
not only for the men who lived through them.
It's good enough and lively enough to be enjoyed
by anyone, whether or not he's ever seen a ship.
Besides that, as a segment of the country's history,
told in terms of people, it's a gem."

THE CORVETTE NAVY

the way it really was in World War II—
as it should always be remembered.

"*A grand book . . . brings alive the horror and
humor of Canada's war at sea.*"
—OTTAWA CITIZEN

"*Vivid and fresh descriptions of strife and circumstances at sea.*" —BOOKS IN CANADA

"*A fine book, with some truly magnificent moments . . . exciting and enriching!*"
—HALIFAX LOYALIST

THE
CORVETTE
NAVY

~~~~~~

True Stories from Canada's Atlantic War

James B. Lamb

Ⓞ

A SIGNET BOOK
Published by
Macmillan—NAL Publishing Limited
Scarborough, Ontario

PUBLISHED BY
THE NEW AMERICAN LIBRARY
OF CANADA LIMITED

DEDICATION

~~~~~~~~~~~~~~~~~~~~~~~~~

The little ships of the corvette navy have
vanished from the oceans of the world, as
quickly and quietly as they came. They
live today only in a few fading
photographs, and in the memories of
middle-aged men scattered across the
breadth of Canada who once sailed them
through the winter gales of the wartime
North Atlantic.

To these men, and especially to the Naval
Reserve officers from the merchant
service who taught and led them, this
book is respectfully dedicated.

AUTHOR'S NOTE

To the best of my memory, all the
incidents related in this book are true.
The chapter "Slip and Proceed" describes
a typical escort group sailing, rather than
a particular convoy; the convoy number
used is fictitious.

CONTENTS

~~~~~~~~~~~~~~~

The Last Corvette   1

The Two Navies   6

Slip and Proceed   19

The Band of Brothers   43

The Characters   61

Ports of Call   74

The Old Firm   96

The Cruel Sea   111

Them and Us   126

Signal Log   140

The Channel War   148

The Graveyard of the Elephants   162

I Remember, I Remember . . .   175

Glossary   177

1
THE LAST CORVETTE

~~~~~~

As these words are written, a small steel steamship lies deserted in a corner of the dockyard at Halifax, her work done, her future uncertain. Years of toil as a tender to an oceanic research institute have altered her silhouette, replacing guns with winches and adding excrescences of various kinds, but there is no mistaking that raked, circular-sectioned funnel in its cluster of ventilators, that jaunty duck's-bottom stern or that long, flaring fo'c'sle. Her origins have been long forgotten on today's busy waterfront, but this work-worn little drudge is the last survivor of one of history's proudest fleets, the last Canadian example of a Second World War creation as famous and successful as the Spitfire or the jeep.

This ship was once His Majesty's Canadian Ship *Sackville*, and for all her obscurity and neglect she is as significant a survival to the people of Canada as HMS *Victory* is to the British or USS *Constitution* to the United States. For she is a corvette, the largest and most successful class of escort warship ever built, and she and her sisters once made Canada one of the major naval powers of the world. More than that: this little ship, and all the others like her, were the principal weapon which brought victory in the war's longest, bitterest, and most vital battle, and thus assured the survival of the free world.

It is appropriate that this last vessel should have lingered in a Canadian wartime port, for the corvette played a greater part in the growth and character of the Canadian navy than it did in any other naval force, and its influence can be seen in the Canadian naval service to this day. More than any other ship, weapon, or aircraft, the corvette had a distinctively Canadian connotation, her limitations and capabilities reflecting to a remarkable degree those of a new and growing Canadian navy, so that she came almost to reflect the character of the men who sailed in her. For both corvettes and their crews were to blossom like so many Cinderellas; from humble origins, despised by the professional crews of regular naval ships, they were destined to become the belles of the ball, the backbone of the victorious Atlantic escort fleet, and the developers of a tradition and an expertise uniquely their own, which was to be the envy of their regular-navy sisters.

The corvette was born of the Munich crisis of 1938, which convinced the board of the British Admiralty that war with Germany was inevitable and imminent. The Royal Navy began at once to gear itself for war by 1940, and its first requirement was for escorts to protect the huge and vulnerable overseas trade carried in British ships to every corner of the world. Existing types of warships were far too elaborate for quick production; hundreds of escorts were needed which could be built and ready in a year's time. As it had in the First World War, the Admiralty turned to the well-known Middlesbrough shipbuilders, Smith's Dock Company, for a design suitable for emergency production, and again this famous firm came through with an effective solution.

The design it proposed, and the Admiralty accepted, was based on the lines of a recently built whale-catching vessel called *Southern Pride*, but with more powerful engines and consequently greater speed. She was to be of approximately 1200 tons displacement with an overall length of 205 feet, a beam of 33 feet, and a draught of 15 feet. Driven by a single three-bladed propeller, she was to have a maximum speed of 16 knots and a really remarkable endurance of 4000 miles at 12 knots on only 200 tons of oil fuel. Her machinery—four-cylinder triple-expansion reciprocating engines of 2750 horsepower, and twin cylindrical Scotch boilers—was deliberately kept simple, for ease both of manufacture and of operation, and the whole design was intended from the beginning to be capable of production by every sort of engineering firm other than the big shipbuilders, which were now crammed to capacity with large warship orders.

Main armament of the new escorts was to be the depth-charge, discharged both from traps in the stern and by mortars—"throwers"—in the waist, with a surface armament of a single four-inch gun and a two-pounder pom-pom, backed up by machine guns, for anti-aircraft protection. Named "corvette", the French word for "sloop", the new escort with its modest 47-man complement was intended only as a stop-gap until something better could be provided.

But all unrecognized in these plans was a touch of genius; the dowdy maid-of-all-work had been endowed by her Good Fairy with a wholly unexpected range of qualities. For this ship of humble design proved to be capable of amazing versatility, able to carry more than twice her designed complement and a seemingly endless accumulation of ever more sophisticated armament and instrumentation. She could keep the sea in weather that overwhelmed huge merchant vessels and reduced destroyers to water-logged hulks; she could be used for anything from minesweeping to anti-aircraft protection. But, greatest blessing of all, she could turn on a dime, the only Allied warship with a turning circle tighter than that of a submarine, and in consequence she was the master of the U-boat in manoeuvring duels that would foil any other surface escort.

Adaptable and flexible in an ever-changing war, the corvette became the backbone of the Allied escort force, going through endless modifications and improvements in the course of the building of no fewer than 269 ships, the largest warship class ever built.

Ultimately she evolved into a new class; two sets of corvette engines were jammed into a lengthened corvette hull to gain a little more speed, and the resulting super-corvette was called a "frigate". By the war's end, frigates and corvettes made up almost the entire strength of the Allied escort forces in the Atlantic, and their crews of reservists had brought the techniques of convoy escort and submarine detection and destruction to new heights of expertise. But they had also founded a tradition of colourful character and eccentric individualism a world away from the stereotype of the professional serviceman; a tradition cherished to this day in moments of nostalgia by middle-aged men in cities and towns across Canada.

Right from the beginning, there was something suspect about corvettes in the eyes of right-thinking professional navy men; what was one to make of a man-of-war that looked like a fish trawler and called itself HMS *Pansy*? For the Admiralty, in a moment of inspiration, had designated the new ships as the Flower class, a tradition in escort vessels begun in the First World War. Each Royal Navy corvette was named after a flower, and the world was enriched by sea-stained fighting

ships glorying in the name of His Majesty's Ship *Pennywort,*
Crocus, or *Tulip.* There was a *Convolvulus,* a *Saxifrage,* and
a *Cowslip.* But even a Board of Admiralty has a heart; eventually, HMS *Pansy* was allowed a change of name by a repent-
ant Ships' Names Committee. She became HMS *Heartsease.*

By the time the Royal Navy had built more than a
hundred corvettes, flower names were becoming difficult to
come by; HMS *Bulrush* probably reflects the growing desper-
ation of this latter period, while HMS *Burdock* and HMS *Ling*
show just how far the naming committee was prepared to
cast its net. In Canada, HMCS *Poison Ivy* was openly
conceded to be a possibility, but cooler heads prevailed; the
Canadians decided to name their corvettes after towns and
villages, although a handful of flower names—*Spikenard,*
Snowberry, Windflower, etc.—were incorporated with ships
originally built for the Royal Navy but taken over by the
RCN.

It was widely believed in the wartime Allied navies that the
naming of the Flower class was part of a form of psychological warfare practised on the enemy by a vengeful Britain;
there must be an added ignominy, it was felt, to being sunk
by HMS *Poppy,* as U605 was, or to bring outfought and captured by a fierce HMS *Hyacinth,* as was the Italian submarine
Peria. It was one thing to perish in the Wagnerian splendour
hankered after by Hitler, but quite another for the proud
Teuton to be vanquished by *Rhododendron,* as U104 was, or
sunk by *Periwinkle,* like U147.

From the beginning, there was something faintly comic
about corvettes, and it was an element which their own crews
were to cherish and embellish as part of their jealously
preserved attitude of enlightened amateurism in a world of
professional inanity. The name of their ship was, for the
stockbrokers and students, clerks and farmers who manned
Violet and *Gladiolus* and *Marigold,* a snook cocked at the
whole professional establishment, and in particular at the
vainglorious German U-boats with their brass bands and "We
are sailing against England" nonsense. There was nothing
fancy about corvettes, either in their names or in their crews,
and this was just the way corvette men chose to have it.

Although Canadian crews were spared the blushes of those
who manned HMS *Pink* or HMS *Wallflower,* they had a few
names of their own which were considered a little peculiar.
Nobody thought much of HMCS *Asbestos* as a name for a
fighting ship, while HMCS *Norsyd* and HMCS *Stonetown* raised

a few eyebrows in the escort ports. But by and large, corvette types took pride, however perverse, in the name of their ship, and did their best to associate it with the ship's crest, usually painted on the gunshield of the forward four-inch. These designs, though they would have been the despair of the Royal College of Heralds, were nonetheless lively, if not downright lurid; it would be hard to conceive anything more apt than the five aces displayed as the crest of HMCS *Baddeck*, or more vivid than the crowned lady falling on her backside into a puddle on the gunshield of HMCS *Wetaskiwin* (Wet-ass-Queen).

Whether named for flower or village, the corvettes, and later those super-corvettes, the frigates, were churned out in dozens by shipyards and engineering firms in Canada, some of whom had never before built a ship. More than 130 corvettes and half a hundred frigates were built in this country alone, and the British built even more, including ships for the Free French and United States navies. The trickle of new corvettes began in Britain in 1940, and in Canada by the spring of 1941; within a year it had become a flood of fat-funnelled, jaunty little ships. They grew to become a force that ruled the Atlantic; the seas were covered with them, and they clustered thick about the quays and trot-buoys in every naval port in the northern hemisphere.

Today they have disappeared as if they had never been; they survive only in the memories of aging men, and in this single forgotten veteran in a dockyard backwater. This is the story of that vanished fleet of ships, and of the colourful crews who sailed them across a wartime North Atlantic.

2
THE TWO NAVIES

~~~~~~

Canada had two navies in the Second World War. First, of course, was the Royal Canadian Navy, the big navy, the "real" navy, the "pusser" navy. It was, as its corps of public relations officers endlessly reiterated, a very big deal indeed. Thousands upon thousands of uniformed men and women filled teeming offices and training establishments, vast and ever-growing complexes of brick and concrete, representing the investment of hundreds of millions of dollars. Its organization, embracing dozens of commands, hundreds of departments, and thousands of experts and specialists, ranging from physicists to dietitians, from jurists to journalists, was a triumph of administrative genius which represented one of the nation's major wartime accomplishments.

It is fashionable in peacetime to deride the capacity of service bureaucrats, but not even General Motors or any other of the civilian corporate giants has ever managed, in time of peace, anything to compare with the administrative miracle of the wartime RCN, which grew from eighteen hundred officers and men into a vast and complex machine of almost a hundred thousand men and women.

Here was the repository of naval tradition, the showcase of talent and ability, the dynamic centre of thrust and growth and expansion. Vast though it was by mid-war, it yet thrived and grew in every direction as busy men were driven to seek more assistants, more space in which to operate. Here was pay and pace and promotion, here was where it was all at.

Each morning, at parade grounds across the country, on prairie and seacoast, scores of white ensigns ascended proudly into the clear Canadian air; bands played and gunner's mates shouted and thousands of feet marched in unison. Dozens of gym floors and paved parking lots earned the respectful salute traditionally accorded the quarterdeck, the abode of authority. In Ottawa and Halifax, and indeed in every city throughout the land, hundreds of uniformed naval officers dumped their briefcases in hundreds of office cubicles, eased themselves behind their desks, and opened their morning newspapers to begin yet another day.

A vast fleet of vessels of every sort was attached to this great navy; literally hundreds of coastal mortar launches, harbour craft, and training vessels, armed yachts and gate ships, harbour minesweepers and picket boats; all the endless numbers and variety of the "9 to 5" fleet.

But the real strength of the Big Navy lay ashore. Its admirals flew their flags from office buildings, and its officers and men, ratings and Wrens, had their wardrooms and messdecks in shore establishments, land-bound battleships these, bearing old and famous naval names.

It was a tremendous force, embodying some of the best brains in the country and involving a significant proportion of the nation's wealth and manpower. Although manned by reservists in their thousands, it was directed by professional naval officers, and its operations were oriented to a hierarchy which included every senior officer the country possessed, or could borrow from abroad. What it all accomplished would be difficult to define, but of necessity it was preoccupied with recruiting, training, housing, feeding, administering, and caring for itself, a great and endless task.

Canada's second navy was a much different force: a bunch of amateur sailors, recruited from every walk of civilian life, manning ships deemed too small for command by professional naval officers. The ships—Algerines, corvettes, frigates, Bangors—were as cheap as they could be built, and their officers and men were involved, not with admirals and captains, but with characters like Two-Gun Ryan, Harry the Horse, Death Ray, Foghorn Davis, and The Mad Spaniard. It was an amateur, improvised, cut-rate navy, but its purpose and accomplishment were clear: it fought, and won, the Battle of the Atlantic. This was the corvette navy, the little navy, Canada's other navy, manned by amateurs like me.

The division between the two navies was surprisingly complete and clear-cut; few regular career Canadian naval officers ever kept watch aboard a corvette, and only a handful of corvette crewmen were RCN ratings. For shortly after the outbreak of war, a strange process began. The little handful of professional naval officers—all that the country possessed and the only Canadians trained over long peacetime years to fight a war at sea—were bustled ashore into offices. There they presided over clerks and typists in a series of administrative posts for which they had received no training at all. Most of them never went to sea again.

Their places afloat were taken by a handful of former merchant seamen, now officers of the Royal Canadian Reserve, and by young men in the Royal Canadian Naval Volunteer Reserve, many of whom were culled from offices ashore and most of whom had never been to sea before. It was a situation worthy of Gilbert and Sullivan: trained seamen were put in offices ashore and trained office managers were sent to sea. As a result, Canada's professional naval officers were to play an ever-diminishing role in the Battle of the Atlantic.

This curious situation had been brought about by a miscalculation of the role the corvettes could play in the naval war. Originally they had been regarded as a stop-gap, and, as such, unworthy as commands for Canada's few, and precious, trained naval officers. Apart from those allowed afloat in the RCN's handful of pre-war destroyers, permanent-force officers were hoarded ashore against the time when the new superships would appear to fight the glorious Armageddon against Germany's powerful surface fleet. Meanwhile, the little jerry-built corvettes were filled up with reservists and packed off to do what they could in the squalid brawls with U-boats around the herds of merchantmen. While waiting ashore, RCN officers accumulated experience in positions of responsibility, and the promotions that went with them; a few years ashore could do more for a fellow than a lifetime afloat.

But a funny thing happened to the regular navy while it waited for the Big Ships that were to fight the Big Battle. For as the years wore on, it became clear that the little battle, the U-boat thing, was in fact the Big Battle after all, and the little ships that were fighting it were all that were going to matter. The RCN pursued its original "big ship" notions to the very end: after weary years of construction that had earned them the names of *Moses* and *Methuselah*, the two Tribal-class destroyers that had been building in the Halifax shipyards since before living memory were finally commissioned and in the closing years of the war joined their British-built sisters in operations with the British Home Fleet; and as the German war ended, the RCN took over two British cruisers. Canada's Tribals covered themselves with glory, particularly in Channel shoot-ups along the invasion coasts, but for all that, their operations, however exciting were a sideshow. The main event was fought out, month after exhausting month, in the North Atlantic. For the issue was, simply, command of the sea; whoever held it held the initiative, and could fight where, when, and how he chose.

The Germans picked the U-boat as their weapon in the duel for ocean supremacy, and consequently it was the anti-submarine forces of the Allies, not their battle fleets, which were principally involved. Thus, it was the little work-worn corvettes, frigates, and over-age destroyers of the escort groups which contributed most to the Allied victory, rather than their more glamorous and heavily gunned RCN sisters.

From the very beginning, the men of the little navy were left largely on their own. A bewildered RCNR lieutenant, only a month or two away from his second mate's berth in some merchant ship, his two interwoven curly strips of gold lace still bright on each cuff, was dumped off at a shipbuilding yard to take over his new corvette command, with three or four officers as green to the navy as himself and sixty or seventy young men fresh from the prairies or city pavements who had never seen the sea before. If the new captain was lucky, one of his officers might have some practical experience of pilotage or navigation, if not too seasick to care. If his chief engineer had worked in a locomotive roundhouse and knew a little about steam engines, the captain felt himself to be fortunate indeed.

In the ensuing purgatory, the corvette captain learned to depend chiefly on his own resources, with help and advice from his fellow corvette commanders or, if he was lucky enough to have a good one, from his group senior officer, who in the early days of the war was usually a professional naval officer commanding a destroyer, either RN or RCN. Certainly he got no help from the shore establishment, not even from those officers who were supposedly responsible for the administration of his ship; I was myself commissioned into one of the early corvettes, and in all the subsequent years at sea we were never visited by any of the Canadian Captains Destroyers, or "Captains D", as they were called, whose direct responsibility we were, or for that matter, by any officer above the rank of commander.

Ah, yes; there was that one occasion . . .

During the preparations for the invasion of Europe, a

flotilla of Canadian fleet minesweepers lay off Spithead working up for the assault on Normandy, where they were to precede the landing craft carrying the first wave of troops. It was an exciting place at an exciting time; the Channel ports were jammed with shipping and Britain was crammed with troops, all trained and keyed-up to the highest pitch for what everyone knew was to be the turning point of the whole war. There was a sense of occasion abroad; all about us were the preparations for the greatest combined operation ever attempted by man, and here, at first hand, were the great leaders of the free world.

From our vantage-point alongside a dock wall, we had seen our king, George VI, and felt our hearts surge as the slim figure in naval uniform drove past us. From the beginning we had "fought for George"; now here he was, in person, and we stared, with awkward reverence, at the earnest, dedicated man whose faith and purpose had so inspired us in far-off Canada. Churchill came next, with his jaunty wave and jutting cigar, and in the days that followed we saw a succession of the great commanders who were to lead us. There was the hawk-faced Admiral Vian of the Royal Navy, an unsmiling Admiral Kirk of the United States Navy, and then the familiar Monty, in his black beret with all the badges, leaning out of an open car as he toured his cheering troops. From the ships we caught only a glimpse of Eisenhower, but like everyone else we were fiercely proud to be led by Ike, who, more than any other leader, awoke instant affection, loyalty, and respect in the servicemen of every country.

But in all this parade of Allied personalities, Canada felt itself to be missing the boat; her servicemen abroad were being seduced by the glamour of foreign, if Allied, powers. The word went out to London and we received, at last, our first and only visit by a representative of the Real Canadian Navy. Vice-Admiral Percy Nelles, a nice little man who looked a bit like radio comedian Ed Wynn and who had spent the greater part of his wartime career in Ottawa, came down from London to visit us. We followed him dutifully as he trotted about our immaculate decks and inspected our paraded crew, and then saw him piped over the side back to his waiting car. A short, plump little man with very thick glasses, he was not exactly a warrior leader calculated to fire our blood on the eve of this great assault, but he represented a Canadian presence in the big-brass department; Ottawa had countered Washington and London admiral for admiral. In the battle of the big guns, Vice-Admiral Percy Nelles rated as Canada's Answer.

The occasion, however, was unique; in all the long years of war, no other Canadian senior officer ever trod the decks of any ships of the corvette navy that I served in, and even a commander was a rare event indeed.

Corvette crews were young; officers and men were mostly right out of high school, and anyone over thirty found himself nicknamed "Pappy" and the oldest man in the ship. Consequently, corvette people were all junior in rank and rate, most of their upper-deck crews being ordinary seamen, and with leading seamen often carrying out the jobs normally assigned petty officers, and the engine rooms filled with youngsters right out of mechanical training school. Early in the war, a corvette would be commanded by a Naval Reserve (ex-merchant navy) lieutenant, with a Volunteer Reserve lieutenant as executive officer or "Jimmy the One", and two other officers—junior lieutenants or sublieutenants—as watch-keepers. The corvettes were cobbled together, half a dozen at a time, into escort groups, led by an old destroyer usually commanded by a lieutenant or lieutenant-commander of either the RCN or, especially in the early days, the RN.

When you first joined a ship in the corvette navy, you passed from one world into another. You left behind the Big Navy, where you had done your training, the shoreside navy with all its braid and bands and bumf, and you joined an outfit that was run along the lines of a small corner-store. For corvette types were "family"; you soon got to know the characters in your own ship, and in the others of the group. There were chummy ships, whose destinies seemed always to be bound up with yours, and there were rivals, usually commanded by officers senior to your own. Months would go by, grow into years; the shoreside navy became a memory, although there were always officers and men joining ship for a trip or two before going back ashore to the other world where they were busy building careers.

For most of us, the corvettes, the frigates, the Bangors, and the old four-stackers and other obsolete destroyers of the escort fleet became home.

At the end of the war, some of the fellows I'd stood watch with in the early days were still around, most of them in different ships, in different jobs, but still accustomed to spending their days slumped against a bridge dodger, with an elbow hooked around a voice-pipe while the old bucket rolled her guts out beneath them. The corvette navy was more a way of life than anything else.

It was a way of life a world away from anything the Real Canadian Navy had envisaged, and the training accorded us reflected the gap between the two. With dozens of other keen young types, I'd done a course at the Royal Military College's Stone Frigate in Kingston, at that time the only naval officers' training establishment available in the country. We were trained there to take our places in the Grand Fleet that fought at Jutland a generation before; we became proficient, after hours on the parade ground, at drilling in fours, only to find when we emerged that some brass-hat had changed the rules and everyone—had switched over to drilling in threes. We were none of us much good on parade grounds after that, and gunner's mates, those spit-and-polish tyrants, were an especial nightmare. To this day I can recall with real fright the fearful aspect of a veteran gunner's mate whose attention had been drawn to the wavering performance of a platoon led by myself during morning divisions on the parade ground at Esquimalt. Divisions is the morning ceremonial parade that begins the day in big ships or land bases of the Real Navy, full of stamping feet and shouted commands and brass bands, and, when properly done, is pretty stirring stuff, what with all those gaiters and bayonets and bugles. My lot, a raw bunch of new entries fresh from Brandon and Swift Current, lacked the snap and precision of the Brigade of Guards, and after drawing upon ourselves the censure of the gunner presiding on the dais, we were horrified to see the burly form of the most irascible of all the gunner's mates descending upon us, black as a thundercloud.

In a moment he was in our midst; I can see him now as he ducked down so that he was invisible to the official eyes on the dais. He marched along backwards, bent over like some malevolent Quasimodo, and mouthed at us in a sort of hiss that pierced us to our chicken hearts. He was a fearsome sight; his eyes glared at us from beneath beetling brows, his visage was like raw, bloody beef (he was reputed to shave with an axe), and his features were contorted with a rage he seemed able to assume instantly, at will.

"If you effing young bastards don't effing well smarten up, by the holy old Jesus I'll have your effing guts for my effing garters," he said, and made violent pulling motions with his hamlike hands.

No words could convey the infinite menace of that fearful

figure, its red face, pocked and seamed by years of exotic excess with the China squadron, thrust into the pale ranks of my pimply schoolboys. Having imparted his frightful warning, he vanished from our midst like some pantomime demon; doubling smartly to one side, he resumed his position on the perimeter of the parade ground, a rigid, upright figure staring unseeingly to his front, his thumbs behind the seams of his trousers.

God, how we marched, ashen-faced and green of gill, through the remainder of that ghastly rigadoon.

Not the least of the attractions of the escort navy was that parades of any sort played no part in its daily routine. In corvettes, we did not parade; we "fell in" and "fell out", and life was immeasurably eased thereby.

It was the same with just about everything the Big Navy imparted to us. A dear old stick of an Edwardian naval officer, gallantly returned to duty after years of retirement, initiated us into the mysteries of celestial navigation, using a sextant and a laborious system of sines and cosines which took hours to work out, and with which any of Nelson's officers would have been familiar.

We used to be tested in our proficiency by being sent out to establish the position of the RMC jetty with a series of star sights, but such was the toil involved that many of us—I blush to admit it—preferred to work it out backwards. After all, we *knew* where we were; we simply looked up our latitude and longitude and worked backwards through the tables to find what our sextant angles should have been, with a trifling error added to impart verisimilitude; too precise an observation might arouse suspicion.

Our instructor was old and tired; so tired that the circles which he endlessly chalked on the blackboard all ended as untidy ellipses, and he mumbled and muttered rather than spoke, communication being rendered even more difficult by a plummy upper-class accent. Inevitably, he was known to all as "Rumbleguts", and it was widely affirmed that he never spoke, he simply opened his mouth and let his guts rumble.

"From this point—heah—" he would mumble, his chalk screeching dustily, "we draw a line down to—" and a dozen of us, heads bent over desks, would interpolate for him with the unconscious cruelty of youth an audible "thayah". He was a delightful old party, beloved of us all, but when we went to sea we found that the escort navy navigated by the new air-force "intercept" method, an infinitely faster and simpler technique; all Rumbleguts' laborious processes became just a memory among the chalk dust.

Even our warlike exercises, enormously enjoyed at the time, proved to have little practical application in the curious force we were destined to join. Revolver practice had a particular attraction for us; in my mind's eye, I pictured myself, Webley in hand, waving my gallant lads on as we swarmed over the decks of some cringing foeman. Alas for reality; in all my years in the small-ship navy the only non-practice revolver shot I heard was that fired in the dark watches of a refit port by a bored sentry who got to fiddling with the revolver in his belt and put a bullet in his foot, thereafter being reduced to carrying an empty weapon, with the bullets in his pocket.

But gunnery school was the highlight of our training, the very heart and essence of the Big Navy. Everything was done with snap and precision; we moved at the double, and the moment we halted, anywhere, we would number off or dress our line or sort ourselves out according to height. (Tallest on the left, shortest on the right, *size!*) My particular day-dream grew out of the calm precision which prevailed in the big-ship gunnery communication we practised in school, with each gun in a ship's armament reporting its state, in set ritual phrases, to a central control transmitting station, called "T.S.", deep in the armoured bowels of a great battleship.

"Number One gun, T.S.," the rating from Number One gun would call.

"T.S. Number One gun," the transmitting station officer would reply.

"Number One gun cleared away, bore clear." And so each gun would report in, ready for action, as the turrets trained around and the mighty ship prepared to annihilate some distant foe. Then would come the thrilling command: "All guns, with a full charge and armour-piercing shell, load! Load! Load!"

In the clinical calm of the transmitting station of the gunnery school, we would be borne into battle with the chanted orders and responses intoned like some litany, and in our daydreams we saw ourselves at our moment of triumph or glorious sacrifice, serene and unruffled in the eye of the storm.

The reality of corvette gunnery was a fearful blow. The gun on our fo'c'sle, a four-inch, turn-of-the-century antique, was a sad come-down from all the gleaming monsters of gunnery school, but it remained for our first gunnery action to completely dispel my dreams of glory. There'd been a fearful bang in the convoy one dark and windy night, and as we tumbled up to our crowded bridge the captain was sucking his teeth and wondering audibly what the hell the hold-up was with the bloody star shell, for we were by now supposed to be illuminating our sector of water in search of a surfaced U-boat.

Stung into fury, our bearded Number One, who was also gunnery officer, leaned over the canvas dodger and addressed the blackness below, where rattles and bangs and muffled oaths indicated the gun's crew was clearing for action.

"Get cracking with that effing gun," he roared, "or I'll come down there and boot your effing backsides up through your effing teeth!" So much for the ordered calm, the chanted litany, the unruffled precision of the gunnery world in the escort navy.

Yet, for all that, the Big Navy taught us much that was of use: seamanship and signalling, pilotage and boatwork. ("What a shower of useless clots," our hardcase old Petty Officer instructor had moaned as he watched us, oars astraddle, attempting to come alongside. "You come crawling up like an effing great spider!") Most important of all, it taught us pride; a great, overweening pride in the Navy, the best, the oldest, the senior service, and in our association with the Royal Navy, *the* navy, with its glorious traditions of victory going back into the mists of time. It was not taught us in class, but was simply acquired by a sort of osmosis; one picked it up unconsciously from association with instructors steeped in the Old Navy, and of all the lessons learned ashore, it stood us in greatest stead at sea.

There was little enough to be proud of in the early days of the corvette navy. With experience and direction in such short supply, everything in a corvette depended upon the character and competence of the captain. If you were fortunate enough, as I was, to serve in a new ship commanded by an experienced merchant seaman, able to adapt to naval routines, you were one of a lucky minority; most of the new ships in the early months of the war were a shambles, and some were downright disgraceful. There was incompetence of every sort, at every level; some of the ships were barely able to get to sea, and once there, were fortunate to find their way back to port without mishap. Indiscipline was chronic, drunken captains, useless officers, mutinous crews were commonplace; those of us in well-run ships grew to dread the prospect of new Canadian corvettes joining our group and tarnishing our Canadian image in the eyes of thunderstruck friends in British ships or bases. It was often all too easy to pick out the Canadian from a group of corvettes alongside; she was the dirty one with rusty sides, and with half her crew in tattered clothes of every sort, playing catch on the jetty.

But with the passage of time and growing experience, we Canadians came of age. The drunks, the cowards, the incompetents wheedled berths ashore; abler officers took command and abler men qualified as leading seamen and petty officers. Discipline, and with it the contentment of crews and the efficiency of ships, improved tremendously, and once they had acquired the confidence born of experience, the superior education and intelligence of Canadian crews began to make itself felt. In the closing years of the war, Canadian frigates and corvettes were conceded to be the best there were, and the maple leaf on the funnel, the unofficial emblem first adopted by Canadian ships abroad, indicated the new pride in their nationality.

It was in these years that a new relationship developed between Canada's two navies. As the new techniques of antisubmarine warfare evolved, it was the reservists afloat in the corvettes who achieved expertise in mastering their challenge; people like Nelson Earl, Canada's top seagoing anti-sub officer. By the war's end, the best and most highly qualified specialists were reservists to a man. The endless versions of asdic (sonar) sets, the development of creeping attacks, of hedgehog and limbo ahead-throwing weapons, of high-frequency direction-finding, of vhf communication, of radar and acoustic torpedoes and sono-buoys; all these familiar features of the escort navy were a closed book to old-line officers of the Big Navy ashore, save for a handful at sea in destroyers.

But not only ships and weapons had changed since the Big Navy came ashore; crews had changed too, both in character and in competence. The new discipline of the escort groups was based on a team concept, rather than on rank structure; as in a bomber aircraft, officers and men worked in close association in positions that were often interchangeable. In such a context, the old parade-ground discipline was out of place; officers did not bellow orders to acquiescent automatons. In a sub hunt, the directing officer sought information from this rating, passed an instruction to that one, listened to a caution or suggestion from another. All were engaged in a common effort to resolve an urgent problem. It was commonplace to hear the officer directing a hunt steady his team of operators and plotters much as a coach might steady his team: "All right, fellows, let's steady down and take this baby!"

Nobody saluted anyone in a corvette at sea, yet there was unquestioned obedience throughout any well-run ship. It was a discipline based on respect, and a hierarchy based on responsibility rather than on social order.

The old discipline of the Big Navy, inherited from the Royal Navy, was based on an officer class whose education, character, and social background were worlds removed from those of the seamen. On the lower deck, thought was not encouraged; a man did as little as he could get away with, and the whole disciplinary system was geared to produce an acceptable standard of performance from an indifferent crew. It was a system measured in outward show, with lots of stamping and shouting and saluting.

But a new discipline evolved in the North Atlantic escort ships. It stemmed from the fact that, in many cases, officers and men came from the same level of society; often they lived across from one another in the same street, had attended the same schools. There was still the old need for obedience and deference to responsibility, but it could no longer be based on the class structure of the old-fashioned navy, or on the system of enforcement through marine guards and regulating officers and the noncommissioned hierarchy of big-ship routine. The new escort-ship discipline was effective, if not showy. Officers were still segregated from men, an essential to any discipline, but they ate the same food, prepared in the same galley, in the wardroom as on the messdecks.

When the Big Navy attempted to enforce the old discipline in the old way as it returned to sea in the big cruisers and carriers at last available at the war's end, it ran into trouble. A dashing pre-war destroyer officer found himself unable to command a Tribal-class destroyer when he returned to sea late in the war, and was taken ashore with his crew in a state of mutiny. Trouble persisted after the war, but this time it was the professionals who found themselves learning from the amateurs. For in the end it was the team-style discipline, developed in the escort navy, which prevailed in both Britain's Royal Navy and the Royal Canadian Navy, and this acceptance was an indication of the curious reversal of roles between amateur and professional which had taken place during the war years. For the Battle of the Atlantic turned its amateur reservists into the true professionals of antisubmarine warfare, and reduced the shore-bound officers of the Big Navy to beginners who had to re-learn their trade before they were fit to go back to sea. In the North Atlantic, the little-ship navy had become Number One.

3
SLIP AND PROCEED

~~~~~~~~~~~~~~~~~~~~~~~~~~~~~~~~~~~~~~~

"Four-thirty, sir!"

We are snatched from the warm world of sleep by the rough hand on our shoulder and start up, blinded by the light, to find the quartermaster, cowled and hooded like a medieval monk in his fleece-lined watch-coat, bending over us. For some reason which we never understand, Operations ashore always sail escorts at some ghastly hour, never quite night or quite day; it is part of the traditional horror of sailing day. Always it is the same: the stuffy cabin, the dazzling light on the white paintwork, the oppressive, all-pervading sense of foreboding, the certain knowledge of misery to come.

Pull on the old sea-going uniform; hump yourself into the heavy winter sheepskin, stiff with salt, and the zip-fastened flying-boots, while overhead the thumps and muffled bumpings tell that the deck party is going about its work of "singling up". The heavy ropes, stiff with frost and black with use, are being lifted off the wharfside bollards in readiness for departure, leaving us secured by only a single set of warps to the shore: head and stern lines, breasts and springs. The after winch gives a few appropriately hollow groans before reluctantly settling down to its task of reeling in the frozen weight of the stern lines; you can hear the voice of the leading hand as he directs their stowage under the pom-pom bandstand. Bells clang deep in the bowels of the ship; they are testing the engine-room telegraphs and bridge communications as His Majesty's Canadian Ship *Trail* prepares for sea.

Out on deck it is black as Toby's arse, as a cowled figure remarks as we make our way forward; that is Bill Harvey,

19

the sublieutenant in charge of the quarterdeck party. There is a light dusting of snow on the steel deck, making it dangerously slippery, and as we climb the steel ladders up to the bridge we become aware of the biting wind whistling in from the east. God, it'll be nasty outside with this gale still blowing! The sudden serenity of the asdic cabin is welcome; Clarke, the HSD and the senior asdic rating aboard, is checking out his set, and the chart table behind its black-out curtains is a warm pool of light. It's all there, just as it was laid out yesterday: the chart, with its pencilled course from St. John's to the rendezvous point where we're to meet our convoy well out in the Atlantic, south of Cape Race; the notebook, with its estimated courses and speeds and times of arrival, in accordance with the secret signal received from Operations the day before, its traditional preamble going back to the days of Pepys's navy: "Being in all respects ready for sea, slip and proceed at 0500. . . ."

"Hands to stations for leaving harbour!" That's the bosun's mate making the pipe through the crowded messdecks, and already the fo'c'sle is alive with hooded figures. There's the captain coming up onto the bridge, and we make way for him as he peers over the dodger into the icy blackness. The tug has hauled off the two sleeping corvettes that have been berthed outside us; at the corvette berths, ships are crowded three and four deep alongside and at the trot-buoys in the centre of the harbour. Figures take their accustomed places; the yeoman of signals takes charge of his signalmen, and from the bridge-wing voice-pipe a steady voice announced from the wheelhouse: "Coxswain at the wheel, sir!"

The engines are rung to standby; at a word from the captain, all the lines aft are cast loose and hauled in, the headline is taken in, and men stand by with fenders along the break of the fo'c'sle as the captain orders slow ahead. We are steaming against the spring line, which alone attaches us to the shore; the torque of the propeller turning over slowly walks the stern out from the wharf. When it is well clear, the captain stops engines, then orders slow astern, with the helm amidships. Responsive as a motorboat, the ship begins to gather sternway; the wharf slips by with gathering speed as the siren blasts three times to warn any traffic that we are proceeding in reverse. The helm is put over and the stern moves obediently to starboard until we lie in midstream, our bows pointing toward the wharf, where the tug is already returning the two outer corvettes to the berth we have just va-

cated. The engines are stopped, and we lie silently, still
turning, our sidelights gleaming red and green in the oily
water beneath. Then "Half ahead", and the ship swings rapidly as the rudder bites under the impetus of our new mo-
mentum, and we steady with our head pointing directly at the
distant harbour entrance. Now the wind is strong and cold,
blowing directly into our faces. Below us the fo'c'sle party is
already stowing lines and fenders, securing for sea; in daylight, they would have been fallen into line, facing to port,
like the seamen on the quarterdeck, ready to honour the Admiral's flag when the bosun's pipe shrilled the "Still".

Ahead of us, a confusion of dim lights shows where our
sisters of the escort group are leaving their berths; we stop
and wait while they sort themselves out. That will be HMS
Montgomery, the old four-funnelled former American
destroyer, built late in the First World War and handed over
to the Royal Navy in the destroyers-for-bases deal. Her captain, a professional RN lieutenant-commander, is our senior
officer, and he leads the parade as he takes us out to sea: five
Canadian corvettes and a Juicer four-stacker, a typical mid-
ocean escort group in this winter of 1941-42.

All about us is the sleeping city of St. John's; the barren
hills of the South Side rise unseen to starboard; the snow-
dusted streets gleaming fitfully in the lights of a passing car
are all we can make out of the city itself, climbing its hills all
along our port side. There is enough light to pick out the
rocks of the narrow entrance: the dim, flashing light of Chain
Rock to port and the concrete bulges of the entrance battery
burrowed into the rock to starboard. As we reach the entrance, a red signal-light blinks blearily from the ship ahead:
"Order One, speed 12 knots." We find our place in the line-
ahead formation, crank up the engine revolutions for 12
knots, and we are off and running.

In Newfyjohn, as the sailors call St. John's, you are either
in the harbour or out of it; there is no long estuary leading to
the sea. The transition is brief and dramatic; one moment
you are trundling along in the comparative serenity of harbour, and the next you are in the open ocean, amid all the
fury of the North Atlantic winter. As we leave the narrow
entrance, we stick our bows into a great black sea, and we
climb upwards, only to come crashing dizzily down in a
welter of breaking water. We ship the end of a sea over the
bows just as the fo'c'sle party is putting the finishing touches
on the securing of the upper-deck gear, and they scuttle for

safety in their sodden sheepskins, in a flurry of boots and bad language. The sea is getting up under the impetus of that shrieking wind; for the next few hours we shall be punching into the teeth of the freshening gale, and already a lot of us are having sudden doubts about our stomachs. There are retching sounds from behind us on the bridge, where one of the new signalmen is bringing up his innards as he greets his first Atlantic gale; in anticipation, the yeoman has thoughtfully provided a bucket lashed to a stanchion, and I can feel my own stomach heave in sympathy.

I mentally review what I had for dinner last night. We'd had a couple of rums in the Crowsnest, that marvellously contrived club for seagoing officers on the draughty upper floor of a Water St. warehouse, before going on to the Newfoundland Hotel for the traditional last-night bang-up dinner. We'd dined in sombre state in the great, glacial dining-room, topping off a fine dinner with Drambuie, sipping that amber ambrosia in order, we assured ourselves, to settle the stomach. Two of our five at dinner had Scots blood in them, and they assured us that Scots never drank for pleasure; it would be contrary to their dour Presbyterian upbringing. But it was only prudent, mind, to take a wee drop to whet the appetite or settle the stomach, to aid digestion or steady the hand, so to speak. We had, accordingly, taken prudent precautions, but as the ship crashed and plunged into the rising head sea and the signalman behind retched and gasped, I wondered if we had been prudent enough.

Once clear of the harbour, the watch closed up to begin the seagoing routine which would last until we berthed on the other side of the Atlantic; one-third of the ship's company manning the engines, boilers, wheel, asdic, wireless, and lookout positions, the other two-thirds below trying to catch what sleep they could before their own four-hour stint began. It is my watch until eight, but the captain lingers anxiously, worried about the rising wind and sea.

A green one crashes aboard; peering over the dodger we can see its dark shape engulf our foredeck, and we crouch for shelter as the ship plunges thunderously into it. A wall of water, tons of it, sweeps across our fo'c'sle to hurl itself against our bridge structure with a resounding thump. Water sweeps overhead; even in the shelter of the dodger we are drenched, and from below comes a series of bangs and crashes, from messdecks and galley and upper deck, where a hundred items, big and small, have bumped and smashed and clanged and rattled under the impact of the heavy sea. A great murmur of protest, of oaths and groans and bitching, rises from the ventilators and voice-pipes, and from the wheelhouse we hear the bosun's mate, loud and clear: "This effing bucket! Roll on, our refit!"

The captain grins, catches my eye: "Hearts of oak!" he grunts.

But it is clear that we cannot go on bashing into it at this speed. Up ahead *Montgomery* must be semi-submerged, those old fourpipers being notoriously the world's worst sea-boats. Sure enough, back comes the signal: reduce speed to 10 knots. It is going to be a long run, just to meet our convoy, and it has all the earmarks of another sticky crossing.

For us, our watch eventually comes to an end, as they always do; we hand over to Bill Harvey, his face still puffy from sleep, and give him our course and speed and show him our position on the chart. A last look round before going below. A grey, lumpy sea, flecked with white, fills our universe, under grey, scudding clouds. There is no land to be seen, anywhere, only our little handful of ships in all this mad world of wind and sea and driven water. We are steaming in line abreast now, at intervals of a mile. There is *Arvida* to starboard, and to port are *Chilliwack* and *Dauphin* and *Kamsack*, with *Montgomery* just visible, now and again, far on the horizon beyond. But although the sea is worse than ever, the wind seems to be dropping, not quite so fierce as it seemed at the beginning of our watch. But then, the wind never *does* seem so bad at the end of your watch as it does at the beginning.

Breakfast in the wardroom below is a cheerless affair; the deadlights dogged down over the ports and the carpet stowed away, as it will be until we make port again, reduce the cheerful clubroom of our dockside days to a sort of clinical tank. The big armchairs are lashed to stanchions to keep them from crashing about, and we eat our greasy egg and tomato, our burnt toast and marmalade sitting bolt upright on the hard leather settee which runs along one side of the table. Number One is just finishing his breakfast as we arrive for ours, and is off to go rounds of the messdecks with the coxswain.

Better him than me! The messdecks of a corvette in bad weather are indescribable; it would be difficult to imagine such concentrated misery anywhere else. Into two triangular compartments, about 33 feet by 22 feet at their greatest dimensions, are crammed some sixty-odd men; each has for his living space—eating, sleeping, relaxing—a seat on the cushioned bench which runs around the outside perimeter of each messdeck. There is a locker beneath the seat for his clothing, and a metal ditty-box—something like an old-fashioned hat-box—holds his personal things in a rack above. The space where he slings his hammock—carefully selected by the older hands and jealously guarded—is 18 inches beneath the deck-head, or another hammock, which are slung in tiers between stanchions and beneath pipes, wherever there is room. Most of the deck space is taken up with scrubbed deal tables, one to each mess, where you eat or write or play interminable games of cards.

Crowded in harbour and stuffy, the messdecks at sea are like some vision of Hades. There is absolutely no fresh air; all the ports, open in harbour, are dogged down and blanked over at sea, and in heavy weather even the cowl ventilators from the upper deck have to be sealed off. Dim emergency lights, red or blue, provide the only illumination in the dark hours, and around the clock there is always at least one watch trying to catch a few hours of oblivion, while about them the life of the mess goes on: men coming and going from outside, or snatching a meal before going on watch. With the hammocks slung, there is hardly room anywhere to stand upright, and there is moisture everywhere—water swirling in over the coamings when the outside doors open, sweating from the chilled steel of the ship's side, oozing from the countless pipe joints and deck-welds and rivets and deck openings, and all the other manifold places where water forces an entrance from the gale outside. Plunging into a head sea, the noise and motion in the fo'c'sle must be experienced to be believed; a constant roar of turbulance, wind, and water, punctuated by a crashing thud as the bow bites into another great sea, while the whole little world is uplifted— up, up, up—only to come crashing down as the ship plunges her bows over and downward, to land with an impact which hurls anyone and anything not firmly secured down to the forward bulkhead. With a rolling, corkscrew motion, the nightmare world of the fo'c'sle starts to climb again, up, up, up. . . . In their navel pipes, the twin anchor cables rattle and clank at each movement, a dominant note in the endless, maddening din.

In such a place, under such conditions, corvette crews endure for days, weeks, years, a degree of discomfort and hard-

ship which they could not have sustained for an hour in
civilian life; wet, cold, bruised, sleeping in their clothes, with
never a moment's privacy or quiet. When they are keeping
watch, getting up at all hours to brave the elements, night
blurs into day in a misery too great for words. In everyone's
mind is the surcease to come when we make port, when the
motion and misery stop, and everyone can sleep, sleep, without interruption. No one thinks beyond that; to endure this
crossing is our chief aim, and the ship is impelled onward by
the mind and heart of every soul aboard.

But there are degrees of misery, as with anything else;
when eventually the long bash to windward is done and we
reach the point of rendezvous, we turn to comb the track
along which the convoy will come. We are taking the seas on
the quarter now, and while the ship rolls heavily, right over
on her ear, there is no more pitching, and the surcease is like
a kind of heaven. The wind is easing and everyone is more
cheerful. Life settles into its accustomed seagoing routine; the
seasick are either better now or beyond hope. In every escort,
there are always one or two individuals, the chronically seasick, whose endurance becomes a matter of proud boasting by
their shipmates, and who live at sea in a sort of half-world,
between life and death, sustained only by a handful of crack-
ers or soup for all the days and weeks of a voyage. Seasickness—real seasickness—is endured by these few with a
resolute bravery that sometimes awes their heedless and
healthy shipmates.

We have arrived at our rendezvous on time, but the convoy is a little late, delayed by weather. We are now at Wes-
tomp—Western Ocean Meeting Point—where the convoys
change escorts, much as trains change crews ashore at divi-
sional points. Our eastbound convoy here will shed the Local
Escort Group which has brought it from New York, Boston,
and Halifax to this point, to be replaced by us, the Mid-
Ocean Escort, who will stay with it until relieved by the
United Kingdom escort somewhere south of Iceland and west
of Ireland.

And suddenly, there they are. First the cluttered mast of a
destroyer pierces the horizon right ahead, then her whole
bridge heaves into view; her signal lamp flashes a greeting,
to which *Montgomery* responds. Now, right across the horizon, masts and funnels appear, rapidly climbing over the
heaving seascape to reveal themselves as merchant ships; out
on each flank is the tiny silhouette of an escort.

A convoy at sea is an awe-inspiring sight, even to us, who spend most of our days at sea hanging about the flanks of them, and as we draw rapidly up to this one, even off-duty crewmen climb out on our deck to have a close-hand look at HX 142, as it has been officially designated—forty-two ships, bound from Halifax to the United Kingdom with food, weapons, machinery, oil, petroleum, and all the manifold munitions of war.

A convoy is a live thing, a collective entity greater than the sum of its parts. There is an unmistakable sense of purpose about this enormous collection of ships as it forges relentlessly to the eastward, its vast bulk covering the sea from horizon to horizon. Its ships are in nine ordered ranks, its flanks five ships deep, and as we draw closer to its starboard wing we can make out the individual ships, the characters of the convoy, so to speak, whose eccentricities of appearance and behaviour are to become a part of our lives in the long days and nights ahead.

It is always a thrill to see a convoy at sea in the brief role of spectator before one's horizon becomes limited by responsibility for some single sector, and as we pass down the side of the great armada we are again moved by its sense of might and purpose, and by an appreciation of the enormous human energy and miracles of organization which have assembled this force of great ships, flying the flags of virtually every maritime nation, bound from ports all over the world to an embattled island, now besieged and surrounded. Here is one of the concentrations of power that are shaping our destiny; here in these ships are the essentials which can sustain a whole nation: food for millions of people, and fuel and arms for their defence. Millions upon millions of dollars are represented by these ships and their cargoes, the accumulated man-hours of countless men and women toiling in farms and factories in a score of countries, in hundreds of towns and cities.

This convoy, manned and escorted by more than a thousand seamen, assembled and equipped and directed by staffs who even now are plotting its position in operations rooms on both sides of the Atlantic, represents a significant portion of the wealth of the free world, the end result of millions of dedicated man-hours and a triumph of human organizing genius. More to the point, it represents a very important factor in the war between freedom and tyranny, and as we watch it surge past us we are reminded yet again of our own responsibility for its safe arrival.

The sense of power invests this collection of rusting ships with an almost elemental quality; one can sense that it will steam on, regardless of loss, regardless of weather or attack, like some great leviathan scorning the assaults of lesser creatures of the deep.

At the head of the centre column is the commodore's ship, a fine "Blue Funnel" cargo liner, one of Alfred Holt's great ships, her halyards a mass of bunting as she signals a pending course change to her charges. Behind her, sheltered by the columns on either side, are the three precious tankers carrying the fuel oil and petroleum that is perhaps the most valuable of all the varied cargoes being carried here to a besieged Britain. They are so deeply laden that they seem at times to be largely submerged, like some half-tide rocks, but as they forge into the great rollers they occasionally rise ponderously, like monstrous sea-beasts from the depths, streaming tons of water from their rusting decks.

Some of the leading ships in the columns have Spitfire and Hurricane fighters mounted on long catapult structures on their bows; these are to give us some measure of air protection as we cross "The Pit"; that enormous sector of mid-Atlantic which lies beyond the zones of air-cover extending east from Newfoundland, south from Iceland, and west from the British Isles. Strictly a one-way trip for their pilots, of course; once their job is done, the enemy aircraft shot down or driven off, they must either crash-land in the sea close to an escort and hope to be rescued from their sinking plane, or simply abandon their aircraft at a safe altitude and bail out by parachute, hoping to be plucked from the sea by an escort. Normally, escort commanders try to conserve them until sea conditions give the pilot a fighting chance of ditching or bailing out safely.

The escort carriers, converted merchantmen able to fly on and off a handful of aircraft and thus provide air cover to the convoy all the way across, are still a year in the future in this winter of '41-'42.

The ships themselves represent the whole spectrum of maritime trade. Although we do not have the older, smaller ships that sail in the slow "sc" convoys, there are ships here of every class and vintage, from trim Blue Star and Ellerman liners, still with their peacetime promenade decks amidships, to the ugly ore-carriers and the new utilitarian "Empire" and

"Fort" wartime-built ships. Mostly they are painted grey and streaked by rust and salt, but here and there are trim Scandinavians, bright in peacetime livery, with huge flags painted on their sides. Some of these neutrals still sail independently, trusting to their lights and flags to earn them safety from U-boat attack, but so many have been lost that now they tend to sail in convoy through the dangerous North Atlantic along with Allied ships.

Here and there, one can see an exotic newcomer to the grey Atlantic: a Ben liner from the Far East, a Fyffe banana boat, a Royal Mail ship from the blue Pacific, the little English Channel packet steamer sailing as rescue ship to the convoy.

We notice something missing: there's no battleship escort to give big-gun protection against a surface raider. We've grown accustomed to having one of the old "R"-class battleships, usually HMS *Revenge*, along for the ride across, but this time we've got an armed merchant cruiser, a former liner armed with six-inch guns, to add a bit of punch to the escort. Somebody makes out her name; it's *Worcestershire*, the fine old Biddy liner, and the name brings a grin all around on the bridge. For *Worcestershire* is famous for an incident involving her doctor's hideous revenge on a group of Canadian army officers who had taken passage aboard.

The doctor, who, as is traditional in HM ships, was secretary of the wardroom mess, had cautioned the Canadian army types against what he considered excessive drinking, and muttered darkly about damage to the kidneys and other possible effects. The Canadians, enjoying a respite from their usual responsibilities, were in no mood to heed these mutterings from the doctor, and when they discovered that he was a teetotaller and at the same time in charge of wardroom wines and spirits, their merriment knew no bounds. Goaded by their incessant teasing, the doctor determined to wreck a horrible revenge. With the considerable resources of the ship's big peacetime passenger dispensary at hand, he began to introduce into the Canadians' drink and food a chemical compound which turned their urine a bright orange.

This had no noticeable effect on the Canadians, other than a marked aversion to oranges and citrus fruits, so the doctor played his second card. He switched to a compound which changed his victims' water to a vivid green, and after a few days, to a rather attractive electric blue. He was now producing real results; green slowed the Canadian drinking to a trickle, and blue brought it to an absolute standstill; the Canadians sat about the wardroom morose and silent, each man alone with his thoughts, and waving away any proffered drinks which the doctor, now assiduous, pressed upon them. Pale and wan and worried, they were a pitiful sight.

But by now the doctor's blood was up; not content with the sad state to which he had reduced his hapless victims, he determined on one final brutal stroke to complete his revenge. Overnight he changed their urine to a deep black.

It was the last straw. With half-remembered tales of blackwater fever crowding to their fevered minds, and pale from lack of sleep, the Canadian officers one by one called in at the ship's hospital in the morning "to have a word with the doctor".

The doctor claimed that he then made it clear to his victims that it had all been a harmless prank, but the Canadians had versions of how they had extorted details of the plot from him under duress, and with promises to have him disgraced by his fellow practitioners for violation of his Hippocratic oath. However that may be, the doctor's ingenious plot has established him as a character, and has made his ship a famous and welcome addition to any North Atlantic escort force. We are pleased to have *Worcestershire* sailing with us.

Our escort group breaks up on a signal from *Montgomery*, and each of us heads for an allotted place in the screen. We work our way gingerly across the front of the oncoming herd to take our station out on the starboard flank. *Montgomery* has positioned herself, *Arvida*, and *Chilliwack* across the front of the convoy, with *Dauphin* opposite us on the port side and *Kamsack* as Tail-End Charlie covering the rear. We are stationed so as to be able, in theory at least, to cover our sector with our asdic beams overlapping, zigzagging but maintaining station on the eight-knot convoy.

We are rapidly closing *Fort William*, a steam Bangor designed as a fast fleet minesweeper but converted into an ocean escort; she is making heavy weather of the big sea still running, shipping a good deal of water over her short fo'c'sle and low quarterdeck. Her skipper is an old friend of our own captain, and as we take over from her and begin our outward leg, our captain signals: "THERE IS A VERY YOUNG, VERY PREGNANT GIRL ON THE JETTY ASKING AFTER YOU."

Back comes the prompt response: "SHE'LL JUST HAVE TO WAIT HER TURN LIKE ALL THE OTHERS."

It raises a smile as the Local Escort hauls away for the

fleshpots of St. John's, and we settle into the familiar routine of convoy escort. Quickly our little world takes on its distinctive shape: the diminutive silhouette of *Chiliwack* far ahead, and the five ships of the wing column stretching down our port side. We come to know each detail of those five ships: their silhouettes, their peculiar groupings of funnels, masts, and derrick booms, their varying colours, and even their distinctive rust streaks and patches. There is one in particular, the third in line, which is of special significance; a modern motorship, she is fitted with goalpost masts to handle her cargo, and it is the distinctive silhouette of these great rectangular projections and the thick, squat funnel which makes our job of night station-keeping easier. *Montgomery* has the only radar yet fitted in the group; the rest of us keep station visually, zigging outward until the convoy becomes invisible behind us, then altering course in until, at the limits of our inward leg, the convoy becomes visible to us again. On a black, rainy night or in a shrieking blizzard, a glimpse of those ungodly goalpost masts helps to put things in proper perspective, and a quick bearing tells us whether we're in proper station.

Another help to station-keeping, but a nuisance in every other way, is the inevitable Smoky Joe, the last ship in our line. An old coal-burner, and only just able to keep up with her newer, faster sisters, she frequently commits the cardinal convoy sins of straggling and making smoke, often at the same time. She is a case-hardened tramp of First World War vintage, her overworked stokers attempting to keep her antiquated engines running at close to her maximum speed on inferior coal, and she quickly establishes herself as our particular problem child. Once she falls behind, it is all she can do to catch up, emitting clouds of black smoke which can be spotted by a questing U-boat far over the horizon, thus risking the survival of every ship in convoy. Yet if she falls back beyond the escort coverage, she is herself a sitting duck to be snapped up by the first U-boat which sights her.

Time after time, in those first days, we close her with our loud hailer going and signal flags flying from our yardarm—cautioning, cajoling, pleading, threatening. To all our exhortations, we receive the same response: a wave of acknowledgement from her skipper at the open door of her wheelhouse. We want him to do the best he can, but of course we know what he is trying to cope with, and for all our lecturing we feel a deep sympathy for his predicament,

But he is Trouble, the weak link which could mean disaster for us all, and we curse the officer ashore who included him in our lot instead of grouping him with the slower ships where he belongs.

Slowly, painfully, HX 142 inches eastward; the noon positions crawl across the chart of the western ocean in half a hundred chart rooms. Each day at noon Howard Wallace, our diminutive red-bearded navigator, emerges, sextant in hand, in the hope that the constant cloud cover will thin enough for him to get a noon altitude and thus establish our latitude, to complement the occasional star shot he may sneak in a clear patch in the night watches. On a rolling, pitching corvette bridge, with a horizon lumpy with heavy seas, it takes both luck and skill to produce satisfactory results, and for days on end bad weather reduces us to estimating our position simply on course steered and distance run. Each midday the convoy commodore, operating from the stablest platform and with the best facilities, indicates by a flag-hoist his observed or estimated position, which automatically becomes the official one of the convoy, but every self-respecting escort and merchantman commander likes to arrive at his own independent calculation, which allows him then to sneer at the figures arrived at by the commodore.

In good weather the commodore may exercise his ships in convoy evolutions, carrying out turns by signal, or exercising gun crews in firing close-range weapons.

A convoy is like a small city at sea, full of minor or major crises: a man is injured or falls sick, and the destroyer's doctor may have to be transferred to a merchantman—not fun in bad weather; one ship has engine trouble, another has a bad leak, or problems with cargo shifting. There is a constant flow of information back and forth between commodore and convoy, convoy and escort. Daily our senior officer checks out the fuel remaining to each escort; under the best of conditions some of them, particularly destroyers, can only just make the other side of a mid-ocean crossing with a slim margin of fuel remaining, so that bad weather or prolonged high-speed steaming means refuelling at sea, always a bit dicey in bad weather. But the overriding concerns, overshadowing all else, are weather and U-boats, and threatening situations in connection with either call for consultation between commodore and escort.

Each evening our wireless office gives us the latest Admiralty appreciation of the U-boat situation. Daily, with Teutonic punctuality, each U-boat at sea tries to signal Doenitz's headquarters its position and situation, so that the master in his Berlin bunker may guide them to a chosen target. These U-boat transmissions are monitored by shore stations in Britain, their messages decoded by the secret "Ultra" decyphering machine, and the position of each U-boat is plotted and broadcast to Allied escorts. Each evening, as we crawl steadily eastward, we plot the positions of known U-boats on our chart, and it becomes ever more apparent that we are in for a brush with them; half a dozen are scattered right across our path, and although we are routed ever more to the north, up toward the Arctic Circle itself, no amount of course alteration seems able to take us clear. Bad weather, which makes it impossible for U-boats to operate on the surface, may yet see us through. And bad weather there is in plenty.

Gale after gale shrieks down upon us, howling out of the north as we approach Cape Farewell, southernmost tip of Greenland. Fierce winds tear at our rigging, snatch the tops off waves and send them flying above our mastheads, stinging our faces and blinding our eyes. Mountainous seas crash inboard, making our upper decks impassable, sweeping over our forward gun and crashing against our superstructure with an impact that jars us to the keel. Life below is a hell of wet clothes and fitful sleep, of sandwich meals and constant violent, bruising motion. Even the plumbing is impossible; to use the toilet is to risk a cold douche as the head seas overpower valves and piping.

On a wild night watch, I see the lighter rim of the sky blotted out and realize, in a moment of mind-numbing panic, that the wall of blackness that towers ahead of us is an enormous, an unbelievable, sea, the "67th wave" dreaded by every sailor. I duck beneath the dodger as the bows rise, and commend my soul to God. There is a thunderous roar, and the whole world is blotted out in water, filled with a myriad crashes and crackings. Miraculously, the wave passes, and I emerge, soaked and scared yet unscathed. But in the sudden silence I can sense something wrong: the ship is falling off into the trough and I can get no answer from the wheelhouse voice-pipe. Mad with fright—if the ship falls broadside to the waves in this mountainous sea we shall surely be rolled right over—I dash down the ladder and burst into the wheelhouse, and into a scene of utter chaos. The rogue sea had burst in the shutters and windows of the wheelhouse, flooding and gutting it and knocking helmsman and telegraph rating against the after bulkhead. They are still there, paralysed with fright and shock, but at the wheel is the captain, brought from his tiny sea-cabin off the wheelhouse, now spinning the wheel hard over to get the ship back head to sea. I ring the engines to emergency full ahead, and we wait, frozen in an agonized tableau, our eyes riveted on the pool of light that is the steering compass. The ship rolls heavily, deeply, right over on her side; if she gets another sea in this position we are all gone for sure. But the engine beat quickens; we can hear the stokehold bell below as the engine room opens all the taps, and at last we can see the compass card begin to move. The crisis is past; it is just a matter of shoring up our shattered wheelhouse covers and we are back in business.

The wild weather may be keeping the U-boats down, but it is also taking its toll of the convoy; under its thunderous blows, HX 142 begins to disintegrate. The gaps between ships increase as ships seek greater sea-room. There is a tremendous collision near the centre as a great bulk carrier becomes unmanageable and sheers out of line, her bows colliding with those of a new Empire vessel in the adjoining column; in the black night we hear the rending screech of fractured metal above the howling of the gale.

Fortunately, it is a glancing blow, but even so it has torn a gaping hole in the starboard bow of the Empire ship, and although the hole is well above the water-line, in this wild weather it is a dangerous wound. Both ships fall astern to examine and repair damage as best they can, and *Kamsack* is told off to stand by them until they can rejoin the convoy. But there is no respite; all the next day the gaps between ships steadily widen, although the commodore has reduced speed to a signalled four knots, which is more like two over the ground. At this speed some ships are virtually unable to maintain a proper course; they fall out of line and peel off to either side, seeking sea-room. They give us in the escorts some grey hairs, for there is nothing which can bring one's heart into one's mouth faster than the sight of a great black shape looming out of the night when one fancied oneself safely distant a mile or so from the nearest merchantman. Next morning Smoky Joe is far behind, now just a smudge of smoke astern on the horizon, and *Kamsack* is directed by *Montgomery* to take him under her wing as well. By the morning of this third day of the gale, HX 142 is scattered over miles of ocean, its shattered ranks broken into two shapeless huddles of storm-lashed ships, its escorts now running dangerously low on fuel with a thousand miles of stormy Atlantic still ahead and the U-boat gauntlet still to run.

Fortunately, at this desperate juncture the wind begins to ease; by afternoon it is no more than a fresh breeze and by nightfall the enormous sea has begun to subside. Dawn next day reveals a North Atlantic restored to something like normalcy. Immediately *Montgomery* drops back to fuel from the aftermost tanker in the centre column, signalling as she goes the rotation in which we, the other escorts, are to leave the screen to top up our depleted tanks. By mid-afternoon our turn has come; we steam down through the re-forming ranks of the convoy and approach the tanker from astern. Our fo'c'sle party grapples and picks up the long grass-line streamed behind the huge tanker, together with the empty water-breaker used as a buoy on the end of it, and haul it on the empty fuel hose, filled with air so it will float, which the tanker pays out like a great serpent astern. We close up until we are broad on the tanker's quarter, the buoyant hose streaming astern of the tanker and then up onto our fo'c'sle in a deep U-shape. The hose end is quickly fastened to the pipe-nozzle which had just been fitted for the purpose at our refit last fall, and at a flat signal from us the oiler begins pumping. We steam along at convoy speed, protected from attack by ships all about us, keeping station easily by maintaining the U in the bight of the hose, which in effect cushions any small failure in station-keeping caused by wind or sea.

This is a method of fuelling at sea developed by mid-ocean escorts in the teeth of regular-navy opposition, for in peacetime oiling had been regarded as an evolution, something to be carried out on calm seas as a display of smart seamanship. Destroyers were required to close the tanker alongside and to steam, beam to beam, a few feet apart, while a short length of hose was passed directly across. Station-keeping had to be perfect; the slightest yawing resulted in a broken hose or a collision, sometimes both together, so that the evolution became impossible with any sort of sea running. Even the astern method had its dangers; more than one escort had been covered with thick black oil from bows to bridge, from masthead to water-line, as a result of a hose breaking during fuelling and the broken end, flying madly about under great pressure, squirting tons of heavy bunker oil over everything.

Such a nightmare was always possible in bad weather, but the large amount of slack in the fuel hose represented by the deep U-shaped bight provided a safe degree of leeway for any well-handled ship. In less than an hour we have topped-up, had pumping stopped, let the hose blow clear, capped it, and cast it off, and we are on our way back to our screening position on the starboard flank of the convoy.

All day HX 142 has been re-forming, the commodore maintaining slow speed while stragglers hurry back into position, and the ranks slowly close up and regain cohesion. Last to return is Smoky Joe, clouds of smoke belching from his tall, thin funnel. As night closes in, convoy speed is increased.

Next day brings a new enemy. We are approaching the area, just beyond reach of air cover from Iceland or Ireland, where the U-boats maintain their patrolling line. It is a thin affair nowadays, as more and more U-boats are hurried down to the happy hunting grounds off the American coast where American shipping, unprotected by convoy as a result of an almost unbelievable miscalculation by Admiral King and his staff, can be butchered like so many sheep. But the evening U-boat report shows plenty of activity still in our area, and the Admiralty, in a special signal to us, warn that at least three U-boats are in the immediate vicinity of our convoy.

We take every precaution; lookouts are especially vigilant, guns and depth-charges are checked out, and we close in to abjure Smoky Joe to throw on his best lumps of coal in order to keep in station and make the minimum amount of smoke. We receive the mandatory wave of the hand—reassuring? resigned? resentful? Who could say?—and return to our position on the screen, maintaining our zigzag in meticulous station. The night passes without incident.

Next day it becomes clear that we have been spotted. Unusual U-boat wireless activity from our immediate area indicates we are being tailed by at least one U-boat, and the pack is gathering. Late that afternoon, as visibility fades, *Montgomery* leaves her station and sweeps astern at high speed; half an hour later the commodore alters convoy course drastically to the northward. *Montgomery* hopes to force any shadower to submerge and thereby not be in a position to detect our new change of course. *Montgomery* returns early in the evening without having spotted anything, but it is hoped that we have shaken off, at least temporarily, any U-boat attack. It is standard practice for U-boats to maintain contact at visibility limit astern, on the surface or at periscope depth according to circumstances, steering convoy course and speed by day and surfacing at nightfall to overtake at high speed and gain an attacking position on the bow of the convoy. Attack is usually from this position on the surface, the boat trimmed down so that virtually only her conning tower is exposed. A spread of torpedoes is fired, with the attacker then either running right through the convoy, or turning to escape at high speed on the surface while the convoy steams on.

It is a black night; there will be a moon later on, if the cloud cover permits, but meantime the darkness favours us in our attempt to avoid detection. We steam on, everyone on tenterhooks; on the bridge and in the messdecks the tension is almost palpable. Yet at sea we are all fatalists; when I turn in after an austere supper—all our fresh supplies are long gone and we virtually live on Spam—I quickly fall into deep and dreamless sleep.

Good God, what was that? I sit upright in the pitch-black cabin. There it is again: the rumbling bang against the ship's side of an underwater explosion, and as I switch on the lamp there is another one. Not depth-charges, these; they can only be torpedoes, and as I fling my legs over the side of the bunk and pull on my seaboots, the alarm bells suddenly go off overhead, sounding action stations, and the whole sleeping ship explodes into pandemonium. Racing for the bridge, I cannon into dark figures, bulky with lifejackets; the night is filled with drumming feet, muttered curses, the metallic sounds of clips being loosened, hatches flung open, guns and depth-charges cleared away, and over all the insistent, mind-maddening clangour of the alarm bells.

Up on the bridge the atmosphere is tense with suppressed excitement; the captain is at the voice-pipes, bringing the ship around to point directly away from the convoy, his voice clipped, controlled, urgent. And the convoy, ah God, the convoy—

We must have been at the inner limit of our zigzag when the torpedoes struck; the dark shapes of the outer column tower darkly above us, seeming frighteningly close. But just beyond them is a terrifying sight: the leading ship of the second column is afire, and flames can be seen all along her upper deck. Even as we watch, there is a blinding flash, and suddenly she bursts into a towering pillar of flame. Across the water comes the sound of the explosion, and a new, horrifying sound: the roar of the inferno that has engulfed her. She must have been carrying high-octane petroleum as deck cargo; only this could have turned her into such a tremendous torch. It is as bright as day; the flames light up the sea all around us, throwing the ships of the intervening column into bold relief, illuminating the pale, tense faces on the bridge behind me. All eyes are on the doomed ship; nobody speaks, we are struck dumb by the fearful majesty of the terrible scene before us, by the unbelievable roar of the holocaust. Slowly, serenely, she passes down the column, isolated now from her grubby sisters ploughing past in the splendid beauty of her destruction. It is a voice up the pipe from the wireless office which breaks the spell: "From *Montgomery*, sir: Raspberry!"

It is an order to all escorts to turn outward and illuminate their sectors with star shell—one of the new group tactical evolutions embodied in the escort "Bible", the big blue-bound volume known as Western Approaches Convoy Instructions, or simply "Wackey". From our inward position, the captain swings our bows around until we are steaming directly away from the convoy, and at a word from him Falconer, our gunnery officer, calls down the foregun voice-pipe: "With star shell and reduced charge, load! Load! Load!" There are orderly scufflings from the gun's crew, and we can hear the breech being swung open and closed, and then Falconer passes down the arc to be covered. "Illuminate from red 45 to green 45." The gun is trained and reported ready, and as all glasses on the bridge are readied and we cover our eyes with our hands, there comes the order "Shoot!" A blinding flash, a hot whiff of cordite, and in the sudden blackness that follows, everyone peers intently out into the dark void on the port bow. After what seems ages, the shell bursts, high and far, and instantly turns night into day. As the magnesium flare, dangling from its parachute, slowly descends, it lights up the empty sea beneath it. Even as we watch, the gun fires again, and after another ageless interval, a second flare appears, further ahead, and now higher than the original, which has been drifting evenly down. And then another, and another; in the space of a minute we have hung a curtain of star shell over a wide arc of the sea, and as the flares drift lower they light up the surface in unbelievable detail, throwing into relief every tiny wavetop. All around the convoy the other escorts are lighting up their sectors; already we can benefit from the outermost star shell fired by *Chilliwack* ahead and *Kamsack* far astern. If, as *Montgomery* believes, the U-boat attacking us is making her escape on the surface, we should be able to catch a glimpse of her, with any luck. Luck, because the area to be covered is huge, and the arcs can never be simultaneous; the first star shell is dipping into the sea, to be snuffed out before the arc can be half completed, and the gaps between areas covered by individual escorts are many and large. And yet—there is a lot of light up there, a lot of sea laid bare for the scrutiny of hundreds of searching eyes. *Montgomery* has radar, a sort of Stone Age contraption; one of her officers told me that they don't put any faith in any object it reports unless they can actually see it, and that its main use was in giving a distance off the convoy for station-keeping, but for all of that they'll be chasing every back-echo and will-o'-the-wisp wavetop in reports right now.

And then—there it is! Far out to the right of the last star shell I catch a glimpse through the binoculars of something in the wavetops, and as my heart almost stops with excitement I see, for the first time, the unmistakable outline of a U-boat conning tower. My shout is simultaneous with that of the captain: "There she is: green 45!" and then everything happens at once. The captain cannons into me, leaping for the voice-pipe. "Starboard twenty!" Falconer calls for another star shell on the same bearing as the last, and Harvey rushes for the asdic set to give his operators the bearing of the surfaced enemy; the moment he dives he becomes their responsibility. As the ship steadies on her new course, heading directly for the submarine, the captain issues a string of orders. A sighting signal is cracked off to *Montgomery*, the gun's crew bangs off its last star shell and then loads with high-explosive shell and a full charge, and down in the waist and quarterdeck the depth-charge crews rush to put shallow settings on their first pattern of charges, for we hope to be up with the U-boat before he can dive deep. The captain calls for emergency full ahead, and even on the bridge we can hear the double ring of the engine telegraphs in the wheelhouse, and up the stokehold ventilators behind us we can hear the answering bells ringing and the stokers shouting as they open all the taps.

I keep the glasses glued on the U-boat, now brightly illuminated as the star-shell flares fall closer; under our feet the ship vibrates madly as the engines reach for their full power. We are closing rapidly, but suddenly there is a welter of white water all about the tiny black conning tower towards which we are charging.

She's diving! I turn to the captain, but he has already seen for himself.

"She's blowing ballast tanks," he mutters, and calmly takes a bearing of her over the standard compass.

In a matter of seconds, she is gone, her position marked by a swirl of foam, and moments later our last star shell dips into the sea and blackness locks us in on every side. The captain moves into the asdic house to direct the search, and as we approach the diving position we reduce speed to ten knots, our asdic beam searching beneath the surface for the vanished enemy.

"From *Montgomery,* sir; *Kamsack* to close and assist *Trail* in hunting U-boat," reports the signal yeoman from the wireless cabin voice-pipe. This is welcome news; with two escorts, one to hold contact while the other attacks, we should be able to kill this U-boat. On the silent bridge, on the darkened decks, men stand in attitudes of tension, all minds on the softly lit compass in the asdic cabin, where a ray of light and the persistent ping! of the set indicate that our supersonic beam is probing the blind depths for the hidden killer of our ships.

"Echo bearing red 10, range eleven hundred yards!" Out on the windswept bridge, I hear the report we have been aching to hear on the chart-room voice-pipe. The report is from the operator on the set; from Clarke, his leading hand and the ranking asdic rating on the ship, comes the qualifying report: "Echo low," and then, after the cut-offs have been established, the confident, unequivocal report: "Target is submarine, sir, on an opening course."

From the captain, then, the low words that put it all together: "Start the attack!"

The attacking signal is made to *Kamsack* and *Montgomery,* we accelerate to a fifteen-knot attacking speed, settings for depth-charges are confirmed and their crews put on standby for firing. As officer of the watch I keep a lookout on the bridge, but my mind is with the little group huddled about the soft-lit instruments inside the cabin behind me, where the operator is holding contact, Clarke, our senior specialist, is keeping the captain posted, and the deep black marks of the chemical traces mark the roll of paper on the set each time an echo is received back from the U-boat, and thus indicate its range on the marked scale.

Bang!

Jesus, what was that! I whirl around toward the convoy, and then, seconds later, comes the sound of yet another explosion. Lord, more torpedoes; we've walked into a second submarine. I pass the word to the captain inside, who simply nods, too intent on our own developing attack to waste words. Moments later, *Kamsack* is diverted from us by *Montgomery*, and detailed to sweep astern for the second U-boat. The commodore reports the pennant numbers of the latest ship attacked, and corrects those an earlier report; despite those first three explosions, only two ships have been torpedoed in the earlier attack—the extra bang was just one of those things.

At six hundred yards, the captain makes a bold throw-off, based on reports from the set and our plot, where the courses of target and ship have been carefully plotted. We alter thirty degrees to starboard in order to cross ahead of our unseen antagonist, so that our charges may sink through the water in his path and, hopefully, explode as he heads right to them.

Now the reports come thick and fast, the whole intensity of our effort stepping up as the range closes quickly. This is the climactic moment of the whole attack, when this ship justifies the purpose for which she was built and for which all her crew have trained and endured. The next few seconds can make it all worth while, can redeem the endless manhours and effort which ship and crew represent. Except for the chanted litany of the asdic team, intoning its bearings and ranges, there is utter silence throughout the ship, every man keyed up to the breaking point. In the asdic cabin, the black line of the echo traces will be moving along the paper tape, being aligned with the perspex firing bar; when they coincide with the etched line on the bar the firing will begin.

There it is: "Fire one!" And seconds later, "Fire two!" and then "Fire three!"

From the blackness behind us, we hear the splash of the charges from the traps into our wake, the "whoosh! whoosh!" of the throwers on each side as we drop our charges in an elongated diamond pattern of ten, with six charges in pairs on the centre line and four from the throwers, two on each side.

"Simultaneous echoes!" comes the report from the asdic operator; the target is so close that no ranging is possible, and moments later, as the target passes astern and our transmissions are blanked out by our own wake, "Lost contact, sir."

"Boom! Bang! Whoorumph!" The tremendous detonation of our charges is like a giant hammer striking our hull; the whole ship lifts and is borne aloft as a great fountain of water, sensed rather than seen, rises from astern. The ship is given a ferocious shaking, and on deck we clutch for support; in the engine room, we must have broken every pipe we have. The captain reduces speed, and we circle around to give our asdic set a clear field in which to regain contact. But in the asdic cabin there are bitter oaths; the main gyro which directs our compasses has been unseated by the explosions, and everyone works desperately to get it back in service, for without it our asdic compass is useless. The captain paces in a fury of exasperation.

How was it? we ask ourselves. In the waist, the depth-charge crews are jabbering with excitement as they reload their mortars, and all of us wait for confirmation of our success. Surely no U-boat could have survived the accurate explosion of three tons of amatol? From the plot comes confirmation that the attack seemed a good one, but still, as we circle around, comes neither contact with the U-boat nor signs of its destruction. Unless—surely that smell was not there before—surely that is the smell of oil! I call the captain out, and he sniffs excitedly, but then the smell is gone, as quickly as it came.

"Not enough for a kill; more likely she's sprung a rivet or two in her fuel tanks," the captain cautions, and moves back to the set. At long last, our gyro is operational again, and the asdic team buckles to its job. Still no contact; we begin a square search, directed by the plot, and the minutes grow, and with them our chances of regaining contact dwindle. Time is now crucial to us, for if we are not firmly in contact we cannot delay much longer. Our convoy is under attack, our escort hard-pressed, the sea perhaps covered with survivors awaiting rescue or death, men whose life in the sea is measured in minutes.

The issue we are already beginning to agonize over is resolved in a moment by a peremptory signal from *Montgomery*. We are to rejoin at best speed, and sweep astern as we do so while *Kamsack* screens the rescue ship, lying stopped

and vulnerable as she hauls shaken and sodden men from the
sea.

In dejected silence we huddle at our action stations. In an
inspired moment, somebody lays on a cup of "key" all
around, and as we sip the hot chocolate, so thick that it is
barely liquid, we fortify ourselves for the long hours of vigilance which still lie ahead of us before this night is over. Our
burning motorship has disappeared, her flames presumably
snuffed out by the invading sea, and everything else has been
swept away from our world, the dark shapes of the convoy
having long vanished over the horizon ahead. We increase to
fifteen knots; it will be all we can do to regain station by
early morning.

In the event, we come up with part of the convoy earlier
than expected. At first light, the air becomes rank with a
familiar stink, and as the light grows we find ourselves steaming through a vast pool of oil, a slick of glossy slime that
seems to cover the whole ocean. It is fuel from the bunkers
of our torpedoed merchantmen, and scattered about in it is
the indescribable debris left by sunken ships. We pass
gratings, and boxes, and nameless hunks of timber, hatch-
boards, bloated canvas covers, bits of white-painted wood.
Boats, too; one of them with bows stove in and half full of
water, two others in good shape, but empty of occupants.

In silence we stare from our decks at the debris streaming
past; clusters of faces at the break of our fo'c'sle show that
even the watch below has come out to look, in shivering
silence, at these pitiful fragments from the shattered house-
holds of friends and comrades. There are worse horrors to
come; my stomach rises as I see, white in the black water, the
bloated sacs and torn flesh of what I am forced to recognize
as the lungs and viscera and abdomen of a human being, and
a little further on, a sudden pointing of arms from our onlookers below indicates a man, only his head and shoulders
visible in the filthy sea. He is dead, of course; his eyes are
open, like his twisted mouth, but he sags lifelessly against his
oil-stained lifejacket, his face as grey as the soiled canvas supporting it, his hair and cheeks plastered with the fuel oil
which has suffocated him. We steam past in awed silence; for
our first-trippers, it is a startling glimpse of the Death which
up to now has been one of war's abstractions, distant and
impersonal, something to be read about or glimpsed in a distant explosion.

Oppressed by our failure, in the bleak grey dawn we steam

through a filthy sea laden with reproach, our decks slippery with the disorder of a night action, squalid with dirty cocoa cups, blistered paint, broken glass, and fallen corking. Sullen, sleepless, and silent we rejoin HX 142.

4
THE BAND
OF BROTHERS

The real heroes of the Battle of the Atlantic were the officers and men of the Merchant Service; everyone who served at sea knows that. Even the name, "Merchant Service", was a misnomer; these men served in no organized force, wore no uniforms, earned no recognition or awards. They were civilians, and although they earned a far higher rate of pay than any naval man, no wage scale could possibly have recompensed them for the hardihood and endurance which kept them at sea, in helpless and often inadequate ships, in defiance of the terrors of the wartime North Atlantic.

But the Merchant Service made another great contribution to the winning of the Battle of the Atlantic; it provided the experienced core of men who, as Naval Reserve officers with the interwoven gold lace on their sleeves, commanded the ships of Canada's escort fleet. In the early years, every Canadian corvette was commanded by a Naval Reserve lieutenant; by the closing stages of the war a good many Volunteer Reserve officers had replaced them in corvette commands, and the more senior Naval Reserve types had gone on to take over frigates and destroyers. From first to last, though, it was the officers of the Naval Reserve, the fellows with the twisty bands of gold lace on their cuffs, who imparted a distinctive character to the seagoing Canadian fleet, an ambience quite different from that of the shoreside navy.

In the early years of the war, each corvette was a distinct and separate world, whose character reflected the personality of her captain, and whose cleanliness, discipline, and fighting

44

capacity often varied widely from that of the sister ships alongside her.

All too often, she was a grubby, rust-streaked mess, manned by a scruffy, undisciplined crew and drunken, incompetent officers, her deplorable state reflecting the incapacity of her captain, who might be anything from a River Plater or a China Coaster to a second mate from some Great Lakes sand-sucker. I was fortunate enough to serve in clean, well-run ships commanded by capable officers, but I also served under alcoholics who used to drink up the crew's rum issue, and under thieves who used money from the ship's contingency funds for their personal expenses on a run ashore. In time, of course, the incompetents drifted off, often after running their ships ashore or running afoul of the law or of a shocked escort commander, and with their passing the seagoing navy began to shape up into an efficient and effective fleet moulded by the best of the Naval Reserve captains.

Canada was fortunate to have attracted to her navy a good number of British merchant-ship officers who had served before the war in well-run shipping lines—Canadian Pacific and Canadian National, Cunard, Royal Mail, Ellerman, British India, to name a few—or in the British-run customs and hydrographic services of China and other Asiatic countries. It was these officers, drawn to the Royal Canadian Navy on the outbreak of war by the pay, higher than that of the British Royal Navy, who not only took Canada's corvettes to sea, but imparted their rich fund of seamanship to the thousands of Volunteer Reserve officers and men who had come to sea for the first time, from Canadian schools and offices, factories and farms.

There were, of course, some memorable lapses. I was one of the group of Volunteer Reserve officers undergoing a short course to fit us to take command which was marched down to the Halifax waterfront for a lesson in ship-handling. We were in the charge of Ben Sivertz, a short, stone-faced little Icelander with the curled stripes of a Naval Reserve lieutenant on his cuffs, a piercing blue eye that never wavered, and a deliberate manner of speech; he seemed always to be speaking in capital letters. We called him "Sea-Biscuit".

He was taking us out on a little wooden-hulled auxiliary vessel, he told us, to practise bringing her alongside various wharves; presumably her light timber hull would inflict less damage on our surroundings than a conventional steel hull could be expected to do. He cautioned us to observe the manner in which the little ship's captain, an NR skipper lieutenant and formerly a Newfoundland fisherman, handled the ship. "HE MAY SEEM TO YOU A BIT ROUGH, BUT WHAT HE LACKS IN POLISH HE MORE THAN MAKES UP FOR IN HIS MASTERY OF SEAMANSHIP AND PRACTICAL SHIP-HANDLING. HE IS A MASTER OF HIS CRAFT," Sea-Biscuit intoned, and we were all suitably impressed. We watched in reverent silence while this master of the ship-handling art brought his scruffy little vessel into the berth while we waited on the jetty.

To begin with he chose to bring her in with the tide astern, instead of stemming it in the normal manner; a cardinal error, roughly equivalent to landing a light aircraft downwind in a gale. Heading into a tidal current helps to push the ship alongside its desired berth; if the ship approaches with the tide astern, the current tends to push it along parallel to the wharf. At first incredulous, then appalled, we watched as the little grey-painted ship made a lunge at the wharf before being borne irresistibly along on the tide into the sharp prows of two old destroyers secured in the berth ahead. She came to rest at right angles to the jetty, broadside on the sharp destroyer bows, and from all appearances she was there to stay for quite some time.

It was then that we were vouchsafed our first glimpse of the Master Craftsman in the flesh; a balding head, a crinkled cigarette dangling from its lower lip, was thrust out the pilot-house window; beneath it we could see the crumpled monkey-jacket, hands thrust deep in its pockets and cigarette ash down its lapels. There was no sign of alarm or distress; instead the Master sized up the situation at a glance and withdrew into the cool depths of the pilot-house. Surely, we thought, we are now about to see how a ship can be plucked from even so awkward a position as this by consummate seamanship and cunning ship-handling; we watched with bated breath.

There was this to be said for the Master Craftsman: he did not waste time with shilly-shallying, or flinch from paying the inevitable price in scraped paint and splintered wood as a more sensitive man might. He put his wheel hard over and his engines full ahead, and dragged his ship by main force across the bows of her encumbering destroyers while stanchions bent and broke, lifelines tautened bar-hard before flying apart, and great shavings of grey-painted wood were scraped from her battered sides. For a moment the bow of the innermost destroyer caught on a davit of the little ship's lifeboat, but as the propeller bit deep the davit was lifted out of its socket and parted with a screeching clangour, and the ship was free. A couple of deckhands in dirty T-shirts tossed lines onto the wharf, and the ship was made fast.

If someone had giggled, or so much as simpered, we would all have exploded with laughter, but as it happened Sea-Biscuit simply collected us with an icy glance and led us aboard over the tatty gangplank, his face a mask. We trooped dutifully aboard, and prepared to follow in the steps of the Master.

This incident, of course, was merely the exception that proved the rule; most Naval Reserve officers were fine ship-handlers.

They included some rough diamonds. One of the best of the early corvette commanders used to astound visitors to the wardroom meals by removing his false teeth for what he considered "the easy bits" and dropping them into his water-glass until they were required for masticating something more challenging. Yet another had acquired a fascinating array of tattoos during the course of long service in the Far East, and would exhibit them, in progressively more intimate areas, when plied with drink during the course of a lively wardroom evening. The pièce de résistance was a magnificent serpent, coloured in vivid shades of blue and green and scarlet, which coiled around his waist and whose head, complete with hooded eyes and scarlet tongue—but enough, enough.

Yet whatever their individual eccentricities, these ex-Merchant Service officers provided the solid core of experienced seamen on which the Canadian seagoing navy was built. It was they who shaped a force whose discipline and attitudes and standards were to prove equal to the rigorous demands of North Atlantic warfare, and which survived, to a remarkable extent, into the postwar Canadian navy.

The strain of command, particularly in the early years, was almost more than men could bear. Not only were the ships ill-armed and under-equipped, the crews inexperienced and undisciplined, the escort groups uncoordinated and ill-trained, the weather, particularly in the winter months, simply indescribable, but the shortage of escorts and the size of convoys—up to a hundred ships—imposed intolerable demands on the early corvette commanders. Each convoy trip was a test of endurance; two to three weeks of gales and sinkings and collisions, of escorts trying to take in tow huge disabled merchantmen ten times their size, of excruciating discomfort and agonizing decisions. Sleeplessness was the rule for the corvette captains; with no other experienced officer to lean on, all decisions, night and day, were thrust on to his shoulders. In the days before oiling at sea became standard practice, fuel shortage was chronic among escorts on a long convoy run; did one risk leaving a convoy under attack to dash away for fuel, or did one remain to fight it out tonight and risk becoming a helpless hulk tomorrow?

After weeks of nightmare, a corvette would limp into Iceland, or, later on, Londonderry, for a layover of three or four days, during which the exhausted crew had to refuel, load food and ammunition for the return voyage, and attempt to repair and maintain their battered ship and armament. There was simply no time, in those early days, for proper training ashore during the brief and hectic layovers. In no time, it seemed, the ships were steaming out to sea to escort a westbound convoy, with the prospect of an equally frantic stopover in St. John's at the end of it. It was like a continuing bad dream, an endless round of misery and hardship and strain which tested officers and men, but above all, captains, to the limits of human endurance, and sometimes beyond. The wonder is, not that a few cracked under the strain, nor that hard drinking ashore during the few nights in port became a customary feature of too many commanding officers' routines, but that so many captains endured the fearsome ordeal month after month, year after year.

The aging process was fearful; who could have recognized, in the grizzled frigate captain at war's end, the feckless young second mate who had joined up only three years before?

As captains, these officers imparted their own character to the ships they commanded; a good officer ran a good ship, a poor one ran a miserable ship. You could tell them apart at a glance; a good captain ran a happy ship, a clean ship, an efficient ship. You could tell the incompetently run corvette by her slack and grubby air, by her sloppy and sullen crew, by her disordered decks. A good captain had to teach his methods and standards to his first lieutenant, had to hound him and coax him until he learned to keep his ship orderly and clean, his men content and obedient. Because experienced petty officers available for sea-duty in almost all branches were virtually non-existent, and officers and crews were green as grass to the ways of the sea, corvette captains had to concern themselves with a thousand details of ship maintenance and organization which would never concern commanding officers in peacetime warships, or even in the wartime Royal Navy, where a backbone of experienced ratings and petty officers could be depended upon to establish routines in every ship, even in emergency-program corvettes and frigates.

The key factor, to the surprise of those volunteer officers and men who looked for more martial qualities to set their ship above all others as a fighting ship, was cleanliness. With so many men crammed into a small space, sleeping and eating and operating their tiny vessel in conditions of indescribable and often chaotic discomfort, orderliness and cleanliness were absolutely essential before any sort of operational efficiency could be achieved. It was an obsessive, never-ending business; always, at sea and ashore, there were things to be cleaned—messdecks, bulkheads, washrooms—or greased—guns, winches, deck gear of every sort—or scraped and red-leaded and painted—decks and shipsides, funnels and upper-works. There was never enough time to catch up with all the work of maintaining a ship as she should be; as fast as work was done it was eroded by weather and usage. But the measure of a ship's capacity was the degree to which she was able to maintain herself, and the moment you stepped aboard a corvette you knew whether she was a happy and efficient ship or one in which even the simplest voyage would be an ordeal.

There existed a myth, particularly on the lower deck, that equated indiscipline with a happy ship, and scruffy crews of scruffy ships would excuse their shortcomings by maintaining that theirs was a "fighting ship", with no time left from battling the enemy for such frills as cleaning and painting. But the reality was quite different; cleanliness and good order spelt both contentment for the ship's company and operational efficiency. I never knew a ship which could gleam in harbour which did not also shine at sea.

Although the curly-stripers of the Naval Reserve, the ex-merchant seaman, provided the commanding officers of the new corvette navy, it was the Volunteer Reserve, the landsmen, who furnished the officers and men who manned it. Most of them had never seen the sea until they joined the navy, and their nautical experience, if any, was limited to a little freshwater yachting. In time they were to equal both merchant navy and regular navy officers as anti-submarine tacticians and corvette commanders.

This outcome was not as surprising as it might at first appear, for the tactics of U-boat warfare were as new to experienced naval officers as to the VR officers newly arrived at sea. The VR's simply gobbled up the new techniques faster than their older RCN and RCNR contemporaries, and their inexperience in the ways of sea and navy was more than counterbalanced by keenness and enthusiasm. After all, the very fact that they had chosen to go to sea in corvettes from safe and comfortable homes ashore indicated that they were anxious to give of their best, and it was this eagerness to learn which was their greatest asset. A second characteristic was a quick intelligence; some of the sharpest and brightest young men in Canada joined the new navy, and they brought to wardrooms and messdecks a feistiness which thrived on the new challenges and techniques of an ever-changing war.

But if they had certain innate virtues, the young VR officers also had certain lamentable defects, quite apart from the lack of experience which made them almost useless on early voyages. Chief among these was an almost total lack of "power of command": the ability to assume responsibility for a group of men and to impose one's will by simple, clear orders. Few Canadian VR officers in the early days had the moral courage to issue orders which they knew would not be well received; instead, too many emulated "Popularity Jack", that most despicable of officers, and attempted to curry favour with the men for whom they were responsible. Another example of this same weakness was the VR martinet, the petty tyrant who delighted in bellowing orders and extracting salutes for the sake of savouring his new-found power. Both the cringer and the strutting posturer reflected the inherent inability of most Canadians to exercise power responsibly in a service hierarchy so alien to the "democratic" institutions of Canadian civilian society.

Not the least of the contributions made by the experienced seamen of the Naval Reserve was their success in knocking this nonsense out of the VR officers who came under their command. My first corvette captain, suspecting me of "sucking up" to the signalmen on watch, told me bluntly to make up my mind whether I was to berth in the messdeck or in the wardroom, for in this ship I wasn't going to do both. At the same time, he insisted that none of his officers was to eat or sleep or go ashore until he first ensured that the men for whom he was responsible were able to do likewise, and it was this two-way lesson which made officers of young Canadian civilians.

For it was discipline which, from first to last, was the chief problem of the war-born Canadian navy. Lacking the stratified and established society of older nations, Canadians had not grown up "knowing their place", like their British counterparts, and did not take kindly to having people no better than they telling them what to do and how to do it. Saluting some fellow who'd grown up just across the street came hard to the free spirits of raw new entries, and the whole service system, hedged around with restrictions and regulations affecting their every waking moment, seemed intolerably confining to men fresh from free-and-easy civvy street. Sailors of no other nation, not even those of the United States, were so resistant to discipline as those of Canada, primarily because of the lack of seasoned petty officers, leading seamen, and commissioned officers. The combination of recalcitrant, inexperienced seamen and inadequate officers plagued the early days of the corvette navy, and was chiefly responsible for the indifferent performance of so many Canadian ships.

It took the experience of conditions at sea, of the frightening ordeal of a North Atlantic crossing, to instill in both officers and men the sense of collective identity that lies at the heart of good discipline; once it became clear that they sank or survived as a ship's company, not as individuals, the need for organized communal effort to serve a collective purpose became clear to even the most independent soul, and indiscipline ceased to be a problem. In ships blessed with good officers, particularly commanding officers, a rapport was quickly established between all ranks on board which established the vessel as that most blessed of institutions, a "happy ship". And while the standard of performance of the average Canadian ship was below that of the average British ship, particularly in the early years of the war, there was nothing afloat in the Allied navies that could touch the performance of a happy and efficient Canadian ship. In a state of good order and discipline, the Canadian sailor proved himself to be the best there was.

But he was never one to be trampled upon, as one officious commanding officer discovered to his cost. This fellow had made himself something of a martinet, and he ran afoul of the unwritten rule of seagoing etiquette that requires commanding officers to limit their strictures to their own crews. Returning to his ship one night, berthed alongside several others at a congested escort jetty, he discovered that the quartermaster of the inboard corvette was not at the gangway as he was supposed to be. In order to teach him a lesson, this pompous fellow confiscated the quartermaster's book and the small table on which it lay, and took them with him aboard his own vessel. Next morning, he sent a message to the captain of the inboard ship, an officer junior to him, notifying him that the missing articles were on board and could be reclaimed by him only, in person. The resentful fury of the humiliated captain was shared by his entire ship's company, and found expression in a revenge that became celebrated throughout the Western Approaches. That same morning the crew of the inboard ship were overside on stages and floats, touching up the paint on the bows of their vessel, and hidden from observation above by the flare of the fo'c'sle.

Next morning, the outside corvette sailed, her captain bustling importantly about his bridge—and awoke the mirth of the whole harbour. Men poured up onto the decks of ships alongside to gesture and hoot with laughter; whole ship's companies lined the rails to jeer and shriek with mirth. Ribald signals were sent to the mystified captain; drawn up on deck fore and aft, his ship's company could only wonder what all the merriment was about. It was the same when the corvette joined her convoy, long after the harbour incident had been left behind; she seemed to arouse derision wherever she went. It was not until a pointed signal from one of her fellow escorts had been received that the officious captain peered over his fo'c'sle rail to discover the full extent of his injured junior's revenge. For there, in great black letters six feet high, had been inscribed on his bows the legend: "I'M A SHIT."

A great many factors played a part in the transformation of the wartime Canadian navy from its shaky beginnings into the experienced and effective force it was to become, but the three principal elements were time, training, and—Mainguy. Time—each passing week after those first corvette commissionings in early 1941 provided experience for green crews, better armament and equipment, and more ships to build up the first puny escort groups. Training—a new Commander-in-Chief, Admiral Sir Percy Noble, emphasized training, training, and more training for the hard-pressed crews of Western Approaches escorts. Mainguy—Edmund Rollo, Captain RCN, took over as Captain D commanding the escort groups at Newfoundland and fashioned a great fighting force almost single-handed.

Looking back to the beginnings of the escort fleet, the

changes wrought upon both ships and crews by the passage of even a few months seem almost unbelievable. The first corvettes were fought from a bridge which consisted of a skimpy edge of planking fringing a glass asdic house and chart-house, protected from weather and enemy only by a painted canvas dodger and obscured from astern by the funnel top, which poured fumes over it with a following wind, and from ahead by a large foremast, which showered watch-keepers with condensation in fog, rain, or heavy dew. There was a large open gap in the main deck between bridge-house and fo'c'sle, which ensured that crew members going on and off watch, and food being brought forward from the galley, could be sure of a drenching in any head sea. Secondary armament was limited to a Lewis machine gun or two and perhaps a fellow who could throw rocks. There was no radar, no room, and not enough storage even for the depth-charges which were an escort's main armament, but there was an enormous winch and other minesweeping gear on the quarterdeck—it was thought that corvettes might double in brass as minesweepers—and an interminable wireless aerial slung between the two masts, a legacy from another still-born notion to use corvettes on the Northern Patrol between the Faeroes and Iceland. Once the true role of the corvette as ocean escort was established, changes came thick and fast. First, splinter mats were hung on the bridge railings, and a flimsy "monkey island" was improvised, by the ship's own efforts, atop the asdic house, where officers could keep watch, impeded by the direction-finding radio aerial but free from funnel smoke and the worst of the mast and rigging. Eventually, the canvas bridge dodger was replaced by wood; a spindly radar aerial, a real plumber's nightmare, snaked up the mast to serve the Canadian sw 1 c radar set, glumly viewed at the time as Hitler's Secret Weapon.

Within a year the wretched foremast had been moved aft of the bridge, where it ceased to be a curse to all; the mainmast was replaced by a stump on the pom-pom bandstand or a gaff on the funnel. A proper destroyer-type bridge had emerged, complete with windscreens and compass platform, and with asdic and chart-room space built into its leading edge. The fo'c'sle deck had been extended aft to the waist, providing both much-needed room and improved sea-keeping qualities. Armament had multiplied, with two-pounder guns (pom-poms) aft and quick-firing cannon (Oerlikons) added to the bridge wings, and depth-charges in rails and four throwers arranged on a main deck cleared of sweeping winches and gear. But best of all, radar—the reliable, efficient British 271 set—was fitted in its distinctive lantern housing above and abaft the bridge, and, with its later embellishment of repeaters in bridge and plot-room, transformed the whole technique of convoy escort.

In a matter of months the corvette was transformed into an efficient and effective warship, becoming ever more complex with each new vessel launched until it spawned, in later years, both the Castle class and, ultimately, the frigate.

The transformation wrought in a few months on the crews of Western Approaches escorts was phenomenal. To begin with, a determined effort was made to ensure that ships were given an extra day or two in harbour before turning around for the long fight back. In the early days, there was never enough time for crews to catch their breath, particularly those in the junior ships, which would always be given the dirty jobs, such as filling in for some missing escort in another group just sailing as the incoming group arrived. Most of us remember too well the terrible depression which gripped everyone on board at receiving a signal, on arrival in harbour at long last after a tough crossing, to "fuel, water, and store with all despatch", in order to catch up with some outward-bound group sailing short-handed.

As more escorts became available, such occurrences became less common; instead, an effort was made on both sides of the Atlantic to ensure that crews were given time to train, as well as repair and maintain their ships, during turn-around periods in harbour. There was individual training for gun crews, which often included a shoot at targets afloat and in the air, as the group sailed to join a convoy. Asdic teams exercised every trip in mobile "attack teachers" installed in buses at every escort port, and whole bridge teams, including captains, navigators, plotters, asdic and radar operators, signalmen, and wireless crews were tested in the marvellously sophisticated tactical tables and night action rooms.

The tactical table was a large plotting floor, where movements of model ships were plotted in accordance with actions taken by each ship's bridge team, isolated in cubbyholes all around the floor. Asdic and radar teams were given realistic contacts on their sets, signals were given, and attacks were carried out as the escort commander manoeuvred his group to cope with simulated subs; afterward, everyone trooped out to see what a shambles they'd made of things on the big plotting floor outside.

It was great fun, and marvellous training; all the situations actually met at sea could be reproduced, and for the first time a really cohesive and instinctive team reaction was developed. A set of standard group tactics was developed, most of them built around the need for illuminating the area of attack in order to spot a surfaced escaping U-boat and force him to dive, and teamwork between individual ships was developed into a fine art. It was desirable to put at least two escorts in contact with a submerged submarine, so that one could retain contact while the other attacked. Quick thinking by escort commanders in allocating precious ships to cope with attacks from several directions at once was developed on tactical tables ashore and played an increasing part in convoy battles at sea. We in the corvettes looked forward to our turn at the tables in Londonderry, St. John's, and Halifax, although we seldom emerged from the post-mortem discussions with much credit.

We were not alone in this respect. Admiral Max Horton, who took over from Noble as Commander-in-Chief of Western Approaches, was a former submarine commander who prided himself on his ability to escape from surface hunters. In an exercise at the tactical table in Liverpool, Max undertook to run the U-boat in a confrontation with a single escort. He was sunk, in short order, three successive times, and stamped out of the room in such a fit of temper that nobody had enough nerve to tell him that the "captain" of the ship which had sunk him with such ease was one of the WRNS girls who served as plotters at the unit, a little Third Officer who'd never been to sea and had been in the navy less than a year!

But the real "big time" in shore training establishments was the Night Action Room, known to one and all as Panic Incorporated. This was an enormous darkened room in which actual seagoing conditions, as well as situations, could be simulated. Every action team of a ship was closed up on bridge, guns, asdic, radar, wireless, depth-charge rails and throwers, and so on. On the bridge, it was dark as night, with a howling gale, simulated by giant fans and a pitch or roll in heavy seas as the ship altered course, and even from time to time a bucket of cold water in the face as the ship pitched into a head sea. When a gun fired, the noise was as deafening and the flash as blinding as at sea; on gun platform and quarterdeck, crews fought their guns and depth-charges on a rolling, pitching surface in all the discomfort of wind and water experienced at sea. The convoy could be discerned through night glasses, or on the radar screen, just as at sea, and torpedoings, star shell, or explosions lit up the horizon in a most realistic manner. But in Panic Incorporated everything happened at once; no sooner did one detect a submarine under one's star shell than two ships went up in the convoy and an urgent message was received from the escort commander, while up a voice-pipe came the cheerful news that one's engines had broken down. After a session in the Panic room, everyone was happy to totter off to sea for a little rest and respite. But it was marvellous training, and it engendered a growing confidence in the groups that they could cope with anything.

But shore training of ships' crews was only part of the constant exercising which steadily raised the level of escort efficiency. At sea, individual ships' companies were exercised daily at evening quarters, weather permitting; crews were closed up at action stations before dinner, in the first dogwatch, and tested armament and communications with a few mock emergency drills. In the latter half of the war, escort groups sailing out of Londonderry would be diverted to nearby Larne, where they did intensive exercises with HMS *Philante*, formerly Tom Sopwith's luxury yacht and later to become the Norwegian royal yacht, together with a couple of tame submarines (our own, that is).

But the really soul-testing experience, the one that every old corvette type still recalls today with a shudder, came with the two-week work-ups of newly commissioned ships, designed to make a collection of odds and sods into an efficient ship's company. There were such bases at Bermuda, St. Margaret's Bay, and Pictou on the Canadian side, but the one that really left a lot of scar tissue was the old original, the Dante's Inferno operated at Tobermory on the northwest coast of Scotland by the redoubtable Vice-Admiral Gilbert Stephenson, Royal Navy. This legendary character, variously known as "Puggy", "The Lord of the Isles", or more commonly "The Old Bastard", inhabited a former passenger steamer, *The Western Isles*, which lay at anchor in the quiet, picturesque harbour, surrounded by a handful of newly commissioned corvettes, like a spider surrounded by the empty husks of its victims. He was a daunting sight, smothered in gold lace and brass buttons, with a piercing blue eye that could open an oyster at thirty paces, and tufts of grey hair sprouting from craggy cheeks, and he preyed like some ravening dragon upon the callow crews and shaky officers served up to him at fortnightly intervals.

From dawn to dusk his signal lamp was never still. Send away both boats! Lay out a kedge anchor! Rig sheer legs and hoist in one boat! You are on fire aft! Send an armed boarding party to *Western Isles*! Prepare to take your next astern in tow! Youngest officer aboard is to take the ship to sea!

At the end of each day, an exhausted crew would tumble into their hammocks, but there was no assurance of uninterrupted slumber. On the contrary; the monster stalked its unwary prey by dark as well as by light, and seldom a night passed without an alarm of some sort. For the Admiral delighted in midnight forays; more than one commanding officer was shaken awake to find himself staring into the piercing eyes of a malevolent admiral and learn that his gangway had been left unprotected, that his ship had been taken, and that his kingdom had been given over to the Medes and the Persians.

But occasionally—just occasionally—the ships got a little of their own back. There was the occasion when the Admiral in his barge, lurking soundlessly under the fo'c'sle of what he hoped to be an unsuspecting frigate, waiting for the sailor whom he could hear humming to himself on the deck above to move on, suddenly found himself being urinated on, "from a great height", as gleeful narrators related the story in a hundred rapturous wardrooms. There was the other frigate he boarded one dark night only to be set upon by a ferocious Alsatian dog and forced to leap back into his boat, leaving, in the best comic-strip tradition, a portion of his trouser-seat aboard the ship, which ever after displayed the tattered remains as a proud trophy, suitably mounted and inscribed.

And there was the Canadian corvette sailor who worsted the fiery admiral in a hand-to-hand duel. Coming aboard this ship, the Admiral suddenly removed his cap and flung it on the deck, shouting to the astounded quartermaster: "That's an unexploded bomb; take action, quickly now!"

With surprising sang-froid, the youngster kicked the cap over the side. "Quick thinking!" commended the Admiral. Then, pointing to the slowly sinking cap, heavy with gold lace, the Admiral continued: "That's a man overboard; jump to it and save him!"

The ashen-faced matelot took one look at the icy November sea, then turned and shouted: "Man overboard! Away lifeboat's crew!"

The look on the Admiral's face, as he watched his expensive Gieves cap slowly disappear into the depths while a cursing, fumbling crew attempted to get a boat ready for lowering, was balm to the souls of all who saw it.

But if it was time that improved the ships and training that sharpened the crews, it was Captain Edmund Rollo Mainguy who imparted the spirit that fashioned Canada's escort navy into an effective and efficient team, and its officers and men into a true band of brothers, a race of men apart.

I can remember the change. We were one of a number of corvettes sent to Newfoundland in the fall of 1941 to form the Mid-Ocean Groups sailing out of St. John's, and each crossing then was a desperate effort to get our ships across as best we could, using evasive routing, often up to the limit of the Arctic pack ice, to avoid contact with U-boats, and then every kind of ruse to escape unscathed from any U-boat we encountered. Ours was a defensive effort in every way, and our object was mere survival, pure and simple. Yet by the spring of 1943 we were running convoys deliberately right at the thickest concentrations of U-boats, like a fullback running over tacklers, because this was the best way to kill as many U-boats as possible. The convoys had become bait, and our support groups, with their carriers and "hunter-killer" specialists, hung about in the offing hoping for U-boats to kill. We were on the offensive, and it was Admiral Doenitz's submariners who were now more hunted than hunter.

It was morale as well as material that made this dramatic turn-about possible, and nobody played so large a part in fashioning a winning team spirit as Mainguy, Newfoundland's Captain D.

"Newfyjohn", as the sailors called it, was a special sort of place right from the beginning; nothing like it existed anywhere else. Unlike Argentia, some miles to the south, where the Americans carved a vast and elaborate base, complete with swimming pools, out of the virgin Newfoundland forest, quite regardless of expense, the British base at St. John's was a very sketchy affair, all improvisation and make-do; more a state of mind than actual substance. Mainguy and his staff were housed on the top couple of floors of the Newfoundland Hotel, which stood on a convenient height overloking the harbour; signals were passed to ships below by signal lamp from an upper-floor window. Escorts were berthed, half a dozen deep, at the shaky jetties already standing on the South Side, across the harbour from the little city of St. John's. To this day, an old corvette type can chant their names like a sort of litany: Cashin's and Bowring's, Job's and Harvey's . . .

But whatever the base lacked in physical assets, it more than made up for in drive and energy. From the first, Mainguy oriented it and everyone who worked in it, high or low, to the service of the escort ships. This was a revolution in itself; other bases, and particularly Halifax, regarded themselves as being of primary importance and significance, with little time to spare for groups of scruffy ships and the interminable war they seemed to be involved in. But in St. John's, Mainguy insisted that the ships came first; when a corvette berthed there, battered and breathless from the fury of the Atlantic outside, staff men would be waiting on the jetty to help make good her defects, replenish her stores, and generally aid and comfort. To ships' officers accustomed, at other bases, to stand cap in hand outside office doors to await the convenience of the shore staff, this was a miracle in itself, but Mainguy did much more than that.

For one thing, his base never closed; twenty-four hours a day, seven days a week, arriving ships could be sure of full attention; none of that Halifax weekend shutdown, "try again tomorrow", sort of nonsense in Newfyjohn. But above all, Mainguy was the first Canadian Captain D to concern himself with the men as well as the ships they sailed, with morale as well as material needs.

We had been based at Halifax before Newfoundland became operational, and were accustomed, on arrival from sea, to be treated as a pestilential nuisance. Halifax Port Orders, like the Ten Commandments, were heavy on "Thou shalt not", and the negative was emphasized throughout in base attitudes to us. We were not to dump garbage overside, we were not to appear out of full uniform, we were not to go beyond this street or into that area, we were not to interfere with this or that or the other thing, and, as an appropriately repressive finale, we were required to land an armed sentry on the jetty whose function, we inferred, was not so much to defend our ships as to protect the shore from our licentious and unruly seamen.

Newfyjohn was a different world; as you arrived in harbour a signal lamp would flash you, along with berthing instructions, news of the night's dance or concert party. For the men, Mainguy established a rest camp where an exhausted crew could forget the sea in a lovely woodland setting, living in tents and huts and busying themselves with baseball and fishing and swimming, the forgotten recreations of civvy street. There were dances and shows and parties of one sort or another every night in the Caribou Hut or the Knights of Columbus Hall or elsewhere, especially laid on for the fellows from the ships, and the Salvation Army had something going every day for the sailor home from the sea.

For ships' officers Mainguy obtained the loan of the fourth floor of an old Water Street warehouse; working parties of ships' officers cleaned it up, rigged a bar and a fireplace, and inaugurated the Seagoing Officers Club. With its fifty-nine steps up a spidery outside staircase, its crest-covered walls— each ship, on arrival, was required to design and furnish an appropriate ship's crest if it did not already have one—the club became famous throughout Western Approaches as The Crowsnest, where you could forgather with friends from other ships, free from the starchiness of shoreside messes, and where women were admitted, Tuesday nights only, on condition "that they did not clutter up the bar". Mainguy himself used to preside every Saturday afternoon at his celebrated cocktail party in the Newfoundland Hotel; "Captain D's cocktail party" became a social highlight of the escort officers' routine as enjoyable, in a different way, as the raffish Saturday night "Rat Race" at the Nova Scotian Hotel in Halifax.

But more than anything else, Mainguy instilled a sense of team spirit, of pride in one's ship and in one's escort group. He did it by fostering inter-ship and inter-group competition in every sport and pastime imaginable: softball, swimming races, rowing races, even huge tug-of-war matches, involving half a ship's company against half another crew, on the jetty alongside their ships. Such tug-of-war competitions, often in winter snow, with literally hundreds of men involved and with many hundreds more watching from crowded ships alongside, had to be seen to be appreciated. Enormous and complicated wagers were made between ship and ship, mess and mess, wardroom and wardroom; indeed, the paying off of the wagers was in itself a recurring spectacle at the escort berths.

A ship sailing out of Newfy quickly became a proud ship: proud of itself, of its group, of the Western Approaches escort force. We were by no means all Canadian; British, Free

French, Polish, and Norwegian ships were among us, sometimes as distinct groups, more often mixed in with ships of other nationalities. Ships would be moved from one escort group to another, on occasion, and it was commonplace for a Canadian group to have a British senior officer, particularly in the early years when Canadians were short of destroyers. Little by little, each group evolved a distinct identity, usually reflecting the personality of its senior officer. There were serious groups and light-hearted ones, and ships were proud to show their affiliation by distinctive group flags, songs, and funnel markings.

Most of the early Canadian groups were known by the nicknames of the veteran River-class destroyers which carried their senior officer. There was the "Guts", or "Rustyguts", for *Restigouche*; the "Sally", or "Sally Rand", for *Saint Laurent*; the "Bones" for *Assiniboine*; the "Sag" for *Saguenay*; and so on. Over the years we sailed with most of them, and for our money the "Sally", when she was commanded by that austere, black-bearded patriarch Herbert Rayner, Commander RCN, was far and away the finest senior ship to sail with we ever knew. But the best-known was probably the Canadian escort group known as the Barber-Pole Brigade, variously led by *Ottawa* and *Skeena* over the years, with their distinctive barber-pole funnel stripping and their famous song, written by *Skeena*'s medical officer.

Perhaps nothing else is more redolent of the wartime camaraderie and team spirit of the old western ocean escort days than the Barber-Pole song, sung with rousing verve to the tune of "The Road to the Isles":

It's away! Outward, the swinging fo'c'sles reel,
From the smoking sea's white glare upon the strand;
It's the grey seas that are shipping under keel,
When we're rolling outward bound from Newfoundland!

Chorus (much waving of glasses):
From Halifax to Newfyjohn or Derry's clustered towers,
By trackless paths where conning towers roll;
If you know another group in which you'd rather spend your hours,
You've never sailed beneath the Barber Pole!

5
THE CHARACTERS

~~~~~~

The big wardroom at HMCS *Halo,* formerly the clubhouse of the Pictou golf club, was warm and crowded; the undertone of conversation was still subdued but becoming more animated as the crowd of officers and guests steadily increased. The officers of the training base were playing host to a very important guest on this summer Saturday afternoon, none other than Captain D himself, come all the way from Halifax on an official visit of inspection, and the base commander had pulled out all the stops to do him suitable honour.

In addition to officers of the establishment and their wives, all that was fairest and best in nearby Pictou had been invited to take part in the festivities, "and bright the lamps shone over fair women and brave men."

To grace the occasion, some of the magnificent wardroom silver had been brought down from the officers' mess at HMCS *Stadacona* in Halifax; in the centre of the room a tremendous silver punchbowl, alive with mermaids and porpoises and Neptune himself, dominated a table laden with flowers and crystal and snowy linen. The guests were animated but decorous, awaiting the arrival of the great man, who was expected at any moment.

Attention was suddenly drawn to the entry of a slim VR lieutenant. It was not so much the officer himself who drew the eye, but rather the expression of stern resolve on his pale features; here was a man, it was clear, who had some fixed purpose in mind and was determined on its execution, whatever the obstacles, whatever the cost.

After a moment's hesitation on the threshold, the young officer fixed his eyes on the central table. The die had obviously been cast, and his course now lay clear before him. With quick, purposeful steps he crossed the polished floor and stood before the massive punchbowl, which was flanked by a glittering mountain of glasses and vases and gladioli.

Tony "Tiger" Turner, for it was indeed none other, drew himself to attention with the exaggerated solemnity of the performer. Every eye was now upon him, and in the sudden hush one could sense the instinctive awareness of everyone present that they were about to witness something out of the ordinary, something really memorable. There was a snap and precision about the young officer's every movement which held the attention of the most casual, while in the minds of those who knew him, a sense of impending disaster paralysed the will. In mingled wonder and fascination, the distinguished gathering watched the performance now unfolding in its midst.

And what a performance it was! Staring straight before him, body erect and heels together, Turner placed a hand, palm downward, on the immaculate linen cloth on either side of the brimming silver bowl. He rose, poised, to the balls of his feet, paused, and then with a little cry, such as circus performers give, he sprang into the air, feet pointing ceilingward, supporting his weight on his arms. For an instant, he fought for control, then, gaining full balance, he stood inverted in a perfect armstand on the table, a magnificent living centre-piece.

There was not so much as a breath in the enraptured audience, as Turner, fighting to maintain control, slowly bent his elbows to lower his head into the punch and into the classic perfection of the headstand. Down, down went his curly head; up, up rose the iced pink of the punch, until it brimmed the bowl, lapped over onto the snowy white of the linen cloth. For just an instant—an instant that will live forever in the minds of all who beheld it—Turner held the full headstand. Then, like some mighty forest giant at the moment of its fall, the figure wavered, began to sway, to move, to topple.

God! What a fall was there—In one magnificent, mindboggling crash, Turner, glasses, vases, flowers, punchbowl, cloth, and table smashed to the floor in a tidal wave of pink punch, and inundation that engulfed and swept away all pretensions and inhibitions. The party that ensued, and into which a startled Captain D was swept on his arrival a few moments later, was of truly heroic proportions; nor was it in any way diminished when the founder of the festivities was discovered asleep an hour or two later, reclining at length, in full uniform, in a bath half-filled with tepid water. He had been ill.

Tiger Turner's headstand was widely celebrated in the wardrooms and messdecks of the corvette navy, but it was only one of the feats and triumphs of a band of characters who added such savour to life in the North Atlantic escort ships. Indeed, it is of these characters and their doings that old corvette types like to reminisce, at rare moments of reunion, long after serious aspects of the war at sea have been forgotten. It's not of admirals or achievements one likes to gossip, but rather of Harry the Horse, Pavillard, the "Mad Spaniard", Foghorn Davis, Two-Gun Ryan—

Was there ever such a centre of gleeful stories as Two-Gun Ryan?

Two-Gun—the origins of this nickname are lost in antiquity, but he was so known to everyone, everywhere, of high and low estate—had had a colourful and adventurous past long before he came to the Canadian navy in the Second World War. As a young officer in the Royal Navy, he had taken part in minesweeping operations in Russian waters in the ill-fated White Russian campaign against the Communists at the close of the First World War, and had been decorated for his services. After leaving the navy, he drifted into the Black and Tans, the para-military police force so execrated by Irish nationalists, and after a brief service in Ireland he turned up in New York. Making the most of his minor medal, his English accent, and his shadowy service in Ireland, he presented himself as a former undercover officer of Scotland Yard, decorated for various hush-hush missions in the service of the state, and on the strength of this he secured employment in private security work, eventually launching out on his own. When war broke out, he came to Canada, and because of his RN service twenty years before, he was commissioned as a regular-service officer with enormous seniority as a lieutenant-commander, later rising to commander.

For his superior officers, life became an endless problem of what to do with Ryan; he was perpetually in hot water, but his seniority had to be respected.

Two-Gun was a swashbuckler of enormous panache, blessed with outrageous gall, and with a disregard for the pretensions of authority which won him instant fame in the escort fleet. Once, when the Canadian destroyer in which he was serving was berthed alongside HMS *Vulcan*, the British depot ship in Iceland, an immaculate Royal Navy lieutenant, carrying his brass officer-of-the-watch telescope under his arm, came aboard to complain, in plummy upper-class accents, that smoke from the Canadian ship's funnels was fouling *Vulcan's* pristine paintwork.

Ryan's response was instantaneous. Sending for the enormous range-finder telescope mounted in the ship's gunnery director tower and girding himself with a borrowed sword, he hastened aboard the British vessel. Sword clanking on the deck from his sagging belt, and with a prodigious six-foot telescope clutched precariously under one arm, supported at each end by the smallest ratings he could find, he presented his compliments to the plummy-voiced paragon. He then begged leave to lodge a complaint against *Vulcan's* officers, who were in the habit of smoking and dropping their cigarette ash overside, thus befouling his destroyer's immaculate decks.

Two-Gun's career in command was brief but dramatic. As a result of the sudden illness of his captain, Two-Gun was put in charge of his destroyer for a convoy crossing, and instantly assumed the airs and honours of a very senior officer indeed. Arriving to join his convoy, he found it already under escort by the British group which Two-Gun's destroyer was instructed to join, and he proceeded to flash stationing instructions to the nearest British corvette. Stung by this assumption of authority by a Canadian interloper, the British escort commander at the head of the convoy asserted his seniority to Ryan and instructed him to take up a subordinate position on the screen. This did not sit well with Two-Gun; he would brook no ordering about by some RN puppy half his age. Firing off a signal to the senior officer, informing him that serious engine defects compelled immediate return to harbour, he cranked up to full speed and charged off homeward.

In response to an infuriated signal, ordering him to return to the convoy forthwith, Two-Gun, as he disappeared over the horizon, sent a blithe farewell: "Good-bye and good hunting!"

It cost him his command, of course, but in a rare moment of inspiration some appointment officer ashore found the ideal spot for Two-Gun. He was appointed technical advisor for a navy film being made by John Huston, and arrived in Hollywood, where he found himself in his element. He spent a good deal of the war there, starlets on each arm, cutting a dash as the swashbuckling wartime naval hero, full of salty stories of derring-do.

Unfortunately, even a Hollywood epic eventually gets completed, and Ryan then found himself out of a job. A desperate appointments officer, clutching at any straw, next sent him to act "in an advisory capacity" to a group of West Coast minesweepers being sent around from Equimalt to Halifax, via the Panama Canal. Ryan's wide acquaintance on the California coast, it was piously hoped, might prove useful to the little flotilla.

Useful was an understatement; the flotilla arrived at San Pedro, the port of Los Angeles, and, with Ryan as master of the Revels, settled down to the time of their lives.

Day followed festive day; the flotilla would have been there yet if indignant naval authority had not routed out the Canadian consulate and bundled the ships back to sea.

After passing through the Panama Canal, Two-Gun, who had by now appointed himself senior officer of the flotilla, with the eager acquiescence of all concerned, headed for the Caribbean, and the flesh-pots of Jamaica. Once arrived, the flotilla virtually disappeared so far as Canadian naval authorities were concerned; Two-Gun had settled in for a long stay and with the Glass Bucket, the Ligunae Club, and the Myrtle Bank under his lee, and with rum punches and sun and surf and rafts of lonely Wrens close to hand, no amount of signalled spleen from the Canadian snows was going to prise the ships out of Kingston harbour.

Eventually, an outraged headquarters was forced to send a senior officer to Jamaica to take over command of the flotilla and restore it to its duty. A chastened Two-Gun trailed back to Canada, and it was there that his naval service was abruptly terminated, thus bringing to an end a saga of glorious misadventure that still lives in the memory of old corvette types.

I have had the privilege myself of sailing with a few notable characters. One such was known to one and all as Sam, although this was not his Christian name. There was a craze for Damon Runyon in our group at this time, and our shipmate had been dubbed Sam the Goniff after one of Runyon's Broadway characters.

A delightful shipmate, Sam was the hero of a dozen notable adventures; he was born to trouble as the sparks fly upward. For one thing, when inflamed with the grape he had a tendency to overestimate his pugilistic prowess, and this cost him heavily, more than once. On one occasion, escorting a lady home from Captain D's cocktail party, he took exception to some coarse jests passed by a gang of toughs lounging around a Water Street lamp-post.

Their remarks, he told them, were an insult to the lady he was escorting; once he had seen her home, he proposed to return and teach them a lesson that would make finer, better-spoken men of them all. And by George, if he didn't attempt to do just that; depositing the lady at her home, he returned to the scene of his encounter, and to an astounded gang of roughs who could scarcely believe their good fortune. They were willing workers, however, and quickly fell to the congenial task of thrashing him, with fist and boot, to within an inch of his life.

This strain of physical abuse seemed to run, like a dark thread, through most of Sam's misadventures; no man shed more blood in the service than he. But his greatest moment was undoubtedly the dark night when, returning to the ship from an eventful run ashore, he missed his footing in stepping across to our fo'c'sle from the ship inboard of us, and fell between the two vessels.

He hit the water immediately opposite the open porthole of the first lieutenant's cabin on the inboard ship; a small tidal wave of oily water slopped over the port and splashed onto the face of Bill Ferguson, sleeping the sleep of the just in his berth below. Starting up in the pitch-black cabin, still only half awake, Bill realized where the water had come from and slammed the portlight shut, clamping it down to keep out any more waves, and promptly relapsed into slumber.

Angered by such a callous response, Sam pressed his face against the scuttle, shouting at the top of his voice and beating with his free fist against the steel ship's side. Alarmed and puzzled by this outcry, Bill sat up in his berth, switched on the light, and, turning toward the porthole, beheld a sight which he later maintained he would bear with him to the grave. Pressed against the streaked glass was a demonic face, its features writhing in the grip of some powerful passion, its black beard soaked and snakelike, its mouth snarling some fearful threat, inaudible through the thick glass. It was as though some demon of the deep struggled without, thirsting for his blood, and yet there was something vaguely familiar about those contorted features, those knotted whiskers—

It was a shaken, white-faced Ferguson who, moments later, assisted the quartermasters of the two ships to hoist a sodden, swearing Sam up and inboard. Restored to his own deck, Sam trailed off below without another word, his soaked cap hanging limply over his ears, leaving a little trail of oily water and the occasional orange peel behind him on the deck. It had been a full evening.

Jimmy Davis must surely have been one of the best-known, and certainly the best-liked, of all the officers of the escort fleet. With a face like a torn boot and a voice like a bull's bellow, he was everywhere known affectionately as "Foghorn Davis", and his inspired whimsy gave rise to some of the most cherished anecdotes of the ocean war. Like the Norse sagas, which they somewhat resembled, they tended to become embroidered and amended by legend, so that some of the details came to blur a bit with the passage of time, but the gist of them has survived innumerable re-tellings. Because his first command, the Fairmile motor launch Q 60, had been built in Orillia, the "Mariposa" of the celebrated Leacock *Sunshine Sketches,* he christened her *The Mariposa Belle.* Determined to make the most of his commanding officer status, even in so tiny a vessel, he had the four stripes of a full captain stitched onto a pyjama jacket he wore at sea, along with a row of bottle tops fastened, like service stars, across his manly chest.

He cut an even greater dash as a corvette captain; once, backing out from his berth and finding it awkward to turn his ship around in a busy Halifax harbour, he took her to sea stern first. The spectacle of his ship, with all hands correctly fallen in and standing to attention on fo'c'sle and quarterdeck while he saluted the Admiral, brought crowds of astounded onlookers to line the jetties and decks of ships alongside; sure enough, there was Foghorn Davis going to sea arse-end first, piping the Admiral in proper seamanlike fashion as his ship slid by at increasing speed.

Once, on a Christmas afternoon at sea, fellow members of the escort group were astounded to see Foghorn close to the convoy, bringing up alongside a big troop-carrying liner in the centre column. Through their glasses they could see the big ship's decks lined with troops, all eagerly looking outboard; faintly over the water came the sound of music and delighted cheering. Closer scrutiny revealed the cause of all the merriment: on his fo'c'sle deck, to the accompaniment of music blared over the ship's loud hailer, Foghorn was putting on a regular revue, with a chorus line of husky seaman, in brief skirts and elaborate head-dresses and the biggest false bosoms ever seen on land or sea. Foghorn's Christmas show for a shipload of delighted troops bound overseas became an established part of the Davis legend.

But equally famous was the anecdote of the earrings. During a run ashore in one of the escort ports with a fellow corvette type—was it *Calgary*'s skipper Hank Hill?—Foghorn is supposed to have conceived the notion that a small gold earring, such as Drake's sea-dogs used to wear and such are still seen in the ears of seamen in the Portuguese fishing fleet, would add a certain salty swagger. Accordingly, the two each had an ear pierced and wore in it a tiny gold ring, to the immediate consternation of their fellow-officers. But consternation gave way in time to secret admiration, then emulation; in no time, small gold rings began to appear in the two ships' companies.

It all came to an end one night when Foghorn was returning to his ship. The sentry who saluted him on the jetty, he noted, was wearing a gold earring. The quartermaster who met him at the gangway was wearing an earring, too, and so, he noticed, was every one of the group of returning libertymen just ahead of him. But the final straw came as he made his way along the deck; there, outside the galley, was the ship's cat, and in its ear was a small, glittering ring.

"That does it!" bellowed Foghorn, reaching for his ear. "Off they all come!"

But while Foghorn Davis was the hero of a dozen stories, lesser men had to be content to be associated with some single episode in the folklore of the corvette navy. Johnny Poulson, for example, is always remembered for his famous demonstration of football tackling, Canadian style. Poulson, a notable athlete, was discussing with a British contemporary in a Greenock pub the principles of good ankle tackling, as executed by a top Canadian outside wing like Wes Cutler, for example, compared with the clutch-and-grab method all too prevalent in British rugger. The argument that ensued continued after closing time, as the two made their way through the now-deserted streets toward the escort berths. As they turned into the top of the last street along their route, they encountered a milkman making his early-morning rounds, with a metal basket full of clanking bottles under each arm and his wagon following on behind, pulled by a large, somnolent horse.

"The idea behind our sort of ankle-tackling," continued Poulson, "is to knock the feet cleanly out from under, thus letting the victim's own weight and the law of gravity do all the work of bringing him down. Minimum effort for maximum effect."

As they made their way down, Poulson's eye was drawn to the milkman across the street, who was proceeding in the opposite direction complete with baskets, bottles, wagon, and horse. With sudden interest he measured the closing gap between them with a speculative eye. In an instant the fateful decision was made: now! Now was the time!

"Watch this!" he said, unbuttoning his jacket and handing it, together with his cap, to his astounded friend. Before any protest could be made, he was off; his friend could only watch, aghast, as the burly figure of the Canadian flew across the street and bore down upon the unsuspecting milkman, with his fragile load and plodding horse. Powerless to intervene, the sole spectator could only shout a warning to the intended victim, his mind reeling from the prospect of the coming collision, with its inevitable aftermath of broken glass and spilled milk.

Straight as an arrow the big Canadian flew until, nearing his quarry, he bent forward and launched himself, outstretched parallel to the ground, with all his force and weight directed the ankles of his hapless victim.

There was a crunching impact, clearly audible to the stunned spectator on the other side of the street, and then the bulging horse, watched by its astounded master, toppled backwards into a sitting position with a look of pained surprise on its long face, and with the legs of its tackler projecting from beneath its massive backside.

"Poulson's tackle" became a legend; the price of such immortality was three broken ribs.

Some characters are remembered for a word, a remark; "Pappy" Old was such a one. Back from an interlude on the Aruba oil run in the Caribbean, Pappy endeavoured to bring his corvette alongside ours with the tide, instead of stemming it, not an easy feat with a single-screw ship at an awkward berth. Pappy, a delightful, diminutive little man with a round, pink face, peered anxiously over the bridge dodger as his ship bore down on us at an alarming rate of knots; his first lieutenant, Jim Elmsley, a friend of mine, collected large numbers of men with fenders on the fo'c'sle for what he considered the inevitable catastrophe.

What followed had the quality of an endless, repetitive nightmare. The ship came to rest with stern sticking out and her bows riding over our fo'c'sle, grinding stanchions against anchors and rivets. Pappy would nip up and peek anxiously at the scene of carnage below him, then bob down to pass an order down the voice-pipe. He would go astern, and his bows would drag and grind along ours, to the accompaniment of twanging and crunches, while Elmsley and I, each on our own fo'c'sle, leaped about with fender parties.

A moon face, pink and worried, over the dodger: "Slow ahead." Twang! Bang! Boom! Crunch! Screech! Again the pink moon: "Slow astern." Screech! Crunch! Boom! Bang! Twang!

Minute after agonizing minute, Pappy's corvette sawed away at ours, while Elmsley sucked his teeth reprovingly and his anchor played hopscotch with our fo'c'sle railing.

In the middle of this ghastly performance, Pappy popped his head over the bridge and uttered his deathless remark: "You know, Number One," he said, addressing Elmsley, "I never should have tried this."

Ever after, even to this day, when landed in the soup on the golf course, in the office, or at home by an over-confident move, one can hear this classic remark from an old corvette type. There were many such situations in the corvette navy, and Pappy Old's remark was so apt that it was instantly caught up, and its creator became an overnight "character" on the strength of it.

Ivan Edwards was a character, too, but of a unique kind. He must surely have been the best-loved man in the navy, and certainly one of the few padres in the service still remembered. Protestant clergymen in the navy were generally a poor lot, either callow kids fresh out of college or failures unable to secure a good church ashore. The Salvation Army and the Roman Catholics did much better; they sent us keen young men of ability and understanding, and won trust and respect thereby. But the rest were a nondescript lot, incapable of comprehending the traumatic spiritual and mental experience of corvette crews in a North Atlantic winter. They would approach a harried first lieutenant in the middle of a hectic working morning with a request to "have a word with the lads", then loaf about the wardroom to cadge drinks and lunch.

Edwards was the opposite of these tiresome nuisances. An impressive fellow physically, he had been a first-class football player at college and in the Big Four, and he was tireless in organizing games and relaxation for cramped corvette crews.

But it was his sympathy and understanding of what these kids were going through, thrust from sheltered homes into a harsh, uncaring ocean as remote and elemental as outer space, where every treasured human value counted for less than nothing, where reason reeled and faith was tested to its utter limits; it was his instinctive comprehension of the gulf that separated lonely sea from comfortable shore that made Edwards unique. He was truly a Christian, and a delightful fellow to boot, destined, alas, to die before his time.

Like most men of the cloth, he had a relish for jokes with a clerical flavor, and it was he who first told us the joke that was later to become famous. The Protestant husband in a mixed marriage, it seems, was being taken by his Catholic wife to her church for the first time, and was nervous about the unfamiliar protocol. "There's no need to worry," she reassured him. "Just watch me closely, and do what I do."

Sure enough, things went swimmingly; the husband had no trouble in conforming to his wife's lead. Until, that is, he kneeled a little too far forward, and the hassock on which he intended to rest his knees slid backward, coming to rest between his shins. As the prayer went on he became uncomfortable kneeling on the hard floor, and reaching furtively between his legs, he groped for the hassock behind him. His squirmings distracted his wife, who hissed in an irritated whisper:

"What's the matter? Is your fly undone?"

"No," responded the husband, and then, as the thought struck him: "Ought it to be?"

Some people became characters because of a nickname— one of the founding fathers of the Volunteer Reserve was known affectionately to everyone as "Useless Eustace"—a disability, an affectation. Chummy Prentice was famous for the monocle screwed into his eye, but Ted Orde's eye was as celebrated as Nelson's. (You could always win a drink on the strength of Nelson's eye. He wore a green shade over his good left eye to shield it from strong light, not over the sightless right one.) Ted Orde had a glass eye, and at parties he would turn up with a supply of spare eyeballs in his pocket. As the evening progressed, he would pop in a replacement from time to time, each one successively more bloodshot, supposedly, he claimed, to match the progress of his good eye. At the climax of the evening, he would pop in an eyeball which had a bright Union Jack on its pupil, a spectacle so shattering as to cause women to faint and strong men to turn pale.

Not all the corvette "characters" were funny fellows; there were some nasty ones, and some tragic characters, as well. I was shipmate in one of the early corvettes with an intelligent, sensitive, high-spirited fellow, with an infallible flair for landing himself, and all about him, in trouble of one sort or another. He was the sort who would miss the last train back, who'd oversleep an early sailing, who'd discover, a thousand miles from friends, that he'd left his wallet on his bureau. A terrific fellow to be at a party with, as I used to tell myself when I'd haul him up from under the table at the Old Colony Club and half carry him outside. Once in the frosty air, he'd bounce up, all bright-eyed and sober, only to do an el foldo back in the warmth inside.

He missed a sailing once, and we were short-handed on a long convoy crossing over and back; everyone was furious at him. The captain thought he needed a better influence than the rest of us were providing, and was glad to see, on our return to Newfyjohn, that our boy had made friends with the bright young priest who'd just been assigned padre to the groups. Two nights later the priest, well sozzled, together with our friend, also brightly illuminated, drove an expensive automobile, not his own, into the harbour, whence the two—but not the car—were extricated by the gendarmes. The young priest was banished in disgrace to some clerical Siberia, and we had to leave our boy behind to face another court—an experience with which we became increasingly familiar.

After a reprimand, and a loss of seniority, he was posted to another ship, only to repeat the performance; a great fellow to have around at sea, but totally irresponsible when he was on the old juice, which was just about every time he was ashore. We'd hear of his escapades from time to time: how he'd lost all his uniform except a pair of trousers in Boston, and then, more serious, how he'd missed his ship again.

It was the last straw. A friend, staying at the Admiralty House for a course, told of meeting him there.

"What, here for a course?" he had inquired brightly. "I'm here for a court"

That was to be the last of all the gaiety that endeared him to us all. On New Year's Eve in the mess, with the sounds of merriment all about him, he had gone upstairs to the washroom. There, in some private purgatory of his own, this bright, erratic, and lovable youth, only a few months before peace would make a joke of all his troubles, blew out his brains; a crueller tragedy to all of us who knew him than the deaths of any who went down with their ships.

6
PORTS OF CALL

Esquimalt—Squiggley, the matelots called it—the lonely
landlocked harbour just outside Victoria, B.C., was the first
naval base we had seen, and we arrived there for gunnery
training early enough to enjoy it in its peacetime innocence.
Japan had not yet entered the war and the Pacific was just
that, thousands of miles away from the Battle of the Atlantic.
With its low, galleried brick barrack buildings enclosing the
upper parade ground, its polished brass, its white-painted
perimeters, its flowers and tennis courts and aura of sunlit serenity, Esquimalt's naval base, HMCS *Naden*, was a delightful
relic of the Edwardian Royal Navy that had somehow survived, like a living fossil, into another age, another continent.
Its wardroom had collected some of the most incredible eccentrics to be found anywhere. I still remember the introduction of a new chaplain dining in the mess for the first time,
who was asked to say grace by the presiding senior officer, a
red-faced Royal Navy type brought back out of retirement,
and grudging every moment of his service.

"For what we are about to receive," muttered the padre, as
we sat with bowed head, "thank God." It was the traditional
naval grace, brief and to the point, we thought, but it seemed
to infuriate the presiding officer. Hurling down his napkin,
his face an even brighter scarlet and his neck bulging with
rage, he bellowed: "By God, padre, we'll have none of your
papist nonsense in this mess! A simple 'Thank God!' will suf-
fice!"

It was an appropriate introduction to a collection of retired
RN types, of former China Coasters and assorted characters
as colourful as any we were ever to find anywhere; as very

junior VR sublieutenants, the lowest form of animal life, we tiptoed about the place and did our best to keep out of the way of all these choleric, hard-drinking characters who seemed to be in perpetual dudgeon, and endowed with vocabularies that opened ever new and more fearful horizons to our innocent ears. They included a mean, black-visaged type reputed to be a black-belt judo expert, a good man to keep clear of. We were to run into him later as a corvette commander in the Atlantic, where he was to go off his head and have to be locked, shrieking, in his cabin. There was the moon-faced retired lieutenant with the medal of the Victoria Cross on his chest, the only one we ever saw. He viewed the world through thick, frog-like glasses from the depths of his leather chair, and was reputed to have taken a motor-launch into Zeebrugge, after everyone else had left in the famous First World War raid, and brought away a lot of stranded big brass through a hail of lead. Nowadays he put away a bottle of Scotch a day. There was the old submariner who, glass in one hand, was perpetually wriggling the other about to demonstrate how he would slip away and evade the furious attacks of brother officers, all keen and determined submarine slayers. There was the crusty old gunnery type, whose ancient black leather gaiters and tiny Jellicoe cap were right out of a Victorian Whale Island, as were his muttered parade-ground asides, picked up by the newfangled loudspeaker microphones and made audible to a startled and astounded ship's company daily at morning divisions. But above all there was Commander Kingscote, base executive officer and the presiding genius of the place, surely the most delightful officer and finest gentleman to ever grace the naval service. A tall, rangy figure, with a craggy face and bushy, beetling brows, he had been a champion boxer in his day, and looked as if he could still handle anyone who came his way, but he had a warm heart, a ready sympathy, and a quick understanding, as well as a sunny disposition and a salty sense of humour. We all loved him, and would cheerfully have died for him; lacking suitable occasion, however, we carried kelp for him from the harbour edge to his garden on Saturday afternoons, and were rewarded afterward with tea in his pleasant home. Kingscote was the finest officer we ever met, a credit to Britain where he was born and to the Royal Navy which moulded him, and everyone, officer and man, who ever passed through *Naden* cherishes his memories of him.

Our West Coast service was a sort of idyllic interlude in a grim wartime period; a kind of never-never land where the most curious things seemed to happen. Being all dead keen, we made the most of every emergency. Like the day the boom-defence scow caught fire, and we volunteered for the fire-fighting party that went swooshing off, at a great rate of knots, to the little vessel lying in a cloud of smoke in the harbour entrance. Will we ever forget rushing around a corner of the narrow deck and coming face to face with a livid Commodore Brodeur, Commanding Officer, Pacific Coast, and ranked second on the Pacific only to God Himself, with his foot in a bucket of grey paint and filling the air with guttural French-Canadian curses!

Apparently Vic (as we called him behind his back) had decided to liven the boredom of an Esquimalt weekend by dashing off in his barge to oversee the firefighting efforts in person. He'd come hurrying around a corner and put his foot right into the open pot of paint some crewman had been using a few moments before. The spectacle of the Commodore shaking the pot from his foot and, without a backward look, getting stiffly down into his boat in a splatter of battleship grey we shall carry gratefully to our grave.

And who will ever forget the furious aerial sneak attack on the tugboat *Haro*, a day of infamy second only to Pearl Harbor? One Saturday morning we'd all been loaded aboard the *Sans Peur*, formerly the Duke of Sutherland's yacht and the largest warship we had at Squiggley, and had dashed off to sea, where we cruised up and down off William Head, with all guns crews closed up and lookouts eagerly searching the sky. It seemed there was to be a combined air-sea operation; the air force were sending over some planes to practise dive-bombing on us while our gunners practised laying and training on fast-moving aircraft. Minutes ticked by, lenghtening into hours; after tracking seagulls in their sights for a few minutes, even the keenest gunners grew weary, and relapsed into sullen, tooth-sucking silence. Finally, at eleven o'clock, it was clear to all there'd been a hitch somewhere and the air force were not going to put in an appearance; cranking up to full speed, we hustled back to harbour in time for afternoon make-and-mend, and the harbour entrance relapsed into its usual weekend somnolence.

The only sign of life, if it can be called that, was the ancient steam tug *Haro*, drifting on station as examination vessel at the port approaches. A solitary seaman on watch sat in a chair propped against the wheelhouse and picked his teeth in the sunshine; everyone else was below taking things easy.

An angry sound disturbed the noonday silence, grew louder, closer. Glancing skyward, the *Haro*'s watch-keeper caught sight of a handful of aircraft, flying high in tight formation; he watched with idle interest as they approached, opened out, began to circle overhead.

The air force, as usual, had arrived late; had someone misread the appointed time? In any case they had arrived for their exercise, loaded for bear, or at least with bags of flour for their dive-bombing markers. A ship, to these air-force types, was a ship, and there below them, in the designated area, was a ship, the only one in sight. The leading aircraft peeled off and screeched down in a shrieking dive, straight at the hapless *Haro*.

With wondering disbelief the *Haro*'s watch-keeper watched the plane hurl its flour bag straight at him, then pull up, only feet above the mast, and go screaming off, level with the far horizon. The bag burst squarely on the bows of the sleeping tugboat; in an instant its wheelhouse, its tarry deck, its whole forepart were covered in snowy white. The impact brought every crewman to the open doors and scuttles of the poor old *Haro*; in silent wonder they stood gaping while plane after plane came swooping down on them, sending bags of flour hurtling into the sea about them, or bursting on decks and upper-works. To the dumbfounded crewmen, it was as if the world had gone suddenly mad, a meaningless maelstrom of snarling planes and bursting bags, wrapped in clouds of swirling white.

The nightmare ended as quickly as it had begun; suddenly, all was silent again, and the dazed crew could take stock of the old *Haro*, now converted into a white ghost of herself, like some old spectral turtle. Squiggley's "Pearl Harbor" was over.

Not the least of *Naden*'s assets was a rich collection of colourful petty officers, nearly all of them long retired from the Royal Navy's Eastern Fleet and China Station, back doing their bit by shaping up this new lot into something like proper seamen. Just as the centurions made the Roman legions what they were, and ferocious drill sergeants built the Brigade of Guards, so it was petty officers who really made the Royal Navy. Who could ever forget Charlie Sweet, who taught us PT? "If I can do it," he would say, hurling his incredibly muscular frame into some impossible contortion, "you can do it." Who does not bear scar tissue inflicted by the tongue and eye of the redoubtable gunner's mates, the fearsome "One-Way" Street, the man-eating "Dickie" Bird? With their obsessive spit-and-polish, their fetish for doing everything by numbers, they were of the classic mould of the RN cruiser gunner's mate who, detailed to parade the ship's company before the medical officer for what was euphemistically called "shortarm inspection", concocted the famous drill for the occasion.

All hands were to be fallen in, he told them beforehand, in rig of the day, "with open vents". When the medical officer appeared they would be brought to attention and begin the drill, to a two-part cadence. "On the order 'One!' " he bellowed, "place the right hand smartly on the crotch. Then—wait for it!—on the order 'Two!' out cocks, and I wants to 'ear them foreskins come back with a click!"

From *Naden,* we proceeded up the British Columbia coast to Comox, where we lived under canvas on a sandspit and built a rifle range in sweltering heat while hundreds of burly ratings lay about in the shade, picking their teeth. This was the notion of our commanding officer, an incredible ex-RN lieutenant (retired) who, because of his enormous boots at the end of a long, skinny frame, was known to all simply as "Feets". It was Feets' fixation that officers should command entirely by example, not by orders, and he ran his lot of young toughs like a Girl Guide camp leader. He would attempt to get a boatful of midnight libertymen, returning from the beer parlours of Comox, to sing improving songs, even hymns. Nothing so coarse as "Roll Out the Barrel", of course, or "I've Got Sixpence"; no, he would start off on "Keep the Home Fires Burning", in a quavering falsetto, and insist that we, as officers, pitch in "to show the chaps how". To lift our own shaky tenor into the damp night air before a boatload of snickering sailors while Feets led us in what he believed to be "Onward Christian Soldiers" was an ordeal that left scars we bear to this day.

But we exacted our revenge upon Feets. The culmination of our musketry course was a field exercise; we were divided into two forces, one invading, the other defending, and turned loose to creep about the scrub and do one another in with tins of pebbles, which we rattled when we had a target in sight, to simulate light automatic fire. A third group was told off as umpires, and rendered verdicts, "Dead" or "Alive", on any close or questionable calls.

In practice, of course, once turned loose in the woods we all found a shady spot and settled down, as comfortably as we could, until somebody should blow the whistle and call "Time!" A group of our more desperate spirits who had settled down in a thicket with a deck of cards, peered out on hearing thrashing sounds and spied Feets himself, his ungainly frame bent nearly double, creeping through the underbrush seeking whom he might destroy. The card-players could scarcely believe their good fortune; waiting till Feets was right abreast of them, they let him have it right in the sweetbreads with a furious rattle of their tin of pebbles.

Feets gave it the big effort. Drawing himself to his considerable height, he placed a fluttering hand over his heart, then toppled headlong into a weed patch, as dramatic and moving an exit as any battlefield has ever witnessed.

"Dead," pronounced the umpire, and rejoined the card-players.

Prince Rupert, or simply "Rupert", as everyone called it, was our next port of call. We were based there in a patrol boat, formerly a twin-screw motor yacht, alternating patrols about the virgin wilderness of the Queen Charlotte Islands with long spells swinging around a buoy off Barrett Rock or Metlakatla Pass as examination vessel. When you could see the mountain tops, you knew it would rain shortly; when you couldn't see the mountain tops, it was raining.

The presiding genius of Rupert, and a most appropriate symbol, was a huge and very old totem pole which stood atop the highest hill looking out over the town. It was an incredible thing, signifying heaven-knows-what crisis in the life of the Haida Indians who had put it up there more than a century before. On the top stood a feathered chieftain, grasping his private parts in one hand and brandishing a tomahawk aloft in the other. Obviously, he was about to perform a rather drastic bit of surgery upon himself. Local legend had it than when a virgin should touch the pole, the chief's axe would fall. For years, every girl above the age of ten had touched the pole, but still the axe had not fallen . . .

Rupert in the war years still had much of the aspect of the gold-rush boom days; at night its streets were crowded with fishermen and lumbermen, together with sailors from the Fishermen's Reserve, gunners from the coast artillery battery, and soldiers from the Rocky Mountain Rangers, as hard-bitten a regiment as one could find this side of the Foreign Legion. In Rupert's rain-soaked isolation, drinking was the primary recreation, followed, not necessarily in that order, by fighting and fornication. The red-light section on the outskirts of town was known as "Over the Hump", and the girls there took time off every Wednesday afternoon to attend the weekly matinée at the movie theatre downtown; they would arrive in a body, amid cheery greetings, whistles, and feet-stamping from other spectators, and occupy a central section of seats set aside for them.

Rupert was a base of the Fishermen's Reserve, a body of fishermen enrolled by the navy, together with their boats, for patrol duties. They wore naval uniform and painted their ships grey, but otherwise bore their naval responsibilities lightly. The rum, intended to be mixed with water and issued daily as grog, and supplied to the ship in large kegs, was used instead as a sort of communal replenishment for the individual bottles which every man took with him for a run ashore; it was common for a Fishermen's Reserve vessel to go through its quarterly quota in a single night on the town.

Early in our stay at Rupert, a Fishermen's Reserve vessel arrived one evening, and instantly disgorged its entire crew uptown; by the time the last line was secured the only one left aboard as duty watch was a raffish tomcat, and he only because he'd been locked in the gallery. Next morning, the scene on the jetty was like something out of Kipling's "Danny Deever"; the ships' companies of every naval vessel in port were drawn up in hollow square while the base commander himself, resplendent in gold lace, slowly paced along the ranks in the wake of a heavily made-up young lady, a waitress from the Boston café. Someone in naval uniform, she claimed, had pulled her into one of the café's curtained booths and had his way with her; not, one should have thought who was familiar with that café's waitresses, such a difficult thing to do. Still, she had lodged a complaint and the commander himself, anxious for his service's public image, had come down to bring retribution, harsh but just, swiftly home to the miscreant. The little party paced along the pallid ranks, the girl, powdered and petulant, searching every face, the commander glowering in the rear.

By the time they reached the fishermen reservists, everyone present knew that they were close to the mother lode; surely somewhere among all those black eyes, those split lips, those bent noses, was her assailant. Surprisingly, the girl sailed right on past the worse of the walking wounded; the Rocky Mountain Rangers had been in town too, last night, and there'd been the usual friendly punch-up. But she found her man at the end of the line, and stood pointing, with an accusing finger, at the ship's captain himself! With a sheepish smile, the skipper was led away to his fate amid the admiring whistles, hoots, and catcalls of his crew.

It was on the West Coast that we were introduced to the bottomless fund of local knowledge drawn on by veteran coastal sailors. For years, ships of the Canadian National and Canadian Pacific, and of the old Union and Blackball lines, had gone charging through narrow, rock-strewn passages at twenty knots or better, even in thick fog. They did it by precise timing, carefully clocking passage time in good weather at every state of the tide in order to run the same route safely in bad visibility, and by a variety of practices based on the most detailed local knowledge.

We had seen for ourselves how ships traversed steep-sided narrow passages in fog by whistle echoes. The ship blew its whistle frequently, and steered towards the side from which the last echo was received. When the echo came back simultaneously from each side, the ship was in mid-channel; nothing could be simpler.

But the extent of local knowledge possessed by coastal pilots is best illustrated by the story of a steamship official taking passage on one of his own ships, and standing nervously beside his captain, who was taking the ship along at tremendous speed on a thick, foggy night.

Aware that soon a right-angled turn would have to be made, and anxious about the complete lack of any visible shoreline, the worried passenger asked the captain how he would recognize the turning point when it was reached.

"Ah, there's nothing to it," the captain reassured him. "Billy Harrison runs a grocery right on the point, and keeps a dog. I blow the whistle when we get close, and it makes the dog bark. When I hear Billy's dog. I know its time to alter course."

The shore official was appalled to learn that the ship's safety was dependent upon so seemingly slender a thread, but could only hope that the captain was right and that he would hear the dog in time. He joined the captain in the bridge wing, and strained his ear to catch any response as the ship began to sound its whistle.

Nothing. The whistle blew again; still no bark. A third

time—and there, far off, he could distinctly hear the barking of a dog! Excitedly, he turned with a smile to congratulate the captain, but his face fell when he noticed the captain still listening, a hand cupped to his ear.

"But captain! Captain! It's time to alter course! I heard the dog barking just now!"

"No! No! No!" the captain responded impatiently. "That's not Billy's dog!"

Hundreds upon hundreds of Canadian seamen enjoyed the experience, as we did, of bringing a newly built ship from the West Coast around to the Atlantic. Their ports of call—San Diego or San Pedro, or perhaps one of the Mexican ports—may have varied a bit, but one place they are sure to remember is Panama, on the western side of the isthmus pierced by the famous canal. Actually, there are two Panamas, and it was the older, ruined city, rather than the modern one, which fascinated us. For this was the city founded by the Conquistadores, those impossibly romantic figures with associations going back to Drake and Hawkins and the age of pirates. But it was Morgan, the most successful pirate of them all, who finally ended the reign of the old city; it never recovered from his devastating sack, and its great stone ruins lie, overgrown with jungle, all about the native shack-town that lingers on the site.

To someone like me, brought up on pirate stories in countless *Chums* and *Boy's Own Paper* serials, Panama was the most romantic place I had ever seen, and its great gold cathedral altar, once painted white to escape the attentions of Morgan's pirates, and representing the lives of who knows how many Indian slaves and Spanish soldiers, seemed the stuff of pure fantasy. But Panama is also famous for its Cocoanut Grove, a notorious red-light section lined with tiny wooden "cribs", where half-naked little Indian girls displayed their coppery charms and cried out for custom to the passing throngs. VD is endemic among the natives; indeed, it was from the Spanish Main that Columbus's sailors were supposed to have brought syphillis home to Europe for the first time. As officer of the day, it was my job to caution our libertymen about the dangers that lay in wait for the careless or unwary ashore. It seems curious, in retrospect, that a set of grown men, which included grizzled old salts from the China Coast and the River Plate meat trade, steeped in the curious vices of Yokahama and the Reeperbahn, should have accepted the prudish vapourings of a beardless youth with only the sketchiest notions of feminine plumbing, and whose encounters with the opposite sex were limited to a few crowded moments in a parked car. But the bonds of naval discipline are all-pervasive; my strictures were accepted with no more than the usual amount of eye-rolling and smirking. As my libertymen shuffled sheepishly ashore, I doled out condoms with all the sang-froid I could muster; after all, as seagoing sailors, weren't we all men of the world?

For the passage through the Canal, we were boarded by an armed guard, a swaggering fellow with a great service revolver carried assertively on his hip. As a non-belligerent, he said belligerently, the United States was taking no chance with the passage of armed men-of-war through the Canal; he was aboard to ensure there was no monkey business. We gave him a hard time, poor fellow. It was bad enough that we had to fight a chicken-hearted America's war for her without armed guards being sent aboard to terrorize honest sailormen, we told him, and plied him with rum and food. He fell asleep after lunch in the wardroom, when Harvey, the junior sub-lieutenant, and I, representing the baser element in the mess, stole his revolver and substituted a large, overripe banana in its holster. Such a dither when he awoke to find his beloved pistol gone! We took pity on him at last, of course—it would cost him his job, he assured us—and restored the weapon to him in time for him to hasten ashore in Colon, a thoroughly chastened man.

Kingston, Jamaica, was our next port of call. Italy had just come into the war, and we were based there for a time as one of a force patrolling the Caribbean to intercept Italian ships trying to make a run for home from the U.S. Gulf ports. With all its buccaneering connections, it was a most romantic place, particularly the naval dockyard at the harbour entrance to Port Royal. Now it ruins, it was once home for a host of famous British admirals. Lord Howe had been there, of course, and so had Rodney and Hood and Cornwallis, Saumarez and St. Vincent and the great Nelson himself. A tablet in the wall of Fort Charles, an old battery defending the harbour mouth, reminded us that we were walking in Nelson's footsteps, and urged us to honour his name and remember his fame. With its old signal tower, its sagging roofs and crumbling buildings, the deserted dockyard was a place of infinite romance, enormously appealing to us.

Indeed, we enjoyed our stay in Jamaica; the Myrtle Bank, biggest and best hotel in the island, had been taken over by a branch of the Admiralty and was full of paymasters and nice British Wrens, while a Canadian regiment, the Winnipeg Grenadiers, was on garrison duty there. The regiment was later to be sent to Hong Kong, to be decimated in the horrors of Japanese prison labour camps, but they were lively company for us in Kingston and we saw a good deal of them in the wardroom, particularly the resoundingly named Captain Hook. At Kingston we made the acquaintance of bum-boat women, twentieth-century versions of Little Buttercup, who came aboard to hustle our laundry and set up little stalls alongside to flog souvenirs to gullible matelots. They also dished out cards advertising a wide variety of services ashore—tailors, cleaners, and the like—including such coyly worded invitations as that for "Daisie's Drinking Parlour—drinks, dancing, and you guess the rest!"

But what fascinated us were the cards listing barber services: "Hair dresser to royalty", and then would follow an impressive list of royal notables, from the turn of the century to the present. It turned out that these were princes who had been barbered while serving as naval officers in visiting men-o'-war. We hastened ashore to the establishment with the most resounding list of royal personages on its card, and had our hair cut in a funny little shop looked down upon by a whole gallery of faded photographs of Edwardian admirals and young sprigs of royalty, all bearded like the Pard and all, we thought, viewing the proceedings with a decidedly fishy eye.

Jamaica was beautiful, but the natives were something else; they struck us as surly and morose, with none of that cheerful bounce and light-heartedness that seems so characteristic of the people in the smaller Caribbean islands. A lot of them seemed perpetually dazed with drink or drugs, and there were too many glazed eyes and sullen mutterings for comfort.

Bermuda, our next stop, was a pleasant contrast: small and civilized after all the vivid colour and latent violence of the tropics, and with surely the most pleasant and prosperous native community. We berthed here at Ireland Island, a vast dockyard complex which had been the base of the Royal Navy's West Atlantic Squadron—the one with the rumbustious song, famous in naval messes the world over—during all the long peacetime years of the British Empire. Now used only to service birds of passage, like ourselves, it was a fine example of that amazing chain of superb naval bases spread all around the world by the Royal Navy for its coal-burning fleet, each link within handy steaming distance of the next.

Lying in an enclosed dock while we were there, we could not use the ship's heads and relied instead on toilet facilities built on the shore alongside, and designed to accommodate the ships' companies of a whole squadron of large capital ships. A veritable pantheon of plumbing, it stretched in a long row as far as the eye could see; an endless line of toilet cubicles, all neatly segregated and labelled into a rigid hierarchy.

Such variety of choice. We strolled past dozens of doors, all properly labelled; not for us the seamen's or signalmen's or stokers' facilities, nor those set aside for chief and petty officers. The label "Gunroom officers"—as lowly one-stripers, we were technically such—made us hesitate, but why should we share facilities with scruffy RN snotties and subbies? Next door were premises for lieutenants, but from observation we knew they were not up to much. "Commanders", now—that had a nice ring, and you were likely to meet a nicer class of people there, but it was next door to the facilities set aside for commanding officers, and we did not wish to poach on the privacy of our own skipper. Further on—ah, there was our proper niche! "Flag officers"—it had a nice ring to it; if you're going to go, go first class. It became a point of honour for us henceforth to use the facilities set aside for flag officers; just sitting there, on the seat used before us by all the admirals, was to savour the greatness of our imperial past. We sat, like as not, on the very seat used by Cunningham and Pound, by Beatty and Jellicoe, Fisher and Lord Charles Beresford. Why, surely King George v himself must have been there before us? It was fascinating to conjecture, so that a visit to the shore heads quite made our day.

The presiding genius of the base was Trammy Lee, a lean, elderly Royal Navy lieutenant-commander who seemed to run the whole base himself. Certainly nobody else seemed to be about except this gangling figure, who used to appear, pedalling his bicycle down the deserted quay, with a small terrier carried in the metal basket on the handlebars. Trammy—his nickname, famous throughout the fleet, was due to the circumstance of his having been born on a tram—was one of the RN's eccentrics and something of an old woman, but it was surprising what he could get done in the way of stores or repairs when he got down to it. He was a little severe to us on arrival, having just had an unhappy experience with a

Canadian armed merchant cruiser whose crew had proved a
bit fretful, but we got him down in the wardroom and he
mellowed a bit. He was full of an impending move to
Jamaica; he wasn't at all sure that Susan would settle in
there, he told us. He wanted to move, but Susan was dead
against it; they had until the weekend to make up their
minds. We muttered something sympathetic about wilful
wives, only to learn that Susan, on whose decision everything
seemed to hinge, was not his wife but his dog, the little terrier
who went everywhere with him.

Bermuda was lovelier then than it became in the postwar
years; apart from a few service vehicles, there were no cars
on the island, and the blight had not yet carried off all the
beautiful cedars. A little narrow-guage railway ran from St.
George's at one end of the island to Hamilton at the other;
the ride, along the very edge of the coast, was a delight in the
little open-air coaches. The Canadian navy took over part of the
base later in the war as a base for winter work-ups of
newly commissioned ships. Most of us, at one time or another, were to experience the high winds and driving rain that
are a feature of a Bermuda winter, while huddled at an exposed anchorage in the tiny harbour of St. George's or outside in Five Fathom Hole. Bermuda is a terrible place to
approach, with fearful coral reefs far off the land, and only a
narrow, buoyed channel winding through the coral around to
the capital, Hamilton. One fellow we knew, making the journey around in his new corvette, had been desperately searching for the next buoy marking a turn through a torrential
downpour. Spotting the marker in the driving rain, he altered
course around it and put himself high and dry on the coral;
the "marker" had been a floating crate.

Ireland Island was abandoned when we saw it after the
war; grass was growing through the cracked pavements, and
roofs were beginning to sag. Its great days as a naval base
were a dream, its admirals so many ghosts in the echoing
buildings. But surely, if it was haunted, it would be by the
shade of a spectral bicycle, bearing an elderly rider and his
elderly dog along the lonely jetties and basins over which
they watched for so long.

New York, farther north, was a base we were to come to
know well. Most Canadian ships and seamen were put on the
triangle run, at some stage in life, for their sins. You were
based at Halifax, sailed out to Western Ocean Meeting Point
south of Newfoundland with an eastbound convoy, traded

that for a westward convoy bound for Boston and New York, then trundled back with a third convoy bound for Halifax, home, and beauty. You got the worst of the weather—it got colder and the seas grew steeper as you neared the continental shelf—and all the trouble of meeting and forming up three convoys instead of one on each trip, but the one redeeming feature of the hated triangle run was that you had a good chance of a few days in New York. Gene Kelly and Frank Sinatra sang it for all of us: "New York, New York, it's a wonderful town!" Well, in the war years, at any rate.

If you needed repairs, you went upriver to the Brooklyn Navy Yard, but for most of us the escort berths were all in Staten Island, across the harbour from the big city. It took a long time, but the ferry ride across was lots of fun; after all, that spectacular skyline is something to see, and the harbour traffic, with its big liners and battleships, was always exciting. The long, long rides on the shabby subway weren't much fun, and they meant that any run ashore was going to take some time, but we got accustomed to a night on the town, a long run back to the ship, shave and shower and breakfast, and so ready for the new day. Being young helped.

Of course, we did all the mandatory tourist sights, Radio City, and so on, as well as the big tourist traps like the Latin Quarter. But with expérience we managed to carve out some particular niche for ourselves; each group had some particular nightspot where each run ashore wound up. A marvellous officers' club operated at Delmonico's, with food and drink and music and the most dazzling girls imaginable; a great place to get acquainted. For some reason or other, our escort group adopted Jimmy Kelly's as its rendezvous, a little bistro in Greenwich Village that vibrated to a solid beat that virtually eliminated conversation. With other ships, it was other places; the *Mina*'s wardroom, for example, headed in a body for the Hotel Pierre, where Xavier Cugat, the Cuban king of the rumba, held sway. Cugat was an accomplished cartoonist as well as a bandleader, and he ran off marvellous crayon caricatures of his *Minas* fans; in return, their wardroom in harbour resounded to "one, two, three, kick!" records night and day, and any visitor on entering was likely to be tossed a bongo or a pair of maracas by Johnny Kingsmill and expected to pitch in. New York was everyone's favourite port of call, although a bad place to be in its frequent fog. I remember heaving to off the Ambrose light-vessel, waiting for some unseen ship to get clear of the channel. Nearer and nearer she came, her deep-toned siren so loud and close that it seemed to shake the very air. Suddenly, only feet away, a tremendous cliff towered over us, so high that it cut off the sun filtering through the fog. For a heart-stopping moment the *Queen Mary* hung above us, so close that we could see every scuttle, every rivet-head, filling the world with the roaring sound of her passage through the water. Her siren boomed out, high above, and then she was past us, bellowing out to sea like some maddened bull elephant. If you ran into anything off New York, it was likely to be something pretty solid.

To most corvette types, St. John's, Newfoundland, was home. Western base of the mid-ocean groups, frequent port of call for escorts on the triangle run, and supply base for the support groups of frigates and destroyers, its jetties were jammed with the fighting craft of every Allied nation, and the harbour centre was cluttered with merchantmen in for emergency repairs. For months, a ship was berthed at the trot-buoys with a torpedo hole blasted clean through her at the water-line, a hole so vast and cavernous that motorboats crossing the harbour used to take a short cut right through her. Even now, after the passage of so many years, one has only to close one's eyes to see—and smell—and hear—it all again: the reek of cod, the shrieking gulls, the rows of salt-stained hulls, three and four deep, along the South Side wharves; the misty sun, warm on the pale greens and pinks and whites of Western Approaches camouflage, the shades of grey of ships from other commands. Escorts berthed on the south side of the harbour, at the foot of the bare hills which fruit-starved sailors used to comb for blueberries in season. Astern of us the big Portuguese sailing ships, crammed with cod from the Banks, would lie before making the long passage home, their decks crowded with friendly brown-faced seamen from the Algarve. Merchantmen berthed at the quays along the north side, or in the city itself, or underwent repairs at the yard at the top of the harbour. Huddled in out-of-the way corners were the antique steamers of the sealing fleet, pencil-thin funnels rising from clipper-bowed wooden hulls. Lying derelict at a dilapidated wharf was the hulk of the *Calliope*, once a famous sloop-of-war in the Victorian Royal Navy and later a drill-ship, now housed over and used as a salt-storage hulk, with an old Hotchkiss gun drooping forlornly from a casemate. It was a busy, animated scene, full of the sights and sounds and smells of the wartime North Atlantic, and a fascinating place to be.

We were a polyglot bunch at the escort berths; British and Canadian ships mingled with Polish and Norwegian destroyers, Free French corvettes. The Poles were fire-eaters, and their ships, named for thunder and lightning and the like, reflected this flair. They also enjoyed a reputation as tremendous womanizers; the standard joke was of a Polish officer who, after exchanging names with a girl he'd just met, exclaimed: "Enoff of thees loff-making; let's fock!"

The Free French were something else; their ships stank like a stable, and they thought nothing of urinating on the deck. We would watch, fascinated, as sweaty French seamen would struggle out of dirty clothes, douse themselves in fragrant lotion, then pull clean jumpers over their unwashed torsos and go ashore looking like a million dollars. With their striped jumpers and red pompoms, their uniforms had a flair and flamboyance all their own. But their emphasis was on panache rather than cleanliness; even on a lowly corvette, they saluted their ensign at "Sunset" and morning "Colours" with a bugler. Although the bugle itself was green and battered, and the bugler grubby in shabby gaiters and stained uniform, it completely outclassed our measly bosun's pipe. And they got the job done; their corvette *Aconit* bagged two U-boats in a single crossing.

The cream of the crop were the Norwegians; they had so many top officers and experienced men for so few ships—a handful of old British destroyers loaned them by the RN— that they were reputed to use full commanders as watchkeepers. It was a treat to watch them come alongside, with hardly a word spoken; everyone knew his job and did it quickly and quietly.

In the later afternoon, when the day's work was done, we used to poke along the jetties seeing what ships had arrived, and visit with old friends. In couples or in groups, off we'd trudge for the long walk around the head of the harbour to the city, and the fleshpots of Newfyjohn. These were few in number and austere in amenities, but nonetheless they were savoured to the full. One could—and did—send a telegram from the cable office to one's girl back home in Canada or go shopping in Bowring's or one of the other delightfully Victorian emporiums along Water Street; where else could you select a pair of Eskimo-made sealskin boots out of an odoriferous barrel?

A favourite café along Water Street advertised "The best milkshakes east of Boston"; since they were also the *only* milkshakes east of Boston, the claim was a valid one. As a concession to the curious tastes of Canadian and American customers, hot dogs were also prepared at a steamy glass partition behind the marble-topped counter, but upstairs in the dining-room everything was starched British gentility. Groups of sailors from Poland, Norway, and Senegal mingled with cropped Canadian youngsters at the little tables, behaving with the decorum expected in such surroundings; flowered wallpaper and potted palms provided the decor and elderly waitresses in starched uniforms served the tables. From time to time a little phonograph in the corner was re-wound and another Strauss waltz was played as a discreet background for polite conversation.

It was all like some vanished English tea-room, glimpsed in a fading sepia print in a Victorian snapshot album, and we loved it. Nothing could have been in greater contrast to the rough masculine world of the messdecks than this primly spinsterish place, and fellows from the ships packed it, night after night. After that, one could climb the steep hills to either of the two movie theatres; Jimmy Cagney was very big at "The Popular Star", as one of the houses modestly called itself. There were lots of big and bouncy and popular dances for enlisted men at the Caribou Hut, or at the fine modern hostel run by the K. of C. people. The terrible fire which destroyed it, and snuffed out so many young lives, was one of the war's real tragedies. For the escape arrangements had broken down, and youngsters died in queues at the very exits.

Choice was more limited for officers; mostly we picked our way down to Water Street to make the great climb up the famous fifty-nine steps of the spindly outside staircase that led to The Crowsnest, in a loft high above the old Outerbridge warehouse.

If any single place could be said to be the heart of the corvette navy, the Crowsnest, officially entitled the Seagoing Officers Club, would be it. Certainly it was home to all of us in the escort ships; a place you could drop into at any time of day or night and be assured of a welcome, a drink, or a simple snack—the hot ersatz eggs and Spam sandwiches were always good—from the assiduous Gordon and his wife, who presided there. Dozens of enormous leather armchairs were scattered about the bare floor, and grouped about the fireplace, with its comfortable padded fender. The walls were resplendent with the crest of every escort ship in the western ocean; original works of art, most of them, and always worth a tour of inspection to see what new ones had been added since the last visit. In a corner, the head of a large spike, "Spikenard's Spike", protruded from the floor; it had been driven in there by Shadforth, commanding officer of the corvette *Spikenard*, during a nail-hammering contest on his last night ashore before *Spikenard* sailed. She was torpedoed and lost with all hands, and her spike in the Crowsnest floor was retained as a memento of absent friends.

Although Newfyjohn was a naval base of world significance, it wore a curiously impermanent air, like a travelling tent show. Unlike the vast and inconsequential base built by the Americans in the wilderness of nearby Argentia, there were no naval shore facilities at St. John's. Mainguy and his staff operated out of the Newfoundland Hotel, the ships berthed at the rickety South Side wharves, and training and repair facilities were housed in a depot ship provided by the Royal Navy. HMS *Forth*, a magnificent modern depot ship with every sort of machine shop and repair facility as well as crew training and amenity space, was our first ship's home on the South Side, and she was replaced by HMS *Greenwich*, an older, smaller vessel. Unlike the army and air force, both with big permanent installations, the navy at St. John's seemed to operate out of its hat; when it closed up shop at the war's end it left nothing to mark its passing but a tradition and a few genes in the Newfoundland bloodstrain. But for all of that, Newfyjohn lives on in the memory of thousands of corvette sailors as a warm and outgoing place, the home of hospitable and friendly people and of the finest, most efficient escort base in all the North Atlantic.

Its counterpart at the other end of the mid-ocean "milk run" was Londonderry, in Northern Ireland. To arrive at Derry after a hard east-bound crossing was a little like approaching the pearly gates. After rounding Inishtrahull, you picked up the green and pleasant coast. The sea calmed as you approached the estuary, and off-watch officers and men shaved and changed into smart shoregoing uniforms. Carpets and linen cloths reappeared in the wardroom, open scuttles admitted air and sunlight to stuffy messdecks. An air of cheery expectancy filled the ship, and it was wonderful to feel the luxury of clean, soft shirts after living for weeks in clothes stiff with salt. And then you entered the mouth of the river Foyle, and the wonderful green land enfolded you.

God! How green Ireland was; the Emerald Isle, for sure! After weeks of flat, grey horizons, grey seas, grey skies, how marvellous to be wrapped about with green hills, trees, fields! Even the old ruined castle tower on the nearby shore was draped in ivy and called—what else?—Greencastle. The sounds of the shore were indescribably sweet: the ecstasy of soft birdsong, after shrieking seabirds!

The Foyle must surely be one of the loveliest of rivers, an escape from the sea unmarred by industrial ugliness. In the escort groups, we filed upriver in a state of bliss, enraptured by the beauty of fields and flowers and trees growing right to the water's edge; truly, Mother Earth had clasped us to her warm bosom after all the perils and privations of the sea! We fuelled at a tanker off Moville, a little estuary village, then picked up a pilot from his tiny skiff for the trip up the narrow, winding river to Derry itself, a beautiful old city in a lovely valley setting. On the outskirts, in a stretch of walled gardens running down to the water, we would come in sight of a fine old country house lying in extensive grounds. Instantly, from an upper window would come the bright officious winking of an Aldis signal light, for this was Boom, or Broome—nobody seemed sure of its correct spelling—Hall, home of the Wrens who staffed the base so efficiently, and who also included some of the finest and fastest signallers in the business. The winking light would send along time and place of that night's dance—there was always a dance in Derry—and our signalman would respond with the number of fellows we would be landing to attend, and another fine party would be in the making. If we were arriving after office hours, the lawns would be alive with uniformed girls waving and calling out to the passing ships. It was the final touch needed to bring us back to the wonderful world of the shore; by the time we rounded the final bend and came in sight of the escorts crowded at their berths along the western bank, all our weariness, all the fatigue of the long trip behind us was forgotten. Home is the sailor, home from the sea. . . .

Everyone loved Derry; the shops of Shipquay street, the battered beauty of the old cathedral, the cheerful chatter of the Shakespearean Cellar bar, the soft laughter, lilting voices, and fresh complexions of its Irish girls! Nice, old-fashioned girls, too, who took a dim view of any "larking about", but were always ready for a dance or "the pictures" or a Sunday picnic in the soft green loveliness of the Irish countryside.

Stop-overs in Derry were all too short, and busy with

painting and storing and training, yet they had an idyllic quality that captured the imagination of the most prosaic. It is said that when the last of the escort groups sailed down-river from the empty base at war's end, every Wren lined the lawns of Boom Hall, waving—and weeping—as the ships filed by. And the men waving from the ships—they wept, too.

Earlier in the war, we had been based at Greenock, a suburb of Glasgow which, with its streetcars and cheery bustle, seemed a sort of Scottish Toronto. Later, at Iceland, we were based at Hvalfjord, around the corner from Reykjavik, or Rinkeydink as everyone called it, and a more dreadful anchorage it would be hard to find. There were no shore facilities and everyone tried to anchor off in a fjord so deep that good holding ground was impossible to find. Mid-winter gales would be funnelled down the anchorage from the mountains all about us, shrieking blizzards that blotted out everything and sent ships dragging down into each other or into the minefields. The destroyer *Skeena* was blown onto the reefs in a midnight gale and was lost with fifteen men, drowned in blinding snow and sea. This nighmarish place had an appropriately eery sentinel; far out at sea a great tooth of jagged rock stood out of the grey waves, its towering top swirling with seabirds, their plaintive cries somehow em-phasizing the desolate loneliness of this tiny pillar of land in the vast desert of the ocean.

Iceland was a ghastly place, particularly in midwinter, and the people there, even the frosty blondes at the Hotel Borg's dinner dance, were as cold and inhospitable as their barren land. Our only touch of warmth was to be found in the wardrooms of *Hecla* and *Vulcan*, the American and British depot ships, respectively, where good food and good company brought a ray of civilized comfort into this bleak and savage place. We made a lot of friends, too, among the American destroyers stationed there in their pre-war "neutrality patrol" days: the *Reuben James* and the *Kearney*, both later tor-pedoed; the *Simpson* and the *McCormack* and the *Broom*. They seemed to us, with their peacetime complements and primitive instrumentation and weaponry, like something out of the Stone Age; who will forget the shock of seeing their funny little "Y" guns, as they called their depth-charge throwers, used as a rack for securing mops and deck gear? The truth is, the Americans never did catch up in anti-subma-rine warfare; after the bloodbath off their Atlantic coasts following their entry into the war, all Atlantic convoying was taken over by British and Canadian escorts, with a few U.S. coastguard cutters thrown in, because the United States needed its ships in the Pacific. The Pacific belonged to them, we felt; the Atlantic to us.

Apart from the principal bases, most Canadian seamen had some particular favourite port of call. For some it was Horta or Ponta Delgada in the Azores, those mid-ocean mountain tops where escorts would sometimes visit briefly to refuel. Being Portuguese, they were neutral, and a little gunboat would puff out fussily to check out the most powerful man-o'-war arriving off the breakwater. The contrast between these semi-tropical paradises, with their flowers and fruit and music, with the wintry wastes of the North Atlantic we'd left behind was unbelievable. To leave a hard-pressed convoy one night and be dining ashore on an open-air terrace the next, amid good food and wine and with the moon rising behind the awesome peak of Pico, was like a kind of magic, as was the Merry Widow setting of sidewalk cafés, mosaic pavements, and gold-laced officers in tasselled knee-boots from the turreted fort, sipping hot chocolate in tall glasses.

For some seamen, Quebec was the favourite port of call. We were based there briefly, escorting troopships to the new air bases being built at Goose Bay in Labrador and Thule in Greenland. Quebec City, with its pretty girls and gaiety, its Grande Allée and Dufferin Terrace, its parties at the baronial Château and picnics at Montmorency Falls, was a delightful place, and the war seemed far away. About the only "military" we saw were the "Quebec Highlanders" as the local girls wryly referred to the loose-gowned monks from the city's numerous religious orders. Yet it was out of this bright and beautiful city and its placid St. Charles basin that we lost a lot of ships, and one fateful night on the Labrador coast, our "chummy ship", the corvette *Shawinigan*, vanished in a moment, torpedoed and lost with all hands; so many friendly, familiar faces we would never see again.

My own particular favourite was the old naval base of Devonport at Plymouth in England. It was a wonderful place to come into from the sea, turning sharp left at the Eddystone and sailing into the beautiful Sound, surely one of the world's loveliest harbours. We always felt the drama of the war at sea when entering or leaving that harbour, steaming past the great natural grandstand of the Hoe and its terraces, thick with crowds of strollers. With the ship in good trim and crew fallen in, fore and aft, in smart rig of the day, we felt ourselves the cynosure of all eyes in a real showcase of a place after the drab anonymity of most naval ports. Then up into the Hamoaze, an estuary heavy with history, and the dockyard, cradle of half the British fleet, with its great basins and drydocks filled with vast battle-wagons bearing famous names and in various states of disrepair, like duchesses caught with their hair down and their corsets off. In a grubby little office ashore at Flagstaff Steps, an elderly Captain D, with an even more venerable Wren as apparently his sole assistant, ran a good part of the Channel war, sending flying squads of cruisers and heavy-gunned destroyers off on raids against enemy shipping, and escort groups of fearsome power and prowess off to make life miserable for any U-boats rash enough to enter his part of the Channel. The contrast with our own base staffs, where every assistant had several assistants and it took an act of God to authorize movement of a garbage scow across the harbour, was a refreshing one to us, as was Captain D's brisk and informal greeting when you called at his office for orders: "Morning, *Camrose*; little job of work for you today!" He'd then send you halfway round Europe on the most complex operation.

Lying at Devonport, you were in the heart of a great naval base, with a big city fire-bombed into a kind of garden centre, behind it. Yet you could drift off in the ship's whaler in the opposite direction, and sail up the St. Germans river into the most idyllic of English countrysides.

Devon, glorious Devon. For our money, Plymouth was the best base of all.

7
THE OLD FIRM

~~~~~~

We met the Royal Navy's Home Fleet returning to its Iceland lair after hunting *Bismarck* to her doom. Our group were bound in for Hvalfjord after bringing an eastbound convoy across, steaming along in line abreast in the gathering darkness of the late Arctic afternoon.

The fleet caught up with us from astern, their silhouettes popping up above the misty grey of the distant horizon. First there had been the aircraft, carrier-borne planes these, rather than the long-range aircraft we were accustomed to meet so far out at sea. In tight circles they thundered low over the water, searching ahead of the fleet on a broad front, and after them had come the destroyers: big, modern, heavily gunned fellows, not the salty veterans we were familiar with in the Western Approaches. On they came, a dozen or more, zigzagging by a timed pattern, lean and hungry and ferocious, like a pack of hungry hounds. Behind them came the cruisers, the most beautiful of ships, the triple turrets and raked funnels of modern light cruisers mingled with the rather Victorian silhouettes of the bigger County and Town classes. Our bridge quickly overflowed with officers, some with binoculars and others bent over our dog-eared copy of Jane's, identifying these new and glamorous visitors to our realm. Famous names they wore, but look there, astern of them! Here came the big fellows, the great battlewagons with their attendant carrier: the twin-funnelled silhouette of the *King George* V, and the prodigious, triple-turreted mammouth that could only be HMS *Rodney*.

It was an awesome sight as the great fleet swept up our starboard beam and passed us; a blend of speed and power, of science and fighting purpose, the like of which none of us had ever seen before. The fierce destroyers, the magnificent cruisers, all speed and swift striking force, and then the awful menace of the great battleships and the hulking carrier, the very embodiment of brute strength and punishing power.

It was *Rodney* that drew our fascinated gaze: that prodigious fo'c'sle, seemingly half a mile long, dominated by those three immense turrets, mounting nine of the greatest guns ever fitted in a battleship, the enormous sixteen-inchers which had literally shot *Bismarck* to pieces. Behind this endless fo'c'sle, that pyramid of turrets, rose a huge tower of armour plate—and then the ship came to an abrupt end. She was all bows, all bite up forward, with nothing behind it; a great, misshapen, malformed monster waddling past, yet so awesome in her pugnacity that she was utterly magnificent. The great dark shapes swept past us, disappearing in the gathering dusk ahead and leaving us bobbing in their wake. It was dark night when we crept up Hvalfjord into our anchorage; nothing could be seen of the fleet that we knew lay all about us.

But such sights—and sounds—as greeted us next morning. Hvalfjord must be one of the grimmest, bleakest anchorages in all the world, rimmed about with snowy wastes and great ice-peaked mountains. Yet this ghastly place was gay with colour and sound; all about us lay the great capital ships of the Home Fleet, their quarterdecks bright with sauntering officers and pipeclayed marine guards. Marine bands marched and countermarched across the vast teak decks as if on parade, the bright brass and silver of their instruments winking in the pale northern sunshine, the music bright and gay as they played popular light music and brisk Sousa marches. From the corvettes, we stared enthralled at this cloud of butterflies that had settled into our bleak base. Speedy motorlaunches plied from ship to ship, surging alongside spotless teak gangways, or lying at the boat-booms rigged out from each ship's side. It was the magic half-hour before the ceremony of Colours began the working day, and officers promenaded their quarterdecks, taking the air after breakfast, and sailors leaned over the rails, enjoying the last cigarette before turning-to.

From a dozen ships, a dozen bugles, amplified by a hundred loudspeakers, sounded; the ritual of Divisions was about to begin the official service day.

We watched spellbound as the beautiful pageantry unfolded, so familiar from our training days ashore but so much more significant here at sea, in its proper setting. At a word, ten thousand men were suddenly capless, their heads bowed in prayer. At a command, soundless from our distance, the sun flashed on the serried steel of hundreds of bayonets as marine guards presented arms. And then, across the water from each ship, came the slow, measured, mellow music of "The King". From each ship's deck enormous white ensigns, startling in their purity and vivid with the red and blue of their crosses slowly climbed the great stern staffs, each capped with a bright gilt crown. Never had the symbolism of this moment, the reverent act of subservience by all the ship's company to the great standard which embodied nation and sovereign and service, impressed us so deeply; for the first time we could understand the worship which the legions of Imperial Rome had rendered to their legionary standards, enshrined in their own chapels; to men bound in disciplined service, the standards which embodied their corporate dedication were objects of compelling devotion. The moment quickly passed; the ensigns were made fast, the ships' companies dispersed to their myriad duties, and the marine bands marched themselves off parade to a lively quick-step.

We had been privileged to see the two faces of the Royal Navy. The reality of sea-power; the raw, brute force concentrated in a fleet of enormous ships and aircraft, we had seen on a dark winter's afternoon; this force, lying in this remote place, embodied the command of the seas of the western world, controlled the destinies of millions of people unaware of its very existence. The other face was that of the hallowed routines and traditions and pageantry which the Royal Navy carried about with it, bringing order and beauty and civilized standards to the bleakest Arctic anchorage, the hottest sun-baked atoll.

It was easy to lose sight of the purpose behind the charm, to regard, as some silly people did, the navy as effete, a Victorian anachronism in a harsh twentieth-century world of air power and total war. But nobody who served with the Royal Navy had any such illusions; they knew from experience that the RN was not merely tough and competent and professional, but ruthless, too. What other navy would snuff out a potential threat from a former friend, as the British did at Oran when they attacked the French fleet, or send a battleship through all the hazards of a narrow fjord to exterminate a nest of German destroyers, as the Admiralty did with *Warspite* at Narvik? For all its old-world grace and charm, the Royal Navy would cut the throat of its grandmother if it served its interest, and you'd better believe it!

The truth is, the Royal Navy is not a mere fighting service at all, in the ordinary sense of the word. It ranks, with the Catholic Church and the Roman legion, as one of the supreme creations of human organizing genius, an institution which simply defies comparison with its contemporaries. It is the mother and father of all the world's navies; there is not, today, a single navy whose organization, uniform, terminology, tradition, and technique does not stem from that of the British Royal Navy.

The Royal Navy is as much a state of mind as a collection of ships. For all its traditional reticence and modesty, "winning" is what the Silent Service is all about, and all the long centuries of accumulated triumph have induced in the service an assumption of ultimate victory particularly galling to rival navies which know themselves to be superior by every material standard. The Italian battle fleet was a superb, modern force, for example, vastly superior to the First World War antiques which were all the British could muster in the Mediterranean, yet always it was the British who sought, the Italians who dreaded, an all-out confrontation. There was never the slightest doubt in British minds—or in Italian!—as to the ultimate outcome, whatever the apparent disparity in material strength. The RN had tremendous élan, enormous confidence and morale, and we found that it rubbed off on the least of us who flew the white ensign. We were proud of being Canadian, of course, and painted maple leaves on our funnels to make sure we got the message across to the Limeys, but for all of that we were very proud to be a part of the big show, a Canadian branch of the old Grey Funnel Line, a member of the White Ensign club, and a sharer of all that marvellous mystique that went with it.

The Royal Navy's air branch demonstrated another curious aspect of the Senior Service. To visit the Fleet Air Arm was to walk back in time to the beginnings of military flight, when the first scout planes were flown over the trenches of the First World War by daring young men from the Royal Naval Flying Corps.

So far as we could see, nothing much had changed in the Fleet Air Arm since. At the RCAF base in Dartmouth we had watched, without interest, a succession of sleekly modern aircraft thundering off to go about their various chores, their an-

nonymous crews concealed inside their great cabins. These
were air-force machines, but in a lull between their comings
and goings we saw a knot of men wheel a little airplane out
onto the tarmac. A few minutes later it went whizzing along
past us and soared aloft—a tiny single-engined biplane, all
canvas and wire and open cockpit. Its two-man crew were
gloved and helmeted, its observer in the rear waggling an
old-fashioned Lewis gun on a scarfe mounting, and, by God,
its pilot even had a long silk scarf trailing back in the slip-
stream. Up, up, and away! After the Red Baron! We had just
been privileged to see the navy's Fairey Swordfish in action,
and to anyone brought up, as we had been, on a diet of boys'
stories of Spads and Fokkers and Sopwith Camels, she was
simply irresistible. Why, it was *Wings!* and *The Dawn Patrol*
all over again; like Richard Barthelmess we knew it was
madness to send a boy up in a crate like that.

On closer acquaintance, of course, we grew to respect the
little Swordfish and her skilled and gutty crews. We watched
them land on the rearing decks of tiny Woolworth carriers
swept by winter gales, saw them tip the balance of the U-boat
war in our favour as they bridged the "Pit" far from land-
based air cover. But always we adored them as an anachronism, a reflection of the instinctive RN tendency to cling to
the old, the tried-and-true.

But if the Swordfish took one back to the brave days of the
First World War, the navy's Walrus transported us back to
the very Stone Age of flight, to the primeval beginnings of
the powered aircraft. The Walrus had to be seen to be believed, as we found for ourselves when we inspected one
aboard HMS *Rodney* in the anchorage at Hvalfjord. It was a
stubby, two-winged amphibian not much bigger than a can-
vas-covered canoe, which it closely resembled, and it was
powered, if that is the word, by a tiny engine mounted behind the pilot and his observer, turning a wooden propeller
which *pushed* the aircraft, rather than pulled it in the normal
manner accepted by God and man. It was sometimes suggested by irreverent sailors that its crew also had to pedal with
their feet to keep it aloft, but this does not appear to have
been the case.

Yet whatever the Walrus may have lacked in speed and
power, it more than made up for in its method of launching,
as we found when our host aboard *Rodney*, glancing at his
watch, urged us to down our drinks and go on deck to see
the fun. We did so and joined the crowd, all in carnival

mood, gathered about the old Walrus perched on its catapult amidships. The two Fleet Air Arm officers who formed its crew were checking out final details, assisted by suggestions from the onlookers. (Be sure to wind the elastic, mind.) In their oil-spattered overalls and air of dedicated purpose, they were regarded by their shipmates with affection and not a little awe, appropriate to the practitioners of an art bordering more closely on the occult than on modern science.

Eventually, the plane's crew aboard, catapult trained outboard, and spectators removed to a respectful distance, the engine was started and the wooden blades whirled around to a noise like that of an outboard motor. In his open cockpit, protected only by a tiny windscreen, the ashen-faced pilot gestured with his hand. There was a tremendous explosion, a cloud of acrid smoke, and the Walrus was no longer with us. We had just a glimpse of two goggled heads being snapped backward by the explosion and of the little machine being hurled into space like a sack of potatoes, and then there was simply nothing there.

The Walrus had been projected overside by the force of a gun-cotton explosive charge, only to fall like a stone out of sight. But from somewhere beneath the deck came a sound like an angry wasp; there was a rush for the rail, and from there we could see the Walrus, its engine flat out, skimming bravely over the sea at a pace markedly faster than a man could run. Minutes later it had gained masthead height, and was still climbing manfully upward. It was scheduled to circle the anchorage before landing on the water alongside and we wanted to stay and watch, but our host was wiser, in the ways of the Walrus.

"Come on below and have the other half," he urged us. "It takes the ruddy thing half the day to fly all the way around the anchorage."

His advice proved sound. When we stole a peep outside five minutes later, the Walrus was only just beginning its circuit, and it was not until nearly lunch-time that the little machine landed and taxied across the water to the ship's side. It was quickly hoisted inboard by the ship's crane, and the two intrepid birdmen were gently led below by sympathetic shipmates who pressed restoratives into their hands. The whole thing had been a harrowing adventure, fraught with every sort of peril, and we were conscious of having witnessed an achievement comparable with the first flight of the Wright brothers at Kittyhawk.

There was a whiff of the primeval in everything the Royal Navy did, from flying to flushing a toilet; it was another facet of the legendary Royal Navy mystique.

I remember a glimpse of a man who, perhaps best of all, was the living embodiment of that mystique. He had been knighted and made an admiral by the time we saw him, and ours was surely the smallest ship in his whole command, but for all that it was a great thing to have served under him and we were proud to make the claim. Rear-Admiral Sir Philip Vian was the very image of the dashing naval officer—bold, resourceful, and, above all, successful. More than that, he looked the part—tall, lean, hawk-faced.

It was Vian who had taken *Cossack* into Alten Fjord, laid her alongside the prison ship *Altmark*, and sent a boarding party *armed with cutlasses* to carry off scores of liberated British seamen in the teeth of hostile gunboats and vacillating politicians. It was Vian's destroyers who had hung on to *Bismarck* all through that long, fatal last night, snapping at her heels and delivering her, exhausted and without hope, to her waiting executioners next morning. It was Vian who, with only a handful of light cruisers and destroyers, had held the Italian battle fleet in play and brought his vital convoy through unscathed in the Battle of Sirte: "The most masterly naval action of the war", according to his superiors. It was he who commanded a thousand ships—nine hundred and ninety-nine and *ours*!—in Overlord, the greatest amphibious assault in history, and who went on to command the British carriers in the final operations against the Japanese fleet. Oh, he was a great man, right enough, but what finally established him as a living legend was an incident that happened when he was commissioning a new ship in Scapa Flow, and had assembled the ship's company about him on the quarterdeck for the traditional first-day pep-talk.

As he spoke, a diesel drifter, one of the boats that lugged potatoes and brussel sprouts and other vital supplies out to the anchored ships, went plugging along near by, its one-lung diesel engine growing louder and more obtrusive as it approached.

"Now listen to me, you chaps," said Vian.

Punga! Punga! Punga! went the diesel, louder than ever.

It was too much. Vian stopped, turned dramatically, and bent his fierce glare upon the offending drifter. Incredibly, impossibly, the drifter's engine choked and stopped; it drifted on in sudden silence.

Without any further ado, the great man turned back and resumed his address. Henceforth, his reputation was made; on the lower deck, they knew he could walk on water if he wished to do so; success would attend his every venture.

Yet for all his dash and glamour, Vian, like Cunningham and the rest of the great admirals, had to yield pride of place to a relatively junior officer who had risen from peacetime obscurity to become the one real naval genius of the Second World War. No one man won the Battle of the Atlantic, but certainly no one man did more to win it than Captain Frederick John Walker, Royal Navy. It was one of the war ironies that this great man, the Nelson of his age, should have lived and died virtually unknown outside the service, while lesser men enjoyed public acclaim and world recognition.

Walker was, in every sense of the word, a genius, and all his many and remarkable gifts were concentrated in the special field of hunting and killing U-boats. He had an uncanny gift for anticipating the moves of his underwater antagonists, but it was his original mind, which devised new and devastating anti-submarine techniques, that truely set him apart. It was Walker who was the first, and most enthusiastic, proponent of the support groups: forces of highly trained ships which would act outside the close escort of convoys and, freed of any responsibilities for the safe passage of the convoy, could concentrate on hunting and killing U-boats. It was Walker who refined the depth-charge attack into a fine art, a matter of infinite precision and deliberation, and who developed the famous "creeping attack," in which one ship steamed slowly astern of her submerged prey in constant asdic contact, and directed a consort onto the target, where it subjected the invisible U-boat to a devastating and concentrated rain of depth-charges. It was Walker who developed the notion of an élite group of specially designated ships, the finest available, fitted with the latest devices and crewed by specialists.

Walker built his famous Second Escort Group into the most efficient, the most successful, team of sub-hunters and killers ever seen. His group simply annihilated all the U-boats in its path as it swept across the Atlantic, or lurked "in the deep field" astern of a threatened convoy. On a single trip across, his group sank six submarines, and took the entire crew of one of them prisoner. He became the dread of the U-boat crews; once in contact, he never gave up, turn and twist as the U-boat would. "The Boss", as he was called, would preside inside a ring of escorts established about him, and, the U-boat contacted, he would call out ships one at a time to "have a go". If the ship failed to produce results, he would send her back to the patrolling ring and summon another in her place. A brooding, solitary man, he was given to moments of inspiration, and he had the courage and confidence to act on them.

But above all, it was the precision of his attacks and his resourcefulness under difficulties which set him apart from lesser senior officers. In a celebrated instance, gaining contact with a U-boat late one night after an arduous and tiring day, Walker detailed two ships to maintain contact with the enemy while off-watch officers and men got some much-needed sleep. "We shall attack at 7:30 a.m. and sink her before breakfast," he announced, and the following morning he did just that. The attack began precisely on time, and at ten minutes to eight the group were gathering bits of flotsam from the destroyed U-boat as evidence of another kill, before sending hands to breakfast.

On another occasion, off Iceland, he was faced with a U-boat operating so deep that the group's depth-charges were unable to get below her before detonating. Depth-charges are fired by a hydrostatic pistol; water enters a tiny hole as the charge sinks and detonates it at the desired depth. Walker solved the challenge of the too-deep U-boat in his own way. He put a dab of soft soap in the hole of his depth-charge pistols. The extra sinking time required to wash away the soap was sufficient to take his charges deep enough to destroy the U-boat; "The Boss" had done it again!

I remember late in the war, seeing EG 2, Walker's renowned group, leaving St. John's harbour for sea. Beautiful ships they were: new Bird-class sloops, with lots of free-board to carry the armament and instruments in the wild Atlantic weather.

Starling was Walker's own ship; the others bore names like *Woodpecker, Wren, Wild Goose, Cygnet, Kite*. They were beautiful ships, beautifully maintained, but it was the élan and esprit de corps of the crews that really set EG 2 apart. As the ships turned into the wind, the pennant numbers hoisted at one yard-arm would suddenly vanish and simultaneously be broken out on the other and leeward side, so that the pennants should at all times stream clear of the rigging. Everything was done at the jump; lines and fenders disappeared like magic; as the group filed down harbour, in tight formation, crews fallen in smartly fore and aft, the ship's loudspeakers blared a brassy rendition of "A-hunting we will go". It was a tremendous spectacle, and I was lucky to see the group at its peak; within days Walker, who virtually lived on his bridge night and day, was dead of exhaustion. But his spirit and techniques were an inspiration to all of us in the Western Approaches.

He was borne out to sea for the last time in the destroyer *Hesperus,* to the shrilling of bosun's pipes, while the crews of ships in the Gladstone dock lined the rails, with heads bared and bowed. In the funeral oration earlier in Liverpool Cathedral, Admiral Sir Max Horton, commander-in-chief, Western Approaches, had delivered his epitaph: "His spirit returns unto God who gave it. Not dust nor the light weight of stone, but all the sea of the Western Approaches shall be his tomb."

A different sort of naval occasion was the August 1941 Atlantic Charter meeting of President Roosevelt and Prime Minister Winston Churchill at Argentia in Placentia Bay. Our group was taken off its usual mid-ocean milk run, and sent round instead to Argentia, then just a fog-shrouded dent in the south coastline of Newfoundland, as escort to the Shell tanker *Clam.* We soon learned that the *Clam* was to rendezvous with *Prince of Wales,* the big new British battleship, which would be carrying Winston Churchill together with the chiefs of staff and the British cabinet to meet with President Roosevelt and their U.S. opposite numbers. When we arrived *Clam* went in and anchored, like a placid cow, off the thickly forested coast; the rest of us stayed outside and patrolled the wide, fog-bound entrance.

The Americans were first on the scene: *Augusta,* a cruiser, with the President aboard; the cruiser *Tuscaloosa*; and the ancient battle-wagon *Arkansas,* a strange old relic with those distinctive American basket-work masts. They went in and anchored while the destroyers of the escort joined us in our endless quadrille across the harbour mouth, their senior officer, the *McDougall,* nattering away to our senior officer, Desmond "Bejeezes" Piers, in the destroyer, *Restigouche,* about the upcoming revels.

Eventually, the principal guest showed up, the dark outline of the big battleship looming out of the fog. But she was ahead of schedule; the Americans had neglected to shift onto local Newfoundland time, and weren't expecting Winston's lot for another hour and a half. Accordingly, the PM and whole platoons of politicans and top brass had to pace up and down outside in cold dudgeon while their hosts finished the breakfast dishes and got everything ready. Promptly at nine a.m. *Prince of Wales* showed up again on the doormat and was welcomed in, and since she came with even more destroyers, we thankfully handed over our screening chores and went inside to join the party.

And quite a party it was, with bugles and bands all over the lot. The big marine band aboard *Prince of Wales* played "The Star Strangled Banner", as Bill Harvey insisted on calling it, and *Augusta*'s band responded with "The King". Winnie waved the V-sign across the narrowing gap between the ships, and Roosevelt gave him the famous big smile, complete with jaunty cigarette holder, and sent a boat loaded with cigarettes and other goodies from peacetime America for the crew of *Prince of Wales*. The contrast between war and peace, between rationed austerity and peaceful plenty, was apparent in the ships themselves. The *Prince* was dark and somber, her brass painted over; the U.S. ships sparkled with bright brass and white decks, and at night—miracle of miracles—they shone with light. It was incredible to realize that this could be done safely here; with a feeling of something like guilt we opened our own scuttles and black-out screens to let the cool fresh air in and the light out to shine on the dark water. It was a strange, dreamlike interlude in the dark ordeal of war.

Although she carried Winston and a regiment of top brass, it was the *Prince of Wales* herself who was the hit of our show. She was then the most modern battleship afloat, and we couldn't wait to get aboard for a look over her. Fortunately, Ralph Ripley, a former great Varsity quarterback and a friend of ours, was serving aboard as a junior—very junior!—radar officer, and we wangled an invitation to lunch, and were duly impressed as Ralph led us on a tour of her electronic marvels, blinding us with science at every turn.

She was vast and complex, infinitely sophisticated, but she lacked the brute strength, the sense of primeval power that we'd felt in *Rodney*. We were awed by the ingenuity and intricacy of *Prince of Wales*' control systems, but all the same their very complexity made one slightly uneasy. In the stress of war, simple things are best; we'd learned to distrust some of this over-sensitive electronic gear, which always seemed to pack up when it was most needed, and we gathered from Ralph that the *Prince*'s teething troubles, which had so humiliated her in her brush with *Bismarck* before she was properly worked up, had still not been completely resolved.

It seemed significant, somehow, that when the crunch came half the marvellous gear aboard *Prince of Wales* collapsed in a shower of sparks and blue flame, while the simple, straightforward slugging power of the *Rodney* shot great chunks out of *Bismarck*.

Still, for simple country boys fresh from a corvette, the *Prince* was strictly Buck Rogers stuff, and we enjoyed her hugely, so much so that the following morning, a Sunday, we were happy to return with church parties sent over by each ship for the elaborate services to be held on *Prince of Wales'* vast quarterdeck. Like everyone else, we goggled at all the bigwigs sitting in chairs in the front row, along with Franklin Roosevelt and Winston Churchill, or immediately behind; there was a good bit of shuffling about among the luminaries to get themselves into a position befitting their rank and status, a kind of gold-laced version of the navy's old evolution of "tallest on left, shortest on right, *size!*" Between hymns, there was a good deal of surreptitious whispering as onlookers tried to identify the more prominent of the many personalities here assembled; was that dyspeptic really Admiral King, and if that fellow who looks a little like Joe E. Brown is General Marshall, who's the little runt in air-force braid and buttons? There were all our own chiefs of staff, of course—Dill and Pound and Freeman, Cherwell and Cadogan—but the President had brought a group of civilians with him whom we recognized from old copies of *Life* magazine: Harry Hopkins and Sumner Welles and Averell Harriman, as well as his own armed forces chiefs. One way or another, it seemed that all the principal talents, political and military, of the western world had been assembled on the quarterdeck of this tremendous ship, anchored in total wilderness completely isolated from the civilized world beyond. Everybody present was keenly aware of the historical significance of this occasion, that this meeting of powers was unique in our time and obviously of the greatest consequence to the future course of world events.

Everybody that is, except for the two chaplains, one British, the other American. Between them, they conducted one of the most interminably tedious services it has ever been my misfortune to have to squirm through. Neither seemed to have any concept of the uniqueness, the significance, of the occasion, neither conceded so much as a passing reference to the great events here in train. Instead, we prayed for everyone and everything under the sun: for politicians, great and small, and for all the usual intangibles so dear to the hearts of clergymen—wisdom and peace and understanding, etc. On and on they droned, while the matelots in the back rows fidgeted and sucked their teeth, and even Winston seemed restless. It was a frightful bore, but it was enlivened by two rousing hymns, chosen, as it later appeared, by the PM himself. We all stood and roared out "O God, Our Help in Ages Past", which seemed to draw both Yanks and Limeys into some common cause, and we closed out the service with a real rouser, "Onward, Christian Soldiers". The marine band really laid into this one, and everyone seemed to sort of catch the spirit: at the final, "On, then, Christian soldiers, on to victory!" Winnie was waving his hand about like an orchestra conductor, and all the bluejackets were shouting at the top of their voices. We all ended up out of breath but with a feeling that we'd somehow accomplished something. Score one for Winston.

Afterward the band marched itself off with a rousing quickstep, and all the hundreds of visitors found their way down into the boats lined up alongside to return to their ships. But Debbie Piers, our senior officer, gathered some of the officers from his group under his wing and led the way into the *Prince of Wales'* cavernous wardroom. Here Roosevelt and Winston were holding court in a circle of admirals, generals, and air marshals, with mere captains and commanders scrambling around the fringes trying to catch a glimpse of the great men in their midst.

It was here that Piers showed his mettle. Whatever his other virtues as escort commander—and we had sailed with lots worse—he was second to none on the social circuit, and not one to be put off by a parcel of over-age soldiers who'd picked up their limited social graces sipping bourbon and branchwater at some sun-baked camp in Kansas. Elbowing his way through all the heavy brass, Debbie approached the Great Man, interrupting Winston in mid-sentence; would they, he inquired, like to meet the officers of their escort, the men who brought them here? It was one of those questions which had only one answer; in no time at all we were lined up, furtively wiping our palms on our trouser legs, and introduced one by one to each of these demi-gods, with Piers doing the honours and each of us being treated to a warm handshake and a bright smile.

Afterward we were led away in a kind of daze, and gulped restoratives in a quiet corner, eyed, rather irritably it seemed to us, by legions of regular service officers, whose red faces and gold lace attested to their vast seniority. That a clutch of whey-faced colonials, probably milk-drinkers to a man, with only a spindly single band of lace on their cuffs, should have hob-nobbed with the Lord's anointed, and in *their* wardroom, obviously galled them. And when they caught sight of Jackson's red lapel-patch, you could see them blench: a grubby-collared reserve midshipman, the lowest form of pond life, normally tolerated only in some smelly gunroom; were they to be spared nothing?

The atmosphere becoming distinctly oppressive, we were glad to take our departure, walking, it seemed, about six inches above the deck. In the boat home, we broke into hilarious chatter, elated by our glimpse of greatness, and traded reminiscences of what FDR had said to this one of us, or what Winston had said to that. Jackson, the lone midshipman in our midst, vowed that he would not wash his right hand until the war's end; the hand that had shaken those of President and Prime Minister, he felt, should be preserved in its pristine condition. However, he later withdrew his vow when it was pointed out to him, perhaps unkindly, that snotties' personal habits being what they were, his gesture was likely to go quite unnoticed among his seniors in the wardroom. But we knew just how he felt; all of us could hardly wait to get a letter off home, and for years we could draw all eyes at the bar when we began a conversation with: "The last time I chatted with Winston . . ." or "Franklin told me himself . . ."

For us, after that, all was anti-climax. Even the ringing phrases of the Atlantic Charter with its lofty delineation of human rights, the coping-stone of the Atlantic Alliance drawn up at Argentia, failed to impress men who were, so to speak, personally acquainted with the President of the United States and the Prime Minister of Great Britian.

We were patrolling the approaches when the *Prince of Wales* sailed past us on her journey home; we watched her fade into the evening twilight, tall and sombre and majestic. It was to be the last time that any of us would see her. . . .

Curiously, the news of her sinking, not so many months later, thrown away with *Repulse* by an admiral's miscalculation, an error obvious to the merest middy, seemed shocking but not really surprising. For the truth was that *Prince of*

Wales was a loser; in all we had heard of her, seen of her, she appeared to be a kind of lemon. Ships take on character and personality by some indefinable process; some ships— *Warspite, Cossack, Rodney,* our own *Haida*— "had it"; others, somehow, did not. *Prince of Wales* was tarred with the ignominy of failure from the first, when she was hustled into a confrontation with the world's most formidable warship before she was operationally ready. Her crew untrained, her armament and equipment untried, and with gangs of civilian dockyard workers still aboard trying to complete installations of turrets even as they were being trained on the enemy, she failed to avenge her consort after *Hood* blew up, and was forced to draw off with some of *Bismarck*'s shrapnel in her. She had been humiliated, through no real fault of her own, and unlike the rest of her class she never really achieved a success. We thought that at Argentina she was sloppy and unimpressive for a flagship carrying so many distinguished passengers; that enormous crew should have been able to lick her into better shape for such an occasion.

Her loss didn't move us; what really shook us was the loss of so many friends, new and old, and particularly Ralph Ripley, surely the nearest thing to an All-Canadian Boy our generation produced. A star athlete at school and university, he was a fine scholar and leader of men; we were proud to be his friend. In the Royal Navy, as in any human institution, error was inevitable, but the damage entailed was fearful. For as Kipling remarked, blood is the price of admiralty, and the RN paid it, bravely and unstintingly. Sometimes, as with the *Prince of Wales,* the price was just too high.

Yet it was the Royal Navy itself which wrote the noblest epitaph to Ripley, and to all the other young men of every commonwealth country who went down with its ships. On the Royal Navy's memorial on Plymouth Hoe, where all their names are listed, thousand upon thousand, is the Biblical text: "All these were honoured of their generation, and were the glory of their times."

8
THE CRUEL SEA

~~~~~~

They brought *Candytuft* slowly up the harbour, leaning heavily on the tugs alongside, like an injured player being assisted from the field of play, and berthed her at the ramshackle jetty on the South Side of St. John's. It was there that we visited her later in the afternoon, filled with horror and speaking in low voices as one did in the presence of the dead. There was nothing markedly wrong with her appearance above decks, apart from a marked list, but there was something ghastly about her for all of that. It was her silence, for one thing, and the darkness that wrapped about her deserted messdecks; the ship was absolutely still, with the silence of the dead, without the background hum of fans, the myriad vibrations of busy machinery, which in a ship is the breath of life. Somewhere deep in her bowels a clang reverberated through her, as the shore party probed her inky depths for what they dreaded to find; long power cables snaked from the shore down her stokehold hatch to light them on their way.

But it was the stench that was the ultimate horror—the smell of cooked meat, somehow faintly familiar and odiously appetizing, that pervaded the ship and hung over her jetty; she was like an enormous stew-pot that had cooked her crew in her own superheated steam. In shocked silence we watched from the wharf while the remains, wrapped in blankets and held together in basket stretchers, were winched up from her blackened stokehold, her blistered wardroom flat, her peeling cabins and corridors. *Candytuft* had experienced the ultimate terror, the nightmare that disturbs the slumber of thousands of young sailors, sleeping for the first time among the pulsating pipes and hot fittings of a crowded steamship. Aboard

112

Candytuft, the nightmare we had learned to ignore had come true; her boilers had collapsed and engulfed her sleepers in a burning cloud of live steam. A mechanical failure, an inattentive stoker, and suddenly a disciplined and purposeful man-of-war screening the flanks of an Atlantic convoy had been transformed into a hissing, scorching hell, where helpless men went shrieking to their deaths in clouds of burning steam. The exploding boilers had carved in the great bulkhead separating the stokehold from the wardroom flat and the officers' cabins, flooding the space with superheated steam and killing men as they slept.

Later, in the lime-washed serenity of a hospital ward, *Candytuft*'s young midshipman told us how it had been on that fearful night, his cheerful, fresh young face at odds with his bandaged hands, enormous as baseball mitts, which lay above the blankets. He had been asleep when the boilers had gone, he told us, but had been awakened in his bunk by the noise of the explosion and the collapsing bulkhead. Dazed as he was, he had yet had the remarkable presence of mind to dive beneath the blankets when the first wave of live steam had come shrieking into the flat, and to stay there until the all-engulfing cloud had passed. Wild with terror, he had emerged later to find that the burning steam had risen to the deckhead above, forming a thick and growing layer overhead. He had tumbled out just as the lights died, leaving the ship in darkness save for the faint blue glow of the emergency lighting. Realizing that he would have to make his escape immediately or be trapped in his cabin by the ever-lowering cloud of steam above him, he wrapped himself in a blanket and made for the door. Peering out into the dim-lit alleyway, he found it running deep in scalding water; in his bare feet, he could never have made it to the ladder leading to the upper deck and outer air. It was then that this fresh-faced youngster, the cheerful companion of many of our pleasant runs ashore, showed what he was capable of. With incredible coolness, he had turned back into his cabin, crouched beneath the burning cloud overhead, and rummaged in a locker for his seaboots. He'd pulled them on and then, wrapping his blanket completely over his head and face and body, he had plunged out the door, down the alleyway, and up through the fearful layer of live steam and out into the cool darkness and safety of the upper deck. He had forgotten only his hands; clutching the blanket tight about him, they had been exposed to the terrible heat of the steam as he had fought his way up through it, and they had suffered fearfully. Swollen into gross caricatures of human appendages, they had driven him nearly mad with pain; a quick-thinking officer injected an ampoule of pain-killer from the ship's emergency kit, and doctors, afloat and ashore, had fought to save them. Now, propped up against the pillows, he used them to hold a paper cup to his chest as he sucked fruit juice from a straw and re-lived the terrible night which had taken the lives of so many of his shipmates.

Towed back to port with her survivors and her dead, *Candytuft* lived to sail again; hers had been a freak accident. A more common cause of trouble to wartime ocean escorts was the North Atlantic weather, particularly in wintertime. By shore standards, the usual weather prevailing over most of the North Atlantic is frightful; the sun is rarely seen, obscured by the heavy cloud cover typical of the area, the temperature is rarely warm, and the winds, especially the prevailing westerlies, are damp and cold and boisterous. But it was the comparatively tiny size of corvettes that made them especially vulnerable to the weather. Seamen who had traded across the Atlantic all their lives in merchant ships discovered for the first time just how important a factor weather was to life in the North Atlantic, stripped of the insulation afforded by the size of one's ship. In a corvette, the level of the main deck in the waist is only a foot or two above the surface of the sea, so that almost any sort of wave is high enough to wash down her decks and send broken water over her upper-works. For much of her time at sea, a corvette was, for all practical purposes, semi-submerged, her fo'c'sle swept by any head sea, her well-decks perpetually awash, and her superstructure bombarded by flying spray, up to and over the height of her bridge and funnel.

Yet while they were exceptionally lively, rolling and pitching in the slightest sea, corvettes were remakable seaboats coming to no harm in conditions which damaged or overwhelmed their larger sisters. Theirs was the immunity of the cork, forever bobbing about on the surface but escaping the worst blows of even the most furious seas.

There were, of course, pleasant days, fine weather, even in the winter, but these were interludes, to be cherished in memory after being savoured to the full. Generally speaking, life at sea in a corvette was cold and wet and miserable, with constant violent motion and a background of noise compounded of whistling wind, bashing hull, rattling and clanging fittings, surging and gurgling water. The world outside was perpetually grey; sea, horizon, clouds, even the light itself had a dingy look.

And yet, curiously enough, for all its misery and hardship in really bad weather, life in the corvettes was happy enough at sea. One can grow used to anything, and once you grew accustomed to the incessant motion life settled into a routine. Off-watch in the messdecks men slept incessantly in the really bad weather, shutting out the appalling sights and sounds beyond the blankets, but at other times they read and joked and played cards. In the wardroom, we played an endless game of Blackjack night and day, into which watch-keepers plunged on leaving the bridge. Everyone's score was kept track of in a battered scribbler, and although nobody ever paid off, and it was understood that real cash was not involved, the accumulated debts most of us picked up on paper used to reach such appalling levels that by general consent there would be a devaluation, with debts being reassessed at ten cents on the dollar, and the game could start again.

Even Percy, our ship's groundhog mascot, quickly settled into a comfortable shipboard routine. I had been deputized to bring back a mascot, preferably a parrot, for our refitting ship while on leave in Toronto. We were currently under the spell of a consort's parrot, which used to shuffle about the rim of the wardroom table and screech, "Where's father?" followed by a *sotto voce* muttering of "The old bugger! The old bugger!" But in downtown Toronto I had seen this incredible groundhog, following along at the heels of its owner through all the crowds of a noonday Yonge Street lunchhour, and knew instantly that this was for us. This particular animal, it transpired, belonged to Mr. Skinner, who ran a famous pet-shop in the old Arcade. She was not for sale, but she had a litter of pups back in the store and I bought one on the spot, a toothy little devil no bigger than a squirrel, and arranged for him to be shipped out to us in a box packed with cabbage leaves to sustain his considerable appetite.

He arrived in Newfyjohn in splendid shape, and popped out of his box and sat up on the magazine hatch in the wardroom flat and ate his first sea-biscuit, watched by an admiring throng. He was an ideal mascot; quickly housebroken to a sandbox, which he used like a cat, he dearly loved to play. He went about dragging an old glove, which he offered to everyone in the hope that they would play with him, trying to take it from him as one does with a puppy, while he grunted in mimic fury. He became an adept climber, and would whistle up the wardroom curtain like a cat, or shinny up a voice-pipe if one was foolish enough to take him on the bridge for company, as I was sometimes known to do.

Percy was supposed to live in the cabin flat aft, or in the wardroom, since he was grossly over-fed if he ventured into the galley or the fo'c'sle; he knew this well enough, but he was as cunning as a fox. From the bridge wing, I would see his furry head appear over the coaming of the after flat; two beady eyes would check that the coast was clear. Then, waiting for the outboard roll—for he was as sea-wise as any shell-backed sailor and knew that the waist would clear itself of water as the ship rolled outward—he would leap out onto the wet deck and scuttle like mad for the galley, reaching the sanctuary of its lower step before the next sea came toppling inboard.

Percy survived many vicissitudes—his seagoing diet was notably short of the green grass staple of his shoreside chums—but his most notable triumph of adjustment occurred when he grew overly curious while spying on the engineer's storekeeper and fell down the storeroom hatch. He broke both his big front upper teeth on the steel deck; after vainly gumming his usual cabbage leaf that night, he huddled miserably in a corner in a snit. Nor would he eat the long strips of leaf we cut up for him; we thought he was doomed.

But a remarkable thing happened. His lower teeth, now unopposed by the dominant upper teeth, grew with incredible rapidity, and in no time Percy was nibbling away, as good as new—but now he was undershot, instead of overshot, and so he remained.

Life at sea went on happily enough; it was only when things got a bit "bumpy" that conditions became unendurable. A real North Atlantic gale, viewed from a liner's deck, can be merely unpleasant; in a battened-down corvette, tossed about like a cork, it can try men to the limits. A winter crossing was an endless succession of gales that came shrieking down from the western Arctic; we would no sooner emerge thankfully from one when the next would engulf us. Ferocious winter weather became a part of the experience of everyone in the escort navy; what lived on in memory were the one or two "ultimate storms" which brought home to everyone the enormous, incomprehensible force and fury of the sea. No corvette sailor ever talked of "ruling the waves" or "conquering the deep"; he knew from experience that man crept across the vastness of the oceans, a microcosm in the grasp of forces immeasurably greater than anything he could muster. He learned that man survived, after all his own efforts had been expended, by luck or fate or destiny, or by the Hand of God; take your pick. But no man could go back to sea without a sense of fatalism after once having experienced its incalculable force; a force that could engulf great ships, or crush the stoutest steel bulkhead, as it did when it crumpled the entire forward structure on a four-stack destroyer, killing its captain as he lay in his bunk. The ocean, like outer space, is an element beyond human comprehension, an expression of the infinite power and immensity of the universe.

We experienced its awesome strength in Decembr 1941, heading south from Iceland to pick up and escort a westbound convoy; five corvettes led by the destroyer *Restigouche*. It was snowing when we left Hvalfjord, and as we emerged into the open ocean we went pitching into a full gale, which grew worse hour by hour. By nightfall, when we had still not found our ships, things were getting desperate; we had no radar, and to run into a convoy under such conditions could be disastrous. We turned onto the likely course of the convoy and ran along, hoping to see something before it hit us, our ships spread in line abreast, a mile apart.

In the shrieking blackness of the night, the wind rose steadily as the barometer dropped; by midnight it had passed hurricane force and we could only estimate its strength at over a hundred miles an hour. The world went mad; the snow and sleet, mixed with spray, drove horizontally over the water. No man could face that blast; we doubled our watches, so that one officer could shelter behind the asdic house for a moment before relieving the other crouched behind the canvas bridge dodger, over which he had to snatch a glimpse into the shrieking maelstrom ahead. The seas grew and grew under the frightful impetus of the wind; by midnight they were mountainous, and after that nobody bothered to contemplate their height and weight. They blotted out our world, towering above us in the darkness, shutting off the wind for a breathless moment before thundering down upon us. Miraculously the bows would rise, so that only the top of the sea would come crashing inboard, to sweep across our fo'c'sle and thunder against our bridge and funnel. Everything small or frail had long been swept away by the seas breaking over us; winch covers, vent screens, rope reels. Each mountain that came towering out of the darkness, its crest outlined in luminous foam, would seem to be the last we could survive; peering up at its ghastly immensity, our hearts would sink and, bowing our heads, we would commit ourselves to whatever power watched over us. "O God, help us! Help us!" The captain huddled, grey-faced, beside the officers rotating on watch; nobody spoke, or could have spoken, in the howling madness of wind and sleet and driven spray. Nobody doubted that it must end, one way or another, within the hour; either the hurricane must pass or the ship would break up and be overwhelmed.

It went on, day and night, for four days.

By noon on the second day we were mindless automatons, so numbed mentally and physically by the incessant violence of our world as to have become inured. We no longer cared whether we lived or died; it seemed no longer to concern us. But for all of that, life went on within the beaten hulls of our ships; watches changed, men ate a little and slept as best they could in the frightful din of the hurricane. We had been washed bare of everything on the upper deck; the Carley floats gone, the whaler stove in, but still our ship lived.

Late on the afternoon of the second day, *Restigouche* began to break up. Her mast went overside, her steering gear broke down, her fragile hull long, and vulnerable, began to open up. Her depth-charges were battered from their lashings and swept overside; steering as best she could with her twin propellers, she became a wave-swept wreck. By nightfall she had turned tail to wind and was running desperately before the storm, struggling to stay afloat, with more than six feet of water in her lower compartments. She vanished swiftly from our ken; four days later she crawled, what was left of her, into Greenock.

Left on our own, we punched mindlessly on. On the third day, a signal from the commodore gave our convoy's position as some thirty miles away, and hove to; we crept towards them but by nightfall we, too, were forced to heave to, barely able to maintain our position by steaming slowly into the tempest. Our convoy had become secondary; now our main concern was to survive.

None of us, later, could remember the events of that storm; all the hours, the agonies, the anxieties of those days and nights became telescoped in memory into a blurred recollection of a single experience. But on the fourth day the sky lightened, became patchy; the wind dropped away with miraculous speed. Within hours only the mountainous seas were left to remind us of what we had endured, and apart from the superficial damage to our upper decks, all our corvettes were afloat and sound and fighting fit; we had survived!

Years later, caught by a similar hurricane south of Cape Canso, we were not so fortunate. This time we were on the continental shelf, which heightens and steepens the seas over it, and so far to the westward that the temperature dropped below freezing, a rarity in mid-ocean. To make things worse, the wind veered quickly to put Sable Island, that nightmarish ships' graveyard, under our lee. We could not afford to turn our little convoy of ships, unladen and therefore riding high and vulnerable to the force of the wind, and run before the tempest.

Early in the storm, we lost our "monkey island"; a great sea, a "seventh wave" even taller than the rest, simply engulfed us, blotting out bridge and funnel in green water. There was a tremendous crash, and when the sea passed, our asdic house had been stripped bare of the little wooden bridge we had built on top of it; miraculously Nels Adams, the watch-keeper, was still there, clutching the exposed voice-pipe and grinning down at us.

But the seas were not themselves our greatest danger; our chief menace was the ice that each one left behind, and that enveloped us in a rapidly thickening coat of marble-hard frozen spray. In an hour we had acquired tons of heavy ice on our masts and superstructure, top-weight which made the ship unstable. In no time the ship began to lie over, to recover more slowly each time she rolled; if something was not done, and done quickly, we must inevitably roll over as the weight of our upper-works upset our normal stability.

Everyone in the ship was mustered ready, with something—anything—hard enough and heavy enough to hammer ice. At a word from the captain, the ship turned, rolled agonizingly in the trough, but recovered—just—and then we were running before the storm, the wind and sea whistling behind, and we were into a new and tolerable world. Instantly, everyone was set to work chopping, hacking, hammering at the foot-thick casing of ice that had built up over bridge and rails and boats, masts and rigging. It was desperate, wearying work; the ice was so hard, and there was so much of it. A steam hose was rigged by the stokers, and melted some of the more difficult patches; the atmosphere aboard was one of frantic, desperate effort, for we all knew that we could only run before the storm for a brief time, with the shoals of Sable Island so close in our lee.

In half an hour we had rid ourselves of the worst of it. Her motion now restored to normal, the ship swung back to her old course, and we were plunged again into the shrieking hurricane, the driving spray, the freezing cold. Three times the ship iced heavily; three times we put our stern to it and cleared ourselves of the ice that clawed our ship over and down.

Our ships in convoy were not so fortunate, their long hulls, riding high in the water, were unmanageable in the frightful wind. The convoy dispersed, disintegrated, as each ship steered as best it could. In the grey light of a stormy dawn, I sighted the rescue ship, a little coastal passenger vessel that had once carried holiday-makers to British resorts; from her bridge a red Aldis lamp began to blink a signal to us. A great sea intervened, blotting her from sight; when it passed, she was nowhere to be seen. She had simply been engulfed, and weighted down with ice, had sunk in an instant.

During that day and night we lost three other merchantmen, great, ocean-going ships that had accumulated such enormous weights of ice that they had simply toppled over and been engulfed by the tremendous seas. Their crews were too small, in that freezing blast, to remove the vast areas of ice, and their hulls were too long for the ships, encumbered as they were, to be manoeuvred in the giant sea. All of them sank like a stone; we survivors, merchantmen and escorts alike, were powerless to lift a finger to help.

Yet one of our ships was destined to have a miraculous experience. Helpless and listing beneath a great weight of ice, she had driven before the storm down to leeward, her propeller churning away but unable to steer herself in the grip of that overwhelming wind and sea. Soon, the horrified crew saw the sea white with breakers ahead, a line of white surf stretching right across the horizon. They were driving down onto the shoals of Sable Island, the monstrous seas breaking furiously on the long scimitar of sand that rose from the ocean depths. As the ship drove toward the sands, both anchors were let go, bringing her bows around to face the wind. The anchors held momentarily, then dragged, then held. Little by little, the ship was driven remorselessly backward to her doom, the anchors slowing her progress but unable to get a firm hold in the shifting sands of the great shoal.

It was then that the miracle occurred. There is a shallow

passage, a sort of lagoon, dividing Sable Island from its outlying shoals. The ship was driven by the storm, stern first, through this passage, so that she literally went right through Sable Island to emerge, unscathed, on the other side! In the sudden calm of the island's lee, she anchored peacefully and rode out the rest of the storm in the shelter of Sable itself.

But we had other enemies besides the weather in the North Atlantic. The memories of anyone who served in the escort ships are filled with torpedoings, and the survivors who were the inevitable aftermath of ship sinkings. Nobody who has ever seen human beings struggling for life in the sea can ever doubt the common brotherhood of man; there is an intangible, unspoken bond that links the struggling survivor, battling for life against all the immensity of wind and sea, with the watchers on the ship, a bond that reaches to the very heart of the beholder, so that the swimmer's fight, his fate, become our own. A man swimming in the sea seems unbelievably tiny, lost amid the vastness of the ocean about him; to rescue him from that uncaring immensity seems somehow a triumph of the human spirit against the ordered anonymity of the universe encompassing us. Those sodden, shivering, oil-smothered wretches dragged inboard and restored to the warmth of our messdecks from the darkness of the midnight ocean had been snatched back from the abyss that awaits us all; they had the glazed look of men who had been carried to the outer limits of human experience, and had glimpsed the face of Destiny.

Tales of such men, of those who lived, those who died, filled the reminiscences of corvette crews ashore. There was the haunting story of men plucked in good health and spirit, from a sinking ship by the escort *Minas*. Not long after they had been taken aboard, a couple of men began to cough, to struggle, to fall into delirium. In a matter of minutes they lay dead, and it was only then that talk began about the cargo their ship had been carrying: containers of poison gas for storage in the U.K. for retaliatory use in the event of a Nazi gas attack. Somehow, the torpedoing had loosed some of this fearful gas. Into the eyes of the remaining survivors came the look of dawning realization as coughing began among still others—they were all doomed. Within hours the last one lay cold and stiff. *Minas*, who had rescued a joyous party of live survivors, steamed on with a cargo of corpses.

Our own particular horror concerned the survivors of the American troopship *Chatham*, carrying workers to the new air base at Thule in Greenland. The ship had been torpedoed by the redoubtable Hartwig in U517, the U-boat that wrought so much damage and heartache in the Gulf of St. Lawrence in the summer of 1942, and we were detached from the escort of a nearby convoy to rescue a couple of boatloads of survivors in Belle Isle strait. They were in good shape when we found them; like most American lifeboats, their boats had more gear, and certainly better gear, than we carried in our ship. But lying amongst them on a blanket stained with blood and oil was a man obviously badly injured; we passed him carefully inboard, and took him forward to be worked on.

In our crowded messdeck, our sick-berth attendant and I, as first lieutenant, did our best to save him. We would never forget the horror which awaited us when we cut away his clothes. He had been so badly crushed that he was just a sort of pudding; there seemed to be no bone unbroken, nothing to give human shape to this frightfully mangled mass. And yet he lived; we killed his pain with novocaine, did our best to make him comfortable. I wiped away the oil from his mouth and eyes; strangely, I could not seem to wipe his face clean of the greasy black. It was only when, puzzled, I bent close to examine his poor face that I realized that I had been attempting to wipe a Negro white. Thank God he died quickly and peacefully; crushed beneath a heavy raft falling from the ship above him after he had jumped overside, he was the most fearfully injured man I had ever seen alive.

But Hartwig and U517 had yet more horrors for us. Asdic conditions in northern gulf waters were hopeless for the asdic sets we then possessed; the mixing of salt water with fresh, of cold water with warm, where the vast St. Lawrence empties into the cold North Atlantic, produced a "layering" effect which bounced back transmissions from our asdic sets, masking the submarine beneath. Hartwig soon sensed his immunity from normal detection in these waters, and made the most of it. He was destined to sink several more vessels, including our chummy ship, *Shawinigan,* before being sunk himself by aircraft from the carrier *Victorious.* But on this particular night, he closed our convoy as we entered the Strait of Belle Isle, bound north with supplies for the new air base at Goose Bay on the Labrador coast. The corvette *Weyburn,* on the far side of the little convoy, spotted the wash of his conning tower, but as she turned to attack, Hartwig got away a torpedo which hit the old lake steamer *Donald Stewart*, loaded with airplanes and high-test gasoline.

While *Weyburn* went after Hartwig, we closed the stricken ship. A boatload of survivors managed to get away and were picked up by the ship astern, but no sooner had they left the ship's side than there was a tremendous explosion, and a vast column of flame towered up into the night sky. The high-octane gasoline had exploded, and the burning ship became a sheet of flame from stem to stern, lighting up the scene for miles around. A wave of burning gasoline poured overside; in seconds, the ship was floating on a sea of flame, burning as fiercely as did the ship herself. We closed the scene, appalled by the sight and sound of that frightful inferno, for the roaring suction of the air rushing in to fill that column of fire was deafening.

It was then that the thing happened that was to haunt our dreams ever afterward. A door in the after house of the doomed ship opened, and out stepped a man clad for a city street, in topcoat and hat, and carrying a small suitcase. He looked about him, first at the roaring inferno just forward, then at the sea of flame overside. Then, with no sign of alarm or despair, he turned and stepped back into the cabin flat inside, closing the door carefully behind him. We never saw him again; within minutes the *Donald Stewart* slid her red-hot length beneath the waves, bearing with her her lone passenger.

Who he was we never learned, but the horror of his situation, with death closing in on him from every side, cutting off every avenue of escape, was more than we could bear. The cool and calm acceptance of his fate by that unknown man, so close that we could see his every feature, yet already on the doorstep of eternity, we have never forgotten, can never forget.

Perhaps the blackest moment in the escort navy was the introduction of the acoustic torpedo in the fall of 1943. Two convoy escort forces and a support group, gathered about a single enormous fleet made up of two convoys combined, had been assaulted by a swarm of U-boats using the new weapon and new tactics, attacking the escorts, rather than the merchantmen. The frigate *Lagan*, hot in pursuit of one U-boat, had been torpedoed by another, the shattering explosion blowing off thirty feet of her stern. *St. Croix* was next; the old four-piper, so familar to everyone on the Newfy-Derry run, was shattered and sunk by no fewer than three torpedoes right aft while investigating a contact; most of her crewmen survived the explosion, but were left clinging to rafts in the freezing water for thirteen long hours.

The fatal delay was the result of another disaster; the corvette *Polyanthus*, one of a pair known as "the Anthus sisters, Poly and Di", was sent to pick them up, but she never arrived. She was torpedoed astern and perished in a single great explosion, taking down with her all save one of her men. He, and eighty-five of *St. Croix*'s numbed survivors, were taken aboard the frigate *Itchen*. It was the next night when the greatest tragedy occurred; *Itchen*, loaded with survivors, switching her searchlight on to a surfaced U-boat dead ahead of the convoy, simply disappeared in a tremendous mushroom-topped pillar of flame, torpedoed in her propellers. Only three men survived of more than two hundred aboard; one from *Itchen*, one from *St. Croix*, and the survivor from *Polyanthus*.

The surviving ships of the groups berthing in Newfyjohn were badly shaken; the stories they told us in their normally cheerful wardrooms were full of foreboding. Obviously, Hitler had launched one of his vaunted "secret weapons", and no one was sure that anybody could devise a counter to this dreaded killer, which homed on the noise of a ship's propellers. Yet within days the acoustic torpedo had been reduced to mere nuisance value, first by the issue of "foxer" gear by the Admiralty, and later with our own, better, simpler "cat" (counter-acoustic torpedo) gear; a couple of short lengths of pipe, clamped together side by side close enough to clang incessantly when towed through the water at the end of a long wire, and thus making enough racket to attract any acoustic torpedo away from the lesser noise of the ship's propellers.

The attrition of ships and men went on, month after month, year after year, regardless of the ups and downs of Allied fortunes; in the family of the escort navy, each casualty in the groups removed a familiar household, a distinctive group of characters, a particular friend. The bitterest to bear were the lives lost that could have been, should have been saved; *Valleyfield*'s men, 115 of them, dying in the berg-strewn waters while other ships of her group blundered unknowingly about close by; the long ordeal of *Guyborough*'s men when the bitter sea swallowed up my old shipmate Tommy Holland and so many others, victims of a staff officer's error.

Awe, and fear, of the ocean grew on everyone who sailed over it, winter and summer, year after year. The ultimate bliss in our lives was to escape from the sea for a time to the haven of a refit port, where the ship would be taken in hand for repairs and alterations, and where her ship's company could go off on long leave. In theory a ship was refitted every twelve months; in practice, particularly in the early years when escorts were scarce, it might be eighteen months to two years. But eventually the time would come when we would be ordered to refit, and we could all go home for up to twenty-eight days. Leave, of course, was the big thing; the return to a normal, civilized world, far from the war and the sea, was the great restorative, although home always seemed just a little different from the way one had remembered it. One's parents seemed a little older, a little greyer; the house a little smaller, one's old clothes and books and belongings just a bit naive, a trifle juvenile. But it was wonderful to wander the old familiar streets, to toss a baseball or football about with a kid brother, to learn from the hometown paper and friends how well we were winning the war.

Even on returning to the ship, there was the pleasure in being part of the life of a small community, if you were lucky enough to have been sent to refit in one of those innumerable pleasant little sunlit ports that dot the river-mouths of the Maritimes: Liverpool or Lunenburg, Pictou or Dalhousie or Shelburne. The ship was a chaotic mess of plumbers and painters and riveters, of course, and life aboard during working hours nearly impossible, but you could escape ashore to the pleasant tree-lined streets, the comfortable homes and hospitable people of these most charming of towns.

Life there was never dull. Who could forget Black Maggie, the redoubtable widow who carried on her late husband's coal business with such flair, or the afternoon a guest of hers, an air-force group captain, no less, got out on her roof, for reasons remembered now only by himself, and clambered up to the roof edge, only to find on arriving there that the roof was so steep he could not bring himself to descend it? He sat there, in full uniform, while passersby gathered below, some to shout advice and others, sad to say, to jeer and jest at this gallant officer. Certainly a diverting spectacle, and one that quite made our day; we were sorry when the volunteer fire brigade, with a long record behind them of rescuing tabbies from trees, arrived to add a group captain to their bag.

It was in the same town that I was put in charge of a naval contingent, drawn from the ship's companies of two corvettes refitting there, to march in a Victory Loan parade. We were all duly fallen in on the schoolground marshalling area. As the representatives of the Senior Service, we were of course intent on securing our privileged place at the head of the parade, leaving the army trainees and air-force cadets to scramble for places behind along with assorted Boy Scouts, policemen, our old friends of the fire brigade, and anyone else who could find a uniform to wear. We were duly getting ourselves shaped up, dressing our ranks, shouldering arms, and forming columns of route and that sort of thing, when the band began to step out, playing a jaunty tune. And we were about to move off, in proper marching order, when a crowd of Brownies behind us grew impatient at what they seemed to think was our procrastination. With a simple, single command. "Come along, girls," their bespectacled leader (The Big Brownie? The Brown Lady?) shepherded her tittering flock right past us in the wake of the band, leaving us to follow, at our slow, navy pace in the No. 2 spot. It was a lesson we never forgot; in manoeuvring large numbers of men, or a gaggle of sparrow-legged girls, simplicity of commands is the essence.

Those idyllic interludes in tiny refit ports were so many rays of sunshine in the grim, grey world of the wartime North Atlantic.

9
THEM AND US

~~~~~~

A dominant factor of life in the escort fleet was the "them and us" mentality, which separated the crews of ships from their Canadian counterparts ashore. Partly, this was engendered by the sense of shared experience which bound crews and groups in a common brotherhood, an experience it was impossible to explain or rationalize ashore. The truth was that almost every convoy crossing was an ordeal so gruelling that, once experienced, nothing could induce a repetition of its agonies; nothing, that is, save pride. Pride of ship and service and group, but mainly pride of toughness, of being one of a select company which could face up, again and again, to the terrors and hardships of a North Atlantic winter. It was the same pride, surely, that sustained men in the trenches in the First World War, and produced a similar sense of comradeship.

When we came ashore, to the soft civilian life of the shoreside navy, and were exposed to all its forgotten motivations of status and rank and petty privilege, we felt ourselves to be apart. We felt ourselves to be older, wiser, and tougher than these spoilt and silly people, preoccupied with illusions. They seemed unaware of the harsh realities of the uncaring universe that enfolded their little make-believe society; a universe whose awesome power and certainty could be glimpsed in the moon-lonely wastes of the winter ocean.

Pride kept us at sea, month after month, year after year; to leave your ship and get a berth ashore was to yield, to surrender, to let the side down.

Pride was one factor; resentment was the other. Resentment of the shore-oriented organization of the Canadian

127

navy, which cast everyone in the little ships of the escort
fleet, officers and men, in the role of poor relations of their
counterparts in the big institutions ashore. Not only was promotion difficult for officers at sea, but for enlisted men as
well; ashore was where the courses were that led to higher ratings, higher rank, higher pay. It was commonplace for a ship
to leave a trouble-maker in prison cells ashore, only to return
a few months later and find that he had been made leading
hand, or even petty officer. He had been available ashore
when a course for the higher rating was beginning, while his
more competent shipmates had been far away at sea. This
was the case for officers also; if they were to advance or to
specialize, they had to come ashore. The first of our class
from RMC to reach the rank of lieutenant-commander was an
officer put ashore as incompetent from his only ship. He was
promptly put in charge of a shore training establishment and
raised in rank. An officer who did one trip with us was
landed in Newfoundland suffering from "nerves". When we
returned from our next trip we found him swanking about as
lieutenant-commander, and spinning salty dips to impression-
able nurses about his "experience at sea".

But envy and resentment of the greater opportunities
ashore were only part of the sense of alienation felt by men
in the seagoing navy; it was the attitudes of the shoreside establishment that particularly rankled. Being sent to sea was
viewed by the majority of officers and men ashore as a form
of punishment, or, at best, as a sort of purgatory which had
to be endured for the briefest possible period, as a necessary
prelude to more exalted rank or a more rewarding shoreside
appointment.

To corvette crews, Halifax, or more precisely HMCS *Stadacona*, universally known as "Slackers", was the embodiment
of the shoreside establishment; oh, how we hated to be sent
to Halifax!

The wartime city itself was a curious place. Because of its
long association with military service in general, and the navy
in particular, its inhabitants were indifferent to the thousands
of young men from every part of Canada who crowded its
old-fashioned streets. There was none of the warmth and interest of St. John's to be found in Halifax; a reaction under-
standable in view of the enormous number of servicemen
who had engulfed their city and taken over their meagre
amenities. It is characteristic that Halifax, renowned for its
port, should turn its back on the harbour which alone gives it

significance. Even today the waterfront is hidden from view, virtually unapproachable from the shore. No sweeping waterfront promenades link harbour with city, no great avenues roll down its hills to the seafront wharves. Instead one can approach the port only through mean little streets, twisting alleys, shabby yards, and dilapidated warehouses. Halifax does everything it can to disown its port origins, and to keep the crude seagoing types who berth there at a decent distance.

Personally, I liked the city, with its wealth of historic sites and pleasant places—the North West Arm and Point Pleasant, Citadel Hill and Grand Parade, St. Andrew's Gardens and old St. Paul's—but I knew that most of my shipmates detested the place, with its shabby wooden buildings, flush with the sidewalk, its run-down tramcars, its seedy cafés.

Yet it was not the city itself that made Halifax so universally detested, but rather the base; Slackers was a synonym for everything corvette crews loathed about the shoreside navy. There were, to begin with, those peculiarly precious officers who affected pseudo-British accents and aped the mannerisms of the Royal Navy, with Beatty buttons left undone and a handkerchief up the sleeve. I once overheard a pair of these exquisites in the dockyard canteen, languidly discussing their social round, shopping coups by their wives, and related matters. Eventually they discussed where they might forgather for drinks and dinner that evening; one of them proposed a well-known hotel.

"Oh, not that place," objected the other. "All those fellows off the ships go there!"

Halifax, in a word, was indifference; nobody seemed to care whether you lived or died. Base officers had a way of showing up on the jetties towards noon, to enjoy drinks and lunch aboard the ships before heading back to their offices. They accepted the hospitality of corvette wardrooms as no more than their due, and there were always remarks about "how lucky you fellows in the ships are to get all that cheap out-of-bond booze," but there was no suggestion that hospitality might be returned at their own mess ashore. Oh, ships' officers could lunch or dine at Admiralty House—most of us did—but at your own expense, of course; the fellow who'd drunk your gin and eaten your lunch aboard the day before would likely regard you with a fishy eye and have difficulty remembering your name if you approached him in his mess ashore. You could take in a movie at the regular *Stadacona*

showings for base officers, and our matelots could use the
Stadacona canteen, but always you were an outsider, an interloper in a creased uniform who hadn't seen last week's
amusing picture at the Capitol and didn't know the price of
drinks at the interval bar.

The one big drawing card for ship's officers in Halifax was
the Saturday night dinner dance at the Nova Scotian Hotel,
famed throughout the Western Approaches as "The Rat
Race". Its principal attraction was that it made it possible for
wardroom officers of each ship to go "on the town" in a
body, which was the clannish custom in escort ships, so that
ships of one group might have several adjoining tables. As a
result, the Rat Race was a wonderful place for fellows just
arriving in port to blow off steam, and the resultant high-jinks
gave the Rat Race a raffish reputation still cherished to this
day in the memories of middle-aged men. Everyone has his
own particular recollection of incidents there; the one we recall that seemed most characteristic was the time the shore
patrol made its appearance, caps neatly tucked under their elbows in deference to their surroundings, and made its way
over to our ship's table. The petty officer in charge begged
our pardon in respectful fashion, and then, before our astounded eyes, lifted the linen tablecloth and gently but firmly
removed from beneath it the tousled officer who, all un-
beknownst to us, had gone to ground there to escape the pur-
suing patrol after some run-in with authority. There was the
night one high-spirited officer attempted to swing from a
chandelier, reached by a shaky tower of tables and chairs.
The chandelier, alas, proved to be a thing of straw, but apart
from a little fallen plaster and broken glass, little harm was
done, surely? In wartime Halifax, the Rat Race was where it
was all at, and about the only happy event on the sombre
Haligonian scene.

For men on the lower deck, Halifax was a virtual desert.
Swarming ashore from crowded messdecks at the end of a
long voyage, they found little to entertain them there, apart
from the handful of crowded movies, seedy cafés, and the
wet canteen. In later years there were games on the sports-
grounds ashore and film showings for the duty watch on
board, organized by base sports and recreation officers, but
Halifax, perhaps because of its size and the numbers of men
cooped up in barracks and ships, never got around to providing the range of activites laid on for ships' crews in other
ports, particularly Newfyjohn. Boredom in barracks and frus-

tration in the messdecks of ships alongside bred a growing anger and tension in Halifax, a feeling intensified by the base's "9 to 5" and "long-weekend" mentality, which left the dockyard virtually deserted except for thousands of men cooped up in berthed ships. The shocking and disgraceful riots on VE day which tore Halifax apart sickened us, and most men in the escort ships by then based in Newfoundland or overseas, but for all of that they did not surprise us. Given the poor discipline and frustrations of Slackers, such an explosion was inevitable.

Women, or rather the lack of women, were a major problem which Canadian shore authority never faced up to. Nobody who has not experienced them can appreciate the frustrations bred in strong young men, in the prime of their youth, cooped up for weeks at a time under conditions that tried mind and body to the breaking point, without so much as the sound of a woman's voice, or the glimpse of a woman's face. Certainly, authority ashore seemed unable to comprehend the terrible need bred by such unnatural circumstances; to men living comfortable, well-balanced lives in normal society, the craving of Jack ashore for women was deplorable but rather amusing, an occasion for sly jokes and knowing winks.

European navies, older and wiser, provided brothels, carefully supervised and medically inspected, for men living under discipline and deprivation; the Americans provided dances and entertainment and thousands of pretty, respectable girls, for the sight and sound and touch of a woman can sublimate the basic urge. But in Halifax, the conventional morality of people living conventional lives could neither countenance a licensed brothel nor comprehend its need; and the means and will to provide alternatives such as was done by Mainguy with dances and other distractions in Newfyjohn seemed totally lacking.

The result was that whores, too old or diseased to earn a living on the pavements of other Canadian cities, hustled a brisk and profitable trade on the shabby streets of downtown Halifax, their white galoshes and their decrepitude becoming notorious throughout the Western Approaches. The resultant VD rate (the highest in any of the Allied services) took a greater toll of Canadian sailors than anything the Germans could do; venereal disease decimated the crews of Canadian ships. But the psychological damage wrought by guilt and fear and shame in youngsters deprived of normal healthy feminine company was equally damaging. Private enterprise hastened to fill the void left by official indifference; an enterprising businessman opened a discreet brothel in a big old house on Barrington Street, staffed it with a lot of pretty French-Canadian girls, and did so well that he opened a branch in Dartmouth. But from first to last, shore authorities seemed incapable of appreciating the intense frustrations imposed on thousands of young Canadians by an unnatural life under brutal conditions. The challenge was never met, the problem never faced; medication and punishment were the only responses.

In the ships, we could never understand why it was so difficult to get the essential supplies necessary to maintain efficiency, especially when enormous stocks were on hand. Paint, for instance. Paint keeps a steel vessel from disintegrating into a heap of rust, and in a small ship, constantly at sea in bad weather, painting is a never-ending task. Yet ships were never able to draw enough paint for their needs—even of the poor-quality paint that Canada provided for its navy. (British and American paint was much superior to anything available to us in Canada.) Vast stocks of paint were accumulated in stores ashore; what was it being saved for? How could a ship possibly use too much paint, when paint was esssential to maintain not only appearance, but the durability of the very fabric of the ship? It was the same with cordage, or shackles, or any other piece of equipment; a corvette the stock-keepers assured us, was not entitled to draw the item we wanted for our towing gear. What *were* they saving it for; a battleship? We were the only ships they had, we were the ones that had to tow ships at sea; why not give us the gear we needed?

Two pairs of Oerlikon guns, installed by the British aboard a corvette I was in to beef up our anti-aircraft defence, were taken away on return to Halifax because they were in excess of guns allotted to corvettes by authority. Nobody explained to us why the guns were more useful sitting in storage ashore than in action afloat.

As a result of this kind of negative thinking, corvette commanders were forced to revert to their own resources to fit out and equip their ship for efficiency. Scrounging parties were part of the answer; anything not actually nailed down was considered fair game by roving first lieutenants and bosuns. For a bottle of rum, a storekeeper could be persuaded to look the other way, and provided the operation was carried out with speed and dispatch a gang of husky seamen could

come away with some surprising booty. When the liner
Rajputana was being stripped out at Esquimalt early in the
war for conversion to an armed merchant cruiser, hundreds
of marvellous arm-chairs, mirrors, drapes, and other luxury
furnishings were stacked on the jetty, en route to storage.
From our corvette, fitting out across the jetty, we watched the
mounting piles of goodies with drooling chops; the contrast to
our own threadbare austerity was too much to bear.

Our moment came at the lunch-hour break; all the
dockyard mateys trooped off to munch their sandwiches
somewhere in the shade, and the instant the coast was clear
half a hundred burly matelots were hard at work. Mirrors
and electric fans for the messdecks, a fine pair of brocaded
arm-chairs for the wardroom, and the pick of the lot,
naturally, for the petty officers' mess: a great overstuffed
settee.

The settee was too large to get down the hatch; like some
monstrous caterpillar too large to get down an anthill hole, it
stuck out of the fo'c'sle door while a dozen sweating figures
toiled to squeeze it in. Within seconds the ship's carpenter
took over, slit open the bottom, unbolted the legs, and slid
the gorgeous carcass in and down the ladder, to be reassem-
bled in all its glory within minutes. For the next two years
our corvette was to be famous for the luxury of her fittings,
and as the *Rajputana* was ultimately lost, she never returned
for her missing furnishings.

Sometimes, of course, scrounging led to disaster; consider
the sad case of Ted Briggs, the bearded bird who was later to
head the CBC, and who was already renowned throughout the
escort fleet for his unique gimballed table. The lively motion
of his corvette *Orillia* had prompted Briggs to put in hand an
experiment designed to make it easier to eat in bad weather,
which made dining difficult because of the constantly tilting
table. Since gimbals, or interlocking rings, permitted a compass to remain steady in bad weather, Briggs reasoned they
ought to do the same for a table. Accordingly, he had the
thing done; *Orillia* emerged from refit with the only gimballed table in the fleet, and in the first spot of bad weather, it
was eagerly put to the test. Sure enough, the table remained
level despite *Orillia*'s wildest leapings; what Briggs had not
bargained for, however, was diners who were not in gimbals
too. They went up and down with the ship, their chairs firmly
on the deck, with the result that the table was at one moment
at their knees, the next moment at their heads. Worse still; if

one was caught with so much as an elbow over the table when the ship rolled, the swinging table promptly spilled its entire contents into one's lap. The gimballed table was relegated to an honoured place in the folklore of the corvette navy, and *Orillia*'s officers went back to dining in the lesser discomfort of a fixed table.

Briggs big moment arrived when he was patrolling off the Normandy beaches just after the invasion D-Day, as senior officer of a group of Canadian frigates. In the aftermath of the initial assault, an enormous amount of matériel was floated off the beaches, and the seas were littered with every conceivable item of military paraphernalia. Eagerly checking out this fascinating flotsam, Briggs spotted a DUKW, an amphibious truck which could chug along on both land and sea. The ideal vehicle, thought Briggs, for a seagoing senior officer; one could use it to go ashore from the ship, and then proceed on land as in a jeep. All hands were mustered, therefore, and while the other ships of the group patrolled around him in a protective ring, he attempted to get the thing aboard.

The trouble was, the vehicle weighed tons, and the frigate had no cargo boom, derrick, or davit capable of swaying such an object inboard. With consummate seamanship, however, Briggs rigged a tackle from his mast, giving him the necessary height, and led the tail to his windlass to be heaved in. As the tackle took the weight of the heavy truck, the ship began to heel sharply under the strain, the shrouds supporting the mast tightened bar taut, and everyone aboard held his breath. But not for long; just as the big vehicle started to lift upward from the water, there was a rending crash and overside went DUKW, tackle, shrouds, and the whole mainmast; the strain had snapped it off just a few feet above the level of the bridge. A chastened Briggs was forced to abandon the DUKW to the fortunes of the sea, and retire to port to lick his wounds and repair the damage.

Worse was to follow. The base commander, already up to his ears in repairs to invasion-damaged ships, was so furious at what he considered the frigate's self-inflicted wound that he refused to repair or replace the mast, and Briggs was forced to return to sea with only a stump, from which he constantly flew a single-flag signal. We encountered him in this condition, the group trailing disconsolately astern, and on looking up the meaning of his flag hoist found that it was: "Ships should closely observe movements of their leader, as he may alter course and speed without further signal." The sorry spectacle was a lesson to all of us, arrant scroungers to a man.

What could not be obtained by official action or by scrounging could sometimes be secured by bribery, with bottles of rum as the medium of exchange. Almost every worthwhile addition or alteration, which converted a corvette from its basic Stone Age beginnings to the sophisticated weapon it ultimately became, was brought about by ships' officers, at their own expense, bribing dockyard workmen to effect improvements which would not otherwise be made. So many bottles for a "monkey island", or elevated con position; so many more for wooden bridge dodgers instead of the canvas ones offically called for; for a compass platform here and signal projectors there, for a ladder here and voice-pipes led there. Little by little, the ship was made more habitable, more efficient, more convenient, always at the expense and instigation of its own officers. No two corvettes were exactly alike in bridge or accommodation layout. Voice-pipe location was always a favourite subject for individual alteration to accommodate the particular needs of particular commanding officers. I can remember being intrigued by a voice-pipe fitted in a bridge wing apparently to accommodate a midget, for its bell-shaped copper mouth reached little more than knee-height, only to learn that it led only overside, and had been fitted as a urinal at the wish of a commanding officer who virtually lived on the bridge while at sea.

Yet this official indifference to the needs and conditions of individual men and ships in the escort fleet was probably inevitable, given the inflated size and multiplying concerns of naval authority. It was certainly accepted as such, and in good heart, by corvette ships' companies. What was harder to accept was the manning policy which prevailed in Canada, and which prevented a ship ever sailing with the same complement twice in succession. In British escort ships, particularly in the later years of the war, serious—and successful—efforts were made to retain officers and crew aboard a ship for the length of its commission, or for the year or so between refits. In this way a trained and disciplined team was built up, and the efficiency of a ship raised as close as possible to perfection.

This was never possible in Canadian escorts, particularly in ships working out of Halifax. As soon as a ship's officers and men began to shape up as a team, experienced men would be drafted off ashore. Each time a ship left harbour the process of training and indoctrination would have to begin again. This was to be the single greatest obstacle with which Canadian ships had to contend, and the biggest impediment to operational efficiency. No attempt was ever made in the RCN to concentrate the best-trained, best-qualified men at sea; instead, our finest experienced men and our most skillful specialists were to be found ashore, in training establishments or offices.

How we envied such crack groups as Britain's famed Second Escort Group, developed and trained by the redoubtable Johnny Walker! In these ships every position in the anti-submarine team was filled by the finest, best-qualified man available, a real galaxy of star performers. The formation of such an élite group of picked men was completely alien to Canadian naval authority; right to the war's end the practice of fobbing off problem officers and men from big shore bases to ships at sea, particularly those going overseas to another theatre of operation, was carried on. When I asked for a competent watch-keeping officer for a ship about to take part in the Normandy assault, Halifax authorities sent me the spoiled son of a Toronto millionaire, who'd been a disciplinary problem ashore, and who was afraid to go to sea. When he jumped ship before sailing; we were sent as replacement another problem child from barracks; this one proved to be not only incompetent and insubordinate, but a homosexual to boot.

Yet for all the differences between ship and shore, between "us and them", it was not until the closing months of the war that any real bitterness began to show itself in the ship's companies. In part the increasing sourness was due to the inevitable disillusionment and cynicism following a time of high emotional involvement. Our crusade, begun as a clear contest between freedom and tyranny, a picture painted in sharp black and white, was ending in a confused scene of drab greys. Tales coming back from Murmansk showed our Russian ally to be a tyrant at least as odious as the Nazis. Our own clear goal, to survive and keep freedom alive, had now long been swallowed up in squabbles about postwar spheres of influence. Even more upsetting from our point of view was the new wave of braggadocio, of boastful national assertiveness, inaugurated by public relations officers for the benefit of "the folks at home". This clashed violently with the traditional low profile, the almost obsessive understatement, of the Royal Navy, "The Silent Service", which we had absorbed, and which valued a modest demeanour above all else. We were first amused, then embarrassed, and eventually sickened, by the vainglorious accounts of the new breed of PR men, which exaggerated and distorted the role of Canadian servicemen and made us ridiculous in the eyes of Allies with whom we'd shared so much. (The first 1,000-bomber raid by Britain's RAF was headlined by our paper as "Halifax Man Bombs Berlin".) We all thought it uproariously funny when Vice-Admiral George C. Jones, a solid, unspectacular officer of vast seniority known to everyone as "Jetty Jones" (presumably because of all those peacetime years spent lying alongside), was given a "new image" by the PR people and launched in the media as Admiral George "Tiger" Jones! We did not think it so funny when we began to realize that we were being manipulated to accord with political purposes ashore, and that the public was accepting the ridiculously excessive accounts of media men at face value. Sourly, we refused to wear the gaudy shoulder flashes and meaningless service medal ribbons now being dished out, and we treasured still the civilian plainness of our sombre naval uniforms, which contrasted with the pomp and panache and boastfulness of the Americans that seemed to have infected our people ashore. Yet it remained for a couple of incidents overseas, in British ports, to deepen the growing cynicism and alienation of long-service men afloat into something like real anger.

In 1944 a large number of Canadian ships were based in Devonport for the Normandy build-up. When the commanding officers of these ships attempted to use the dockyard chapel for the funeral of half a dozen men killed aboard our *Haida* during a raiding action off the French coast, we were told by a plummy-voiced RN chaplain that only he could preside there; our own Canadian padre could not conduct a service within the sainted precincts. And, he added, only the Church of England man could be buried from there; we would have to take the others somewhere else.

This pedantic reaction was typical of the growing administrative obsession with form and forms which was blunting our fighting edge at sea. It did not seem to matter to those ashore just what you achieved at sea, so long as you filled in the correct returns ashore, and in quadruplicate, of course.

Our mounting resentment and confusion were heightened

by the inability of Canadian authorities to comprehend the conditions under which we were operating abroad. For months at a time, the ships of the two Canadian Normandy minesweeping flotillas were based at anchorages miles from the nearest shore facility. The motorboats we once carried had been removed in Canada and replaced with Carley floats. To get ashore, even for the most urgent business, we had to make a long pull in our whaler against strong tides, or rely on the hard-pressed boat services provided at long intervals by the port authority. Our grumbling was not improved by a signal received from some officious ass in Ottawa, who ordered us to land every curtain and tablecloth in the ship, because of a potential smoke hazard should the ship catch fire!

To tiny ships like ours, smoke from a burning curtain was the least of our concerns, but what rankled with us was not so much the stupidity of the signal as the incomprehension of its sender. Didn't he know that a ship was more than a weapon; that it was also our home? Didn't he know that to the more than one hundred men cooped up for months in this cramped metal box a bit of curtain, a cloth on the table, meant the difference between civilized standards and mere animal existence? Needless to say, we disregarded the signal in the finest Nelson tradition; but its dispatch, at a time when we were nerving ourselves to accept fifty-per-cent casualties in the coming assault on Fortress Europe, seemed indicative of the blindness to our realities of a shore authority obsessed with its own petty concerns.

In the hectic days following the first landings on the Normandy beaches, the British cable-ship *St. Margaret*, escorted by the Canadian corvette *Trentonian*, was laying a communication cable to the beach-head when they were attacked during the night by an American destroyer. The attack, of course, was inexcusable; the American commanding officer had failed to read the signal informing him that the cable-ship would be at work in his patrol area. But it was his persistence in the attack, once the identity of the cable-ship was clear, that was positively criminal. The destroyer lit up the civilian ship with star shell, then pounded the unarmed vessel with salvoes from close range, shifting fire to the Canadian corvette when she attempted to intervene. Eventually American bridge officers prevailed on their captain (a glory-hunter, they later explained to us) to cease fire. The American vessel then attempted to come alongside its shattered victim, but the fury of the British seamen, and of the Canadian corvette crew, prompted its crestfallen captain to make a prudent exit into the blackness of the night. The cable-ship was a shell-torn wreck, littered with badly wounded men; her captain died in the arms of Bill Harrison, *Trentonian*'s commanding officer. The shattered ships—*Trentonian* had a hole through her engine room—limped back to Portsmouth.

The American destroyer carried on unscathed. But when corvette and cable-ship made harbour, they were immediately isolated in a remote corner of the port, denied all liberty, and cut off from any communication with the shore. For some authority had become obsessed with the idea that if their story ever became known, it would create anti-American feeling in Britain and Canada, and accordingly the two inno-cent crews were imprisoned aboard their ships. After her Portsmouth exile ended, *Trentonian* was sent to sea. Shortly afterward she was torpedoed and sunk, thereby relieving shore authority of any further embarrassment.

The incident was soon common knowledge, and our fury at this monstrous injustice was deep and abiding. It was not directed so much at the U.S. captain—Americans were noto-riously trigger-happy and it was accepted as the other side of their aggressiveness—as at the ruthless and cynical manipula-tion of ships and men by our shore authority. It convinced us at last that it was not what happened that really mattered, so much as what you told the public had happened. We had learned the lessons taught by Goebbels, and now the pupil was besting the master.

With disbelief came disillusion; a growing cynicism soured our attitude to the whole vast image of Allied success. The enormous torrent of words, celebrating our glorious achieve-ments on land and sea and air, engendered only a mounting bitterness. Ironically, we found ourselves almost envying our old antagonists, the U-boat crews; they, at least, had been able to maintain their integrity and firmness of purpose, and had fought bravely to the end against hopeless odds. I can remember the real admiration we felt on visiting, after VE day, the surrendered U-boat that we had hunted, with no fewer than thirty-one other ships, right in the approaches to Plymouth, where it had just sunk a small fishing vessel. The guts of these German kids, shaken and shattered by bombing in port and depth-charging at sea, impressed us deeply; their demeanour robbed me of any savour in our triumph, now usurped and corrupted by boastful politicans, both service and civilian.

The little world, the private war, of the corvette navy was coming to an end, and all we wanted was out.

10
SIGNAL LOG

The little coal-burning trawler, the smallest member of our escort as we shepherded our convoy off the Scottish coast, was investigating an under-water contact; the large flag attesting to this fact fluttered from her foremast. She was hardly moving as we watched her through the glasses, probing beneath the surface with her primitive asdic. Then her hoist went close-up to the yard-arm, indicating she was attacking with depth-charges. "My God, at that speed she'll blow herself out of the water," someone gasped on the bridge beside us. We watched in mingled horror and incredulity as suddenly the ocean all about the little ship erupted in towering fountains which blotted out all sight of her.

After what seemed an eternity, the little trawler came into view again—but what a change! Her stern staff had disappeared, blown clean off; she had a list to port and her steering gear had been damaged, so that she described a slow circle as she lost way through the water, finally coming to a stop with clouds of steam pouring from her engine-room skylight.

The spell which had gripped us was broken as her signal lamp began to chatter; we read the simple message as it spelled out: "I HAVE BUSTED MYSELF."

Signals like this, which capture a whole situation in a few terse words, are treasured by everyone who served in the escort ships, and everyone has his own particular favourite. Signals best embody the wit and humour of the navy, sometimes erudite and apt, sometimes coarse, but always pithy and to the point. After all, when each letter, word, or phrase has to be signalled by lamp or flag, one is at pains to be as brief as possible, and the consequent sharpening of wit and style led to some gems of bantering brevity.

What could be shorter, for example, than the greeting flashed by the destroyer *Restigouche* ("Rustyguts" to her friends, "Guts" to her group), whose pennant number was HOO, to the little auxiliary vessel bearing the identifying number YOO:

From HOO to YOO: "YOO HOO."

In the interest of brevity, a number of senior officers of escort, particularly those from the RN, developed the habit of sending signals to errant ships in the group which contained merely a biblical reference of chapter and verse; the recipient would have to have recourse to his Bible and, after looking up the quotation, would "get the message". This business of biblical signals became a great cult, so that it was necessary to keep both a Bible and a concordance, which grouped references under various classifications, handy on the bridge at sea. We received a typical example of such a message one night when we had inadvertently strayed out of station. As we scrambled shamefacedly back into station in broad daylight our senior officer blinked a biblical reference to us which, on being checked out, gave us: "MY GOD, MY GOD, WHY HAST THOU FORSAKEN ME."

Almost every situation, every nuance of meaning, could be found in the vast reaches of the Bible. A treasured example was the signal sent by Commander-in-Chief, Plymouth, to a corvette towing a damaged merchantman:

From corvette to C. in-C. Plymouth: "ROMAN EMPEROR IN TOW, BADLY DAMAGED, PLEASE SEND TUGS."

From C. in-C. Plymouth: "REVELATIONS CHAPTER 3 VERSE 11." ("Behold, I come quickly; hold that fast which thou hast, that no man take thy crown.")

Then there was the classic which went the rounds of the wardrooms: the signal sent by a commanding officer in response to a message of congratulations upon his receiving promotion to lieutenant-commander. "VMT. PSALM 140, 2ND HALF OF VERSE 5." ("Very many thanks. They have set gins for me.")

The destroyer *Skeena,* seeking assistance to check out a poor asdic echo which yet seemed suspiciously like that of a submarine, sent a signal to the corvette *Wetaskiwin* which touched off a famous hunt. The signal was simply: "ACTS 16, VERSE 9." ("And a vision appeared to Paul in the night;

There stood a man of Macedonia and prayed him, saying, Come over into Macedonia and help us.")

Eager for the fray, *Wetaskiwin* came pelting over the horizon, sending as acknowledgement the brief signal: "REVELATIONS 13, VERSE 1." It was *Skeena*'s turn to thumb furiously through the pages of the bridge Bible, to turn up the reference "And I stood upon the sand of the sea, and saw a beast rise up out of the sea, having seven heads and ten horns, and upon his horns ten crowns, and upon his heads the name of blasphemy."

Not so apt and precise as some of the best of the biblical signals, perhaps, but considering it was done in the heat of the hunt, a hunt which was to result in the destruction of U588, it was pretty quick work, and raised a smile in many an escort yardroom and messdeck.

Some of the most savoured signals were at the expense of ships' names, of which there was an endless variety. Ships named for ladies were a favourite source of funny signals, including these gems from escorts: "GRACIE FIELDS MAKING WATER, OUT OF CONTROL," and "LOUISE EJECTED FROM CONVOY FOR EXCESSIVE SMOKING."

There was a good deal of archness in signals about Wrens. The first and most famous signal was said to have been sent with no double meaning intended in 1940. There were serious shortages of cloth at that time, resulting in conflicts between various branches of the service for the limited supply of material for uniforms. Indignant that his sailors were still in civilian clothes while girls entering the service were drawing uniforms without hindrance, an irate admiral made the following signal: "WRENS CLOTHING IS TO BE HELD UP UNTIL THE NEEDS OF SEAGOING PERSONNEL HAVE BEEN SATISFIED."

In Portsmouth, however, a reverse condition prevailed: uniforms for Wrens were in such short supply that over a thousand servicewomen were still in plain clothes. The C.-in-C. Portsmouth complained by signal: "AT SOME ESTABLISHMENTS NEW ENTRY WRENS ARE NOW WORKING IN BARE LEGS TO SAVE THEIR PAIR OF STOCKINGS FOR WALKING OUT. IN DUE COURSE A LARGE NUMBER OF WRENS WILL BE WORKING IN A STATE OF NATURE WHICH ON MANY GROUNDS WOULD BE UNDESIRABLE."

The sly response came from C.-in-C. Plymouth. "SUGGEST YOU APPLY FOR FIGHTER COVER."

References to women, of course, provided a constant source of humour in a force starved for their company. Everyone recalls the joyous disbelief of the escort returning to base on receiving the signal: "HAVE WOMEN FOR YOU." Inevitably, of course, a correction followed: "HAVE TWO MEN FOR YOU."

Perhaps the most famous signal of this sort was sent on the occasion of a squadron's arrival at an overseas station:

From Flag Officer to Senior Officer, Port: "WHO DO YOU RECOMMEND FOR ADMIRAL'S WOMAN."

The recipient of this signal, naturally dumbfounded, asked for a repeat of the message, and received the following amendment: "REFERENCE MY SIGNAL, PLEASE INSERT WASHER BETWEEN ADMIRAL AND WOMAN."

To corvette crews, of course, signals from shore authority sometimes seemed out of touch with the realities of the situation, and a particularly obtuse example was something to be treasured. But there were few that could match a famous exchange between the Admiralty and a destroyer in the earliest days of the war:

From Admiralty to destroyer: "PROCEED WITH ALL DESPATCH."

From destroyer to Admiralty: "REQUEST DESTINATION."

From Admiralty to destroyer: "ADEN, REPEAT, ADEN."

From destroyer to Admiralty: "AM AT ADEN."

Another classic was the interchange between a corvette, inward bound from sea, which had been damaged by a mine and had reported her conditions to shore authority as she limped into Liverpool. Feeling very much the battered warrior, home from the wars, bloodied but unbowed, and secretly wondering if they might not even be cheered into harbour by crews of ships alongside, the corvette crew were considerably miffed to receive, as the only acknowledgement of their suffering, the following terse signal from an unfeeling authority as they passed the Bar light vessel: "DO NOT SINK IN SWEPT CHANNEL."

In Canadian groups, a kind of cult would grow up around the style of signals between ships in the group. In some groups, for instance, the jargon of Damon Runyon, whose Broadway argot and guys and dolls were then very popular, was often used, and individual officers were known to one and all by Runyon nicknames: Harry the Horse, Good Time Charlie, etc. Other groups would use an affected British style for inter-ship signals, à la Bertie Wooster and Jeeves, while in other signals would be couched in a sort of burlesque Jewish style.

A couple of Canadian escorts were making their way into an East Coast anchorage blocked by pack ice; the first ship, forcing a passage, anchored inside and sent the following signal to her consort outside:

First ship to second: "ABIE, ABIE, ABIE, MINE BOY, WHAT ARE YOU WAITING FOR NOW."

Reply from second ship: "ICEHOLES."

Then there was the signal from one Canadian escort overhauling another, racing for port: "DON'T LOOK NOW, BUT YOUR SHIP IS SLOWING."

Canadian reservists were notoriously impatient of the service nomenclature used in the Royal Navy, and hallowed by centuries of use; they would talk of "rowing" a boat, for instance, instead of the proper "pulling". The following signal is typical of such reproofs:

Canadian corvette to base: "AM TIED UP AT NO. 5 BERTH."

From base to corvette: "SHOE LACES ARE TIED UP. HM. SHIPS ARE SECURED."

A host of signals made in response to fussy authority were cherished by ships where "respectful irreverence" was a sort of art. One such pearl was the response of a corvette on being asked by an impatient base authority how long he would be before leaving harbour:

From corvette to base: "TWO HUNDRED AND FIVE FEET AS USUAL."

Or the one which, after making a botch of a mid-ocean manoeuvre, was asked by an irritable senior officer: "WHAT ARE YOU DOING."

Reply from corvette: "LEARNING A LOT."

Then there was the annoyed senior officer attempting to scold the corvette which was rejoining after a hunt astern in very bad weather.

Senior officer to corvette: "WHY HAVE YOU TAKEN SO LONG TO REJOIN CONVOY."

Corvette to senior officer: "IT WAS UPHILL ALL THE WAY."

And then:

From Port Authority to corvette: "WHAT IS ALL THAT LAUNDRY HANGING UP FOR."

Reply from corvette: "SUBMIT, TO DRY."

Signals to other branches of the service could sometimes be fun. Coming in to Portsmouth one evening, we signalled a very warlike-looking MTB growling out on patrol: "GOOD LUCK."

We received the saucy reply: "THANKS. ACTUALLY WE RELY ON SKILL."

And then of course, there was the air force. Towing a drogue for target practice by anti-aircraft gunners in the fleet was always a hairy business at best. Once, when a shell burst in front of the towing aircraft instead of near the target towed far astern, the indignant pilot made the classic protest: "I AM PULLING THIS BLOODY THING, NOT PUSHING IT."

Sometimes, too, the point of naval jokes was missed in the air, or vice-versa. The following interchange took place early in the war, with a ship encountering a coastal command aircraft off Rockall:

From aircraft: "WHAT SHIP."

From ship: "GRAF SPEE."

From aircraft: "ARE YOU NAVAL TYPES STILL SO FAST ASLEEP THAT YOU HAVEN'T HEARD OF THE END OF THE GRAF SPEE."

From ship: "WHICH END."

The besetting worry of ships at sea concerning their position produced many memorable signals, typical of which is the one signalled from one ship to another: "WHAT DO YOU MAKE OUR POSITION, OTHER THAN PRECARIOUS."

Off Omaha beach-head on the morning of June 6, 1944, a single landing-craft, loaded with troops, led an enormous armada, stretching back over the horizon as far as the eye could see, towards the beach ahead. She had been brought to precisely that position by all the marvels of modern science and good staff work; her route was marked by lighted buoys and lit up as brightly as Yonge Street on a Saturday night, her path swept and marked by ships with the most precise electronic navigational gear, and directly ahead a midget submarine lay on the surface transmitting a beam, by light and wireless, on which she could steer. Her arrival, in the vanguard of the greatest naval force ever seen, was both a technological triumph and an historic moment. As she moved past us, where we lay recovering our minesweeping gear off the beach, her signal lamp began to flash; some stirring, inspirational war-cry, perhaps, at this moment of ultimate confrontation?

Signal from landing-craft: "WHERE AM I."

And then there were the private signals. With thousands of homesick seamen writing home, anxious to convey intimate messages to loved ones without incurring the censor's attention, an ingenious system of communication was incorporated into letters to family, and especially to wives and girl friends. Postscripts were the most popular method, beginning with simple o's and x's scrawled at the bottom of a letter.

Censoring mail aboard ship was a thankless task, traditionally assigned to the most junior officer in the wardroom; it was his job to delete from all letters any mention of ship movements or military operations which could conceivably be of use to the enemy. As the war went on, censoring officers noted a growing trend to enigmatic postscripts, usually merely a few capital letters at the bottom of a page, or on the envelope itself. The cracking of these codes was perhaps the sole redeeming pleasure which censor officers derived from wading through dozens of letters home from lonely sailors, and even today the recollection of some of those messages can raise a smile. There was a simple H and K— Hugs and Kisses, and the equally ubiquitous SWALK—Sealed With A Loving Kiss. But a great cult developed later in the war, the so-called WICH message, introduced by RN ratings writing home to their wives. These posed a real challenge to censor officers, and ran the full gamut of the erotic imagination. Everyone's favourite was in the best tradition of the earthy society which had evolved the comic seaside postcard. It was NORWICH— (k) Nickers Off Ready When I Come Home.

Memory's logbook retains mostly the light, the frivolous, messages, sent from ship to ship; the great moments, the signals that initiated historic events, are mostly forgotten. The best signals were passed on as anecdotes, so that the ships actually involved tended to be forgotten and only their cheeky banter survives:

From ship to ship: "PLEASE SEND YOUR ARTIFICER TO SEE OUR FORWARD GUN."

Reply: "OUR ARTIFICER CAN SEE YOUR FORWARD GUN FROM HERE."

From senior officer, whose ship has just been run into, to his crestfallen assailant, now backing off: "WHAT DO YOU INTEND TO DO NOW."

Reply: "BUY A FARM."

Two escorts approaching Portland in thick fog, visibility nil:

First escort: "WHEN DO YOU EXPECT TO SIGHT PORTLAND BREAKWATER."

Reply: "FIFTEEN MINUTES AGO. ESTIMATE MY POSITION FOURTH FAIRWAY GOLF COURSE."

And then, of course, there is the marvellous old turkey about the new ship berthing for the first time under the approving eye of the port admiral. The ship made a good approach to an awkward berth, and appeared to have judged matters to a nicety, so the admiral signalled, approvingly: "GOOD."

But then everything went wrong; a breastline parted, and the new arrival ground along the bows of the ship astern. A horrified admiral made another signal: "ADD TO MY PREVIOUS SIGNAL, GOD."

Aircraft carriers of all sizes were ungainly ships, a favourite target for insulting banter. When a fleet carrier appeared from refit, gleaming in fresh paint, she signalled a passing escort:

From carrier: "HOW DO I LOOK."

Reply from escort: "GO BACK TO LOCH NESS."

A Canadian escort carrier, disabled at sea and entering harbour under tow, took an awkward sheer and set down upon the gate vessel as she passed through the boom defence, doing considerable damage to the little vessel's paintwork. Weeks later, after the carrier had been repaired and headed down harbour for sea, a waggish corvette lying near by signalled to the boom-defence gate vessel: "LOOK OUT, HERE SHE COMES AGAIN."

A senior officer escort, dispatching a damaged corvette to base for repairs, sent her on her way with a fond wish:

S.O. to corvette: "HOPE YOU FIND FACILITIES YOU NEED IN BELFAST."

Despondent corvette to S.O.: "HOPE I FIND BELFAST."

But of all the signals ever made by ships of the escort navy, surely one of the last was one of the best; certainly the best-remembered, and in its cheekiness and brevity, typical of the wartime corvette navy. Newfoundland in signal jargon was N.F.; the flag officer in command of the base was Flag Officer, Newfoundland, or F.O.N.F.

At the war's end, a corvette leaving Newfoundland for home made the following famous signal:

From corvette to F.O.N.F.: "REQUEST PERMISSION TO F.O. FROM N.F."

11
THE CHANNEL WAR

In the spring of 1944, a wonderful thing happened to a lot of us in Western Approaches; after years of bashing into North Atlantic gales, we transferred operations to the English Channel and its approaches from the Bay of Biscay and the Irish Sea. In preparation for the coming cross-Channel invasion, Canadian frigates and corvettes set up patrol lines at the western entrance of the Channel to deny the assault area to any U-boat intrusion, or reinforced the escort of the vital strategic-cargo convoys now entering British ports. But for those of us in steam Bangors, the change was even more welcome; after weary years of escort, these fine twin-screw little ships were to be fitted out for the fast minesweeping duties they were designed for, and sent across to lead the way through the minefields and on into the invasion beaches. Our quarterdecks heavy with new floats and sweeps, and bristling with new high-angle three-inch guns forward and power-operated twin Oerlikons aft, we felt capable of taking on the Luftwaffe single-handed; in the event, we were not called upon to do so.

It would be difficult to conceive a more dramatic change in circumstances than the transfer to the Channel from the North Atlantic. Gone were the frightful winter weather, the incessant gales, the long, wearying hauls across the endless reaches of featureless ocean. Suddenly, things got much more civilized; distances were shorter, passages faster, the weather better; always there was a choice of ports under your lee in case of trouble. Reinforcements were only hours, sometimes even minutes away. By getting on the blower, you could whistle up air cover or call over a couple of support groups to bear a hand, while tugs and pumps were always available in case of collision or torpedoing. Ships could make port with damage that would have meant certain loss in the vast Atlantic; fuelling became a mere harbour function, and we could complete a whole trip without running out of bread.

Equally intriguing was the nearness and variety of the enemy menace. You had to be concerned about him, even in harbour; he could bomb you there or strafe you in the Channel, or blow you up with the guided glider-bomb, Hitler's latest. There were doodle-bugs in season, along with E-boats, fast, and R-boats, slow; Elbing (small) and Narvik (big) destroyers, flak ships, U-boats, and miniature submarines; mines (moored), mines (pressure), mines (acoustic), mines (magnetic), mines (electric), mines (controlled), mines (contact), mines (theirs), and mines (ours); most surprising and most dangerous of all, there were the heaviest and most accurate and most belligerent shore batteries imaginable.

After the dreary, boring months of shepherding convoys across the briny, the variety and proximity of the enemy was most stimulating; you could leave harbour, have a rousing punch-up with Adolf's lot in one form or another, and be back in harbour without missing a meal. Navigationally, too, it was a whole new ball game; gone were the noonday observations and star-shots. Now we were back into doubling angles on the bow and running fixes, for not only land but usually a prominent lighthouse or two was in sight. We stowed our sextants away and quickly became familiar with the characteristics of a new set of landmarks, set out like lamp-posts along a busy street; the Wolf and Bishop, Longships and the Lizard, the Eddystone and Start, Portland and Beachy Head.

And oh, the change in weather. It could get nasty in the Channel, of course, with lots of wind and steep seas and bad visibility, but the Channel chop was a world away from those giant Atlantic combers, and the radar we had nowadays removed many of the terrors of fog in convoy, although the great volume of traffic through the Channel and the close quarters could make things a bit dodgy on a thick night.

Everyone welcomed the change, and for those of us lucky enough to be in a Bangor, these were great days. At sea we applied ourselves to mastering the techniques of a new kind of warfare, with its emphasis on tight formation and meticulous station-keeping; ashore we revelled in the infinite variety England—even war-weary, austere, England—offered its visitors. For although our leave was limited to a few hours in port or a run to London during a boiler-clean, a marvellous train and bus system seemed able to transport us almost anywhere in the country in a matter of a few hours. For Canadians accustomed to a train a day in either direction at home, the frequency of British trains was a revelation; you could catch a train to London from Portsmouth about every twenty minutes!

It was an exciting place to be, at an exciting time. The country was a vast armed camp, full of the soldiery of all the free World, and full, too, of an air of exultation. For everyone knew that we were on the brink of a great adventure, an assault, on a scale never seen before in all the world, on the bastions of Nazi Europe. For long, weary years Britain had been battered and beleaguered by the armed might of oppression; now the forces of freedom, from all over the world, had rallied to this war-worn island, and Britain and the British reflected a new and confident mood.

London was the centre of the world in those great days, or so it seemed to us on our brief visits there on leave. Gielgud was in *Hamlet* at the Haymarket, Ivor Novello's *Perchance to Dream* was playing to packed houses, Richard Tauber was filling a battered London theatre with lovely Strauss waltzes and arias from *Gay Rosalinda*, and if you were lucky, you could get to see George Robey or Max Miller and hear the bluest, funniest jokes imaginable. Those stunning girls were still posing in nude tableaux at the Windmill, and some of the finest musicians in all the world were playing every noon-hour at the National Gallery before milling masses of uniforms.

And, of course, all those thousands of servicemen had presented the Piccadilly Commandos with their greatest challenge; they hurried, as fast as they could on their high heels, from their beat in the Circus to their shabby rooms in some bomb-battered building near by to keep up with the demand. "I'll give you ever such a good time, ducks, but just a short time only, mind," It was their finest hour.

But London for us was for the infrequent "boiler-clean" leaves; mostly our time was spent in the rural loveliness of Devon and Cornwall, for we were based out of Plymouth. On an afternoon off, we could nip ashore, into the yawning emptiness of the city centre (for the whole middle of the place, miles of it, had been completely gutted by fire-bombs early in the war), and catch a bus to anywhere, our destination just a name on the bus front. We were never disappointed; we discovered Fowey and Looe and St. Ives, Dartmoor and Cockington and Buckfast Abbey—all those incredibly beautiful little ports and towns, set in the loveliest countryside we had ever seen.

Meanwhile, we were making our flotilla, the 31st, the finest minesweeping group in the Allied navies—or so we thought, at any rate. Our own ship, *Minas,* we rated as best in our flotilla; we could get our gear out or in faster than anyone, and our signalling was sharper and our station-keeping more rigid—or so, at least, it seemed to us, impartial judges to a man.

We were conducting our exercises principally in Tor Bay, a fine, sheltered anchorage, in anything except an east wind, on the south Devon coast, a traditional bolt-hole for British Channel fleets in westerly gales during the French wars. We were supposed to anchor out there each night, or around the corner in Babbacombe Bay, and so we did—at first.

But across the bay from us lay Torquay, with all the fleshpots of England's finest coastal resort. Its inner harbour dried out at low water and its outer harbour was intended only for yachts and small fishermen, but close examination of the chart showed that there was just sufficient water alongside the inner wall of the mole to float a Bangor at all states of the tide, although it quickly shallowed a few yards out toward the centre of the basin. Once we had discovered that, the die was cast; for expert ship-handlers, as we had become, and with twin-screw, handy ships, the thing was a piece of cake. We would approach the end of the mole, one at a time, get a line on the end bollard as a spring, and pivot ourselves around the end of the mole and alongside just as slick as you please, and we nested up alongside, two abreast; the biggest ships, the locals told us, ever to berth inside.

At the end of the pier, immediately opposite, was a superb theatre; five minutes after berthing we were all inside, watching George Bernard Shaw explain the dilemma of *Mrs. Warren's Profession.*

Those exercises were a great time for us. All day, in the endless Devon sunshine, we steamed back and forth across the blue waters of the bay, steaming and recovering gear, laying marker dan buoys, practising precise station-keeping. At night, pleasantly weary, we would repair to the diversions of Torquay, a base we had all to ourselves.

All good things come to an end. Adjudged fit and battle-worthy, we were shifted east to Portsmouth, henceforth our base, and already filled with the shipping readied for the great assault. Here, with vast numbers of other warships, landing craft, aircraft, and thousands upon thousands of soldiers, we engaged in a number of joint exercises in which a large number of men were actually landed on a shelving beach. It all culminated in the vast dress rehearsal (Exercise Trousers) off Chesil Beach, a long stretch of shingle stretching for miles westward from Portland Bill.

It was a schemozzle from start to finish; thick fog came down as the landing-craft, loaded with eager young soldiers, began their run in to the beach. Some of the craft grounded on an outer bar; the fog prevented them from seeing that they had not yet reached the true beach, and they lowered their ramps, disgorging their men into ten feet of water. Hundreds drowned. Adding to the confusion was a German R-boat, with an escort of faster E-boats, quietly laying mines off the beach. Caught by this vast armada looming out of the fog, they took off at a great rate of knots, racing past long columns of landing-craft whose soldiers looked blankly out at them as just another realistic touch to the exercise. It was difficult to say who was the more startled; we stared at the Germans haring past us, and they stared back at us, all of us "filled with a wild surmise". They disappeared into the night, pursued by the corvette *Mimico*, whose commander was henceforth to be known to all his friends as E-boat Elmsley.

"Trousers" was a frightful mess; we atoned for it with "Fabius", the final exercise, and a full-scale one, when we put thousands of men ashore near Selsey Bill, with everything going like clockwork. We were ready for the big one.

On the first of June we moved to our assault anchorage off Poole; all about us lay a vast assemblage of shipping of every kind, including such exotica as the Dutch gunboats *Flores* and *Soemba*, tiny vessels carrying a pair of enormous six-inch guns, and crewed by the blackest Negroes we had ever seen. All the great battleships of the bombarding force—*Warspite, Rodney, Valiant, Texas,* etc.—were there, along with all kinds of magnificent cruisers; the French *Gloire*, which we selected as the most beautiful warship we had ever seen, *Black Prince, Bellona,* and innumerable others. All the endless ramifications of specialist assault ships were there too; the rocket ships, their whole deck covered with hundreds of spigots on which rockets were fixed and fired; gun ships, flak ships, even cook ships, which carried galley facilities to service the innumerable small craft off the beaches.

The Germans sent aircraft over to bomb and strafe this enormous fleet, and the flak in the night sky from our concentrated gunfire was something to behold. The dark sky was filled with every sort of flak, orange, green, red, white; lines of tracer reached upward, bursts of bright luminescence floated high above, bright searchlight beams probed the high cloud cover above. It was an amazing sight, and it brought results; our twin Oerlikons shared honours with a Hunt-class destroyer in bringing down a Heinkel III which crashed right in the town after weaving low over the water.

The next day we, like everyone else taking part, were sealed off from any contact with the shore, and received our orders. Our flotilla was to lead the parade in to Omaha beach in the American sector, cutting a path through the minefields towards the little town of Port en Bessin, where we would sweep out an area in which the bombardment ships could do their stuff. Hopefully, we would then withdraw to let the first wave go past us, but since we would have been fooling around, at slow speed, a mile off the beach and in point-blank range of three big coastal batteries, we did not really expect to survive as a flotilla. In fact, we were told to expect thirty per cent to fifty per cent casualties, and we were provided with spare vessels ready to fill in the formation as required, a rather nice touch, we felt.

Operation Neptune, as the sea-borne assault at Normandy was called, was a miracle of staff work; nobody who saw it will ever forget the incredibly complex and complete volume of instructions and detailed descriptions furnished to each ship in the great attack. Everything was there, including a mosaic of photographs, from air and sea, of the entire coastline of the Bay of the Seine; every tiny landmark, down to individual trees, was clearly indicated. Men had been working for years, from canoes and submarines and aircraft, to gather this information. The depths of water, the obstacles—and they were formidable—even the composition of the bottom, had been learned and indicated; the guidebook to Neptune was a triumph of organization carried to the level of art, of genius.

D-Day was set for June 5, and we would sail in the dark hours of early morning of the fourth in order to reach our rendezvous on time. I cleared lower decks when we had our orders and had a chat with all our people; we would have liked to be taking in our own Canadian troops, but we were enormously proud to be in the forefront of this tremendous affair, and felt it to be a fitting reward for all the endless years of convoy work in the North Atlantic. We made our wills, wrote our last letters home.

It blew hard that night, we weighed at 0245 and headed down channel from our new anchorage off Ryde in the Solent, and as we neared Horsesand fort it was blowing half a gale, with driving sheets of rain. A terrible night for an invasion, and the congestion of traffic, of every ship, great and small, all bound outward round Bembridge Point, was like Number 11 highway south from Lake Simcoe on a summer Sunday night. At six in the morning, just before we were committed to the sweep across, we were recalled; the invasion had been postponed for twenty-four hours, which cost our chief engineer the eight pounds he had won in the ship's D-Day pool, and gave us a wet day at anchor in the Solent.

Our little dan-layer, the former fish-drifter *Gunner,* missed the recall signal; her captain thought it odd that he somehow emerged from the heavy traffic all alone in the world, but he kept on in the driving rain, hoping to catch up the flotilla he was convinced had sailed ahead of him. He arrived off the appointed beach on the Normandy coast, found nobody, so anchored to await the march of events. He sat there, untouched, all that long day, under some of the most powerful guns in Europe; next day, when we arrived, he weighed and took station astern, wondering what had kept us.

The sweep across for us, once we had got clear of the incredible traffic jam east and south of the Isle of Wight, was simple enough. We got our sweeps at 5:30 in the afternoon, and two hours later we entered the enemy minefields, my knees shaking with patriotism as I kept close watch on *Cowichan* ahead for any mines she should cut. By midnight the show was on; the air force began to kick the stuffing out of the coast, and Port en Bessin ahead was a tremendous spectacle, with fires raging below and a fireworks show of flak and searchlights up above.

At three in the morning we did our thing, a slow turn to starboard, with the ship almost stopped, and so close to the beach we could make out every detail in the pale light of a wan moon. When we finished our turn, without a glove laid on us, we knew we were home free; from here on it was downhill all the way, a piece of cake. Behind us stretched a great wide channel of swept water, lit up by lighted dan buoys at regular intervals; off to starboard were two other similar channels, like lighted streets leading to the beaches, cut by "the famous Fourth", a fine old bunch of First World War coal-burners, and the 14th, a flotilla of mixed British and Canadian ships. The roads well and duly cut and blazed, we stood to one side, as the Coxswain said, "to watch the Pongoes get on with the job."

It was full daylight as we recovered our sweeps, right off the beach. To seaward was an unbelievable sight; every ship in the world seemed to be steaming over the horizon, heading for the beaches, now lying veiled under clouds of smoke from the night's bombing. Troop-carrying liners were headed for their anchorages, to off-load their men into assault boats; long lines of landing craft, infantry, and landing craft, tanks, were trundling along in close formation, while the big battleships and cruisers of the bombarding squadrons were taking up position and spitting in their palms, getting ready to buckle down to work.

For a moment we in the sweepers were conscious of an instant of almost heart-stopping intensity; a moment of historical confrontation between what seemed to us to be the forces of freedom and tyranny, of good and evil. Behind us to seaward all was light, the pale flush of dawn on the light paintwork, the bright white ensigns of the ships; ashore all was dark and sombre and sullen, the squat grey concrete of the German batteries, with their black slits and deep embrasures, like so many malformed skulls. For a long moment, we freemen looked for the first time on the dark forces we had fought against for so long, brought to bay at last like some fearful monster of romance; and they, in their bunkers and casemates ashore, surely they looked out at us, and saw at last their doom.

And then, sharp at ten minutes past five, our bombarding ships opened fire, and the fur began to fly. A French cruiser, the *Georges Leygues* ("George's Legs" to one and all), out of position and, as one would expect, in a panic to be somewhere else, nearly ran us down, but we went hard over and cut under his stern, unscathed save for a change of drawers all round. With our battle ensigns snapping in the breeze, we were getting our sweeps inboard, surrounded by assault boats of engineers going after the underwater obstacles in the shallows, when the first salvoes from the shore batteries arrived in our midst, speeding things up considerably among the toilers on the quarterdeck. *Blairmore*, next ship to us, was near-missed, a fountain of water towering up over her quarterdeck, and as she turned she was near-missed again, the water blowing right across her. The noise now was indescribable, with the reverberation of our own heavy guns as a constant thunderous rumble, orchestrated by lighter guns and bombs and bursting shells. Fleets of aircraft filled the air, both bombers and strings of troop-carrying gliders, headed inland; so intense was the racket that we could not hear ourselves speak. *Blairmore*'s mascot, a little white woolly dog and a great favourite, caught up in a world gone mad, went mad, too. He shot at high speed around the quarterdeck, then leaped over the side, never to be seen again; but despite the shells now falling in our midst, he was our flotilla's only casualty.

As we drew out to begin our next task, the headquarters ship *Largs* was flying the hoist "DRIVE ON!" It seemed as good a battlecry as any. Our wardroom steward, best in the navy, brought us breakfast on a tray; I breakfasted on the bridge, with a fresh linen napkin, in almost eighteenth-century elegance, amid all the noise and smoke of furious battle.

This day, and the week that followed, was the most exciting period of my life, so crammed with incident, so filled with tension and toil and exultation and excitement, that time quite lost its meaning. We worked from daybreak to darkness, sweeping the heavy minefields which shielded most of the coast. Mines were thick here; we cut them with the serrated wire of our sweep and with the steel cutter jaws at its end, then sank the floating mines with anti-tank rifles as they bobbed to the surface. Occasionally a round from the gun would hit a horn, and the mine would explode with a bang that would make us all pull long faces, as we thought what they could do to a little ship like ours. Once, manoeuvring to go alongside a tanker, the wash from our propellers touched off an oyster mine, and it went off just ahead of our bows, drenching us in a fountain of water but otherwise doing no damage. All about us the battle swirled and surged; we parted a sweep wire on the old U.S. battleship *Texas*, and had to recover it right under her turrets, the blast from her gun breaking our bridge windows as she pounded the beaches. For our lot had trouble ashore, the only beach that had; Omaha beach commander had fouled things up a bit by off-loading his men so far offshore that by the time they hit the beach the impact of the bombardment had passed, and the Germans were back at their guns and ready. To make things worse, the same commander had disdained the close fire support given the other beaches by amphibious tanks and other ingenious improvisations designed to wipe out the pill-box fire. As a result, his fellows got stuck on beaches dominated by steep cliffs, the most formidable geography of the whole area, and only by sending destroyers and gunboats right into the shallows—one destroyer we saw was so close they were using machine guns to fire at individual Germans running along the beach—and concentrating the fire of the big battleships on the cliff-tops was the assault finally able to get moving again.

The battleships, wreathed in smoke and flame, were stirring sights as we ploughed along past them, clearing mines so that they could move in a bit closer.

We lived intensely, in a chaotic, exciting milieu, and mostly on our nerves; we made the most of each precious hour of daylight and slept on briefly, for even at anchor each night the Germans sent marauding aircraft in under our fighter cover to bomb and strafe just off the beaches. It was exhausting, but after the long hours of shepherding convoys across the Atlantic it seemed wonderful to us.

And through it all, like a kind of theme, ran "Lili Marlene". The Allied Forces radio seemed to play nothing else; on the popular Mailbag show a dozen different renditions, with a dozen different singers, gave us Lili's haunting ballad. But the German rendition, with husky-voiced Lale Andersen, a bass chorus, and all those marching feet in the background, was by far the best. The Germans played it incessantly, and so did we; it had been the song of the desert armies, and now it became the melody of the invasion.

More than any other music, it captured the home-sick sentimentality of everyone who was far from home and his girl: "your sweet face seems, / to haunt my dreams." More to the point, there was a kind of fatalism, a sense of despair, that appealed to men caught up in great events. For whatever reason, Lale sang her song to all of us, hourly it seemed, and turned the imagination to your girl and to your dreams that could never come true, a passing relief from the demands and pressures of the present.

Every day brought its adventures. There was the midget submarine or "chariot" torpedo attack on ships at anchor off the beach, when a sailor looking idly over the side found himself staring at a man in the sea beneath him, in a sort of plastic bubble. There were the innumerable aircraft incidents, usually tragic, for the trigger-happy gunners of the American landing-craft were unfamiliar with European aircraft, and unable to tell ours from the Germans. So many of our fighters were shot down by the men they were trying to protect that for a time our own fighters were pulled right out of the beach-head area.

The night that the second Mulberry, the artifical harbour, broke up became legendary. For it let go at the height of a really disastrous gale, and the great "bombardons", or steel tanks which were coupled together to make part of the floating roadway, came driving down on us where we lay anchored in the lee. What a wild night ensued! There were the most frightful crashes and grindings as the big tanks crashed into anchored ships, and gunfire all over the place, as ships attempted to sink the units before they were themselves bashed into. Eventually we were ordered to weigh and pursue each individual tank, sinking every one we could round up, charging along through anchored ships in driving rain and howling wind, with guns blazing all about us.

There was the day we lay alongside one of the ships destined to be sunk to form the outer breakwater around the Mulberry harbour at Arromanches. All the British ships used for blockships were stripped-out hulks, but this American vessel had everything aboard, just as the crew had left her. When we wondered at the waste of so much fine new material, the watchman told us that in the time, and at the cost, of stripping and sending home all the material, half a dozen ships could be built back in the States. We believed him, and were glad of the dozens of steaks from her freezer and some of the fine navigational gear from her charthouse.

Like everyone else, we were awed by the fantastic size and shape of all sorts of things being towed past us by fleets of tugs; "Winnie's Wonders", as they were called, included huge concrete caissons, like sea-going grain elevators, to form part of the Mulberry harbours, and gigantic drums, like giant spools of thread, unwinding a plastic pipeline as they were towed towards the beaches by tugs in Operation Pluto (Pipe Line Under The Ocean). Soon we were pumping fuel for vehicles in Normandy all the way from England, via underwater pipeline.

The weeks following the initial D-Day assault were filled with varied action. As the armies crunched inland, we swept ahead of the assaults to open up the new ports of Morlaix and Roscoff. There we passed close to the burned-out hulk of a German destroyer, driven high and dry on the rocks by our own Tribal destroyers *Haida* and *Athabaskan*; an action which had cost the latter's life. Lying on his back in the water, *Athabaskan*'s gallant captain, Johnny Stubbs, had watched the dawning day which would spell death for *Haida* if she lingered longer to pick up the remainder of the survivors still in the water. "Get out of it, *Haida*," he had shouted to her bridge, and *Haida* had been forced to do just that, leaving further rescue work to the German vessels already putting out from shore. John Stubbs, who had led us in the Atlantic in *Assiniboine* and who had welcomed our flotilla so warmly when we arrived in Plymouth, was lost with 128 of his crew, and for us the rusting German hulk, high on the rocks of the Ile de Bas, had special significance.

Earlier, we had swept ahead of the force that landed at Cherbourg, after *Rodney* had softened up the coastal batteries with a tremendous curtain of fire. The shattered concrete fragments of the great fort on the outer mole were vivid testimony to the power of her huge guns.

In the early days of the invasion, the waters off the beaches were filled with every imaginable sort of flotsam, including men alive (head up) and dead (bottom up). We picked up the crew of a Liberator early one morning; as we came alongside their rubber raft the flight lieutenant in charge said "Good morning" to us as casually as a man waiting for a bus. They had been investigating a radar contact the night before—probably from one of the many rocks hereabouts—and, flying low over the water, had switched on their Leigh light, a great floodlight of incredible brilliance. In the sudden glare, the pilot had lost sight of the sea surface, and, misjudging his height, had flown his big Liberator right into the sea. Strangely, the only casualty had been the tail-gunner; everyone else had made it clear as the plane sank, although there was a sprinkling of broken legs and arms.

For all of us in the Channel these were momentous and memorable days. The support groups hunting down U-boats, the Tribals raiding across to the French coast everynight, returning next morning wreathed in glory and heavy with dead, the MGB's and MTB's on their nocturnal forays, as well as we flotilla types messing about the coastal minefields—all of us shared a sense of destiny. We felt ourselves to be participating in the freeing of a continent, of being part of a great crusade that would bring to an end this long struggle against an odious tyranny. It was this euphoria which was to nearly bring about our downfall.

For we had received a signal while we lay in Cherbourg:

Minas was to return to Canada to refit, forthwith. Within five minutes the anchor cable was rattling home and we were on our way.

It was then that I made the mistake which nearly cost us our ship and our lives. I was so intent on getting to Plymouth with all dispatch that I laid off our course to pass from port to port direct, instead of taking the safe dog-leg prescribed in order to pass out of gun range of the island of Alderney, where the Germans had a battery of heavy coast artillery. The direct route would cut off a hour, and would take us seven miles off Alderney, safe enough, surely, for a small ship. We had passed the island before at closer ranges without drawing a shot.

We cleared the Cherbourg approaches, and I went down for breakfast.

Bam!

The shattering explosion brought me to the wardroom door, napkin in hand; a towering waterspout was disappearing, close to our starboard quarter. I raced for the bridge, and for the next quarter-hour we played tag with the shore battery firing at us. The gunners were dead on for range, and only slightly off in deflection; I kept altering course toward the last fall of shot and then the gunners would miss on the opposite side, but it was only a matter of time before they fired two rounds with unchanged deflection.

Desperately, we called the engine room to make smoke; normally, we cranked out clouds of it, but this time, when we needed it, not a smudge.

Finally, a desperate quarterdeck party managed to get a smoke-float over and we tucked gratefully behind its comforting shroud. We put over another smoke-float, just as the bridge window beside me starred and broke, pierced by a bit of shrapnel from the shell bursting alongside. An array of tiny holes suddenly appeared in our funnel, and my heart sank.

But as we moved behind the smoke, the gunners' accuracy fell off markedly. Suddenly, a new hazard appeared: we were running into a minefield, the navigator informed me, and we would have to alter back into clear visibility if we were not to be in the middle of it. Better to risk the shellfire than the certainty of blowing up on a mine; we altered back into the bright sunshine out of the safety of the smoke, and I stared at the distant battery with my glasses. I could see it clearly, the low gunpits topped by a huge, skull-like concrete dome, which must be the observation and control position. That great tower on its forbidding cliff was to haunt my dreams for years; long afterward, I was to return and seek it out, to find it still as formidable and sinister in its peacetime decrepitude as it had seemed before its teeth had been drawn.

Fortunately for all concerned, its gunners had decided against wasting any more ammunition on a now-distant ship; we legged it for Plymouth, home, and mother. For us, the great Channel battle was over.

12
THE GRAVEYARD
OF THE ELEPHANTS

As the Allied armies drove steadily through France toward the German border, the war at sea entered its latest and, as it proved, final phase. Equipped with the schnorkel, a long, pipe-like extension which could be raised above the surface allowing a submerged submarine to run her diesel engines, swarms of U-boats were concentrated in the Irish Sea, the Bay of Biscay, and the western Channel, through which the Allies had to transport all their vital supplies for the armies in Normandy. A large number of Canadian corvettes, including mine, were hustled across to beef up local escorts of convoys in the threatened areas, while British and Canadian support groups prowled about the Channel approaches.

The schnorkel, fitted with valves to keep out water from wavetops while admitting vital air, meant that U-boats were no longer forced to surface to re-charge the batteries that drove their electric motors underwater, and hence were no longer so vulnerable to attack by radar-fitted aircraft. Now they became true submersibles, and instead of attacking in packs on the surface, at night, as before, they lay in wait at periscope depth and attacked, submerged, principally by day.

In any sort of chop, it was extremely difficult to spot the few feet of periscope which appeared at brief intervals above the surface.

The last stages of the Battle of the Atlantic, like the first, were to be fought out on the British doorstep. I was glad to be back in corvettes after a crack at minesweeping, for I had left *Minas* at her refit port and taken command of the veteran corvette *Camrose*. But I was happier still to be back in the civilized conditions of the narrow seas, where voyages

were shorter, weather was better, and assistance of every kind
was more readily available than in the far reaches of the Atlantic. And yet, for all that, this new kind of submarine warfare was a particularly frustrating one for the escorts. We lost
ships, in ones and twos, but seldom had the satisfaction of
making a clean kill. In the shallow Channel waters, a U-boat
would lie motionless on the bottom after making her attack,
while we would go probing around with our asdic and even
our echo-sounder, trying to make out which bump on the
bottom could be a U-boat. What complicated matters, apart
from tidal rips and other submerged distractions, was that the
bottom of the Channel and its approaches was simply carpet-
ed with wrecks, literally thousands of them, for ships had
been sinking there since the dawn of history and had continued to do so right up to the present. The wreck chart, on
which the position of every known wreck was plotted, became a key part of our operating equipment, but in case of
doubt we generally attacked a good contact on the bottom
just to be sure; U-boats had a way of cosying up to a known
wreck to shelter in its immunity. As a result, we occasionally
brought up some strange bits and pieces from ships which
had been lying on the bottom for years; a fragment of a
Tudor warship, perhaps, black as coal, or some of the cabin
fittings from a vessel sunk by the Kaiser's U-boats in the First
World War.

Fog became another bothersome factor; there seemed to be
no end to it in the spring of 1945. We once found ourselves
attempting to pass orders to our little fogged-in Irish Sea convoy by Morse on our siren, for althought still a lieutenant
like everyone else in corvettes, I was getting so long in the
tooth as to find myself sometimes senior officer in escorting
these little coastal convoys. We were attempting to button our
Irish Sea section onto the Channel convoy which we'd encountered crossing our bows; in the thick fog, only we escorts
could tell, by our radar, where the other ships were. The
process of signalling a new, safe course to our lot, hidden in
swirling clouds of thick fog, by means of our snuffling,
screeching siren, was guaranteed to put a few more silver
threads among the gold.

Crossing the Bay of Biscay with a big convoy one sunny
midday, there was a tremendous bang and the leading wing
ship nearest to us went up in a pillar of fire. She was a
tanker, heavily loaded with fuel oil, and she burned like a

torch, brighter than the bright sunlight, and covered the sky above with a pall of black smoke. We closed her instantly while the rest of the convoy steamed past and the escort group carried out its proper evolution, each escort searching out its sector. As always, the sight and sound of the burning tanker was appalling; it was the roar, even more than the heat or brightness of the flames, which seemed so daunting. She had been torpedoed in the stern, and as she gradually filled, her bows rose steadily, until they were well clear of the water. She hung there, bows upthrust, in a towering inferno of smoke and flame, while her survivors paddled frantically away in the few rafts and floats they'd managed to get overside.

As we ran in we got a firm asdic contact on a target only a few hundred yards past the doomed ship. It came in, loud and clear, with sharp cut-offs and good definition, moving very slowly left to right, and so hard and clear that the echo on the bridge speakers could be heard all over the ship. In such a position, such an echo could only come from one thing: at last, in this shifting, elusive Channel war, we'd gotten our teeth well into a U-boat!

For us, it was a perfect situation. The convoy was by now well clear, the weather was fine, our set was operating sweetly, and our asdic team, honed to a fine edge by endless drills and a week-long intensive course at the asdic centre in Campbelltown, was eager for blood. We reduced speed and prepared to carry out a textbook attack on this rash U-boat, using our hedgehog. This was a sort of many-barrelled mortar, mounted on our fo'c'sle, which threw a pattern of heavy bombs ahead of the ship. They sank rapidly, and would explode only on contact with the U-boat, or the bottom. An explosion meant a hit, and a hit meant a sinking.

We carried out the prettiest attack we'd ever done; at precisely the right instant, our hedgehog fired, sending its rockets rippling off to fall in a perfect circle, far ahead. In a silence so intense as to be tangible, we held our breaths and listened.

Bang! Bang!

Two hits! We'd done it! We almost burst with exultation; down in the waist the depth-charge crews pounded one another on the back, and from the engine room the Chief called up excitedly to ask if "we'd got the bastard". We had, we had indeed, we assured him, and slowed down still further, as our asdic operator warned us of breaking-up noises just ahead.

And there! Bobbing up fine on the port bow, some large

object surfaced. Wild with excitement, we fixed it with our binoculars, but could make nothing of it. Now there came oil, and we were sure of our kill. But—what was all that? Suddenly, the sea about us seemed to erupt with floating debris. But it was not the splintered wreckage, the little bits of panelling and nondescript domestic flotsam, expected from a sunken U-boat; rather, it was great rectangular-shaped packages of some sort.

Coming close to one, we inspected it minutely; scores of heads craned overside at the strange apparition from the depths. It was a bale of some sort, baled rubber, by George! We were steaming through a sea covered by floating bales of rubber. But it was not until the commodore's signal, reporting not one but two ships torpedoed, that it became clear to us what had happened. Directly behind the torpedoed tanker, a second ship had been hit, and had sunk almost immediately, screened from us by the burning tanker. We had actually picked up her sinking hull, submerged but not yet on the bottom, on our asdic, her twisting motion and increasing depth giving all the effects of a slow-moving submarine. Our attack had been letter-perfect, and the explosion of the hedgehog bombs had broken loose her deck-cargo of baled rubber.

It was a freak occurrence, and a bitter disappointment to us, but it also marked an event of some significance. For although we could not know it at the time, it was to be the last loss, the last U-boat attack, we would sustain; the long attrition of the U-boat war was nearing its end. We were in Portland when the war with Germany ended, and duly celebrated by splicing the mainbrace with a lot of rum for each man, and we were back in Plymouth in time to see the U-boat which had given us so much trouble only days before steer meekly up the Sound, under heavy escort, with her large black flag of surrender flying. But the Channel held one last surprise; for a few days more, convoys still proceeded under escort, and while we were shepherding a Channel section past the Lizard one morning there was a great explosion astern of the rear ship of the outer column, and a fountain of water erupting out of the sea. Instantly, of course, we suspected a torpedo exploding at the end of its run, or possibly an acoustic torpedo inadvertently detonating in the turbulence of the convoy's wake, and we carried out a thorough search after reporting the incident to C.-in-C. Plymouth. We could find no contact, nor could the wing escorts, but in no time at all EG 2, Walker's old group and the cream of the support force crop, came galloping over the horizon, and eagerly sought all relevant details from us. They were hoping, of course, for a lone-wolf U-boat unwilling to surrender and taking one last crack at the hated Allies, and the group longed to tack just one more hide on their barn door. They immediately settled down to comb the waters thoroughly, but they came up empty-handed. The explosion might well have been the detonation of a mine, but we chose to put it down to that category of unexplained detonations described by the late Captain Walker himself as an "ichthyological gefuffle". It allowed us to end our war with a bang.

The whimper was to come later. Summoned into the presence one morning, we were greeted by "Father", as everyone called our aged, delightful Captain D, with his usual: "Morning, *Camrose*; job of work for you this morning."

It was a most unusual assignment; taking the corvette *Lunenburg* under our wing, we were to hop around all the Channel Islands, which had been by-passed by the Allied drive and had only now surrendered, gather up the German men-o'-war which had accumulated there, run them down the Brittany coast to the naval port of l'Orient "and turn them over to the Frogs".

It was a fascinating performance; Woody Thomson of Lunenburg and I went ashore in each of the little island harbours—St. Helier, St. Peterport, St. Anne—and were met by the mayor and a deputation of authorities, who in turn introduced us to the German commanding officers. It was all most awkward; how, after all, did one behave to the vanquished enemy on their home ground, so to speak? Complicating matters was the disparity in strength; during the months following the invasion, all sorts of German craft had sought refuge here, as the other Channel ports fell to the Allied armies. How were two small corvettes to enforce their wishes on dozens of heavily armed destroyers, minesweepers, flak ships, and other odds and ends? Even the armed tug could have blown us both out of the water if he had wanted to make a break for South America.

In the event, everything went swimmingly. We brought our QR2, our senior gunnery rating, with us, equipped with a couple of large gunnysacks. We removed the breech-block firing mechanism from each German gun, popped it in the bag, and suddenly we were dealing with a fleet of unarmed ships. The German officers proved to be embarrassingly subservient. Their fawning, apologetic manner we found enormously disappointing, somehow; we expected resignation, perhaps defiance, from an enemy who had fought so long and so bravely; this smiling servility stuck in our throats. Perhaps it was true that the best of the German navy went into the U-boats.

We put a signalman aboard as many of the Germans as we could staff, and made sure that on these ships there was someone who could translate English into German; these ships we made section leaders, with the remaining ships of that section under their orders.

We then set off for the French port to the south and west of us, our Germans strung out in a long line-ahead formation, with the tug and assorted trawlers bringing up the rear, and Woody cavorting on one flank and us on the other. We shepherded our little flock, a gaggle of ugly ducklings if there ever was one, around the corner and into the approaches of l'Orient, where we turned them, and our bags of breechblocks, over to a French naval escort. What was to become of them we had no idea, but we suspected that for the next year or two the minesweepers would be busy tidying up all the enormous minefields they had been so industriously laying off the French coast for so long. Our operation was over; it had been pure comic opera, from start to finish.

Perhaps appropriately, it was our last "job of work" for Captain D; we got our orders to sail for Canada, and all about us the world of Western Approaches we had known for so long was tumbling about our ears.

The whole command was being run down; its bases were being closed, its ships released to other commands, and its men were queuing up for demobilization. Leave-taking at Londonderry was like a wake; one hardly knew whether to laugh or to cry. We crossed the Atlantic for the last time, with all our lights blazing; the first—and last—time we did so.

We bade Newfyjohn a last, long farewell; already its South Side jetties seemed forlorn, for the mid-ocean types had already taken their departure, and there were few familiar faces left around. We fuelled and backed off into that crowded little harbour for the last time, the three blasts of our siren echoing off the bare hills we had known so well. We took our last look at the pleasant little jerry-built wooden city we had come to love, and where we had made so many friends; in the late afternoon sunshine, the homely buildings glowed warmly, and there seemed not one that did not have some meaning and significance to each of us. We could ever make out the rickety staircase leading to the Crowsnest, scene of so many happy hours. It was with a heavy heart that we took old *Camrose* down the harbour she had known so long and so well, cleared the entrance, and stood out past Cape Spear's storm-battered light. In the gathering darkness of early evening, we took our departure for the last time from Cape Race, its great light flicking like a finger in the northern sky, and headed for Halifax and the inevitable end that awaited us there.

Halifax had taken on a special meaning for us since the disgraceful riots that had disfigured VE day. The news of the drunken debauch which had gone on for days had made us ashamed of our service; once again, it seemed to us, the shore navy, the barracks idlers and incompetent officers and the whole ramshackle edifice of Slackers, had made outcasts of seagoing men, blackening the name of the navy and distorting our reputation. We looked on it as a place to get our discharge as quickly as we could.

We passed through the boom defence, steamed up-harbour past George Island, the ferries, the big-ship wharves, and berthed alongside Jetty Four in the dockyard. *Camrose* was home from the wars at last; home to stay. She was never to sail again as an operational ship.

Yet she was not to die all at once. We landed our crew, and most of our officers and men made their farewells and went off to home and civvy street; a handful of us remained to take our ship on her last journey. We moved her across the harbour, first, where working parties from the shore removed her ammunition and depth-charges, her asdic and other technical equipment, and specialized fighting gear of every kind. When they had done and had gone their way, we raised steam and took her away on her last voyage. We cleared the boom at Halifax with never a backward look, and settled into the unaccustomed routine of steaming a ship, in peacetime, from port to port, with no worries or concerns of any kind save the routine ones of simple pilotage.

Sydney in Cape Breton was our first stop; we went alongside the great cranes there and had our Oerlikons and our four-inch mounting, our surface main armament, lifted out of the ship. Poor old *Camrose*; for the first time she showed her years, a veritable toothless tiger; it was surprising what a difference the removal of her forward gun made in her appearance. We hoisted our long de-commissioning pendant; *Camrose* was ready for her last voyage.

It was a sad business; that evening, the last before we were to sail on the first leg of this dismal trip to the boneyard, we pooled the dwindling resources of our wardroom with that of the corvette alongside and set off, in the ship's whaler, for a final party together.

In the twilight of a pleasant summer evening, we picnicked on a point of land not far from the dockyard. We had a pleasant, reminiscent time, a very quiet affair save for a few rousing songs of one sort or another. Towards the end of the proceedings, a cow joined us; it loomed out of the darkness and shouldered into our circle, where it was made much of by one and all and, in lieu of anything better, was offered a cigar, which it declined. Somebody bet our chief engineer, who was from Kenora in western Ontario, that he couldn't ride the cow for more than ten seconds. (To benighted Torontonians anyone from west of the Humber is a cowboy, born and bred.) The chief could not refuse; standing up, he acknowledged the applause with a graceful gesture and moved towards the cow, now fallen into a light doze. Stroking its neck placatingly, he essayed to vault onto its back, which, since he was built on the general lines of a chesterfield, was no easy task. In the event, it proved to be beyond him; the cow, sensing dirty work afoot, gave a heave, shouldered the chief to one side, and disappeared into the night whence it had come, snorting with indignation.

Since, as the chief pointed out, he had never actually been aboard the cow, his ability, once on, to remain seated for the requisite ten seconds had never been put to the test, and it was conceded that all bets were off; we were regaled instead by the fine baritone voice of Number One.

Shortly thereafter, we returned to our virtuous beds and slept the sleep of the just.

Next morning there was a tremendous flap. I was summoned into the office of some four-ringed captain and given the most scathing tongue-lashing; his cow, he maintained, had clocked in that morning too upset to give of its milk in its usual generous manner. His cow, he claimed, had been interfered with and he intended to have the heart's blood of the skunk who had laid a hand on her. If it had been his daughter, his wrath could not have been greater. We were not to be allowed to sail, he told me, until I had given him the name of the man responsible.

I could simply not comprehend the man's fury about a cow which he obviously was pasturing on navy land at navy expense to furnish him with a little fresh milk for his private use; the kind of petty swindle which shore officers seemed to regard as one of the "perks" of office. Yet this pink-faced little bleeder, now throwing a tantrum about his ruddy cow, was of the same rank as Vian when he led his destroyers against *Bismarck*, of Mainguy when he built the mid-ocean groups at Newfyjohn, of Nelson when he interposed his ship against the Spanish line at Cape St. Vincent.

My disbelief must have showed, because he now became utterly fatuous, with threats about "ruining the careers of those responsible". Since the careers referred to could be timed in hours, there was little to worry about, but I was not about to cause concern to one of the corvette's navy's finest engineers at the end of years of hard and distinguished service. I told this incredible man that as the senior officer present I was responsible for any misconduct at last night's affair, and assured him that there had been none. I told him exactly what had happened, save for the names, and reaffirmed that no injury had been done the cow, who had left our midst admired by all.

The captain, calming down somewhat, asked for a formal written report from me, together with the name of the officer responsible, before we would receive sailing orders. I went back to the ship, typed my report, omitted any names but appended an apology for any emotional upset caused the cow by what had been a foolish prank.

In the end, of course, cooler heads prevailed; we received our sailing orders after a few hours' delay, and left with sighs of relief. All the same, it had been a disquieting reminder of the transition we would have to make between the world of the operational navy, where the issues were life and death, and that of the shoreside navy we were coming back to, obsessed with the most trifling concerns and motivated by a pettiness and selfishness completely alien to the way of life of men living literally in the same boat. The end of the war meant the end not only of the corvette navy but of a whole way of life, and we felt an inward qualm as the nature of the world we were returning to, and in which we must now make our way, was brought home to us.

It was a strange trip we made, through the Gulf and up the great stream of the St. Lawrence, in a mood compounded equally of exultation at our pending return to home and family and all the comforts of peace, and of sadness for what we were leaving behind, and above all, for the approaching end of our ship. One by one, the lights and landmarks made familiar to us years before, in trooping trips to Labrador, passed by: Cape Chat, Matane, Father Point. In the calm waters of the river, we decided to let the old girl show what she could really do. For years, even in the heat of action, the Chief, like all engineers, never let his beloved engines run to their utter limit; always, like any prudent man, he kept a little something in reserve. He had nursed his engines, his boilers, all through the war years; now, at the end of their career, he assented to a full-speed trial. We fixed our position carefully, and laid out a precisely measured course on our chart; then we rang down for full speed, a triple ring, and held onto our hats...

Freed of her heavy burden of guns and depth-charges and extra fuel, of men and supplies of every kind, old *Camrose* fairly flew. With a great bow-wave flaring out on each side like wings, she tore through the water, her wake a ribbon of boiling foam astern. As the Chief and his delighted crew in stokehold and engine room cranked her up and opened all the taps to their fullest extent, a shimmering haze hung over her funnel-top, and everything in the ship shook with the vibrations of her surging propeller. The shore marks fairly whizzed by; as we neared the transit that marked the end of our allotted course, the navigator stood ready with his stopwatch. Click! We had done it; the vibration eased as the revolutions dropped, while cheering came faintly up the engine-room voice-pipes.

A little calculation produced the startling result: *Camrose*, in the last hours of her life, had gone faster than ever before; the 18.2 knots she had just chalked up exceeded even her highest speed achieved on her acceptance trials, when she was fresh from the builder's yard. We all gave her a cheer for that, and wondered what was to become of her.

We were bound for Sorel, roughly halfway up the St. Lawrence between Quebec City and Montreal, where we were to hand her over to officials of War Assets Corporation for disposal. Most of the ships, we knew, were destined to be scrapped, but some at least, we had heard, were being bought up by nations in South America and elsewhere for further service in their navies. Built and launched in 1941, *Camrose* was relatively old as corvettes went; probably the ships chosen for further naval service would be selected from the more recent productions. Nevertheless, our ship was in excellent shape, and there was always the chance that her smart appearance might just tip the scales in her favour. Taking advantage of our sunny summer weather, we turned to with paint and brush, all of us, officers and men, and touched up her paintwork where the removal of wiring and instruments had left bare patches on her bridge, in her wireless and radar cabins. Always well-kept, she needed only a touch or two here and there, and a good scrubbing of decks and messdecks; she arrived at Sorel gleaming and immaculate, inside and out, her teak decks fore and aft as bright as a yacht's, her brightwork polished and her bulkheads and corticene spotless. We had done for her everything we could; her fate now lay with others, and we led her in to her graveyard bedecked in her finest, like some sacrificial maiden led to the fatal altar.

Off Sorel, we picked up our pilot, a voluble little French-Canadian chap, who guided us, with a torrent of orders and cautions and gestures through a channel into a cluster of reedy islands, among which we picked our way before emerging at our final destination.

Ahead of us, a long stretch of water opened up, hemmed in by a featureless line of low, swampy sandbars. And in that stretch, moored head to tail at rows of buoys, lay the entire corvette navy, together with the destroyers and frigates that had led the escort groups. There were hundreds of them, still in sea-worn Western Approaches camouflage, but strangely altered. For one thing they had no guns; for another, there was not a sign of life. They were no longer ships, but mere lifeless hulks, the bare bones of once-great fighting ships, lying huddled in decaying ranks in this dismal place. We had arrived at the graveyard of the elephants.

As we edged to our allotted place alongside a dead corvette, we gazed about in wonder, in awe, in real horror. It seemed a terrible thing, somehow, to reduce this mighty force, which only weeks before had won command of the bitter North Atlantic, to so many rusting hulks.

The sight of so many veteran ships, built at such effort and cost and fought with such hardihood and endurance, lying forgotten in this ghastly backwater was, literally, a terrible sight; nobody who saw it will ever forget it. It was the Battle of the Atlantic reduced to a few hundred thousand tons of rusting metal, and it sobered us as nothing else could.

After this numbing spectacle, all was anti-climax. A fellow in a fedora hat came aboard, knocked back the last of my precious Maderia like so much soda-pop, and wrote me out a little receipt for *Camrose*: "received from the Department of Naval Defence, the corvette *Camrose*, together with . . ." etc. etc. It was a slip of paper, the kind one would expect when a used lawnmower changes hands.

Towards sunset, the ship began to die. The last of the steaming party supplies were embarked, along with most of our crew, in a big motorboat; we had gathered, all of us, a few minutes earlier to splice the mainbrace for the last time. We'd mixed everything potable in the ship—a little rum, some sherry, half a bottle of crème de menthe—and measured it out to each man. We'd toasted the King, of course, and then our coxswain, a grizzled, taciturn old veteran who'd been with the ship since commissioning, stepped forward to make the toast we were gathered for. "To *Camrose*, a great ship!" he said, and we all drank to her for the last time.

Down below now, the Chief had shut off all steam; the exhaust fans, which throbbed aboard day and night, at sea and alongside, stopped, and the silence was so sudden it made us jump. For steam was the lifeblood of the ship, and when it ceased to flow, *Camrose* ceased to live.

We had only a few minutes to wait before the boat arrived to take the last of us ashore. I went up to the bridge, and leaned on the binnacle and looked out at the grisly scene, lit now by the glow of a dying sunset. There was *Assinibone*, the old "Bones" of our early group, and alongside was *Trail*, the corvette in which I had spent two eventful years, and about her were all the ships we had sailed with, in one group or another, for what seemed all our adult life. Each one brought memories, evoked faces—*Morden* there had once startled everyone by bringing in a record ninety-four survivors, many of them women and children, and there was *Moose Jaw*, famous in the fleet for her wardroom Moosemilk. Here was *Port Arthur*, Ted Simmons' old warhorse, and "Sally Rand", the *St. Laurent*, which had made such a name for herself in the Western Approaches. And there was Cowboy Jackson's old bucket, and *Dauphin*, a chummy ship from refit days.

All dead now; not only dead but forgotten. Seagulls perched on the dodger where George Hall, my old captain, once leaned; the rasping screech of a rusty fitting as the ship moved to a slight swell only emphasized the silence of death all around us.

I took a last long look around at those lifeless ships, haunted by so many ghosts, then closed the cover of the voice-pipe to the wheelhouse, severing the umbilical cord which had bound me to *Camrose* for so long. For *Camrose,* which had sunk U757 and shot down two bombers, which had screened the invasions of Sicily and Normandy, which had fought off U-boat packs in a dozen fierce encounters and had helped bring innumerable merchant ships safely to port, this great ship of ours, was dead now, and I must leave her here among the bones of her sisters.

I turned and ran down the ladder, and into the waiting boat. And I left behind me a ship and a fleet, a host of friends and a way of life that I would never see again. The corvette navy was dead, and I walked away into the strange civilian world of peace.

13
I REMEMBER,
I REMEMBER . . .

~~~~~~

We have stood, in the unaccustomed attitude of parade "attention", at more than a score of Remembrance Day ceremonies now, in various parts of Canada. Sometimes it has been cold and blustery, sometimes chill and bright, but the way we remember it is in the rain, when the bugler sounds the Last Post and we are left alone with our memories. Around us are the few from the Old War, with their dreadful memories of blood and mud at Passchendaele or Vimy, Hill 60, Ypres or Amiens. Our own thoughts are of another, newer, war—yet a war which already seems part of a dim past.

It is not the dark memories which come to us now: the terror of ships afire in a black night, of crashing seas in an Iceland gale, of the white-faced crewmen of the destroyer *Ottawa*, the smell of death already upon them; of the shredded, bloated horrors, floating under clouds of seagulls, in the dawn-grey seas after a convoy attack. Years of peacetime pursuits, of family life and television and business pressures, have eased these memories from our conscious mind; it is only in dreams that they live on now.

On Remembrance Day our memories are of a different kind. We remember when the world was an exciting place in which to be young and when, with a thousand others, we were likely to be sent halfway around the earth and back again, without a care for tomorrow. One had a sense of destiny in those days; of being a part of historic events, of helping to mould a new and better world. How innocent, how naive, how pathetic it all seems now!

But we remember only the pleasant times, the high-spirited

times. We remember Tiger Turner standing on his head in the punchbowl at Captain D's cocktail party, and the midnight discussions of the works of Shaw and Chesterton with Tommy Holland over cocoa in a deserted middle-watch wardroom, tossed in a raging sea. We remember the sudden serenity of Lough Foyle, the luxury of fresh linen that went with the end of yet another eastward crossing, and the gay signals to the wrennery at Boom Hall as the escort group filed upriver to Londonderry. We remember warm and happy hours at the Crowsnest in Newfyjohn; aboard the mother ships *Baldur* and *Vulcan* in Iceland's Hvalfjord; in the brass-bound murkiness of the Shakespearean Cellar in Londonderry. Happy, light-hearted times; the happier for their stark and fateful background. One cherishes the few sunlit days all the more in seasons of rain and despair.

They are all gone now: Holland and Millthorpe, Harvey and the rest of them, in the shattered wrecks of ships scattered across the wide ocean floor. We who are left, are young no more; the eager boys' faces of yesterday are creased by time and pouched with civilian living. Yet still, across the widening gulf that yawns between that age and the present, the memory of our shared youth brings a pang to our heart, and moisture to our eyes.

It is not for the dead that we mourn, those bright hearts we have been revisiting in memory. Rather it is for the passing of our lost youth, and for the spirit of adventure and high endeavour which passed with it.

GLOSSARY

Abaft behind, relative to something aboard ship.

Aft, after towards the stern.

Asdic submarine detection gear based on sub-sonic transmission. Later, the U.S. term "sonar" was adopted.

Astern behind, relative to a ship.

Bollard vertical post around which ropes are secured.

Boom defence underwater steel netting, supported by buoys and fitted with a gate, stretched across harbour to keep out submarines.

Boom defence vessels located either side of gate to open and close it as required.

Bosun or *boatswain* senior rating in charge of upper deck.

Bosun's mate messenger who carries or promulgates messages.

Bosun's pipe shrill whistle carried by bosun's mate.

Bow front end of ship or boat.

Breastline warp at right angles to ship's centre-line, used to hold ship close alongside.

Bridge elevated platform from which ship is conned.

Caisson a concrete tank which can be sunk in designated place by admitting water through valves; used for floating harbour.

Carley float lifesaving device with slat floor suspended inside a floating ring.

Coxswain senior petty officer in the ship, who takes wheel for all important manoeuvres. Responsible for discipline in small ships.

Dan buoy float fitted with anchor and pole topmark.

Davit post at shipside used to raise or lower boat, and other objects.

Dodger wood or canvas screen sheltering bridge from weather.

Dog-watch two two-hour watches—4-6 p.m. and 6-8 p.m.

Drogue canvas funnel dragged through air or water.

Flag officer senior officer above rank of captain; flies rank flag.

Flotilla organized grouping of destroyers or smaller ships.

Fo'c'sle, forecastle forward part of ship. In a corvette, it houses most of the crew.

Funnel ship's smokestack.

Gunner gunnery specialist, usually warrant officer.

Gunner's mate petty officer gunnery specialist, navy's drill sergeant.

Guns used as title for officer in charge of gunnery department.

Halyard light rope used to hoist flags to mast or yard.

HSD (Higher Submarine Detection) the senior asdic rating in the ship.

Lee downwind side; in the shelter of downwind side.

Leeward downwind, away from the wind.

Leigh light light of intense brilliance, used by aircraft in night operations.

Main deck the principal overall deck.

MGB motor gunboat.

MTB motor torpedo boat.

Navel pipes tubes carrying anchor cables from upper decks to chain locker.

Oerlikon light rapid-firing cannon firing variety of shell.

Pom-pom single or multi-barrelled gun firing 2-lb. shell.

Pusser naval slang for proper, official, or regulation style.

Quarter diagonally astern and out to one side of ship.

Salvoes system of firing guns by direct order, applying corrections as required to bring fall of shot on target.

Signalman rating who transmits messages by light, flag, semaphore.

Singling up to reduce warps ashore to one of each.

Snotty midshipman, most junior officer rank. So called because three buttons on cuff were traditionally intended to prevent him wiping nose on sleeve.

Stanchion vertical metal support for rail or lifeline.

Star shell fired from gun, it releases flare suspended from parachute.

Stern back end of ship or boat.

Subbie sublieutenant, senior to midshipman, junior to lieutenant.

Trot-buoys or trots midstream buoys used to moor ships fore and aft.

Waist midship section of upper deck.

Warp rope used to secure ship to shore.

Whaler double-ended pulling boat; capable of being sailed.

Yard-arm outer end of a yard crossed on a mast.

ABOUT THE AUTHOR

James B. Lamb joined the RCNVR in 1939 and spent the war on several corvettes. He commanded two, HMCS *Minas* and HMCS *Camrose*. After the war, Mr. Lamb embarked on a career as a newspaper man. His articles have appeared in a wide variety of newspapers and magazines, including *The Toronto Star, The Globe Magazine, Saturday Night, The Saturday Review,* and *The Financial Post.*

Mr. Lamb lives at Big Harbour overlooking the Bras d'Or Lakes.

SIGNET Novels You'll Want to Read

☐ **THE LUCK OF THE IRISH: A Canadian Fable by Harry J. Boyle.** A wild and wondrous novel about a miracle called love . . . "A toothsome story . . . a tale to be savored." —*Hamilton Spectator* (#YE18—$2.25)

☐ **CLOSE TO THE SUN AGAIN by Morley Callaghan.** A great writer's triumphant new novel of a man's final reckoning . . . "Masterful, gripping, powerful . . . Callaghan's best." —*Winnipeg Free Press* (#YE8—$2.50)

☐ **A POPULATION OF ONE by Constance Beresford-Howe.** The exuberantly sexy novel about an unforgettable young woman aching to spread her wings . . . "It rings true!" —*Ottawa Journal* (#YE49—$2.25)

☐ **SANDBARS by Oonah McFee.** A remembrance of things long past—the moving story of a woman's search for herself . . . "Long, luscious, intricate . . . gem-studded all the way!"—*The Canadian* (#YE6—$2.50)

☐ **THE INVENTION OF THE WORLD by Jack Hodgins.** A vividly memorable novel that will take you into a magical world. *The Invention of the World* rings with needle-sharp authenticity . . . a powerful evocation of life in its unquenchable vitality . . . rich, complex, explosive!"— *Toronto Star* (#YE55—$2.95)

☐ **FARTHING'S FORTUNES by Richard B. Wright.** "All the wonderful elements of picaresque adventure including plenty of vigorous sex . . . a pleasure . . . ONE OF THE BEST CANADIAN NOVELS OF THE YEAR!"—*Vancouver Sun* (#YE4—$2.50)

☐ **CHILD OF THE MORNING by Pauline Gedge.** The fiery epic of the beautiful woman who dared ascend to history's most powerful throne . . . "A marvelous saga . . . a torrent of passion and intrigue!"—*Toronto Star* (#YE54—$2.95)

Other Nonfiction Bestsellers from SIGNET

☐ **TRUDEAU by George Radwanski.** The real man behind the image . . . "The most successful exploration of the man so far!"—*Toronto Globe and Mail*. A Book-of-the-Club Main Selection.　　　　　　　　(#YE66—$2.95)

☐ **MIKE: The Memoirs of the Right Honourable Lester B. Pearson, Volume I.** From minister's son to minister of state—a magnificent human odyssey. "This book makes it clear that the Mike Pearson whom the world came to know and admire is the real Mike Pearson. . . . *Mike* is full of stories and anecdotes, threaded with the names of the famous people who were his friends and confidants."—*Time*　　　　　　　　(#J5766—$1.95)

☐ **MIKE: The Memoirs of the Right Honourable Lester B. Pearson, Volume III—1957-1968.** In the climactic volume of his best-selling Memoirs, Lester Pearson tells the story of his difficult, dramatic, but ultimately triumphant years as Prime Minister of Canada.　(#J7272—$1.95)

☐ **I CHOSE CANADA: The Memoirs of the Honourable Joseph R. "Joey" Smallwood, Volume I—Light of Day.** The candid, colourful, compelling personal saga of the making of a man and the molding of a leader.
　　　　　　　　(#J6662—$1.95)

☐ **I CHOSE CANADA: The Memoirs of the Honourable Joseph R. "Joey" Smallwood, Volume II—The Premiership.** The years of power and testing—when a colourful, controversial leader fought to turn a dream of progress into a triumphant reality.　　　　　(#J6663—$1.95)

☐ **TORSO: The Evelyn Dick Case by Marjorie Freeman Campbell.** Canada's most lurid, sensational and suspenseful murder trial, with all its scandals, shocks, and still controversial findings has been re-created—in a fascinating narrative no novelist would dare invent, and no fiction could surpass. "It all comes alive again."—*Hamilton Spectator*　　　　(#W6971—J$1.50

Other SIGNET Books You'll Enjoy

☐ **TWO WOMEN by Doris Anderson.** The passionate novel of a woman consumed by desire for the husband of her best friend . . . "Sparkles with wit and warmth . . . a gripping, topical page-turner."—*Thomson News Service*
(#YE14—$2.25)

☐ **SHREWSBURY by Jamie Brown.** Power and passion, guilt and shame—in the climactic novel of a magnificent Canadian dynastic saga . . . "Remarkable!"—*Toronto Star*
(#E8368—$2.25)

☐ **JOHN AND THE MISSUS by Gordon Pinsent.** A brilliant Canadian writer's roaring novel of an indomitable man and the woman who went with him all the way . . . "Extraordinary, marvelous, shattering!"—*Library Journal*
(#W6779—$1.50)

☐ **THE ROWDYMAN by Gordon Pinsent.** The raw, ribald, and riotous story of a man who can resist everything but temptation! The unblushing, best-selling smash hit novel by one of Canada's brightest storytelling superstars . . . "A winner!"—*St. John's News*   (#W6850—$1.50)

☐ **WILDERNESS MAN: The Strange Story of Grey Owl by Lovat Dickson.** The startling saga of the man of mystery who became the uncrowned king of the Canadian wilds . . . "Beautiful, sensitive, honest!"—*Ottawa Citizen*. Illustrated with unforgettable photos.   (#J6513—$1.95)